SANTA FE
PASSAGE

SANTA FE
PASSAGE

JON R. BAUMAN

T·T

Truman Talley Books

St. Martin's Press • New York

www.stmartins.com

Library of Congress Cataloging-in-Publication Data

Bauman, Jon R.
    Santa Fe passage / Jon R. Bauman.—1st U.S. ed.
        p. cm.
    ISBN 0-312-33348-X
    EAN 978-0312-33348-5
    1. Mexico—History—1821–1861—Fiction. 2. Americans—Mexico—Fiction. 3. Santa Fe (N.M)—Fiction. I. Title.

PS3602.A9625S26 2004
813'.6—dc22   2004046822

First Edition: November 2004

10 9 8 7 6 5 4 3 2 1

To James O'Shea Wade and Susan Collins Bauman, two excellent editors who helped make Santa Fe Passage *a better book*

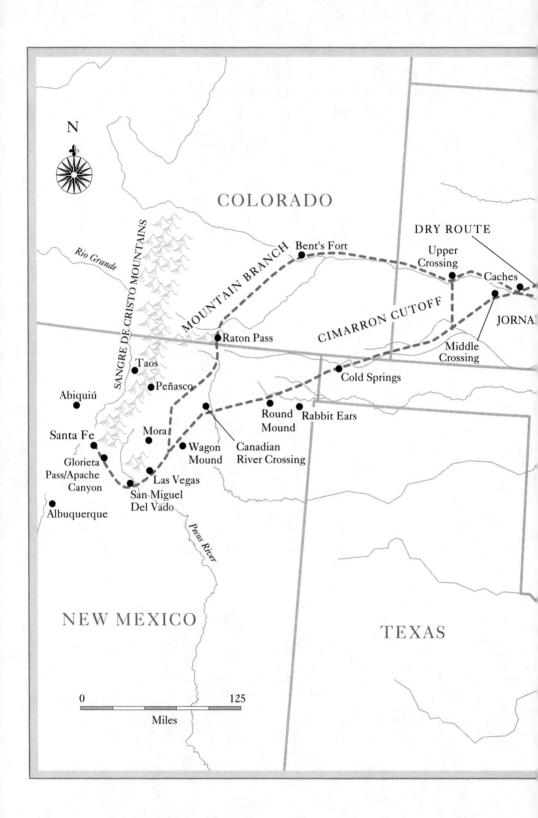

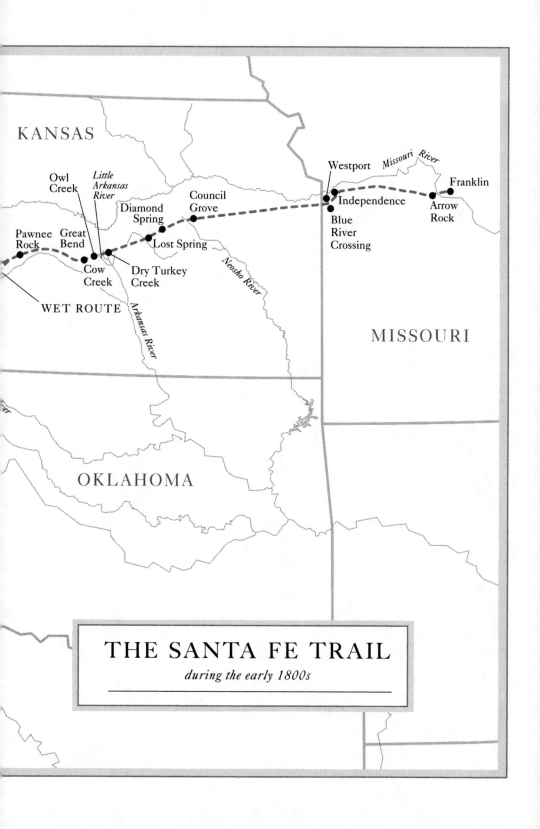

KANSAS

Owl
Creek

*Little
Arkansas
River*

Diamond
Spring

Council
Grove

Westport   *Missouri River*   Franklin

Independence

Arrow
Rock

Blue
River
Crossing

Pawnee
Rock

Great
Bend

Lost Spring

Cow
Creek

Dry Turkey
Creek

Neosho River

WET ROUTE

Arkansas River

MISSOURI

OKLAHOMA

THE SANTA FE TRAIL
during the early 1800s

SANTA FE
PASSAGE

PROLOGUE

1846

"It's a by God act of war, and I'm going to Congress for a declaration."

THE MAN AND THE HORSE WORKED UP A SWEAT ON THE TRIP from Georgetown to the White House. When the president's messenger had arrived at his home earlier on that hot, humid morning, Senator Thomas Hart Benton hurriedly put on a red silk vest and shoved his heavy arms into a swallowtail coat. He donned a battered beaver hat he plucked from the hat rack and heaved his bulk onto his sorrel mare. The horse sucked in a gulp of air and resigned herself to the solid block on her back, but stumbled and almost fell when she crossed the rain-slick boards of Rock Creek Bridge.

The sun came out as he cantered through the federal district, and Senator Benton guessed that something about Mexico had caused James K. Polk to summon him on a Sunday. In the White House drive, the mare stopped to nibble at a tuft of spring grass that was poking up through the gravel. Annoyed, Benton yanked her head up. At the mansion's back door, he dismounted, gave the reins to a stable boy, and followed a stately black butler to the president's office.

The president rose and motioned the senator to a chair in front of his desk. Through the window behind Polk's back, Benton had a fine view of the orange flowers on the trumpet vines and of the just-greened lawn, but the sunlight at Polk's back made it difficult for him to make out the president's features.

"Tom, I need this man—this Collins. What's his Christian name?"

"Matthew, Mr. President."

"The Mexicans have taken the bait. They attacked General Taylor's position on the Rio Grande. It's a by God act of war, and I'm going to Congress for a declaration." Polk hammered his fist on the desk so hard that his inkwell jumped and splashed black liquid onto his blotter.

Thomas Benton and James Polk had been friends and sometimes political allies for years. Benton had staunchly supported the Democratic Party's 1844 dark-horse candidate because the Tennessean had promised to push democracy from Missouri to the Pacific Ocean, and, for years, Benton's had been the loudest Senate voice calling for the westward expansion that was enriching Missouri. His home state was the jumping-off point for traders and fur trappers, and it was booming by selling wagons and oxen, beans and onions to the adventurers, and Benton was always the driving force behind any measure that would bring more money to Missouri.

"Where the hell is this Collins?" Polk asked.

"He's somewhere on the Santa Fe Trail, Jim—Mr. President—but the First Dragoons they sent from Ft. Leavenworth couldn't find him. If Collins is traveling south of the Arkansas River, he's in Mexico and our troops can't cross the border. Even if he's on the American side, the Trail meanders all over hell and back and they could have passed one another without knowing it."

"Wherever he is, we've got to get this Collins to Washington in a big damned hurry. I've talked with General Scott. He's planning to invade Mexico on two fronts—from Matamoros and Veracruz. If your man Collins can't fix things for us in Santa Fe, then we've got a monumental problem."

"Mr. President," Benton said, "you'll recall that I told you that there are people in this town who will question your judgment in choosing Collins for this mission." Benton leaned forward to see whether, from the president's expression, he had picked up on the senator's attempt to shift any future blame away from himself. The lanky president's thin features revealed his pique.

"Damnit, Tom, you're the one who recommended him. He's your man. You vouched for him."

Benton knew that James Polk, a veteran of backwoods, bare-knuckled political wars in Tennessee, had boxed him in. The senator's only choice was to give Matthew Collins his full support. "I think he can do the job, Mr. President, but, with this war coming on, I just wanted to remind you that there are risks. Damn! Sure is humid." Sweat beads rolled down the creases in his jowls.

"Take your coat off, Tom."

Polk, Benton thought while he rose and draped his coat on the back of his chair, was, like him, a Westerner who resented the Easterners' financial stranglehold over the West. But the president knew little of the Missouri frontier and nothing of the Santa Fe Trail. "Mr. President, some of the Americans who've been out in New Mexico a long time have lost their enthusiasm for our democratic experiment. But Collins is pragmatic. He wouldn't want a shooting war that clutters up the Santa Fe trade. He's been a successful merchant on the Trail for twenty years, and he knows he'll make even more money when New Mexico joins the Union."

The senator gave Polk what was meant to be a reassuring smile, one that bared his large square teeth and gave his heavy jaw the set of a mastiff.

"If it's not him, we've got to find somebody who can get to New Mexico's governor," Polk insisted. He stood, put both hands on his desk, and leaned toward Benton. "We don't have enough money or troops to fight on three fronts, and General Scott's plans don't include a full-scale campaign in New Mexico. If we can't control Santa Fe, we can't take California."

"I think Collins will be loyal, Mr. President. I still vouch for him. I know a man here in Washington who's been up and down the Santa Fe Trail two or three times. If you'll authorize funds for his expenses, he'll find Collins."

"How much will he need?"

"Enough for the stagecoach, railroad, and steamboat fares to Independence. He can buy a good horse and tack out there. If we give him something extra for his trouble, five hundred should do."

"Done. Get him moving." Polk walked around his desk and helped Senator Benton struggle into his coat, clapped him on the shoulder, and ushered him to the door.

Matthew Collins halted their caravan so they could water the animals at Six Mile Creek. They had crossed the driest part of the Great American Desert, and had been in the tall grass country long enough for the mules to have put on weight. Matthew rose up in his stirrups and his six-foot-two height gave him a view over miles of the country ahead. He watched with pleasure as the wind set the fresh green stalks to rolling like an ocean. Despite years under the western sun, he still had the fair skin of a redhead. He scratched at the dead skin on his sun-burned nose, smiled, and turned in his saddle to see how far west the sun had traveled.

"If we push hard, we'll get to Diamond Spring by this evening," he said.

"I expect so," Matthew's partner of eighteen years, Edward Water-man, agreed. "The mules are plenty strong enough."

They camped that night at Diamond Spring and, at sunup, Collins & Waterman's three freight wagons began lumbering east, leaving a dust curtain hanging in the still morning air. Matthew rode ahead on his sad-dle mule to scout the trail for muddy bogs and ruts too deep to cross. In the distance, he saw a lone rider silhouetted by the half-risen sun against the prairie sky. When the rider drew close, he slowed his horse to a walk and approached within hailing distance. "I'm looking for Matthew Collins."

"I'm Collins."

The two men rode slowly toward one another and dismounted. "My name's Kinney," the messenger said in a solemn voice that he meant to convey the gravity of his mission. "I have a letter for you."

Matthew took the letter from Jerry Kinney's outstretched hand and broke the wax seal on the White House envelope. Edward rode up with the wagons and the four peons in their party just as Matthew was fin-ishing reading. "You look so serious, Matt. What's it say?"

"Somebody in Washington wants to talk to me. Something about Mexico. It isn't very clear what they want."

Turning to Kinney, Matt asked, "Mr. Kinney, will you be going back East with us?"

"Nope. I'm going on to Santa Fe and then out to California." Kinney gigged his spurs into his horse's flank and turned to wave at the east-bound caravan.

After a long, hot afternoon Matthew and his caravan passed through a stand of large oak trees that bordered the Neosho River at Council Grove. He counted eight freight wagons and a buggy parked along the river, and saw the heads of mules and oxen bobbing up and down, in and out of the tall grass near the bank.

Matthew led his caravan to a flat area close to a campfire surrounded by a dozen men. "Timoteo," he said to his servant, "you and Jesús un-hitch the mules and get us some wood and water." Matthew and Edward walked the few dozen yards to the campfire.

"Who's your captain?" Matthew asked. A short, heavily bearded man dressed entirely in buckskin raised his right hand. "I am. Name's Elijah Blaylock. How's things up ahead?"

"The trail's in pretty good shape," Matthew answered. "It's been drier than a witch's teat, so there's not much spongy ground to mire you."

"We've had some pretty good rains from here on back east," Blaylock said. "The Neosho must've come out of its banks 'cause there's lots of water standing in the low places. I hope you've got some mosquito net. The damned things think we've got brandy for blood."

The two captains gossiped about mutual friends in the Santa Fe trade, two of whom had gone broke, until the talked turned to the war with Mexico.

"We didn't get much news in Santa Fe this past winter," Matt said. "Last thing we heard was that Polk sent somebody named Slidell to Mexico City to try and buy New Mexico and California."

"The newspapers say the Messkins was so mad about the Texas an-nexation in 'forty-five that they wouldn't even talk to Slidell," Blay-lock said. "Them spics give the president's man the back of their hand."

"Look, friend, Mex-i-cans aren't spics," Matt snapped. He debated with himself whether to make an issue of it until Edward tugged his sleeve. Since 1828, when they formed Collins & Waterman, the two men had learned to read the other's thoughts. Matthew recognized the look in Edward's eyes, brown eyes that ran to black when he was in-tense, that told him to drop the matter. *Edward is right*, he thought. *If they know I'm a Mexican, we could be in for real trouble.* Matt smiled at his partner in agreement. He paused and noticed the firelight highlighting the white speckles in Edward's dark hair.

"Sorry, Collins. No offense meant," Blaylock said and held up his hands, palms out in front of him as a sign that he had backed off.

"The Mexicans," Matt said, "were plenty unhappy with the Ameri-cans—thinking they could buy up chunks of Mexico like you buy a farm."

"It's just business," Blaylock said. "Same way as Jefferson bought Louisiana. The Messkins would've been a helluva lot better off if they'd sold. Our army's gonna whip their butts, and we won't have to pay 'em a damned cent. Too bad Andy Jackson died last year and ain't around to see this."

"That's enough about war," Matt said. "Look, we've good a goodly excess of Taos lightning, if that'd be of interest to you boys."

Timoteo brought out a cask of whiskey so raw that it would rasp a man's tongue and poured it into tin cups. "Anything excitin' happen down in Santa Fe?" Blaylock asked, swatting at mosquitoes and squatting on his haunches by the fire.

"We had a shooting at La Dama's," Edward said, laughing. "Dama doesn't like that kinda thing. Disturbs the monte players. And the whores get nervous. You boys'll be happy to know that Dama's got three new girls. One is really a looker, but she charges five silver pesos."

"What about the other two?" a teamster asked hopefully.

"There's a Mescalero Apache. She was a Navajo slave, but she escaped. The other one has bad smallpox scars, but she only charges two pesos."

"Is that dandy from Mexico City—Pérez—still the governor?" Blaylock asked.

"No," Matt said, "our good friend, the honorable Susano Baca, is back in the saddle. Now, we've got somebody we can do business with." Matthew took a sip of Taos lightning and shuddered as the firey liquor burned his throat. He scooted closer to the fire so the smoke could ward off mosquitoes, and cut himself a slice from a deer's hind quarter that was roasting on a spit.

"The salt makes all the difference in the world," Matt said, savoring the meat. "We lost ours when we crossed the Arkansas. The quicksand sucked our front wheels down so fast that the water flooded our salt box. But, say, I'm in a hurry to get back east. I saw that Dearborn parked over there and I was wondering if might be for sale."

The Dearborn's owner turned down Matt's offer of six bales of buffalo hides, but agreed to take thirty silver pesos and a small elkskin pouch of gold dust. The next morning, Matthew picked his two fastest mules and hitched them to the Dearborn, a light-weight buggy that could roll over the prairie three times faster than the ponderous freight wagons. As the sun lifted the gray off the tall grass, he shook Edward's hand, jumped in the Dearborn, and drove east from Council Grove.

———

For one hundred and fifty miles, Matt drove the mules hard—through the Narrows, past the Oregon Trail cutoff—until he pulled into the square at Independence, where he sold his mules and Dearborn to a livery stable.

The next morning, he boarded the *Western Queen* for the journey down the Missouri River. Runoff from heavy spring rains and the ship's steam engine pushed the sidewheeler eastward at a fast clip. Five days later, the *Western Queen* swept into St. Louis, where the pilot guided it to a berth among the Mississippi River steamers that jammed the waterfront.

Matt waited for a slave to unload his baggage and they walked to the Perryman Hotel. His old friend, Jim Perryman, juggled his reservation list and gave him a room that he did not have to share with strangers. The next morning, after an American breakfast of pancakes, gravy, and sausage, he boarded a paddle wheeler headed up the Ohio River to Wheeling, Virginia. From there, he made his way to Washington City. He hired a carriage at the train station and told the driver to find him a hotel close to the White House. In the City Hotel's oak-paneled reading room, he wrote letters to President Polk and Senator Benton, waved the notepaper in the humid air until the ink dried, and tipped a bellman handsomely to deliver them.

The next morning, he dressed in a grey suit that his St. Louis tailor had made for him and a pair of Cordoba leather boots his Mexico City cobbler had fashioned. At eight o'clock, the president's messenger met him in the hotel's lobby and led him down Pennsylvania Avenue toward the White House. *My God*, he thought when they walked up the mansion's driveway, *I've heard about this house all my life. Here I am, an orphan, and now I'm on my way to the president's house. When was it that the British burned it? Just over thirty years ago?*

The White House butler showed him to the president's reception room, where Senator Benton was waiting. Before the two men could exchange greetings, the butler ushered them into President Polk's office. The butler placed chairs in front of the ink-stained desk the president had brought with him when he came to the House of Representatives in 1825.

"Mr. Collins, the Senator has told me a little about you and your ties to New Mexico," Polk said. "I understand that you've been down there a long time?"

"Yes, Your Excellency," Matthew said, bowing stiffly.

"There are no excellencies in Washington, Mr. Collins. Take a seat. Senator Benton says you speak Spanish."

"Yes, sir. I made my first trip to Santa Fe in 1826, and I saw Americans down there who couldn't speak Spanish. They lost a lot of money by not being able to deal with the local people. Now, I'm more comfortable speaking Spanish than English." Matt drew a handkerchief from his inside breast pocket to dab at the sweat that was trickling out of his sideburns.

"And your wife's a Mexican?"

"Her father's family immigrated to New Mexico in the early sixteen hundreds. My children are Mexican, and my business is there."

"And what—let's call them 'affiliations'—do you have?"

"My father-in-law is well-connected. He knows the other *hacendados* well. Over the years, I've gotten to know a few people." Below the desk, where President Polk couldn't see, Matthew twisted his handkerchief into a tight roll and crushed it in his fist.

"Senator Benton tells me that you've become a Mexican citizen."

Matthew's mouth suddenly became so dry that his tongue almost stuck to his palate. "Being a citizen has practical benefits. I can own land and have a retail store, which foreigners can't. And my taxes are lower."

"I know about those damned taxes," the president said, pounding his fist in his other hand. "They discriminate against Americans. Our ambassador tried to do something about it, but the Mexicans wouldn't budge. Mr. Collins, could I have a few words in private with the senator?" Polk pointed to the door.

When Matt left, the president tilted his black leather chair at an angle, put his feet on his desk, and clasped his hands behind his neck. "I don't know about him Tom. He's got the contacts, and I'm guessing that he understands the Mexicans, but he may not know whether he's an American or a Mexican. This mission is too important for someone with questionable loyalties."

Benton fidgeted with his watch chain, annoyed that Polk had challenged his judgment, and instinctively took the offensive, leaning forward and jutting out his chin. "Mr. President, I've know this man for eight years. He may be a Mexican in name, but at heart he's an American. He told me he took on Mexican citizenship as a matter of convenience, and you heard him say it yourself. When I've talked to him about Mexico, it's clear that he's sick of the chaos down there. For Christsake, the presidency has changed hands fifteen times since

Mexico became independent twenty-five years ago. And the government is so weak that it can't protect New Mexico from the Indians. The savages even attacked Santa Fe a few years ago."

"Are you absolutely sure about him, Tom? If Collins can't bring this off, it will jeopardize our entire war effort."

"Mr. President, I assure you that he has no truck with the path Mexico is following. You have no cause for worry." Under the senator's beefy arms, sweat had seeped through his coat and made dark circles.

President Polk rang a small silver bell and his butler opened the door. "Send in Mr. Collins."

When the butler approached Matt from behind and coughed softly to get his attention, Matt almost jumped. He managed a tight smile, followed the butler into the president's office, and took his seat beside Senator Benton.

"There are a lot of my fellow Americans who would tell you that we are going to roll up the Mexicans in a few weeks or months," Polk said. "But I'm here to tell you that this is going to be a long and difficult war. My sources tell me that Mexico has a well-trained officer corps, particularly in the cavalry."

"What you've heard about the Mexican cavalry is true, Mr. President," Matt said.

"What I'm about to tell you, Mr. Collins, requires the utmost confidentiality. If I hear that you've breached this confidence, I'll find you wherever you are. Is that understood?"

"Yes, Mr. President."

"We'll be fighting in Mexican territory, on ground that they know and we don't. Our supply lines will be longer than Napoleon's when he went to Russia. And our army hasn't fought anything more than Indian skirmishes since the 1812 war. We simply don't have enough troops to fight major battles in New Mexico." Polk rubbed his chin and stared steadily at Matt. "What kind of army can the New Mexicans muster, Mr. Collins?"

"Mr. President, there are a few regular troops in Santa Fe, but they are poorly armed and trained. They kill off a few Apaches and Navajos every so often, but that's all they know about war."

"And militia?"

"I'd guess that Governor Baca could raise four or five thousand men. Mostly peons and Pueblo Indians."

"Mr. Collins," Polk said, "there are some folks in Congress who fought like hell against bringing Texas in as a slave state. And some of those idiots don't think that we need to expand to the west. So we'll have plenty of opposition to raising men and money for this fight. We've got to neutralize New Mexico."

"I understand, sir," Matt said, straightening his back to raise himself to his full height.

"How well do you know—what's his name—the governor?"

"Susano Baca. He's related to my wife's family, and I have done business with him for years. He's not exactly an *hombre de confianza*, but I know him well."

"An *hombre de* what?"

"Someone in your deepest confidence, someone you would trust with anything," Matt said.

"This Baca—what kind of man is he?"

"He's the third son of an old family from near Albuquerque that lost its money. He's very—ah—very acquisitive. They tell a story about how, when Baca was a boy, he stole sheep from a blind neighbor and then sold them back a few days later."

"That makes a good story," Polk said, "but—"

Matt broke in, and Polk twisted his mouth in annoyance. "I know for a fact, sir, that he takes bribes from the American traders to cut their taxes or to look the other way if they're smuggling. And there's been a scandal over some land grants that he made. It's not on the record, but everybody knows that he got a secret interest in that land under the table."

"Anything else?"

"If you'll excuse me, sir, he has a politician's need to be liked. And he has a knack for surviving. He has gotten himself appointed governor four times by both liberal and conservative governments in Mexico City. When he's out of office, he knows how to bide his time until the right moment to get back in."

"We might learn a few lessons from this Baca," Polk said to Senator Benton with a half smile. "Anything more?"

"A lot of Americans don't like him. They think he's a political opportunist with no principles and that he's a despot. But I get along with him. We've never had any trouble."

"Anyone else with power?"

"Colonel Diego Zambrano. He commands the army."

"What about him?"

"He's another story. I'm not that close to him, but my partner Edward

Waterman is. Zambrano's from an old, aristocratic family down in Guadalajara, and he fancies himself a Napoleon. He's more than happy to join with the Church and the *ricos* to run the country."

"Do you think the New Mexicans will fight?" Polk asked. He leaned back in his chair and put his feet on his desk. When Matt gave him an astonished look, the president, embarrassed by his rudeness, put his feet back under his desk.

"Baca's likely to do anything. But you can negotiate with him. Zambrano? He's a fierce Mexican nationalist, and he's never gotten over the loss of Texas. He sees Americans as grasping expansionists who have had their eyes on Mexican territory for a long time."

"Mr. Collins, what I have in mind for you wouldn't fit with Colonel Zambrano's view of what is in Mexico's best interests. But, quite frankly, I'm worried about your loyalty to the United States."

Matthew's fair skin flushed as red as his hair, and a bitter, acid taste rose in his throat. "Sir, I think I know where this is headed. Before we discuss this further, I'd like to think it over."

Polk paused for several seconds and let his eyes scan the ceiling before giving Matt a long, assessing look. "Can you be back here in the morning at ten?"

"Yes, sir." Matt stood and looked down at the seated president. He wiped his moist palm on his pant leg and reached across the desk to shake Polk's hand.

Senator Benton was shocked by Matt's hesitancy and his face showed it. "If you'll be in your hotel, Matt, I would like to meet with you this evening."

It was Matt's turn to pause, to consider whether he wanted to listen to the bullying that he was sure would come from the Missouri senator. "I will either be in the bar or the restaurant, Senator."

BOOK I

1822–1827

CHAPTER ONE

1822

"When my indenture's up next month, I'm gone. I hear the Santa Fe Trail's dangerous as hell—eight hundred miles through Indian country."

ON AN AUTUMN AFTERNOON, HANS BANHOFER'S DOORBELL TIN-kled to announce the mother superior of the Sisters of Charity orphanage. His general store's shelves were jammed with merchandise and he had stacked barrels and boxes in the aisles, which forced Sister Marie Thérése to turn sideways to avoid bumping into other customers. She stood in line for over thirty minutes to pay Banhofer for the bolt of black broadcloth and white French linen she needed to sew new habits for her nuns. "Mr. Banhofer," she said while he was figuring her order, "it looks to me like you need an assistant."

Banhofer was so busy that he barely heard her, "What's that, Sister?"

"I've got a boy you might want to take on as an apprentice."

"I try to keep my costs down, but lately I've been swamped. Tell me about the boy," Banhofer said deferentially. Although he never attended church, he had been raised a Catholic and taught to respect nuns and priests.

"He came to us when he was a few days old. His mother was French. The mother, uh—worked on the riverboats," Sister Marie Thérése said, her blushing face set off against her white cowl. "She told me his father's name was Collins, and I picked Matthew for his Christian name. He's a good boy, but he's almost grown, and it's time for him to learn a trade."

"What about his character?" Hans asked. Although he had been in the United States for over twenty years, his "w"s still morphed into "v"s, a legacy of his birth in a southern German village.

"He's very serious," the nun answered. "And he's quick with languages—French, and his Latin is so good he serves as an altar boy. I wouldn't say he's shy, but he doesn't show his emotions much. He tries to keep himself under control, but he'll flare up occasionally."

"What about his reading and writing?"

"He'll read anything you put in front of him. The Bible. Our set of Shakespeare's plays and sonnets. But I must be honest with you, Mr. Banhofer. You'll have to keep after him or he'll be off reading rather than doing his chores."

"And his ciphering?"

"He'll need your help with numbers. But he's a bright boy, and he'll get better."

"Is he clean?"

"He keeps himself cleaner than most boys."

"I'll expect him to bathe twice a week, even in winter. We do a lot of trade with the ladies, and they don't like boys who smell bad or have head lice. Can you bring him in tomorrow, Sister?"

The next morning, Sister Marie Thérése climbed out of her buggy, lifted her black robes above her ankles to keep them out of the mud, and signaled for Matthew Collins to follow her into Banhofer's store. Matt's jugged ears and hatchetlike nose deprived him of handsomeness, and at thirteen he was already tall, but still gawky with his newfound height. His red hair, as it did every summer, had turned almost blond from working alongside the Sisters of Charity in their vegetable and herb gardens.

"Why do you want to work in a dry goods store?" Banhofer asked. "You could make more money in the coopering or saddlery trades."

"Well, sir, Sister didn't ask me where I wanted to go." Sister Marie Thérése clamped her hand on Matthew's shoulder and squeezed until it hurt, reminding him that there was no tolerance for even the slightest impertinence.

"He works hard, Mr. Banhofer," the nun insisted. "He's still a boy, but he figures people out quickly. In short order, he'll know how to keep your customers happy, and who he can and can't give credit to."

"I would want you to sign up for five years, Matthew. You'll get room and board and a little pocket money. But, Sister, I'm not so wealthy that I can pay the Church for his services."

"We just want to get the boy situated," she said. "Three new orphans came this month, and we don't have room for them. We would be in your debt if you would take him, Mr. Banhofer."

Hans gave Matthew a stern look. "Son, when I was indentured, a man with a strict set of rules taught me this business. I run my store by those rules, and I'll expect you to follow them—down to the letter. If you try to run away before your contract's up, I'll have the law on you. Do you understand?"

"Yes, sir," he answered calmly, looking directly in Banhofer's eyes.

"Fine. I'll get a lawyer to draw up the indenture papers. You and Sister can come back next Monday and we'll sign them."

After a few months, Matthew had resigned himself to the tight rules Hans Banhofer set for the running of his business. His master had arrived in the New World in 1799 and joined the tide of immigrants who were rushing west to the frontier. Hans made his living as a store clerk and finally settled in Kaskaskia, a river port that had just been designated Illinois' state capitol. When he first arrived, the Creole river men cursed and joked in French as easily as English, and the priests proudly rang the cast-iron bell that Louis XV had donated to the Church of the Immaculate Conception when Louisiana was still part of France.

As the Americans flooded in, Kaskaskia became an integral part of the Mississippi River network, an enterpôt that supplied the fur trappers and traders who were headed northwest up the Missouri River and southwest to Santa Fe. The city fathers were quick to brag that their Gallic-flavored town was larger than St. Louis and that Lewis and Clark had spent several days there before they left to search for the Northwest Passage.

Hans invested his entire savings in a small dry goods store along the riverfront to cater to Kaskaskia's politicians, merchants, and the rich farmers who grew twice as much corn in the fertile bottom land as did their neighbors on higher ground. The rich soil and the vibrant Mississippi, Missouri, and Ohio River trade routes gave Kaskaskians the money to pay premium prices for Hans's embroidered silks, plush velvets, and English woolens that Negro slaves unloaded from the ships.

By 1822, Banhofer's small store had grown to become an emporium, with a large blue and gold sign that proclaimed BANHOFER'S GENERAL MERCHANDISE. It was a one-story red brick building that had two large, multipane display windows overlooking the wide brown river. For years he had put in long hours, but he was frugal to a fault and had put off getting a clerk until, nearing forty-five, he had almost worked himself to exhaustion. The men he had talked to had demanded what he thought were ridiculously high salaries, so he was happy to get Matthew for room and board and pocket change.

The year before Matt became indentured to Banhofer, Mexico had thrown off Spanish colonial rule and had opened its doors to trade with the United States. At the store, Matt heard the stories that trickled back to Kaskaskia about William Becknell, a Franklin, Missouri, man who had led a pack train loaded with merchandise through the Comanche country and into the newborn Mexican Republic. Becknell, the stories went, came back from Santa Fe with bags of silver and gold—and profits upwards of 600 percent.

Matt and his apprentice friends gossiped about Becknell's enormous profits and longed for the day that they were free to go west. He had made several friends, but, for reasons he couldn't define, an apprentice at Alphonse Larue's blacksmith shop particularly intrigued him. Most of the boys were frightened of Brady Hardin, never knowing when some offhand remark might send him into a rage. He had bloodied boys who had asked questions about the steamboat captain's daughter he had flirted with, and, when he drank, which was often, he radiated danger.

On a Saturday after the shops had closed, a group of apprentices bought a small keg of beer and went to a clump of trees south of town that they called their "club." Pierre Laroche, a printer's devil for the *Kaskaskia Press*, began mocking Matt's shambling gait. Matt kept sipping his beer and said nothing until Pierre, annoyed that he got no rise, shouted, "I hear your mama's a whore." Matt lowered his head and went at his antagonist, but Pierre, a short, husky boy nearing twenty, knocked him to the ground with a powerful blow to the cheek. Pierre jumped on Matt and began pummeling him until Brady, his eyes wide and face red with the excitement of a fight, picked up a fallen tree branch and slammed it into the back of Pierre's head. Brady kicked the unconscious Pierre several more times and walked away, exhilarated.

After that, the apprentices left Matt alone. A week later, Brady banged on the back door of Banhofer's store. Matt opened the door and waited for Brady to say something. Instead, he said nothing, but held up the cane poles, twine, and barbed hooks he was carrying, and nodded toward the river. After several moments of silence, Brady said, "Let's go fishin'. I know a place with still water where the catfish feed in the afternoon."

"I'm reading."

"Readin'? What the hell are you readin'?" Brady almost shouted and his face darkened. "What crap. Damn it, let's go," he commanded.

Matt put his book down, laced up his brogans, and rose.

They walked at Brady's fast pace, stopping only to catch grasshoppers for bait. On a spit of land that broke the river's current, they put their lines in the gray-brown water. Brady raised his shirt and pulled a flask from his waist. "I made the still myself—out of some old tin and copper we had lyin' around. Want a drink?"

"No thanks."

"How old are you, Matt?"

"Thirteen."

"They say you're an orphan boy," Brady said, taking a seat on the bank. "Me too." Without waiting for a response, he said, "When I was a little younger than you, my old lady died of the ague, and the old man run off—just disappeared. Somebody told me the bastard went out west and the Indians killed him."

"How'd you live?"

"By beggin'. And I got a meal ever' now and then from the county. One afternoon, a constable grabbed me. He waved this paper in my face and told me that the county judge had ordered me to be indentured to old man Larue." Brady's expression changed. "You ever jacked off?"

"I don't think so."

"You even know what I'm talking about?"

"No."

"Loped the ole mule?" Brady said, unbuttoning his pants. "Like this."

Matt flushed and wheeled around to stare across the river. When Brady finished, he took another pull on his flask. "You heard about this Becknell fella?"

"I heard he's made huge profits," Matt answered, still afraid to look in Brady's direction.

"When my indenture's up next month, I'm gone. It hear the Santa Fe Trail's dangerous as hell—eight hundred miles through Indian country. But who gives a shit. By the time I'm thirty, I either want to be dead or to have my fortune made. How much longer are you stuck here?"

"Almost five years."

"Banhofer's a tough old German," Brady said. "I wouldn't have lasted thirty minutes with him."

"He's not so bad. He's only laid the rod to me once, when I misquoted the price of some fox pelts and he lost fifty dollars."

———

It was a rainy winter day in 1825 when Brady Hardin walked in the front door of Banhofer's general merchandise store. "My God, it's been three years," Matt exclaimed. "Welcome home."

"It ain't home no more. Kaskaskia's just a place to buy some merchandise and kill some time till the Santa Fe caravans leave next spring."

"I can't talk now," Matt said, picking up an account book and quill. "We're restocking and taking inventory. I'll meet you in front of the Belle Frontiére Bar at seven."

"You old enough to get in?" Brady teased.

"I'm sixteen. Besides, they don't ask."

Since he had left Kaskaskia, Brady had become massive, with thick, heavily muscled arms. The harsh sun on the Santa Fe Trail had tanned his already dark complexion a leathery brown, and, in his broad-brimmed felt hat and ankle-length dust coat, he looked older than his twenty years.

That evening, Brady paced impatiently back and forth in front of the Belle Frontiére, glancing inside at the clock behind the bar, until, at seven thirty, he saw Matt hurrying toward him. "Where the fuck you been?"

"Sorry. Banhofer wouldn't let me leave until we toted up the last box of straw hats."

They went into the Belle Frontiére and took a table near the fire. "Why the hell don't you fix that fireplace," Brady shouted at the barman between coughs. "It don't draw worth a shit."

"It is smoky in here," Matt said, "but it's nothing a beer won't fix."

"What you been doing since I left? Countin' ladies' corsets?" Brady sneered.

"Same old things. Sweeping, stacking, keeping the books. But I've learned what sells and what won't, and about who you can trust and who you can't. I can almost smell it when somebody's out to cheat or he's lying."

"Sounds boring as hell. How you gettin' on with Banhofer?"

"Seems like he's gotten stricter as he's gotten older. Gripes all the time—about everything. Or maybe I've gotten older and don't cotton to all his rules. I can't even pee without his permission. And he hasn't raised my allowance for a year. Skimps on everything. He even waits to buy our dinner vegetables till they're about to rot and the prices come down. The only thing he doesn't mind spending money on is the whores coming off the riverboats."

"Tight-fisted bastard."

"He's like a bitch hound with her pup, watching everything I do. Even if I add up the accounts two or three times, he almost always finds an error. If he doesn't, he gets mad because he's sure there's a mistake he didn't find."

"Fuck him," Brady said, gulping his beer and waving at the barman for another.

"He gets peevish if he catches me reading at night. He says I'm wasting whale oil."

"Can't say as I blame him for that. You oughta quit readin' and start doin'."

"That's enough of the store clerk's saga. Tell me about the Santa Fe trade."

"There's big profits for those who knows what they're doin'." Brady's voice raced to a staccato beat, as it always did when he was excited, and for the first time since they had sat down the scowl left his face, which became happily animated. "When my apprenticeship was over, old man Larue give me a set of clothes, a Bible, and thirty-five dollars. I went straight to Franklin. It's booming. There's lots more chance out on the frontier for people with nothin'—like you and me."

"How did you hook up with the Santa Fe Trail?" Matt asked.

"Met this Englishman. He come down here by way of Canada," Brady said. "He had the money to outfit four wagons, and he needed teamsters. Offered thirty dollars a month. Plus food. I took it. We went down the forest trail till we got to Independence. Not much of a town. From there, we went west."

"What's it like out there?" Matt asked.

"On the prairie, you're cut loose from the civilized world. You're in the wild. Ain't nobody to stop you but yourself. You can do whatever you want if you've got enough balls."

"People say the Indians are dangerous."

"Who gives a shit about some fuckin' savages? You'll see some, and they'll try to run off your horses and mules. But they're like hornets. They don't bother you unless you stir 'em up."

"What about Santa Fe?"

"Their homes is all mud," Brady said. "Lots of cripples 'cause there ain't no doctors to set a leg or birth a baby. If you can do anything proper, you can make out real well. I made fifty dollars shoein' horses 'cause there ain't no smithy in Santa Fe."

"There must be something good about it."

"The good is that the greasers down in Mexico City ship merchandise to Santa Fe. But their prices are so much higher than ours, it ain't no competition. Last year, Captain Vick let me take twenty dollars worth of merchandise, and I sold it in a week for over a hundred."

"Mr. Banhofer's lucky if he makes a twenty percent profit."

"And you can have some good times," Brady said, talking so fast that his words almost ran together. "Everybody in New Mexico knows when the caravans'll get to Santa Fe. And there's some good-lookin' women what come from miles around. Lots of the gals are married to goat herders. They're so damned poor they'll jump through their ass if you give 'em a couple of extra dollars. There's fandangos a couple 'a nights a week."

"Fandangos?"

"Dances—where there's everybody from the governor down to the peons. I met a gal last summer at a fandango. We had us some real fun. A few days later, I takes her to another fandango, and this greaser don't like me bein' with a Messkin woman. Kept makin' these remarks."

"How'd you understand him?"

"It ain't hard to get the idea. You know me, Matt. I don't take shit, I give shit. We went outside and had good fight," Brady said, lifting his shirt to show a ten-inch scar on his belly. "When that healed up, I come on back. Got home with just over seventy dollars to buy a stock of goods for next year's caravan. With any luck, I'll turn that seventy into three hundred." He paused and grimaced. "I gotta piss."

"There's a hole out back with lye in it," Matt said. "It doesn't stink too bad." Matt lifted his beer glass and whisked away the wet circle it had formed on the table. Brady, he knew, reveled in his bravado, but his aggression alienated most everyone. Still, there was something intriguing about him. *Maybe*, Matt thought, *it was because they were both orphans or because Brady had protected him from bullies, or because, wherever Brady was, there was excitement and often danger.* Matt wasn't sure.

"What's it like to be in a foreign country?" Matt asked when Brady came back.

"When the caravans get to Santa Fe in June, us Americans take over the town. Somehow, it don't feel like you're in the real world. It's like you're from heaven or hell or some other world. In a funny kinda way, you feel a lot freer and you get to thinkin' that the Messkins can't do nothin' to you."

"That fellow with the knife damned sure did something to you," Matt said, smiling.

"I got ahold of him too. I beat him with an ax handle so's he couldn't come outa his house for more'n a week."

"The Mexicans didn't arrest you?"

"Unless you kill somebody, they leave the Americans alone 'cause they're makin' too much money off us. Matt, you oughta think about goin' with me. With what you've learned from Banhofer, you know ten times more about buyin' and sellin' than most of them proprietors."

"I've learned a lot from the old man," Matt said, "but he's gotten his money's worth. When he's with his women, he leaves me to run the shop. His river gals make a beeline for the store as soon as their boats tie up. Sometimes, he jumps them in the back room, and I'm sitting out front listening to some gal's butt slapping a stack of buffalo hides and him moaning like a mounted-up bull. Makes it hard to keep my mind on how many new stockings and suspenders we need to order."

Brady went to the bar, got another beer for Matt and a whiskey for himself, and returned to the table. "You gotta figure out whether you're gonna live for old man Banhofer or for yourself. Whether you're gonna spend your life with them ink stains on your hands. Do what you want, but you'll be lettin' one hell of a chance slip by if you don't jump into this Santa Fe trade. There may not be another money-makin' proposition like this one to come along for years. Them goddamned Messkins are so screwed up—changin' governments all the time—they might shut down the Trail or do somethin' else that bungles it up. You never know what'll happen."

"I'd need to think on something like that, Brady."

"Think all you want, but there's something else that's gonna kill this trade in the next few years."

"What's that?"

"You come out to Franklin, and you'll see men swoopin' in from Kentucky, Tennessee, North Carolina, and from as far away as Connecticut and New York. So far, only about thirty-five wagons a year been goin' down the Trail. But, with all the newspapers talkin' about the Santa Fe profits, it won't be long before there's two hundred wagons. There's even a few of the rich Messkins gettin' in on it. *Ricos* they call 'em. Prices are gonna come down, and sloggin' your way down that trail ain't gonna be near as romancey—or as profitable."

Brady took a long, greedy drink of his beer, swallowed wrong, choked, and spit it on the table. He almost doubled over with coughing and went outside to catch his breath and clear his head. While Matt waited, he weighed Brady's dare. He still had two years remaining under his indenture, but his employer had gotten full value the last three years. "When are you going to Franklin?" Matt asked when Brady returned.

"I've got my merchandise ordered up," Brady said. "I'm shipping it on the *Beau Riviére*. She sails the day after tomorrow."

"I don't plan to spend my life being somebody's store clerk. I know I've got to make my move at some point. I just don't know if it's now."

"You think about it, and let me know."

"Let's have another beer," Matt said, his face relaxing into a smile. "How would we get away? Mr. Banhofer'll have the sheriff after me sure as hell."

"You slip out real quiet tomorrow night. Tomorrow's Saturday, and Banhofer won't know you're gone till Monday morning. If we take the inland road and walk all night, we'll be out of Randolph County before they know you're gone. Once we're across the county line, the sheriff can't arrest you. Besides, he'll probably be lookin' for you to take the river road. We'll catch up to the *Beau Riviére* in St. Louis and take her to Franklin."

"All I've got saved up is fifteen dollars," Matt said.

"Captain Vick'll probably be needin' teamsters, and if he don't you can hire on with another proprietor. Matt, you gotta be gutsy."

When the store closed the next day, Matt rolled up his extra clothes, a packet of crackers, and his copy of James Fenimore Cooper's *The Pioneers* in a blanket, and tied it with a rope to make a sling. After sunset, he and Brady walked north, and sometimes broke into a jog along the inland road.

CHAPTER TWO

1826

"I am not making this trip because I like to travel. I am making it because I want to make money."

SPRING RAINS AND SNOWMELT HAD DEEPENED THE MISSOURI so that river traffic could begin. Matthew Collins joined the crowd walking to meet Franklin Missouri's first steamboat of the year. The warm air over the cool river had created a shroud of gray-white fog that cut visibility to almost nothing. The unseen ship signaled with its whistle, while on shore a man banged on a frying pan with a hammer to guide the paddle wheeler to where it could tie up. The crowd cheered when its prow jumped out of the fog and hit the mud flats with a thud.

"God damn it Jed, I told you to bring it in slow," the captain yelled at his first officer on the bridge. Crewmen threw a line to the shore, and Matt grabbed it and snubbed it to a tree. Two sailors jumped off the bow, sank to their knees in mud, and struggled to pull the gangplank to a grassy rise.

"That's him, Matt, the Englishman I told you about," Brady said, pointing to the first passenger off the ship, a portly man in an ill-fitting black wool suit with a red face that looked like it was going to break into a sweat. Amos Vick was a man with a big-boned frame, big enough to carry his excess flesh with ease. He walked down the gangplank with an air of fastidiousness that set him apart from the other passengers. When he stepped on shore and made his way through the crowd, Brady motioned for Matt to follow him. "Good to see you again, Mr. Vick," Brady said. Vick tipped his brown beaver hat, revealing a bald pate that was surrounded by a Franciscan friar's fringe of iron grey hair. Offsetting his lack of hair, however, was a heavy line of bushy eyebrows.

"Brady, I am surprised that you aren't dead," the Englishman said in a tone that did not reveal whether he was joking or serious.

"I been in a few scrapes since I seen you last fall, but I whipped 'em all. You got your goods with you?"

"Indeed, I have. I bought sixteen thousand pounds of merchandise in Cincinnati and Louisville, and I will need help offloading it."

"I'm ready, and my friend here, Matt Collins, will help too."

"Collins? Irish, are you?" Vick asked.

"A little Irish, a little French, sir."

"If you can keep Brady sober, Mr. Collins, I will hire you both to unload."

"I know what you mean, Mr. Vick. Brady's some kind of hell when he's drunk."

"No profanity, son," Vick said, twisting his face in distaste.

"Excuse me, sir," Matt said, embarrassed. "We'll get your job done."

Amos Vick oversaw Matt and Brady while they unloaded his merchandise, stacked it in a vacant lot next to the sheriff's office, and covered it with oiled canvas. Because it was a warm day and they had sweated their shirts black, Vick paid them four rather than the three dollars they had agreed upon. "I'd like to hire on with you again this year, Mr. Vick," Brady said. "And I got about seventy-dollars-worth of goods that I'd like to put on one of your wagons."

"I ordered four wagons in St. Louis. There ought to be room for your merchandise, Brady. The freighting cost will be eight cents a pound."

"That's fair enough, Captain. My friend here wants to hire on too."

"You are big enough, young man. How tall are you?

"Six two, sir."

"Have you worked with mules?"

"No."

"Ever handled a blacksnake whip?"

"No, sir."

"Why should I hire you?"

"Well, Mr. Vick, you took on Brady when he was a greenhorn, and he worked out. I'm as able as he was, plus I can read and write and cipher if you need me to. And, since I've got red hair and I'm taller than anybody else, you'll always be able to find me."

Vick's ruddy cheeks twitched and his mouth broke into a broad smile.

Although he was a staunch Baptist, believing fervently that an avenging God has a special place in hell for the frivolous, he fancied that he had an uncommonly acute sense of humor. "You did a good job offloading, Matthew. It is not often that you find someone so diligent out here on the frontier. The pay is twenty-five dollars a month and, of course, victuals."

"Brady got thirty dollars last year."

"That was last year, when there were fewer men. In this year of our Lord, eighteen twenty six, there are experienced men in abundance who are looking to go to Santa Fe. The pay is twenty-five dollars."

"Mr. Vick," Matt pleaded, "I need that extra five dollars."

"Twenty-five."

Matt read Amos Vick for a man who, when he made up his mind, was not likely to change it. "When do you figure we'll start?" he asked.

"I plan to leave Franklin within a week after my freight wagons arrive and we fit them out—about four weeks."

"That's going to stretch me, Mr. Vick. All I've got is the four dollars you paid me. Any chance of an advance."

"No advances, old chap. When you finish the work, you get paid."

Matt found a job at the Double Eagle Tavern, sweeping and washing dishes in return for meals and a pint of beer a day. Brady introduced him to Tim Creasy, a teamster who agreed to rent Matt space in his tent for twenty-five cents a week. Even though spring was advancing, the nights were still chilly, and Matt traded the thin blanket he had brought with him—plus seventy-five cents—to the barber's wife in exchange for a quilt that she had made of woolen scraps and had insulated with cotton lint.

That night, he wrapped himself in the quilt and went to bed. Long after midnight, Creasy crawled into the tent and closed the flap. Matt awoke to the sound of Creasy muttering to himself and hiccuping, and he smelled his tentmate's body odor and foul breath. Thereafter he slept in the open.

On a Sunday morning Matt followed a crowd to the west side of town, where tradesmen had built homes for their families. Every day for weeks, the Missouri's spring runoff had been nibbling a few inches off Franklin's shoreline. But word had spread that a particularly hard rain upstream had created a tidal wave. Matt heard a roar and, like an amoeba, the crowd rushed back and watched a wall of water slam into the shore. Giant oaks that had toppled into the river acted as jack hammers and excavated fifteen feet of bank and washed away six log cabins.

A few townsfolk predicted that it was just a matter of time before all of Franklin would wind up in the river, but, mostly, the town's shopkeepers and tradesmen were full of optimism. Franklin, they boasted, would soon become the gateway to the West. Its boosters crowed that the town's coopers were working late every night, hewing barrels and crates out of Missouri hardwood to carry Kentucky whiskey and factory-made boots to Santa Fe. Its wheelwrights were making final adjustments to freight wagons that had been prefabricated in Pittsburgh and St. Louis for assembly in Franklin. And its blacksmiths were hammering out iron wheel tires and L-shaped braces to strengthen wagon beds for the journey over the rough trail across the Great American Desert.

Franklin's four tavern keepers were making small fortunes from their poker and billiard tables and by selling liquor and beer to the teamsters, scouts, buffalo hunters, and fur trappers. While Matt was mopping the Double Eagle's planked floor and washing out beer glasses, he overheard the men joking about the sexual talents of Pug-nosed Sally and Black-assed Beth, and he was curious.

The Double Eagle's owner had rented a small room at the rear of the tavern to Raquel, who Matthew recognized from her visits with Hans Banhofer in Kaskaskia. Raquel's advancing age and weakness for alcoholic drink had expanded her to a pink plumpness that earned her the nickname Lady Bountiful. Although she wasn't the most beautiful of Franklin's prostitutes, her adherence to a level of cleanliness far above that of the other girls attracted a steady traffic.

"Miss Raquel, what was it you called yourself when you used to visit Mr. Banhofer in Kaskaskia?"

"I've been Josephine and Babette. I don't remember what name I used with Banhofer. I do remember that I liked him because he was neat and tidy, even if he was a stingy old German. Never gave me anything extra. You know him?"

"I worked for him. I was usually stacking or toting when you came in."

"Now I remember that red mop of yours bobbing up from behind the counter. You used to stare at me."

"Well, a good-looking woman deserves staring at. I always admired your clothes and hats. I especially remember a rose-colored dress you wore."

"I loved that dress. Lost it when the boiler on the *Pride of New Orleans* blew up and burned damned near everything on board."

"I'd say your new wardrobe, especially the yellow dress with the white lace, looks good on you. This may not be exactly polite, Miss Raquel, but it flatters your figure. Not to say that your figure isn't good to begin with."

"You trying to cozy up to me?"

"Well, yes ma'am, I am."

"Won't work."

"Miss Raquel, I'll be honest. I can't afford the three dollars you've been getting. I've heard the men talking, and I'd sure like to try it. But all I can pay is a dollar."

"No money, no deal."

"Now, wait before you make up your mind. You'd be giving me my first ride, and I'd remember you and that yellow dress always."

"Look, son, you've got a friendly way about you, and I like you. And you say nice things. But my work pays for those satin dresses, and there's no way you're getting in bed without paying. So, no, no, and no."

"I take your point. But, if I ever get three dollars in my pocket, I know where I'm going first."

Raquel laughed as Matt picked up his broom and left.

When Amos Vick's wagons arrived by steamboat, he put Matt and Brady on his payroll to help a wheelwright assemble the parts. Vick paid cash for forty mules that a proprietor had bought in Santa Fe and driven back to Missouri. Then he staked out the boundaries of a corral in an open field, and, when Matt and Brady had dug in posts and strung rope, he began teaching his teamsters to break the half-wild mules to harness.

"Brady," Vick said, pointing to a brindled mule, "lasso that one and blindfold its eyes."

Brady confidently tossed a rope around the mule's neck. As he approached with the blindfold, the animal rolled its eyes but didn't move, and Brady quickly tied a strip of muslin in place. The sightless mule's left rear hoof flared twice, searching for an enemy. Brady slapped the animal's jaw a hard blow and yanked the rope to distract it while Matt put the harness over its head and buckled it. When Brady took off the blindfold, the terrified mule raced in a half circle at the end of the rope and let out high-pitched brays of rage.

"I say, the beast is not going to come down easily," Vick said. "So we will break it the hard way. Brady, put the rope around that wagon wheel and haul it in until its nose is an inch or two from the wheel."

The young mule was so strong that, even with Brady's immense strength, he could not move it. "Matthew," Vick shouted, "don't just stand there like a fool. Help him!" Matt dodged the animal's flailing hooves, grabbed an ear, twisted it hard, and tried to force the mule toward the wheel. The squealing and kicking continued until the mule was out of fight and yielded to the rope. "Tie it to a lower spoke so that its neck has a good bow in it. It should learn its lesson by morning," Vick said.

"That's a pretty harsh lesson," Matt said.

"Sentimental rubbish," Vick said. "A mule is a machine. Just like a textile loom. The only thing important about them is how well they work."

The next morning Vick picked out the most experienced animals to be the lead mules that the others would learn to follow, and instructed his crew to harness the experienced animals next to the tyros so they could learn to work in pairs. "'Gee' means right," Vick told the first-time teamsters, "and 'haw' means left. 'Whoa' means stop, and, if you want them to stop in a hurry, it's 'whoa, you son of a buck,'" Vick said, smiling broadly at his own humor.

"That's as close as I've ever heard him come to a cussword," Brady whispered to Matt.

With sharp jerks on the traces and occasional pops from blacksnake whips, the teamsters directed pairs of mules right and left, forward and backward. When the pairs began answering to voice commands, the men harnessed together their best six animals and sent the others to be tended by the drover in the cavvyard, the herd of spare animals that would follow the caravan.

"We depart in two days," Vick told his teamsters. "We will load tomorrow. I know that some of you are thinking that this will be your last chance to drink spirits until we get to Independence, and you are right. There are rules in my caravan, and I enforce them as strictly as a ship's captain. I do not wish to hear any swearing. And any man caught drinking, playing cards, or fighting will get a taste of the lash. We will not travel on Sundays, and I will conduct services which you may or may not attend."

"He ain't kiddin'," Brady said. "Last year he whipped two men for fightin'."

The next morning, the men drew up Vick's four wagons in front of his stacked merchandise. He climbed on a wagon bed and announced, "I am not making this trip because I like to travel. I am making it because I want to make money. And every bottle of perfume that breaks and every box of peppermint candy that gets crushed loses me money. It is our job to pack the wagons so that that does not happen."

Vick methodically supervised the stowing of boxes and barrels to pre-
vent shifting when the springless wagons rumbled over the Santa Fe
Trail's ruts. First, the men heaved crates onto the floor boards. If Vick
could run a quarter-inch hickory stick in the crack between two boxes,
they were too far apart, and he made Matt and Brady push them together,
while others lashed them into place. Beside the boxes, the teamsters
loaded barrels of molasses and paraffin wax for candles. Then came a
layer of mackinaw blankets and bolts of cloth for cushioning, topped off
with boxes of cigars, lace, and ribbons. Even though the wagons had bonnets, the men wrapped the loads with sheets of Osnabrück linen. When
his crew finished tying the ropes, Vick tested them for tightness. If he
could slip his index finger under a rope, it had to be retied. "If I see one
corner of a sheet flapping in the wind I will dock your pay," he said.

For all his professed Baptist piety, it did little to disguise the fact that
Amos Vick was a shrewd businessman who paid attention to every detail. He went over his checklist of food supplies with his outfitter. "Ab-
ner, it appears that everything is here, but let's make sure. You gave us
fifty pounds of flour and fifty of bacon for each man?"

"Right."

"Twenty pounds of sugar, ten pounds of coffee, and salt, beans, and
crackers?"

"It's all there, Mr. Vick."

"What about some petit fours," Brady said, "and chocolate candy."

"Brady, that is not funny," Vick said. Matt had been observing the
two, and had concluded that while Brady's sarcasm annoyed the older
man, Vick overlooked Brady's peccadilloes because he worked hard.

The loaded wagons left Franklin and headed west across the Missouri
River's floodplain. The mules, still cold in their harnesses, struggled up to
higher, drier ground. Before the white men had come, the road had been
a game trail, and then an Indian path, that led to a salt spring. After three
days of jolting over ruts and the stumps of trees that had been cut to
widen the forest road, the freight wagons arrived at Boone's Lick, where
Amos Vick bought salt blocks that were made from the saline springs that
Daniel Boone's descendants had discovered.

The caravan spent the night there, and the next morning a ferry boat
transported the wagons, men, and mules to the Missouri River's south
bank. From there, the road wound through the trees, lush with spring
leaves and skirted by undergrowth so thick that Matt could see no farther than twenty feet into the virgin forest. He remembered an ancient

Sister of Charity who was gifted at telling fairy tales about the fate of naughty children who failed to properly venerate the Virgin Mary and the Holy Trinity. In her heavy French accent, the nun laced her fearsome stories with details of satanic fiends who whisked children to their forest lairs, where the scant light that penetrated the canopy of trees cast a sickly green glow on their demonic rituals. Matt was almost a grown man, but he still shuddered.

The caravan arrived at Independence in late May. Land promoters were clearing the forest for log cabins to house the harness makers, cobblers, and farmers they were certain would come. The promoters were already touting their frontier village as the next jumping-off point for the Santa Fe Trail. This was so, they were quick to say, because Independence was six miles from the Missouri River. Unlike Franklin, there was no chance that floodwaters would wash it away. And Independence was one hundred and fifty miles farther west than Franklin, which allowed proprietors to put their merchandise on Missouri River steamers that made thirty or forty miles a day, rather than using wagons that were lucky to make ten.

After they finished the day's work, Matt and Brady planned their evening in Independence. The village had three taverns. But only two prostitutes had ventured to America's most westerly outpost, and a long line of men outside the whore's tents were rewarding them for their efforts.

"They're getting five dollars," Matt said.

"The price'll go up to seven the night before we leave," Brady said. "Everybody knows it'll be their last look at a woman for ten weeks—or maybe ever."

"Ever?"

"Typhoid and Indians. Or you can cut yourself and die from the gangrene. Ain't no doctors on that desert."

"Damned doctors don't do much good anyway," Matt said.

Brady pulled the peg stopper out of a gallon cask of whiskey and took a long drink. "It gets real dry on the trail."

"Mr. Vick's hates liquor as bad as he hates the devil."

"I'll hide it so's he'll never find it."

"That Puritan gentleman is mighty strict on drinking," Matt said. "He'll have your back looking like red-and-white-checked calico."

"But he ain't gonna catch me."

"If you fall asleep on guard duty, he'll be sniffing your breath, or if you get to throwing up he'll figure it out."

"Matt, you ain't been on the Trail before. You're gettin' ready to go on the longest, most borin' trip of your life. It's hot, and you're suckin' in dust and puttin' one foot in front of the other, and there ain't nothin' to break the monotony. Sometimes, I go to sleep while I'm walkin'. After a while, you get to hopin' the mules'll act up to give you an excuse to whip up on 'em. So you need a little liquor every now and then to set you straight."

"It can't be all that bad."

"You just wait, Matt. I'm tellin' you, it's almost as wearisome as clompin' along behind a plow. So you get all excited if you make twelve miles in a day, and you'll talk about it like you won a horse race."

Matt was irritated. Until then, everything Brady had said about the Trail had been positive, but now, just before they were ready to leave, he had turned negative. "If it's that bad, Brady, why are you going back?"

"If I didn't have my own stock of goods to make some money, I wouldn't be doin' this again. I'm just tellin' you that without a little liquor to break the boredom you'll go crazy. You'd better get yourself a gallon. You can put it with my stuff."

"I'm not giving Mr. Vick a chance at my back."

"Suit yourself. But don't ask for any of mine, 'cause I ain't sharin'."

"Did you teamster for Mr. Vick last year?" Matt asked Bill Sartain between sips of beer at the No Name Tavern, so called because the owner hadn't bothered to put up a sign.

"Naw, trapping's my real business. I'm working for Vick so's I'll have a way back to Santa Fe," Bill said.

"How did you get into that?" Matt asked.

"My family was farmers," Bill said. "They left Virginia and come out to Missouri in eighteen nineteen. I didn't much like farming, so I joined John Jacob Astor's fur company and worked the northern Rockies."

"Why'd you start going to New Mexico?"

"It's too cold up in the Dakota country, and there's competition from them Frenchmen with the Hudson's Bay Company. I quit Mr. Astor after a few years and come down to Santa Fe and Taos. I done pretty good the first few years, but after the Mexicans passed a law that said foreigners couldn't trap, the army arrested me at the Taos Fair with three packhorses loaded with beaver pelts. They hauled me down to Santa Fe, and the soldiers divvied up my skins and jailed me for six months.

Gloria says the troops don't get paid very much or very often, so the governor looks the other way when they confiscate skins."

"Is Gloria your wife?"

"Nope. After I got out of the calaboose, I met Gloria Marquez at a fandango. She'd come on hard times. Her husband was a *cibolero*—that's Mexican for buffalo hunter—but the Comanches killed him. Anyway, I had a little money left over from my good years, so I told Gloria I'd get her a place to live if she'd take care of me. We found a house not too far from the Santa Fe River. The Mexicans don't have much water, so they call it a river, but to us it's a creek, and a small one at that. Gloria's a good cook, and she taught me pretty good Spanish. I tell her she's my talking dictionary."

"If you couldn't trap, how did you make a living?"

"Gloria's cousin Alejandro helped me get a trapping license."

"But you said the government won't let foreigners trap," Matt said.

"I know, but Alejandro has a friend who's a clerk in the governor's office," Bill said, and gave him a look that told Matt not to ask any more questions.

"Have you made good money?"

"Last season, I cleared over six hundred pesos after paying Alejandro and giving my partner his half. I went back to Santa Fe, and I had all that money, and I guess I went a little crazy. I started drinking that Taos lightning and playing monte. But, I gotta tell you, only a Mexican knows how to win at that game. Gloria tried to get me to give her the money for safekeeping, but I didn't. Lost damned near all of it."

"What were you doing back in Missouri?"

"I hired on as a teamster to get back home. I got some family and friends to put up five hundred dollars to stake me for another run at the beaver." Bill and Matt finished their beers and walked back to camp.

Well before sunup the next morning, Mike McGuire, the scout and hunter Amos Vick had hired, rousted the men from their blankets. "All right, boys, let's get going," McGuire said. "Drovers, round up the mules. Mule skinners, pick your teams and get 'em hitched."

When the drovers brought up the mules, the teamsters waded into the milling animals to select their first string. "Where the hell's my lead mule?" Brady shouted. "I can't see a goddamned thing in the dark." Most of the crew had hangovers, and the braying and shouting added to their misery. As the men and animals jostled and slipped on the manure-slicked ground, a frightened mule lifted a leg and showered a drover with a stream of urine. Another teamster caught a flying hoof squarely on his right arm, leaving a large red welt. "You goddamned pissin', shitin', fartin' machine," he bellowed as he pummeled the mule's nose with the stock of his whip.

"Whoa, you hellfire son of a bitch," Brady yelled when his lead mule reared and jerked the halter rope that he had wrapped around his arm. He stumbled and fell to the ground. Choked by the halter, the mule bolted and dragged Brady several yards through the slime.

"It's not too far to the Blue River, Brady," a teamster said, laughing. "You can wash that shit off when we cross the river."

Brady heard Amos Vick's voice and marched over to him. "Damn it, Mr. Vick, leavin' before we could see was a dumb idea. You can fire me right now, but I'm not doin' this again."

"Boy, don't you talk to me like that," Vick said, squaring his stout body.

"I'll talk to you any by God way I please. I don't give a damn who you are," Brady said, his voice rising in woozy anger.

"You are still half drunk, and I will forget it this time. But you look here, son, you'll give me respect and you'll cut out the profanity."

"Fuck you," Brady muttered under his breath as Vick walked away.

CHAPTER THREE

1826

"The way a Comanche gets to be a hero is by stealing horses from some other tribe or from us. To them, running off a bunch of horses is as big a thing as makin' a million dollars is for us."

AMOS VICK'S WAGONS LEFT INDEPENDENCE SHORTLY AFTER sunup. They headed southwest, then turned due west, and, two weeks later, the mules pulled the heavy freighters to the top of a knoll overlooking Council Grove. Below them, Matthew saw a palisade of hardwood trees running north and south along the Neosho River.

Vick turned in his saddle and signaled his lead wagon to head to a clearing near the river. At the campsite, the teamsters unhitched the mules, and the drovers let them water in the river before herding them to a spot a few hundred yards away to graze on the rich bluestem grass that bobbed and nodded in the midday sun.

When the crew had split and stacked wood for the cook fire, Matt went to the Neosho to wash off the dust that had turned his clothes tan and the dried mud that had caked his pant legs up to his knees. He took off his wide-brimmed felt hat and boots, and noticed that two weeks of walking beside his wagon had worn the soles by almost half. *Damned cheap boots*, he thought. Then he plunged head first into a deep hole with his clothes on.

That afternoon, Mike McGuire shot a deer—fat from feeding on the tender spring grass—while it was drinking from the Neosho a mile south of their camp. Giovanni Macconi, the Italian cook who had traveled with Vick on his previous trips to Santa Fe, butchered the animal and set aside the tender tongue and liver for his boss.

While the venison was roasting, Macconi melted deer fat in his smoke-blackened skillet, sliced two-inch squares of deer entrails, and tossed them into the spattering oil. When the squares swelled and crisped, the men ate them greedily. The cook also baked a flat, chewy bread in his outsized skillet, and, for a salad, he served watercress that he had picked along the Neosho's banks, dressed with coarse salt and a harsh vinegar. After their meal, the men sat around the fire, finishing their coffee. "Those Indians we saw this morning didn't seem so fierce," Matt said.

"Between Independence and Council Grove, the redskins are friendly," McGuire said, "mostly Osages and Kansans. Some government men met the Osages here at Council Grove in 'twenty-five and got them to sign a treaty saying they wouldn't bother the Santa Fe caravans. In return, the tribe gets eight hundred dollars worth of merchandise a year. Still, you gotta be on your guard in case they try to sneak into camp and steal something. These Indians are just a nuisance, but farther west the Kiowas and Comanches are a helluva lot more than a nuisance."

"I ain't scared of them fuckin' Comanches," Brady said. "I seen a few last year. They begged some food, but other than that they didn't do nothin'. They're short little bastards, and they wobble when they walk on them stubby little legs of theirs."

"One thing you gotta understand about the plains Indians," said Mike McGuire, who had lived for a year with the Comanches, "is that they only got three ways of makin' a living. They can hunt buffalo, do some trading, or steal from another tribe or from the white man. It's like one of us making a living as a lawyer or a banker. And stealing ain't a sin, 'cause they'll starve if they don't."

"Everybody says the Comanches are fine hunters," Matt said.

McGuire warmed to his role as an expert. "As soon as the boys are strong enough to pull a bowstring," he said, "their fathers are teaching them to hunt with bows and arrows. For practice, they shoot grasshoppers with blunt arrows—the legs are crunchy and make good eating. When a boy kills his first deer or buffalo, they have a big celebration, and, by the time they're fifteen or so, they're men."

The talk tapered off and the men left to find sleeping places, flat ground without rocks or limbs. Matt stayed by the fire, stretching out and leaning against a wagon wheel. *Everyone hates the red man*, he thought, *but McGuire makes them seem almost human*. Matt wondered how he'd react if he got into a scrape with the Comanches, and then decided not to worry about it until he needed to. Instead, he stared at the fire, mesmerized by the blue, purple, red, orange, and yellow flames, and re-membered the kaleidoscopes that Hans Banhofer had ordered for every Christmas season. Relaxed and almost asleep, he listened to the prairie's night sounds. Frogs croaking in the Neosho. Moths' wings snapping when they zoomed in to examine the fire. And the grass rustling as rab-bits and skunks foraged. Matt got his quilt out of his wagon and spread it on a bed of soft grass and fell asleep.

"All right, gentlemen," Amos Vick said when the teamsters and drovers smelled the frying fatback and gathered around the fire for breakfast the next morning. "There is no wood out on the prairie except for some spongy cottonwoods that are worthless for anything but burning. Mr. McGuire, please pick out a couple of good, straight oak or hickory trees to chop down and split into planks. If we break an axle or crack a wagon tongue, we will be glad we have them."

"When are we gonna get started?" Bill Sartain asked.

"Not to worry," Vick answered. "Six more wagons arrived late last night, and their proprietors tell me that there are eight wagons about a day behind them. We should be off in three or four days. And this, gen-tlemen, brings us to the question of who will be in charge of the caravan. I aim to be elected captain, and I want you to help make that happen. None of us wants some fool who does not know what he is doing. One of the proprietors I talked to has never been down the Trail before and the other one has only been once. I would appreciate your easing over to their wagons and talking to their men."

"Any reward for your campaign workers, captain?" Brady asked. "Like a little whiskey." He spit a brown stream of tobacco juice that landed inches from Amos Vick's boot.

The normally red hue in Vick's cheeks turned almost purple, and he refused to look at Brady, giving his answer as if Brady had not spoken. "There will be an extra ration of coffee and sugar." Matt was becoming increasingly irritated by Brady's challenges of Vick's leadership. *Per-haps*, Matt thought, *I have been living too close to Brady for too long. And Brady's flouting of authority is wearing thin.* For a time, he had felt guilty about his waning support for his friend. But Amos Vick had taken an al-most fatherly interest in Matt and he had found himself siding with the older man more and more often.

When the other men dispersed, Vick took Matt and Mike McGuire aside. "While you two are talking to the gentlemen in the other train, keep an eye out for who would make a good lieutenant. Let me know so that I can make him an offer when I am elected captain," Vick said with his usual certainty. "I am going to appoint you, Mr. McGuire, as the chief scout and hunter."

To Matt, Vick's asking him to look for candidates meant that he had gained the Englishman's trust, and he was flattered. To Mike, being the chief hunter meant that others would do the heavy work of skinning, butchering, and hauling meat back to camp, while he supervised. It also meant that he would spend most of his time on his saddle mule scouting far in front of the caravan, away from its cloud of choking dust.

Amos Vick convinced the two proprietors to support him, while his men successfully lobbied the drovers and teamsters in the six-wagon caravan. At mid-afternoon, Matt heard muffled shouts coming from the east and turned to watch eight wagons, which, at a distance, looked like an inchworm crawling over the ridgeline and descending into the Neosho valley. The new arrivals' scout galloped by Vick's camp and stopped two hundred yards to the north. The scout waved his hat, and his train veered toward him, the mules breaking into a trot to get at the Neosho's clear water.

That evening, Vick's vote-gatherers strolled to the new campfire. "Our man, Mr. Vick, will make a fine captain for the trip," Mike McGuire announced.

"Not as good as our man," a short wiry teamster said. "Augustus Klotsche started going down the trail in 'twenty-four and he knows every mound and marker."

"Bullshit," Mike said, his face darkening with anger. "I met Klotsche in Santa Fe last year in a monte parlor. Drunk and gambling like a wild man. He ain't got good enough sense to run a caravan."

"You son of a bitch," the teamster shouted, jumping to his feet. Both men drew knives. Hearing the commotion, Vick and Klotsche, who had been sitting under a wagon away from the fire, ran into the circle of light.

"Mike, put that knife down. Now!" Vick commanded.

"Not till he drops his."

"Put it down," Klotsche said to his teamster. "God damn it, we're all Americans here. Most of us anyway. We'll decide this by the ballot."

"Let's have a debate," someone shouted.

"Fine with me," Klotsche said. "When?"

"Tomorrow morning after breakfast. At our camp," Vick said. "I will make sure the other proprietors and their men are there."

Morning dew clung to the bluestem, wetting the men up to their waists as they walked to the Vick camp. When they gathered around the fire, Vick and Klotsche stepped into the middle of the circle.

"Who goes first?" Klotsche asked.

"After you, old chap."

"First of all, I worked for the United States government's survey party that marked the Santa Fe Trail in 'twenty-five," Klotsche said. "I know every inch of it."

"Excuse me, Mr. Klotsche," Vick said, "I am not sure what the debate rules are. But I must break in to point out that most of the markers that the survey party put up were nothing more than dirt mounds. The wind and rain have already done most of them in. So, I am forced to conclude that Mr. Klotsche's efforts are of little practical use."

"Many a wagon followed our markers last year, and, even if some them are gone, you can tell where the main trail is by the ruts."

"Sometimes," Vick said, "those ruts get washed out, and a captain who does not know what he is doing can bog down in low places or can unwittingly attempt to cross a stream at the worst possible place. This is my fourth trip, and I was captain of my caravans the last two years. Finding and staying on the Santa Fe Trail is not all a captain needs to know. He must locate the best grazing and the purest water. He must know when the mules and the men are overwrought and need a rest. He must know how to read the prairie weather. I do not think this is an idle boast, but I believe that I can conduct us to Santa Fe more quickly than any captain on the Trail. Mr. Klotsche, how many trips have you made?"

"Counting my trip with the survey party, two."

"Have you ever served as captain, Mr. Klotsche?"

"No."

"There is yet another issue here," Vick continued. "It has to do with the Indians. My scout, Mr. McGuire, lived with the Comanches. And I have dealt with the Kiowas, Arapahos, and Cheyennes—always on peaceful terms. Between myself and Mr. McGuire, we are equipped to handle the Indians."

"That is just not true," Klotsche said. "I know for a fact that the

Kiowas stole a bunch of your mules last year. How many was it? Twenty? Twenty mules out of a cavvyard slows you down—"

"That is not all of the story, Mr. Klotsche," Amos Vick said, breaking in on his opponent. "They made off with twenty-two, but we caught up with them. Instead of fighting and getting somebody killed, we gave them honey and beads and let them keep five mules."

"What are you proposing when it comes to discipline, Mr. Vick? I hear that you're a strong religionist."

"It is true that I am of the Baptist creed, Mr. Klotsche," Vick said, his voice rising and his eyes narrowing. "I plan on resting every Sunday, which I find to be a good tonic for man and beast. Otherwise, I pretty much follow the law of the sea. I am strict on gambling and drinking. And I will severely punish with stripes anybody who fights or sleeps on guard duty. But I will give a man a fair hearing. We will set up a three-man court, with you as one of the judges, Mr. Klotsche."

"You gonna be strict on cursin'?" Brady asked with a half sneer on his face.

"Profanity is indeed offensive to me," Vick said. "But you cannot penalize a man for what he says."

"I'd go along with Mr. Vick on those discipline rules," Augustus Klotsche said. "But his accent tells me he's a limey, and I want to remind everyone that it's only been eleven years since Andy Jackson whipped the British at New Orleans."

"It is true that I was born on my father's farm just outside of Bath. But I came to the Illinois Territory when I was eighteen, and I got into the mercantile trade up and down the Mississippi. It may be that our English traditions are a bit different, but I have been in America just over twenty years, and I can assure you that I know when fair is fair. Now, I want to address the most important issue. And that is: Who best knows how to negotiate with the Mexicans to get our goods into Santa Fe with the least tax."

"On my first trip in 'twenty-four," Klotsche said, "I was with the proprietors when they talked to the governor. We got the taxes down by ten percent. What about you, Mr. Vick."

"In a quiet way, the governor is my partner, but discretion dissuades me from discussing the details. I can, however, guarantee that I will deliver much better than a ten-percent tax reduction."

"Let's vote," Matt shouted. He got two tin pails from a wagon and, with the charred end of a stick from the fire, marked one with an X for

Vick and the other with an *O* for Klotsche. He took the pails behind a wagon, and each man picked up a pebble, walked out of sight, and dropped his stone in a pail. After the voting, Matt brought the pails to the fire and began counting. "Twenty-four for Mr. Vick, ten for Mr. Klotsche."

"You won," Klotsche said, shaking Amos Vick's hand, "you're the captain."

Amos Vick looked at his brass compass and set the eighteen wagons' course for due west, passing landmarks that even the first-timers had heard about. Traders had named Diamond Spring, with its cool water bubbling out of the ground, after a famous spring in the Arabian desert. Fifty miles farther on, at Dry Turkey Creek United States envoys had signed a treaty with the Kansas Indians that guaranteed safe passage to the merchants.

When the caravan was four miles east of the Little Arkansas River, Mike McGuire galloped forward to find a crossing. He coursed up and down the bank until he found an almost-level approach to the river. He clicked his tongue and slapped the reins lightly on his saddle mule's neck to urge it into the water. The mule tiptoed into the stream, shying at the unsure footing on the muddy bottom. Its hooves kicked up sediment, and, when it lowered its head to drink, McGuire felt it sinking into the ooze. He tapped the mule's flanks with the rowels of his long Mexican spurs until it lunged and freed its hooves and returned to the shore. *The wagons will never make it across this muck*, he said to himself.

McGuire rode north until he came to a tall, solitary cottonwood tree. He guided his mule down the bank and into the river and let it stand in the stream, where it sank only four inches until its hooves found the rock bottom. He rode back to the caravan, and, sighting on the cottonwood, led it to the crossing.

"We are going to cross this evening," Vick announced to the men.

"The hell with that, Captain," Brady said, "we been goin' since this morning, and the sun'll be down in an hour. The mules is wore out. And my feet are so blistered they're bleedin'."

Vick glared at Brady and turned to speak to the men. "There is a ferociously awful looking cloud to the north. If a rainstorm comes up tonight, the runoff might trap us on this east bank for days. We will cross now."

The west bank was steep, and Vick ordered the men to get their shovels. They dug the bank to a gentle slope and covered the newly-spaded cut with scrub brush for traction. The caravan made it across without difficulty, and, that night, Vick called Augustus Klotsche and Jay Birdsong, his two lieutenants, to his tent.

"Tomorrow is Sunday, so we will rest here," he said, his ruddy cheeks shining in the candlelight. "Some of the men's boots are wearing out, and this will give us time to put new soles on them." Vick opened his saddle-bag and fished out the travel notes he had made on his previous journeys. "Gentlemen, my notes say it is twenty miles to the next water at Cow Creek. We can do it in two days or leave early Monday and try to make it in one. What do you think?"

"It's gonna rain sure as hell," Klotsche said. "You can smell it. If we're gonna try and make twenty miles in one day, Cow Creek'll be running fast when we get there, and the mules won't have enough left in them to pull us across. If we take two days, the creek'll be down pretty good, and we oughta be able to get over without a problem."

"Yeah," Birdsong said, "but, if we take two days, the mules'll be without water for forty-eight hours."

"I would rather do it in two days," Vick said. "We pushed hard today, and it will be better for everyone to rest up. I will send Mr. McGuire to find good pasture a few miles out. If there are some low places, the rain will make playa lakes, and, if not, there will be enough moisture on the grass to keep the animals contented."

The caravan arrived at Cow Creek at four o'clock on Tuesday and had an easy crossing. Instead of parking the wagons randomly as they had be-fore, Vick ordered the teamsters to form them in a defensive diamond. After the teamsters unhitched the mules, the captain motioned for the cavvyard drovers to join him.

"The creek is shallow, so take the animals downstream a quarter mile to keep them from fouling our water. Then, run them back to that good pasture on the east bank where there were some long-stem grasses mixed in with the short."

Vick called Matt to his tent. "I noticed that you like to read, Matthew. If you have run out of books, I have a Spanish grammar you can study and Lord Byron's *Childe Harold's Pilgrimage*."

"The only book I have is a novel by Fenimore Cooper, and I've read it three times, Captain. I'd appreciate reading yours." Vick gave him the books and asked him to summon the lieutenants and Mike McGuire.

"Gentlemen, we are two hundred fifty miles from Independence, and we have entered serious Indian country. We are not in the *Comanchería* yet, but there are Pawnees and Cheyennes who can make trouble. From now on, we are going to travel in four columns, and I am making Matthew a lieutenant. Mr. Klotsche, you head up the most northerly column. Mr. Birdsong, you take the next, then Matthew. I will lead the southerly one."

"Captain," Matt said, "I'm not sure I'm old enough. The men might not like my being in command. Brady's older and he's been on the Trail before."

"Sometimes Brady's individualist spirit is a bit daunting," Vick said, scratching the gray fringe on his bald head, "and he is unpredictable. Out here, age does not mean much. You might be a little green, Matthew, but you do what you say you will. If you have trouble that you do not think you can handle yourself, come to me."

"If we are attacked," Vick continued, "Mr. Klotsche and I will take the outside columns and form an angle at the point. Matthew, you and Mr. Birdsong slant your columns behind us so that we form a diamond, but leave a wagon-length of opening at the back for the drovers to run the animals in the cavvyard through. When they are inside, you lieutenants are responsible for closing the gap with ropes."

"What if the Indians are on us before the mules are inside?" Matt asked.

"If Mr. McGuire cannot give us sufficient warning, you keep the gate open until the animals are in. Without them, our merchandise will rot out here on this wretched prairie. And none of us proprietors is here because we enjoy clogging our nostrils with dust. We are here to make money. Mr. McGuire, tell them about the Indians."

"The first thing to remember," McGuire began, enjoying his role as expert, "is that the plains Indians make their living hunting and stealing. With horses and mules, they can do both a lot better. They can range farther to find buffalo and, when they find them, they can get closer and kill more of them. And they can sneak into an enemy camp at night, take what they want, and be thirty miles away before anyone knows that something's missing. But horses and mules do more than help them conduct business."

McGuire paused and surveyed his audience. When he was sure he had their attention, he continued. "The Comanches love their horses so much that they call them 'god-dogs.' Lots of horses make a brave rich, and the best warriors have two hundred. They can trade them for a wife or a slave."

"I was at the Taos trade fair last year," Klotsche said, "and there were hundreds of Indians milling around. Lots of horses got traded for whiskey and rifles."

"The horse has lots of uses," McGuire said, annoyed at the interruption. "They use the skin to make clothes, and they braid the tail and mane hair for ropes and bridles. If they get in an argument, they can settle it by giving the other man a few horses."

"Well, professor, anything more?" Klotsche asked, smirking.

"You think you're so damned smart, Augustus," McGuire said. "You've seen a few Indians at five hundred yards, and you think you know what you're doing. You'd better listen up so's you don't get a Comanche haircut." McGuire returned to his lecture: "The way a Comanche gets to be a hero is by stealing horses from some other tribe or from us. To them, running off a bunch of horses is as big a thing as makin' a million dollars is for us. They'll brag about it for years."

"What Mr. McGuire has told you," Amos Vick said, "is a long way of making the point that we must be constantly vigilant. I did not set up guard duty until now because there was not much risk of a raid. But from now on we will have three-hour shifts each night. You lieutenants take turns checking on the guards, and if you catch one of them sleeping report him to me."

"What if somebody's sick or hurt?" Jay Birdsong asked.

"He will have to be exceedingly sick before he will be excused," Vick answered. "Now, go make your assignments. And while you are doing that make a list of the men's weapons and the amount of ammunition they have."

"I can't write, Captain," Birdsong said, "and Augustus don't cipher too good neither."

"You two go with Matt and he can keep the tally."

At Issac Penner's mess, a teamster showed them his weapon. "Lookee here at this plains rifle. And look at that beautiful burled walnut stock. It was one of them long-barreled Kentucky rifles that a St. Louis gunsmith sawed off for me so's it'd be easier to handle on horseback."

"I got me one of them smooth bore muskets," a drover making his first trip said. "It's army surplus from the eighteen twelve war."

"Muskets ain't too useful out here," Klotsche told Matt. "They're only accurate to about fifty yards."

"I ain't gonna waste powder and lead on Indians that's out of range," the drover said. "But if those red bastards get close enough, I've got plenty of lead to nail 'em dead."

At Augustus Klotsche's campfire, a proprietor proudly showed Matt the matched pistols he kept in a cherrywood box that was lined with green velvet. "These damned things ain't worth a shit out here," Klotsche whispered as they walked away. "You can't hit a mule at twenty paces with a pistol, even if he's standing sideways."

"It's a real hodgepodge, Captain Vick," Matt reported. "Looks like eleven rifles with calibers from forty-seven to sixty-four, so we'll need all sizes of bullets. There's two shotguns, four muskets, and ten pistols. The men who don't have guns are carrying either Bowie or skinning knives. It's just a guess, but it looks like there's about four pounds of powder and twenty pounds of lead for each man who's got a gun."

"Can they shoot with accuracy?" Vick asked.

"I reckon they've all handled guns since they were boys," Matt answered, "except for one of the drovers. He's from Boston, and he tells me he's never fired a shot."

Vick had the men up before sunrise the next morning to make the sixteen-mile trip to the great bend of the Arkansas River. "We gonna cross over at the bend, Captain?" Klotsche asked.

"No. The south bank is Mexican territory, and I want to stay on the American side as long as I can."

Mike McGuire, who had been scouting the wet and dry routes for two days, returned and reported to Vick, his lieutenants, and the proprietors. A few miles west of their camp, the Santa Fe Trail would split in two; the wet route hugged the Arkansas River and the dry route veered ten miles north, until the routes rejoined into a single road some eighty miles farther along.

"If we take the dry route, Ash Creek and the other watering places are low," McGuire said, "and some of the water up there is pretty brackish."

"I am reluctant to take the wet," Vick said. "When I went that way last year, it was a swamp and the wagons got stuck every few hundred yards. I would hate to wear out our animals, and if we waste a week or ten days working our way through soggy ground, another caravan might get in front of us."

"The wet's got a few low places that could be pretty messy to cross,"

McGuire said. "But other than that the trail's in good shape, and there's a good carpet of buffalo grass."

Vick put the question to a vote among the proprietors and lieutenants. "All right," he said, "pass the word. Tomorrow morning we will take the wet route."

"Catch up! Catch up!" the lieutenants shouted the next morning, signaling the teamsters to fall into the line of march. When the teamsters sang back, "All's set," the blacksnake whips cracked and the wagons creaked as the mules leaned to their tasks. That afternoon the caravan arrived at Pawnee Rock, a one-hundred-and-fifty-foot-high mound with sheer rock faces.

"It's the last landmark you're gonna see till we get down into New Mexico," McGuire told Matt's mess. "Between here and there, it's as boring as the ocean. Just goes on and on. Lots of famous people carved their names on Pawnee Rock. Zebulon Pike. Bill Becknell. For some of them, it was the last time they wrote their names 'cause, sometimes, the Indians hide behind Pawnee Rock before they ambush."

Matt, Brady, and Bill Sartain climbed to the top and looked west at the setting sun. "McGuire's right," Matt said. "I've never seen salt water, but everything out there is just like I imagine the ocean to be. Where the prairie's got a little roll to it, it looks like a heaving sea."

"That's why they call a caravan leader 'captain' and the wagons 'prairie schooners,'" Bill said.

"The horizon," Matt said, "just drops off into nowhere. I wonder how far we're seeing."

"Fifty, maybe sixty, miles," Bill guessed.

Matt pointed to the southwest, where the setting sun's rays were hitting the underside of the single cloud in the sky, flashing on it with a brilliant orange. "That's no cloud," Brady said. "That's smoke. Could be a prairie fire. Could be Indians. Frankly, I don't give a shit. Let's go carve our names."

The sun was almost down, and they could barely see a name scratched in the sandstone. "It must be Spanish," Bill said, "because there's an accent mark over an 'e.' And look here, there's three numbers, 'one—five—four,' but you can't read the last number. Some Spaniard musta been here in the fifteen forties. Damned near three hundred years ago."

The next day, the caravan nooned on a bluff above Ash Creek. It had made good time that morning, and, after a lunch of bacon and beans cooked over a cottonwood fire, the men got into the shade of their wagons and dozed until the lieutenants rousted them for the afternoon march. Toward evening, a murky cloud appeared in the northwest sky. When the mules caught the scent of oncoming rain, they flared their nostrils and pranced nervously in their traces, while the men watched the thunderstorm's vanguard rumble over the prairie's unrelieved flatness.

Darkness closed around the caravan, and lightening left a sulfurous odor in the air. One bolt struck a mule in the cavvyard with a blast that charred its meat and set its hair afire, and the shock wave knocked over a drover who was standing a few paces away. The other mules panicked and ran wildly in all directions.

"Look at that," Matt shouted, pointing at a funnel shaped cloud to the west.

"Shit!," Brady said. "It's a goddamned tornado."

"It's headed southwest," McGuire said, pulling on his raincoat, a cotton duster he had soaked in melted beeswax. "We'll get some wind, but the eye won't pass this way."

Wind squalls toppled a wagon that was parked on an incline. Gusts ripped the crippled wagon's canvass away and scattered merchandise for two hundred yards across the prairie. Just as quickly as the storm had come, it passed.

"Get your butts from under them wagons," Issac Penner shouted at his teamsters, "and help me gather up my things." The men righted Penner's freighter, reloaded his crates and barrels, and unwound and draped his bolts of cloth over his wagons to dry.

After midnight a drizzly rain began. The ground was already saturated from the earlier storm, causing rivulets of water to run down the slightest incline and penetrate the men's blankets and clothes. At dawn the rain tapered off and stopped. The men crawled out of their wet bedrolls and formed into teams to round up the scattered mules. Most of the animals had huddled in a cottonwood grove close to the Arkansas, and stood as sad looking as mourners, with their heads drooping and their still-wet backs sending up curtains of steam. The others were wandering on the prairie. When the men had herded the mules back to the caravan, they had a cold breakfast of raw onions and bread, and got underway.

The four-column caravan had been traveling for less than an hour when Matt's lead wagon sank in sticky mud. Men pushed on each wheel and Matt popped his blacksnake whip over his mules' backs, but the slipping, sliding men and animals only churned the soil into a sloppy quagmire. Matt ordered the drovers to bring up three more pairs of mules from the cavvyard. They succeeded in rocking the wagon forward a few inches, and then it sank up to its hubs, its bed resting on the ground. Matt helped the men unload the wagon and joined them in pushing the wheels. As the wagon began moving, he slipped and fell and a wheel rolled over his left arm. He heard the snap and felt a spiky pain rip up his forearm.

"Captain, it looks like I broke my arm," he told Vick, who had ridden up to see what had happened.

"Bad show. I will get McGuire. He did some curing when he lived with the Comanches. They thought he was a medicine man."

McGuire trotted over to Matt and dismounted. He inspected the arm and sent a teamster to pick up cottonwood branches. "Don't get those green limbs that the storm just knocked down. Make sure they're dry and stiff. I'll need four. Here, drink some of this," he said to Matt, offering a canteen half full of whiskey. "Don't tell the captain."

Matt took a long swallow of the raw whiskey and almost gagged it up. The teamster returned with branches and McGuire cut them to the right length with an ax. Then he grabbed Matt's left wrist and yanked.

"God damn it! God damn it! Son of a bitch! Son of a bitch!" Matt screamed.

"How's it feel?" McGuire asked.

Matt hurt so bad that he could not form words.

"I got it back in the right place and you won't have a crook in it," McGuire said, as he tied the sticks on Matt's arm with leather strips that he had wetted so that, when they dried, they would shrink and the arm would be firmly bound in place. "You won't be usin' that for a while," he said.

Amos Vick knew that Matt was left-handed and would not be able to manage his team's reins and his blacksnake whip. That evening, he relieved Matt of his duties as a teamster and lieutenant and assigned him to work as a scout with Mike McGuire.

"I think we should take the Cimarron Cutoff," Vick told the lieutenants and proprietors.

"That's bullshit," Issac Penner said. "Those damned Indians out in the *Comanchería* have been raising hell lately. I say we go over Raton Pass."

"I take your point, Issac," Augustus Klotsche said, "but nobody's ever tried to get freight wagons over Raton. We'll get to Santa Fe a lot faster on the Cutoff. That'll guarantee that we're the first caravan in Santa Fe and that we'll get the best prices."

"Prices won't mean a damned thing if we lose our hair," Penner said.

"Not to worry," Vick said. "We have thirty-four men and we are pretty well-armed. Even if we do run across the savages, we should be able to handle them."

"I've been on the Cutoff," Penner said, "and that big stretch of the *jornada* is so damned dry and hot that it'll burn the soles off your feet."

"All that is well and good, Mr. Penner," Vick said, "but going by Raton Pass is at least a hundred miles farther and would take two weeks longer. The mules are already getting puny, and that pull up the Pass would kill a goodly number."

"I vote for the Cimarron," Klotsche said. "You can take your wagons over Raton by yourself if you want to, Issac. It's a free country."

When all the proprietors and lieutenants voted to take the Cimarron Cutoff, Penner agreed without enthusiasm to stay with the caravan.

Matt and Mike rode to where the wet and dry routes came together at the Arkansas and then followed the river to the Caches, a famous Santa Fe Trail site where a blizzard had trapped two traders in the winter of 1822–1823.

"Let's see what it's like," McGuire said, quirting his mule into the Arkansas' muddy water. The animal stooped to drink and its front legs immediately sank in quicksand to its chest. The chief scout took the halter in his hand, scooted back on the mule's rump, whirled around, and jumped to the shore. "Matt, come over here and help me pull him out. This stuff's worse than tar." With his good arm, Matt awkwardly tied the stranded mule's halter to his saddle horn and slapped his mule with his reins until the trapped animal flopped and wallowed its way out of the river.

"This crossing ain't gonna work," McGuire said. "Let's go on to the Middle Crossing and see if there's quicksand up there." At midmorning the next day, the numerous ruts heading into the Arkansas told them that they were at the Middle Crossing. McGuire coaxed his mule into the river, crossed to the south bank, and waved for Matt to follow. The water was up to his mule's belly until, in midstream, it stepped off into a deep hole. The mule swam ten yards before it found its footing and trotted to the shore.

"Welcome to Mexico. Ever been in a foreign country before?"

"Nope. It looks the same on this side as it does on the American side," Matt said.

"I can damned well guarantee you that it ain't the same."

Three days later, the caravan arrived at the Middle Crossing and formed into a diamond shape on the high ground. The drovers herded the mules to the river, where they greedily lapped up water, almost as if they knew that the *jornada* was ahead of them. After dinner that night, Matt and Bill Sartain walked down to the Arkansas to wash.

"Matt, you and me have been eating in the same mess for over a month now," Sartain said when they had finished. "And I think we've gotten to be friends."

"I'd agree with that."

"Tomorrow, we're headed into the *Comanchería*, and, I got to tell you, I'm a little worried."

"About what?"

"I'm carrying five hundred dollars on me. Got it strapped around my waist. There's something I'd like you to do for me."

"Of course."

"Remember, I told you how I'd busted out last year? Too much gambling and too much Taos lightning. With this new stake, me and my partner can outfit ourselves for the trapping season."

"Nothing's going to happen to you, Bill."

"But, if it does, I want you to make sure the money gets to Jack Marentette. He's one of the few white men living in Taos, and he stays with a half-breed woman. You can find him easy."

"Not to worry, as Captain Vick says."

CHAPTER FOUR

1826

*"I think I see wings growin' on them red bastards. If they get close enough,
I'm gonna turn 'em into angels, and they'll need them wings."*

By EARLY AFTERNOON, THE CARAVAN HAD CROSSED THE
Arkansas River into Mexico, and Amos Vick ordered the men to camp
on the south bank. The next day, Sunday, the men and animals rested.
On Monday, they began preparations for the dry pull over the *jornada*,
the great stretch of harsh, arid land between the Arkansas and Cimarron
Rivers.

"We're leaving after the sun goes down," Vick told his lieutenants.
"Have your men fill their water barrels. Lash one on each side of the
wagons to balance the load." Giovanni Macconi, using the last firewood
he would have for days, cooked extra food for the trek across the desert.

"This is the roughest part of the trip," Bill Sartain said. "No water for
sixty miles—and very damned little fodder. If we get lucky, there might
be playa lakes, where rainwater is standing in low places."

"And if not?" Matt asked.

"There's been some men who done some pretty desperate things on
the *jornada*," Bill said. "There was a bunch that got so parched they cut
off their mules' ears and drank the blood. A day later, they were sure
they were dead men until one of them killed a buffalo with a stomach
full of water. Before they butchered him, they cut a hole in his gut and
drank it."

"That story makes this muddy Arkansas water taste a lot better,"
Matt said without a smile. "Sometimes, I think I oughta chew it before
I swallow."

With the sun slipping below the horizon after a day of blistering heat, the wagons fanned out into four columns and the mules strained in their collars to pull their loads across the Arkansas River's sandy floodplain to the hard-packed ground above. When a full moon rose, its rays reflected off the white desert and lit the trail with a soft, almost feminine glow. Some mules shied at their shadows, but after weeks on the trail most were so used to the routine of following the wagon in front of them that their teamsters could ride on the wagon tongues and catch naps.

The caravan traveled all night and only stopped when the sun burned off the desert cool the next morning. Matt Collins lay down and slept in a wagon's shade. But when the sun moved, it pierced his clothes and skin like cactus needles. In the late afternoon, he joined his mess mates, squatting on the east side of a wagon to eat before starting another all-night journey.

The windless evening amplified the sounds of wagon timbers creaking, harness chains jangling, and iron tires crunching small stones. The mules, working on short water rations, snorted dust out of their nostrils and teamsters cursed God and man when they stumbled over deep ruts or cactus patches. Well past midnight, Amos Vick found Matt walking beside his saddle mule to keep himself awake. "Ride out six or eight miles and see if you can find water or pasture."

Matt mounted and rode ahead of the caravan, his broken left arm aching when his mule shifted into a bouncy jog. Even though the moon was bright, he saw shooting stars that reminded him of July Fourth fireworks in Kaskaskia. The land was so featureless that there were no echoes, and the sounds of his mule's footsteps dissolved immediately in the darkness. "Sailors must feel like this in the middle of the Atlantic," Matt said out loud, needing to hear his own voice.

An owl swooped so close to his head that its wing beats bounced puffs of air off his cheek. Further on, prairie dogs screeched in protest when he rode through their town. Rather than feeling a closeness to other life, he felt a sadness, an aloneness. "Must be homesick," he said to himself as his mule carefully picked a path through the prairie dog town. "But I don't know what I've got to be homesick about. Got no home to go back to. Funny."

After the moon set and before sunrise, Matt wheeled his horse back toward the caravan. As the orange eye grew out of the east, he reported to Amos Vick. "I covered a pretty good stretch, Captain, and didn't run across any water."

"We are going to make camp earlier than I wanted. The sun is barely up, but it is already getting hot and the mules are looking poorly. Did you find any forage."

"No, sir. Nothing but sticker weeds and sagebrush."

Vick called the lieutenants, proprietors, and scouts together.

"How far did we make last night?" Jay Birdsong asked.

"I'd say fifteen miles," McGuire answered.

"How much longer till we get to the Cimmaron?"

"It's about thirty-five miles."

"Us proprietors think we ought to keep going," Issac Penner said. "These mules is gettin' onery. There's so little grass their ribs is beginnin' to show, and my water barrels'll be emptied out by tomorrow. How many more days we got?"

"Maybe two, but more likely three," Vick said. "There are usually sunflower patches between here and the Cimarron, and we can fill up the mules with green sunflower seeds. If we get lucky, we might find a bit of dew on the grass tomorrow morning."

"It's drier than a hot skillet, Captain, so we ain't gonna find no dew," Penner said. "We say we keep going."

"You know as well as I do, Mr. Penner, that traveling under this vicious sun drains the mules three times as fast," Vick said. "And they are getting footsore."

"Yeah, but, if we do another five or six miles this morning, we'll guarantee that it's no more than two days to the Cimarron."

"If we wear the animals down, Mr. Penner, and they start dying on us, it will take more than three days. I say we stay here and rest up."

"You can stay here by yourself if you want to, Captain, but we're goin' on," Penner said. Other proprietors nodded in agreement.

"I am running this caravan, gentlemen, and I say we stay."

"Look here, Captain Vick," Penner said in a belittling tone, "we elected you captain, and we can unelect you captain. We might be in Mexico, but we still run this caravan like a democracy, and, if you wanna buck the men's will, you can sit out here on this desert by yourself."

"I am ordering this caravan to stop." Vick was calm, but his ruddy cheeks had turned purple.

"You can order all you want, Captain, but we've got a heavy majority that says we keep moving," Penner said and turned to walk back to his wagons.

"Unruly fools," Vick muttered to himself as he gave the signal for the caravan to move.

The caravan pushed on. Three mules collapsed in their harnesses and died, and five others were limping badly with stone bruises when they stopped for nooning. The exhausted animals stood, immobile, with their tongues lolling back and forth in search of moisture. The teamsters soaked their bandannas with the little remaining water and daubed the mules' swollen tongues.

That night the wagons rolled along at half speed. When the caravan stopped to camp after sunup, Amos Vick sent Matt and Mike McGuire ahead to scout for water. McGuire swung two miles to the left and Matt to the right before heading southwest. *There's not a tree or a shrub or even a tall weed to use as a landmark,* Matt thought to himself. *Sometimes this damned desert is scary.*

By noon, the prickling sun was so intense that Matt felt dizzy, and he was certain that the sun had adopted a particular hatred for him alone. He let the last of the water in his canteen drip on his tongue, which had swelled to the size of a fat sausage, and put a lead rifle ball in his mouth to keep saliva in his throat. Cracks split his lips and drops of salty blood from the deepest cuts made him even more thirsty. His lips became so caked with dried blood and skin that he ran a finger up a nostril and smeared mucus on them.

As he rode, mirages of glistening lakes appeared in the distance and quicksilvery waves of heat rose in front of him, until his mule waddled slowly down into a low place. Matt saw fresh buffalo droppings and liquid standing in the depressions the animal's hooves had made. He dismounted and, desperate for water, he found a dried weed with a hollow center, lay down by a buffalo track, and used the weed as a straw to suck up the brackish liquid. When he stood, a hot flash turned his face red and he vomited.

His stomach emptied, Matt remounted and rode south until he saw a flock of small birds darting up and down. *They wouldn't be there unless there was water,* he thought, bringing his mule to a reluctant trot. "God damn it!" he shouted in frustration when he came to a dry river bed. For the first time since he had left the Sisters of Charity, Matt choked up and began crying. He collected himself and gigged his mule with his spurs to head it back toward the caravan, but the animal refused to move. When Matt relaxed the reins, the mule walked slowly down into the striated sand in the river bottom and then up the bottom some two hundred yards until it came to a pool of water no bigger than Matt's wide-brimmed hat.

Matt got off and began digging with a piece of driftwood. Under the surface, he found dark, wet soil, and, after digging a few more inches, water seeped into the hole. His mule nudged him with its head to get at the water, but Matt pushed the animal away and scooped handsful of water into his mouth, flinching as the alkali stung his chapped lips. He drank till his belly hurt, and then moved out of the way so his mule could drink. From nowhere, the small brown and grey birds appeared and angrily chirped at the man and mule that had cut off their access to water.

Refreshed and invigorated, he headed back to the caravan. Two hours before sundown, Matt got back to camp. "I found water," he announced, his voice as triumphant as if he had discovered a lode of gold nuggets.

The teamsters laughed and joked as they hitched their mules to their wagons. Amos Vick shouted "catch up" and the four columns moved out smartly for their night-long trek. When the sun turned from orange to yellow the next morning, the mules pulling Jay Birdsong's lead wagon smelled water and began trotting. Matt heard its teamster shout, "Whoa, you stubborn bastards." The teamster beat his mules with his whip handle, but they only kicked up their heels and broke into a run. The other teams followed, stampeding down the slope to the small pool in the riverbed. The mules lapped the water greedily, and soon fouled it with urine and droppings.

"Get out the shovels and start digging," Vick shouted.

Liquid seeped into the holes, and the men lay on their bellies to drink water so thick with alkali that it looked like milk. To keep out the sand, they clenched their teeth and sucked in water until the grit built up between their teeth and forced them to spit so they could drink again. "Slow down, men," McGuire said. "If you drink too much of that stuff, it'll give you a case of the shits that'll last into your old age."

The caravan followed the Cimarron River on a southwesterly course. There were no trees. No hills. Just interminable flatness, made even more tedious by the heat—and dust so thick that, when the men squinted against the sun's rays, it felt like sandpaper scraping their eyeballs.

The wagons crossed the Cimmaron's dry bed to the south bank, and

Amos Vick sent Matt and Mike to find Cold Spring. When they had been riding for an hour, McGuire stopped beside a patch of yuccas, broke off a leaf, and sucked out the liquid. "Try it, Matt. It's got a strong taste, but it ain't half as bad as that alkali water." Matt sampled yucca liquid and relished the feel of it trickling down his throat.

When he and Mike found Cold Spring, they lay down and sucked in water. Then the mules gulped as fast as they could, until the two men yanked on their bridles and pulled them away from the sweet water before their bellies became distended.

The caravan reached Cold Spring late on Saturday and Vick ordered a one-day halt. Matt shot his first buffalo when it strayed near their camp in search of water, and the men stuffed themselves with its roasted hams, ribs, and loins. Below the spring, where the water ran, the mules feasted on a tightly woven mat of buffalo grass.

Refreshed by the rest, the men and mules moved at a fast pace, making fifteen miles a day on ground that looked like a skilled carpenter had planed it smooth. Three days after the caravan left Cold Spring, Matt saw what looked like a slit in the western horizon. The next day, the slit took on a hazy contour, and, when the caravan stopped for its nooning, he could see humps rising up out of the prairie.

"Rabbit Ears," McGuire told Matt. "We're smack in the middle of the *Comanchería*."

"Doesn't look like a rabbit's ears to me. Just a bunch of mounds."

The next afternoon, the caravan drew up in the shade on Rabbit Ears' east side. Amos Vick waved his black hat to summon the lieutenants, scouts, and proprietors. "Make sure the wagon wheels overlap when you form up the diamond. Tell the cavvyard guards to keep the mules close to the wagons and to sound off if they see or hear anything unusual. Now, Mr. McGuire, kindly tell these gentlemen what you have encountered."

"I seen Indian signs."

"How can you tell that they're Indians?" Matt asked.

"Because there's lots of pony prints, but there ain't no sign of horseshoes. There's marks from their travois poles, and that means there's women and children," McGuire said. "They're probably moving to a new camp, so we shouldn't have any trouble."

Matt awoke in the dark at five o'clock and lay still, listening to a wolf pack howling and the mules' nervous stamping and whinnying. Still groggy, he unwound his quilt and got up to make his round to inspect the guards. He found Brady Hardin on the far side of the cavvyard, awake but drinking whiskey from a tin flask.

"Fuckin' Indians," Brady said. "They're not even half human."

"McGuire lived with them," Matt said, "and he says they aren't so bad."

"Fuck McGuire. What that squaw man likes is that Indian poosey. I wouldn't touch those mangy savages. They stink worse than buzzard shit."

"Brady, let me have that flask."

"The scum don't fight fair," he continued as if Matt had not spoken. "Unless they've got you outnumbered three to one, all they'll do is sniff around your camp and run off a few mules. If you treat 'em decent, they think you're scared of 'em and come after you."

"Brady, give me the flask. I don't want to have to turn you in to the captain."

"Turn me in. Turn me in," Brady said, mimicking Matt in a falsetto voice. "Fuck that limey bastard, and fuck you too, Collins."

"Brady, you're going to pass out if you keep on drinking. We've known one another a long time, and I don't want to fight you over that whiskey. You've got to stop."

"I'll stop," Brady said, taking another gulp, "when it's gone." Matt reached for the flask, but Brady kicked his hand away, jumped to his feet, and swung at Matt. Matt gritted his teeth and whacked Brady with his splinted arm. They scuffled for a few minutes until Brady, too drunk to fight, gave up. Matt poured the whiskey on the ground. "I'm not telling the captain this time," he said. "You go get some sleep and I'll stand the rest of your watch."

The morning sun filtered through a dust cloud, casting a hazy, tan light on the parked caravan. Matt walked to Amos Vick's bedroll and shook him awake. "Lots of dust over there," he said, pointing to the east. Vick sat up stiffly and stretched his muscles before standing. He found his brass telescope and looked through the eyepiece as the cloud drew closer. "I cannot tell how many there are, but it looks as if there are a goodly number of them. They are about thirty minutes away. Matthew, take some men to the cavvyard and herd the mules inside the diamond of wagons."

Matt and five men ran to where the mules were grazing. "Get the animals inside the wagons," he shouted at the drovers. With the mules safely corralled, the men positioned themselves under the wagons, watching the dust cloud and listening to the mules, unhappy inside the unfamiliar enclosure, braying. Otherwise it was quiet. When the sun was at a thirty-degree angle, three Indians rode over a low ridge and stopped just outside of rifle range.

"I think I see wings growin' on them red bastards," Brady said to Matt when he crawled next to him under a wagon. "If they get close enough, I'm gonna turn 'em into angels, and they'll need them wings."

"You better hope they don't see any wings on you," Matt said without humor. "Even if they don't see you, they'll smell that whiskey you been drinking."

Using signs, the Indian leader indicated that he wanted to talk. Then he and the two warriors raised their arms to show that they had no weapons. "Mr. McGuire, you and Matthew come with me," Vick said. "We will see what they want. Leave your guns here, and do not do anything to make them edgy."

"Are they Comanches or Kiowas?" Matt asked as they walked their mules toward the Indians.

"They're Comanches," McGuire said, "from the Liver Eaters band. Those yellow and black feathers stuck in their hair mean they're the bravest."

As they got closer to the Indians, Matt saw that they had no beards or eyebrows and that long braids, greased with buffalo fat, hung below their waists. The chief had a black star tattooed on his chest and another warrior had a fanciful tattoo around a battle scar on his arm.

"Let's stop here so we don't make 'em nervous," McGuire said when they were ten yards from the Indian party. The Comanche leader held up one hand, the signal for peace, and McGuire reciprocated. The chief made several quick signs, which, Mike translated, meant that he wanted to trade. McGuire then broke into Comanche, causing the Indians to clap their hands to their mouths.

"They always do that when something surprises them. They look like young girls at their first cotillion," McGuire said, pleased to divulge his insider's knowledge. "The leader is Ten Bears. He's their boldest. When I was living with the Water Horse band, I heard that he's counted more *coup* than he can remember. He says they're following the buffalo down south."

Ten Bears and McGuire spoke in Comanche for several minutes before the scout stopped to interpret. "He says they've got some buffalo hides they want to swap for gunpowder and cloth."

"Tell him that we only have enough gunpowder for ourselves," Vick said, "but that we have plenty of cloth we can spare."

"He says he wants gunpowder too," McGuire translated.

"Tell Mr. Ten Bears that our supply is very limited. But, as a gesture of friendliness, we will give him some. Ask him to ride closer to the wagons with us so that I can show him our fabrics. We have many colors."

"He says he'll come," McGuire said.

"Matt, ride on in there and get some things for Mr. Ten Bears to peruse," Vick said. As Matt galloped toward the wagons, he saw men kneeling and lying under them and caught the sun glinting off the flask that Brady had refilled from his cask. "The captain says not to shoot," Matt shouted, "they just want to trade."

The three Indians followed Vick and McGuire at a slow trot. They stopped fifty yards from the wagons and waited until Matt returned with swatches of cloth and a keg of gunpowder. While Ten Bears was examining the cloth, out of the corner of his eye Matt saw a puff of smoke rise from under Brady's wagon. Before he could turn his head, he heard the dull thud of a lead ball smacking into Ten Bears' chest, just to the left of his star tattoo. The Comanche leader fell off his horse, hurting but refusing to cry out in pain. A warrior jumped to the ground and threw Ten Bears' body across his horse's rump. He remounted and the two Comanches dug their heels into their ponies' bellies and raced back over the ridge.

"Now we have done it," Vick screamed as he galloped back inside the diamond. "All we had to do was trade them a few things and they would have gone on their way. You lieutenants break your men into two groups. Make sure that the best shooters have the weapons and do the firing. The others will load. Let their first wave approach to within forty yards, and then fire at will. Now, who was the idiot who shot Ten Bears?"

"It was Brady, sir," Jay Birdsong said. "He's drunk. Barely knows what he's doing."

"I will deal with him after we get through with this."

"Yessir," the lieutenants said, and pushed their way through the wrought-up mules to get back to their men.

"God damn," Matt muttered to himself as mounted Indians poured over the ridge. "There's more than a hundred of them." The Comanches advanced in a solid phalanx. A few carried muskets, but most were armed with bows, quivers of arrows, and buffalo hide shields. As they approached the diamond, they turned their ponies to the right and left, forming a circle around the wagons. Matt and Bill Sartain crawled under the wagon next to Brady's.

Matt heard noise coming from Brady's wagon. He rolled over to look, and saw Brady standing in front of his wagon naked, except for his boots and a powder horn slung around his neck. In his right hand, he had a pistol, and, in his left, the Kentucky rifle he had used to shoot Ten Bears.

"You sons a bitches. You half-human bastards," he shouted. He spit a stream of tobacco juice that splattered on the sun-cooked earth and started walking toward the ring of Comanches.

When Brady passed out of musket range, eight warriors charged him. "Look at that," Bill said to Matt. "That crazy son of a bitch has a hard-on. Looks like a stallion ready to mount a mare."

Eight Indians rushed Brady at full gallop. He fired his pistol and missed. He threw it down and aimed the rifle. Flames flew out of the barrel and a Comanche tumbled to the ground. The other seven kept charging, firing a hailstorm of arrows. One hit Brady in the thigh and another in the shoulder. When the warriors got closer, he swatted at them with his rifle. Within seconds, the Comanches pierced his body with arrows from every angle. "He looks like San Sebastian," Bill said.

Brady crumpled and fell. A warrior jumped off his horse and pulled his knife out of its sheath. He made deft slices across Brady's forehead, along each side of his head, and over his ears to the back of his neck. The Indian put his foot on Brady's left ear, snatched a handful of hair, and yanked. He waved the blond scalp in the air and used the Kentucky rifle to crush Brady's skull. With a swoop, the warrior lopped off Brady's still-hard member, grabbed it, and threw it defiantly at the wagons.

The Comanches began riding counterclockwise at a lope, shouting and whooping and shaking their weapons. The pace became faster and faster and the circle grew smaller and smaller. When the braves were within arrow range and their ponies were full out, they disappeared, slinging themselves to the offside of their horses. The only parts of their bodies the white men could see were the warriors' heels over their ponies' backs and the flash of an arm or face when they fired arrows from under their horses' necks.

"Shoot their horses," Vick shouted.

Rifles and muskets boomed through the clamor of shrieking Comanches and of yelling, cursing men inside the diamond. After weeks on the almost-silent prairie, the cacophony brought the mules' ears straight up. They kicked viciously at anything passing near them and as the shouting and firing became more intense they brayed and rolled their eyes in fear.

The drovers tried to calm the mules, but the animals surged from one side of the diamond to the other, trampling one drover. Suddenly they reacted as one and rushed the south line of the diamond. The mules, frantic to escape the terrifying noise, pinned their brothers in front against the wagons. Two wagons separated, creating an escape hatch. Before the men could control them, nine mules leaped through the opening and ran wildly onto the prairie. Matt and a crew of men dragged the wagons back together, and the drovers forced the frightened animals to move in a circle inside the diamond until exhaustion calmed them.

The Indians saw the distracted whites and sent a swarm of warriors to charge the north line of wagons. They laid down covering fire with muskets and arrows, and ten Comanches broke inside the diamond, yelling and screaming as they came. "Sounds like Beelzebub and his darkest angels," Bill said, firing his musket and knocking down a brave.

After the whites fired their weapons, they charged the Indians, using their rifles and muskets as clubs. Others pulled knives or wielded axes or shovels. When five Indians lay dead or dying, the others scooted under the wagons and escaped. Vick and his lieutenants steadied their men and got them back to their positions on the diamond's perimeter. With their forces reorganized and reloaded, sharpshooters systematically knocked down Indian ponies until their chiefs moved them out of rifle range and they disappeared over the ridge.

"Lieutenants and scouts, over here," Vick shouted. "We are not out of trouble yet. Keep the animals inside."

"Can't we move somewhere else?" Jay Birdsong asked. "They've pissed and shit the enclosure full, and every damned fly west of the Mississippi has found us."

"We are not moving anywhere, Mr. Birdsong. Take a party and get those Indians' corpses out of here. Drag them to the north so that the south wind will carry their smell away from us. Matt, get some men and bury Mr. Hardin's body. Do we have any more dead?"

"Bill Sartain, Captain. An arrow in his throat," Jay said. "There's a few wounded that need tending to, and a drover got trampled pretty bad."

"Matthew, bury Mr. Sartain too," Vick said. "I do not care what you do with Mr. Hardin's grave, but take precautions that will keep the predators away from Mr. Sartain's body."

"Bill and I got to be good friends, Captain," Matt said. "I'd like to wrap him up in something before we put him in the ground."

"You can have a few yards of my cheap muslin, but do not use my good quality cottons."

Matt picked six men for his burial party and they carried Bill to where Brady's body lay.

"My God, he's got twelve arrows in him," Matt said, staring at the cap of blue-green flies that were squirming on Brady's head. Matt waved his hand over Brady's scalp and the flies rose for a second and then descended just as quickly back onto the ooze. He looked at the vacancy where Brady's penis had been. "Find his dick and we'll bury it with him," he told a teamster.

"Not me."

"Then we'll bury him like he is. Lets burn some buffalo chips on Bill's grave so it'll be harder for the scavengers to smell him."

The burial crew bent to their work, but snapped to attention when they heard the *pop—pop—pop* of upwind gunshots. Matt looked toward the sound and saw that Jay Birdsong's teamsters had cut off the heads of two Comanches and were using them for target practice. "Stop that," he heard Vick shout, "and get those corpses another fifty yards away from the wagons."

When Jay's men finished their work, they came inside the diamond, romping and happy as puppies. "Lookee here," a teamster said, gleefully holding up an Indian's body skin by an ankle and a wrist, "I can scissors this up and make me a nice shirt." Another teamster pulled his trophy, a Comanche scalp, from his belt and announced, "I'm gonna make me a necklace with these ears when they dry out."

CHAPTER FIVE

1826

"It is not considered polite to launch into your business affairs. . . . If you jump in and start telling them what you want, they will think you are rude. Ill-bred."

A FURIOUS RAIN SHOWER BROKE THE HEAT ON THE AFTERNOON of the Comanche attack. Lightning shot out of a black cloud and rain spattered the mules, invigorating them as they sucked at the water collecting in wheel ruts. When it had rained on the east end of the Santa Fe Trail, the teamsters had cursed the heavens for the mud that slowed their passage to a crawl. But, on the trail's west end, they stood with their heads upturned and their mouths open, leaping about in an impromptu dance, shouting with joy.

Amos Vick decided to stay in place for another day to give the Indians time to move farther south, speculating that they were more interested in following the buffalo herd than avenging Ten Bears. The men used the hardwood they had cut at Council Grove weeks before to patch cracked wagon tongues and to hammer wedges between steel tires and wooden wheels that the dry desert air had shrunk.

That night, Matthew packed Bill Sartain's five hundred dollars in cash and six beaver traps with his own belongings, and wrote the name of Sartain's partner, Jack Marentette, on a ten-dollar bill so that he would not forget it. Matt lay down on his bedroll by the fire and pillowed his head on his saddle. Tired as he was, his mind raced as he looked up at the stars spangled against the coal-black sky and listened to wolves' teeth clacking on the Comanches' bones. A wolf's howl broke the night silence, and coyote yips from all directions answered, creating a prairie roundelay.

He fell into a restless sleep, and during wakeful periods his thoughts wandered. *It would have been nice to have known the fancy ladies' secrets. Ah, Lady Bountiful was so pink and clean.* The images of Brady and Bill floated before him. Brady bloody and scalped; Bill bleeding to death from arrow wounds. It was horrible. *What did my parents look like?* When he fell asleep the last time, night birds were singing their last calls before sunup.

As the wagons moved westward, the land began to roll, and an occasional landmark swelled out of the desert. When the caravan approached Round Mound, Matt and Mike rode to the top and Mike pointed out Sierra Grande. "Tomorrow, we'll scout for a Canadian River crossing," McGuire said. "If we hit the Canadian too far north we'll run into some of the worst quicksand you've ever seen. Too far south, and there's one hell of a gorge." Three days later, Matt and Mike led the caravan down a gentle grade to the Rock Crossing. From the Canadian's west bank, Matt paused and slouched in his saddle to look at the mountain range in front of them.

"This is the very southern tip of the Rockies," McGuire said in an authoritative tone. "The Mexicans call them the *Sangre de Cristos*. Don't sound too bad in Spanish, but it means Blood of Christ. Them Spaniards love their blood and death."

The next day, Amos Vick pointed the caravan southwest toward a promontory he called Wagon Mound. "You scouts get on out there and find us a camping place—and some fresh meat would be nice," Vick said.

Matt and Mike rode fifteen miles in front of the caravan. "Gotta be careful around here," McGuire told him. "The Indians hang around Wagon Mound just like they do Rabbit Ears. Be alert for any birdcalls when there's nothing flying, or coyote barks where there ain't none."

The caravan made good time, passing Wagon Mound the next day and arriving at the junction of the Sapello and Mora Rivers, flowing with clear mountain snowmelt. "This clean water and good grass will perk up the mules," Vick told his scouts. "We ought to make San Miguel in three or four days."

Matt and Amos Vick sat by the campfire and Matt watch the flames reflect on the captain's bald pate. "You say New Mexico's different, Captain, but what's so different about it?" Matt asked.

"It is a foreign—and, for the most part—a barbarous country, my boy," Vick said. "You will soon learn the definition of primitive."

The next afternoon, the caravan approached San Miguel del Vado, where a joyous crowd came out to meet the train. The women walked or rode horses, their skirts tucked between their legs. Rough men with black stubble on their cheeks tipped their straw hats and grinned, displaying brown teeth with dark gaps between them. Two naked children straddling a burro, their upper lips crusted with dried mucus, smiled and waved at the newcomers.

The wagons crossed the Pecos River and entered the plaza. The teamsters parked their wagons, unhitched their mules, and took them to pasture along the Pecos. San Miguel was one of a string of fortress towns on the frontier facing the *Comanchería,* all built to the same Spanish specifications. The windowless adobe houses, government offices, and church faced inward on a plaza that had only one entrance. Because the Spanish, and then the Mexicans, could not support an army to fend off New Mexico's untamed Indians, the government gave away frontier tracts to induce people to move there and serve as the first line of defense against the people they most often referred to as *salvajes,* which was not intended as a term of endearment. Some of the colonists were convicts whom the government had exiled from Mexico's more civilized south. And if the treasury ran out of cash, it paid soldier's pensions with land near New Mexico's most dangerous outpost villages.

When the teamsters and drovers finished their chores, the proprietors made salary advances, and many disappeared behind buffalo-hide doors with women in tow. Matt, Mike, and Amos Vick went a few yards upstream on the Pecos, stripped, and jumped in. "Here," the captain said, "I have a can of coal oil. Apply it to hirsute areas to get rid of the insects." Matt rubbed the coal oil on his armpits and genitals and submerged himself for as long as he could hold his breath. When he came up, he watched with malicious pleasure as surfacing lice and ticks floated down the fast-flowing Pecos.

Captain Vick passed around a bar of lye and sheep-lard soap that he had bought in the plaza. It had a strong animal smell, but Matt gleefully washed the odor off his body and the oil out of his matted hair and beard, a beard so sparse and scraggly that it looked like a circus clown's false red beard. He scrubbed his clothes in the river and used a stick to gouge lice eggs out of the seams. "Gimme that soap and stick," McGuire said, "so's I can get them seam squirrels outa my clothes, too."

"How long till we get to Santa Fe, Captain?" Matt asked, as they soaked in the cool water.

"It is only about sixty miles, but it is an uphill climb. It will take the wagons five or six days, depending on how muddy it is."

"San Miguel doesn't show me much."

"It is not exactly London," Vick said, smiling slightly at his humor.

"Santa Fe's not the Seven Cities of Cibola either," Mike said. "But it's bigger, and got lots more women. Lots to tempt a young buck like you. Or old bucks like me and the captain."

"The women do not tempt me," Vick said, cupping his hands and pouring water over his bald head.

"Maybe you need a little poosey, Captain, just to take the edge off," McGuire teased. "We've been on this damned Trail over two months."

"That is not amusing, Mr. McGuire," Amos Vick said, standing and walking to a sunny spot to dry his pink body.

"Come on, Matthew, I want you to go with me," Vick said, jabbing his boot toe into Matt's bedroll.

"Where're we going?" Matt asked, rolling out of his quilt and shivering in the morning chill.

"You and Mr. McGuire and I are going on ahead to Santa Fe to have a little chat with the estimable governor—Don Susano Baca. This will be a good lesson in the way things get done in Mexico."

Matt and Mike saddled their mules and rode beside the captain until they stopped to camp at Apache Canyon. The next day the three capped a ridge and looked down at Santa Fe. They sat on their mules a long time, squinting in the brilliant sunlight at the provincial capital below them.

"The air feels so light up here," Matt said. "It's fluffy, like fanning yourself with a feather."

"The altitude makes the air thin and dry," Vick said. "It is certainly different from that heavy, muggy air along the Mississippi."

They trotted their mules into town, passing adobe houses. Some were abandoned and had collapsed to reveal earthen bricks underneath a mud-plaster coating. "Santa Fe doesn't look like much," Matt said, disappointed at having made such a long journey to such an unimpressive place.

"You mean you do not see those roads paved with gold?" Vick said with a mocking chuckle.

"All I can see are mud houses."

"There are fine homes and gardens behind some of those blank walls," Vick said. "But you are right, Matthew, they are not like American or English dwellings, with windows everywhere."

The three stopped on the southeast corner of the plaza. Animal dung littered the treeless open space, and flies and rodents scattered when stray pigs foraged through rotting corn cobs and apple cores. Along the plaza's north and south sides, ditches ran with muddy water, *acequias* that formed part of an irrigation system that made existence possible. "It surely is not like leafy green Missouri, where you have enough water to float Noah's Ark," Vick said, responding to Matt's quizzical look.

"Over there," Mike said, nodding his head in front of him, "is the governor's palace."

"That's a palace?" Matt laughed sarcastically as he took in the one-story adobe building that fronted the plaza's north side.

They tapped their spurs against their mules' flanks, crossed the plaza, and tied their animals to a log hitching post. Along the palace's facade, farmers squatted behind piles of dried corn and beans, and looked at the newcomers in hopes of making a sale. Soldiers lolled on benches on either side of the entrance, staring at Matt's red hair and beard.

"May I assist you?" a sergeant guarding the door asked them.

"Would you do us the favor of requesting a meeting with Governor Baca's secretary?" Vick asked in heavily accented but grammatically precise Spanish. The sergeant nodded and disappeared inside the palace.

Matt noticed a corporal slouched on a bench and, between his legs, a surplus musket from the Napoleonic war. "How can they keep them working?" he asked Vick.

"Without spare parts," Vick answered, "those old guns spend most of their time stacked in the armory."

At first the foreign language bewildered the corporal. Then a suspicious look came over his face.

"To the Mexico City dandies," Vick continued, ignoring the corporal, "Santa Fe is the end of the world. It is Siberia. And almost everything they send up here is a castoff."

"I've read a little about Mexico's troubles," Matt said.

"Troubles? That is being very generous, my boy." Vick used the time to explain how, after independence from Spain in 1821, Mexico had been unable to decide whether it wanted to be a democracy, a kingdom, or an oligarchy. It was that political chaos, he said, that kept the Mexico City politicians from worrying about New Mexico, a province so remote that they had little idea of what went on there—and cared less.

But that neglect was not all bad. While the Mexico City crowd was busy with plots and *cuartelazos,* "barracks revolts," Vick translated, Governor Susano Baca was free to run New Mexico pretty much as he wanted. "There is very little that happens here," Vick said, "that Baca does not know about, approve, and get a piece of."

New Mexico's marginal gold mines and mostly subsistence agriculture did not provide the governor with much to work with. But the opening of the Santa Fe Trail after Mexico threw out the Spaniards was a bonanza, and Governor Baca had become expert at extracting enough taxes from the American merchants to keep his province afloat.

The sergeant returned, interrupting Amos Vick's dissertation. "Gentlemen, the governor's secretary will see you now." He led them through a warren of low-ceilinged halls and ushered them into a small office. A man in a dark blue military uniform rose from his desk. *He has a lean and hungry look,* Matt thought immediately, remembering Julius Caesar's description of Cassius. Diego Zambrano's features— his chin, his nose—had the sharpness of a finely honed ax, and his large, dark eyes had the evangelical look of a man certain of his beliefs.

"Lieutenant Diego Zambrano, at your service," the governor's secretary said, shaking hands with Matt and Mike. Vick put out his hand, but Zambrano smiled and opened his arms. "Don Amos, what is this shaking of hands?" The two embraced and clapped one another on the back with effusive slaps.

"Welcome to Santa Fe, gentlemen," Zambrano said and sat down. He fancied himself an heir of Napoleon, and, although he lacked Napoleon's paunch, he cut his hair short and combed it forward on his forehead. As the lieutenant settled back in his chair, Matt almost laughed when he undid the middle button of his military tunic and slipped his hand inside, as the French emperor had once done. "We are always glad to see the first caravan of the season arrive, Don Amos. And it is always good to see you again. You are well, I trust."

"I am well, and I thank you for your interest," Vick replied.

"Your affairs in Missouri are prospering, I hope?" Zambrano asked.

"Yes, quite well. We had an excellent tobacco harvest on my farm last year. And your family is well?"

"Quite well, thank you. Was your journey easy this year?"

"The Comanches attacked us."

"I am sorry. Did they injure anyone?"

"They killed two of our men and wounded a few. But we killed eight savages."

"The Comanches are, indeed, savage brutes, Don Amos. They have given us trouble, too. They have caused terrible ruckuses in Truchas and Taos."

"I am so sorry to hear that, Don Diego. I hope that none of your family or friends were harmed."

"No, thanks be to God."

"What's all this babbling about?" Matt whispered to McGuire. "Why doesn't Mr. Vick get to the point?"

"Shut up," Mike whispered, "the captain knows what he's doing."

"Did your farmers have a good harvest last year?" Vick asked.

"Thank you for asking. Around Santa Fe, it was a little dry, and the crops did not do particularly well. But, up in Taos, they had more rain, and the wheat and barley were good. Along the Rio Grande, the apricot and apple trees produced very nicely."

"Thank you for your kindness in receiving us on such short notice, Don Diego," Vick said, pausing to give Zambrano a friendly, reassuring smile. "Don Diego, at the governor's convenience, we would like to meet with him. Of course, we do not wish to rush His Excellency, but our caravan will arrive in Santa Fe in another three or four days. Is Don Susano in Santa Fe?"

"His Excellency is here. But you understand that I cannot grant you an appointment until I consult with Don Susano."

"Of course."

Zambrano excused himself, bobbed his head in a semi-bow, and left.

"We spent twenty minutes talking about family and friends," Matt said impatiently.

"If you are going to work in Mexico and survive, you must learn their ways," Amos Vick replied. "It is not considered polite to launch into your business affairs."

"It's a waste of time," Matt said.

"Not to them. If you jump in and start telling them what you want, they will think you are rude. Ill-bred. Worse, still, you will not get what you want."

"I have managed to speak with Governor Baca," Zambrano said

when he returned. "He is busy with a number of personal matters to-day. But he could see you tomorrow."

"What time would be convenient for His Excellency?" Vick asked.

"He suggests some time in the middle of the morning."

"We will be here."

"Please come to my office first, and I will escort you to the governor's office."

"Of course. You are very kind, and I thank you," Vick said, rising and bowing deeply.

The three spent the night at an inn, a *posada*, at the southeast corner of the plaza and, after breakfast, Vick suggested a walk along the alameda by the Santa Fe River. "Let's get on over to the palace," Matt said, drinking the last of his coffee.

"There is no rush," Vick said. "Don Susano does not get to his office too early, especially if he has been playing cards or romancing a lady friend. And, no matter what time we get there, he will make us wait for at least half an hour. Besides, the *posada*'s food is inedible, and I want to visit a woman I know and arrange for her to prepare our meals."

They left the *posada* by its back entrance and stepped gingerly around a mound of residue from the previous night's chamber pots. Black-and-white magpies squawked and fought over the morning garbage that had been pitched in the alley, and a few yards farther on iridescent flies swarmed over a dog's carcass. "That doesn't make me want to think about eating," Matt said.

"You'll get used to it," McGuire said.

"Why don't they dig privies like we do back home?" Matt asked.

"Don't know. Just not the custom," McGuire answered.

"There is Florinda's house," Vick said. Smoke and the fragrance of baking bread was pouring out of a beehive-shaped *horno*, an outdoor oven that sat in the yard. Sunflowers and hollyhocks stood at attention in front of the adobe house, sustained by rain runoff from the roof. The yellows and purples and reds were so brilliant that Matt squinted his eyes. *Must be the sunlight*, Matt thought. *Flowers back home don't get that brilliant.* To one side of the home, where an *acequia* ran, Florinda Maestas had cultivated a small plot of herbs and a vegetable garden. "Doña Florinda," Vick called out as he knocked on the door's heavy planks. When the door opened, an attractive woman with a naked child clutching her skirt came out.

"Don Amos," the woman smiled. "It is good to see you again."

"And the pleasure is reciprocal. I have two companions, Mr. Collins and Mr. McGuire. We would like to engage you to prepare us more of those fine victuals that you have so generously served in past years."

"Of course, of course, Don Amos. I have been baking bread, and it should be ready by the time your coffee is boiled. Food prices have gone up, Don Amos, but you will find me to be fair."

"I have no doubt about the fairness of your prices, Doña Florinda. And I know that your bread is the best in Santa Fe."

The three men followed Florinda Maestas and her child into the room that served as kitchen, dining room, parlor, and sleeping quarters for the child. There was no furniture, but Florinda unrolled a buffalo hide on the floor and motioned to them to sit down. She placed a large pot of water in the coals of her corner fireplace and put a generous scoop of ground coffee into it. Then she went outside to check the *horno*.

"Interesting woman," McGuire said.

"Stay away from that," Vick said. "By my lights, she is the best cook in town. But Doña Florinda is also Lieutenant Zambrano's mistress. Most people think that that child is his."

"I thought 'doña' meant a married woman."

"It does in the dictionary, Matt, but out here it is a way to show respect. If there is something you admire in a woman, even if she is not married, you can call her 'doña.' On my second trip to Santa Fe, Zambrano suggested that I might want to take my meals with her. When I discovered the connection, and sampled her food, it was an easy decision."

After the three ate hot bread and fresh goat cheese, they walked to the palace. Amos Vick asked a guard for Lieutenant Zambrano, who appeared immediately and informed them that the governor would see them shortly, *un ratito*, which he indicated by holding his thumb and forefinger close together in front of his nose. After a wait of over an hour, Zambrano reappeared and guided them to Susano Baca's office.

Matt stooped to go through the low door. The room was large, but had only one wall hanging, a *retablo*, a painting on board that a local artist had decorated with a crudely painted image of San Francisco surrounded by swarms of birds. Above each end of the desk, wooden candelabra hung from rawhide ropes that were looped over heavy pine beams and snubbed to wall pegs. The governor's long, narrow desk was made of pine boards that bore the deep scars of hand hewing. His chair legs etched a trench in the hard-packed dirt floor when Baca pushed it back and stood to greet them.

With a broad, jowly smile, he waved an unusually small and delicate hand to indicate that they should sit on the backless bench in front of his desk. Matt was surprised at how young Governor Baca was, maybe late twenties or early thirties. His black hair was slicked back with a perfumed pomade, the sweet odor of which floated across his desk. He parted his hair down the middle and it was as straight as a man's hand could make it. His skin bordered on swarthiness and, even though he was still young, his body bordered on corpulence.

Vick introduced Matt and Mike, and opened the conversation with the required courtesies, questions about families and crops and mutual friends. Baca crossed himself when he mentioned that his wife had lost a baby that winter. "Thanks be to God that she is well," the governor said. "And thanks be to God that the little one died before he was forced to live in a corrupt and evil world."

"Don Susano," Vick said, "let me say that it is a pleasure to be in your company again."

"I assure you, Don Amos, that it is an even greater pleasure for me. I understand from my secretary that your caravan had trouble with the Comanches."

"We did, Your Excellency, and I thank you for showing your concern," Vick replied in the exact, elegant Spanish that formal occasions required. "We have been trying to convince the American government to furnish military escorts up to the border on the Arkansas River. Perhaps Your Excellency might consider some form of protection while the wagons are in Mexican territory."

Matt had spent enough time with Vick's Spanish dictionary to pick up an occasional word, but the rapid exchange made any real understanding impossible.

"The caravans are very important to us," Baca said, "and I consider your suggestion to be a fair one. But we are a very poor province, as you know. We have difficulty getting the central government to send us enough priests, much less soldiers. But let me think about it."

Vick signaled to McGuire to untie the strings around a carefully wrapped package. "I know your love of music, Don Susano, and I have taken the liberty of bringing you a small gift."

"May I have that string? It is very hard to obtain in Santa Fe," Baca said. McGuire wound the string into a ball and presented it to the governor with solemn formality.

"I have brought you a violin made by one of the most skilled craftsmen in Philadelphia," Vick said. "With your fine ear for music, Excellency, I am sure that you will appreciate its tone."

"You are much too kind, Don Amos. I have a peon who is quite good with the violin, and I will have him play this fine instrument tonight at dinner."

"I brought you another gift. I do not have it with me, but I will deliver it when and where you may wish."

"And it is?"

"A case of the finest French brandy. It was made thirty-five years ago, in seventeen ninety-one. I hope that you will enjoy it."

"It is older than I am," Baca replied. "You may deliver it to La Dama's home. Not her place of business—her home. Do you know it?"

"Of course, Your Excellency."

"Tell me about your caravan, Don Amos. How many wagons are with you this year?"

"Fourteen."

Matt leaned forward to interrupt, but caught Vick's eyes, which stared him into silence.

"And what merchandise are you carrying?" Baca asked.

"The usual things, Governor. Suspenders, boots, hats. I also have three bolts of French velvet and two of Chinese silk. And I have several *varas* of Belgian lace. Señora Baca might have a particular interest in them. If you are interested, you would, of course, receive your usual discount. There is a good selection of hammers, wood-working tools, and a barrel of nails."

"We look forward to the safe arrival of your merchandise. Since you are the first caravan this year, you will be getting the highest prices of the season, Don Amos. We have been thinking of adjusting the customs duties," Baca said, rising and turning his back to them to look out the room's only window.

Baca's rump, Matt noted, was broad, and his chubby thighs rubbed together when he walked to the window and clasped his hands behind his back. "We are thinking of seven hundred pesos per wagon this year."

"But, Excellency, it was only four hundred last year," Vick said, stuttering in seeming surprise.

"You know as well as I do, Don Amos, that the proprietors' taxes are almost all we have to run the government. Those idiots in Mexico City give us almost no help, no money. Some people joke that New Mexico is the 'forgotten province.' But it is true. Our troops live in miserable conditions. When the Navajos killed six farmers near Abiquiú recently, we proposed a punitive expedition, but the soldiers refused to go because they hadn't been paid in months."

"Don Susano, you know that I have the greatest sympathy for the situation in New Mexico," Vick said. "I have been here often enough to count many of your countrymen—and yourself—as my friends. The depredations carried out by the Indians must be punished, and your soldiers must be paid. But, Your Excellency, seven hundred per wagon is much too high. That rate of customs duties will only discourage future trade."

"We would consider six hundred, but only if it is paid in cash within two days after the wagons arrive in Santa Fe. This is our final decision," Baca said, wheeling around. He looked gravely at the three Americans and snapped shut his eyelids, which were hooded and coffee brown, contrasting with his much lighter skin.

"Governor, may I confer privately with my colleagues for a moment?"

Baca turned back to the window and twirled the buffalo hide window curtain's tie strap around his stubby finger while Matt, Mike, and Amos Vick huddled at the other end of the room. "That thieving devil," Vick hissed. "I did not just dream up that brandy and violin. He practically demanded that I bring them to him. Now the greedy swine is trying to gouge more taxes. It is time to make him an offer."

Vick walked along a narrow beam of sunlight coming from the window until he was beside the governor. "Your Excellency," he said in a confidential tone, "I was thinking that the proprietors might be able to offer something that would be for your sole benefit—if you could see your way clear to making the customs duties five hundred dollars a wagon."

"What might that be?"

"Four hundred silver dollars, paid to you in cash or deposited in your St. Louis bank account. Whichever is most convenient."

"I will need five hundred. I have to provide for Zambrano and the chief customs collector. Pay it in cash; here in Santa Fe."

"Done, Your Excellency. This is a wise solution to our mutual problem."

"We will allow the wagons in at five hundred silver pesos each. If the proprietors do not pay within two days, we will fine them or confiscate their goods," he said, his voice much harsher than previously. "Tell them that."

"Don Susano, you are most kind, and I thank you for myself and for the other proprietors."

When Baca and Vick finished exchanging elaborate good-byes, the three foreigners walked into the brilliant sunlight in the plaza. "What about the miscount of the wagons?" Matt asked. "We have eighteen, not fourteen."

"That may be," Vick said with a shrug. "Shall we go to Doña Florinda's for lunch?"

CHAPTER SIX

1826

"Los americanos! Los carros! La entrada de la caravana!"

AMOS VICK AND HIS TWO SCOUTS MET THE CARAVAN TEN MILES south of Santa Fe. "I have negotiated five hundred pesos a wagon and a five-hundred-dollar *mordida,* a bribe for the governor," he told the proprietors.

"God damn! It was only four hundred a wagon last year," Issac Penner said. "You let him jack it up twenty-five percent. What the hell kind of negotiating is that?"

"He was asking for seven hundred, but I prevailed on him to accept five. And he approved a wagon count of fourteen instead of eighteen. That saves us two thousand. If you feel that you can do any better, Mr. Penner, go talk to Baca yourself."

"He's upped his bribe, too," Penner complained.

"We can divide the *mordida* among ourselves, based on the number of wagons," Vick said, ignoring Penner.

"These bribes just ain't right," a proprietor, said. "I never paid off nobody to do business back home."

"This is your first trip," Vick said, "and this is how things are done here. And I do not think any of us can afford to be preachy. We both know people who paid off the boys at the land office in St. Louis, and they got some of the best bottom land along the Missouri River."

"I'll pay my share, but I don't like it," the proprietor said.

"That is enough of this genteel ethical debate," Vick said. "We must get down to practicalities. We have to reconfigure our eighteen wagons to get down to fourteen. We will transfer one wagon load to the fourteen we take into town and cache the goods from the other three." Vick called his lieutenants together and instructed them to organize a digging party and find a hiding place. The men buried the three wagon loads of merchandise behind a cedar grove and resumed their march to Santa Fe. Later, they would smuggle the goods into town.

Vick called a halt, four miles outside of Santa Fe. The men could smell the tangy piñon smoke rising from the adobe houses scattered among the corn and wheat fields south of the capital. That night, teamsters, drovers, and proprietors stood and watched their clothes boil in iron cook pots, purging from them the sweat, cook fire smoke, and evidence of their inability to wipe themselves with other than handsful of grass.

In Matt's mess, naked men danced around the campfire, splashing water over their bodies, while others stood in line to use McGuire's straight razor to shave beards that had collected dribbled grease and trail dust for weeks. One teamster, Elijah Blaylock, pulled out a comb that then passed through everyone's hair. The men chewed the ends of cedar branches and used the makeshift brushes to scrub the fuzz off their teeth. A few had brought new socks, underwear, and shirts for the *entrada* into town. The others sewed their torn clothes as best they could. In the cool night air, the men sat close to the fire joking about what awaited them in Santa Fe.

"Poosey! Poosey! The best in the West," Blaylock shouted exuberantly. "Not like that baggage in San Miguel. The best-looking women in the province'll be flooding into Santa Fe just for us. What about you, Matt? You gonna get some poosey?"

Matt shivered in his still-wet clothes and gave no answer.

"No poosey?" Blaylock said, grinning a grin that revealed only four lower teeth. "You turned seventeen last week, and you still ain't had no poosey? Well, boy, here's your chance. When the captain pays you off, you'll have more money than most of them spics'll see in a lifetime. You can buy the finest poosey in New Mexico."

Matt stared at the flames, not sure whether the fire or the thought of sex was turning his face red.

"Damn it, Elijah, leave the kid alone," McGuire said sternly. "He'll have plenty of time to get laid if he wants to. Who knows? He might get lucky at a fandango. One of them pretty Mexican gals might take a shine to him and not even charge. But you, Elijah, you toothless bastard, you'll have to pay no matter what."

Early the next morning, the wagons began lumbering down the road into Santa Fe, and everyone knew that the monotony of trudging beside their wagons for ten weeks was about to end. The teamsters had put new poppers on their blacksnake whips, and the smart cracking sounded like a Fourth of July celebration. In answer, church bells clanged a welcome to the traders. Some men sang in thunderous voices while others shouted hilariously. The mules sensed that the strain of pulling six thousand pounds every day was almost over and picked up their pace to a happy prance.

As the caravan neared town, people lined the road leading to the plaza's southeast corner. *"Los americanos! Los carros! La entrada de la caravana!"* they cheered. Matt felt the excitement as he rode beside Vick, who was more convivial than usual. "We made it with no loss of goods," the captain said with enthusiasm. "We should make fine profits. When we get to the plaza, have the lead wagon stop in front of the palace's main door."

"You think the customs inspector'll make us unload everything, Captain?" Augustus Klotsche asked.

"We will see. At the very least, Don Bonifacio will require us to have the official translators translate our manifests into Spanish. He gets a kickback."

As the lead wagon passed the palace door, a stooped man in a frayed cutaway coat stepped out. Bonifacio Chacón straightened himself as best he could and raised his right hand to stop the caravan. Vick dismounted and greeted the customs chief with a handshake. "Señor Chacón, how good it is to see you again."

"Thank you, Señor Vick. Considering how far they have come, your men and animals appear to be in good condition, which is an attestation to your fine leadership. As always, we in Santa Fe are delighted to receive your fine merchandise."

"You mean that you are pleased to receive our customs duties," Amos Vick said, smiling broadly to make sure that Chacón knew he was joking.

"Yes, we need the taxes, Señor Vick. But, also, the American goods surpass those that come through Chihuahua in variety and quality."

"We have a good assortment this year. I remembered how you loved the smoked oysters I brought you last year. When we unload, I have four tins for you."

"Good, very good. Governor Baca tells me that we will be levying customs duties on each wagon load. Five hundred pesos?"

"That is correct, Señor Chacón. Our thinking was that this procedure would relieve you of the burden of having to count every item."

"Even though Governor Baca's system does not exactly follow the law, it is better, more efficient than our squabbling over the values of ostrich feathers and writing nibs."

"Señor Chacón, I could not agree with you more. Will you require that we unload our goods at the customs house?"

"I too have become more—what is the word you Americans favor?—practical," the customs chief answered. "You may unload your merchandise in your stores. But do not forget that you must have your papers translated into Spanish. I can forego some formalities, Señor Vick, but there are some that I cannot waive. I will need the documents by tomorrow."

"Thank you, Señor Chacón. Of course, we will comply with your wishes."

Chacón smiled politely, turned, and disappeared around the corner.

That night, Amos Vick called together his teamsters, cavvyard drovers, and Matt. "Men, through your efforts, we arrived first with a minimum of mishaps, which means better profits for me. So, I am giving each of you a bonus."

Instead of the sixty dollars in salary that Matt was expecting, Vick counted out seventy-five silver dollars. "Captain, I really do thank you."

"You earned it, Matthew," Vick said, the normally shrewd look on his face softening into warm affection. "Mr. McGuire was very complementary of your assistance with the scouting and hunting. I must admit that your age weighed against you, but you stepped up and did a good job." Vick gave him a good-natured slap on his left arm. Matt winced. His arm still ached occasionally, but he was free of the splint and the arm was straight.

"By the way," Vick said, "if you want to contact Mr. Sartain's partner in Taos, the mail between here and there takes about two weeks. Mr. Marentette is probably illiterate, so you may want to have it translated into Spanish. He can find a priest to read it to him."

Matt and Mike McGuire walked from the *posada* to Florinda Maestas's house for dinner, while Vick left to rent shop space on the plaza. "Let's eat and get down to La Dama's," McGuire said. "There's lots of pleasure halls in Santa Fe, but Dama's is the best. She gets the best-lookin' women."

Florinda pan-fried corn tortillas and served frijoles and a mutton stew laced with chili peppers. "The tortillas and the free holes kinda calm down the chilis," McGuire advised, scooping a chunk of mutton out of his bowl with a tortilla. He turned to Florinda, "*Dulce*, the chilis are really hot this year. Do you have some honey to cool off my tongue?" She brought a clay pot of honey, and the two men spooned it liberally on their tortillas. When they finished, they headed for La Dama's.

The low-ceilinged main room of La Dama's establishment was heavy with cigar and cigarette smoke when Matt and Mike arrived. Oversized candles in four candelabra sent up plumes of smoke that added more layers of soot to the blackened *vigas* and *latillas*, the beams and rafters that supported the mud roof. The candlelight dappled the whitewashed walls with the shadows of American teamsters, government officials, and finely dressed Mexicans who were milling around the bar and a monte table in the center of the room.

The monte players straddled three-legged stools that were so low that only the heads of the shorter men were above table level. La Dama, dressed in a black lace gown that was cut to reveal her bountiful bosom, sat in a tall, regal chair cushioned with a horsehair pillow covered in red velvet. Rather than the crude, hand-hewn furniture that Matt had seen elsewhere in Santa Fe, La Dama's English gaming table was made of highly polished mahogany that, Mike told him, an admirer had brought down the Trail at great expense and given to her. "There isn't another table in Santa Fe of that quality, and she's mighty proud of it," McGuire whispered. "She didn't want anyone tossing heavy metal coins on it and scratching it, so she hired a *bulto* carver to make chips out of soft cottonwood."

"It is a fine piece of furniture," Matt whispered back.

"She'll kick you out if you spill coffee or liquor or even sweat on that table. See that girl over there? She's not one of the whores. Her only job is to wipe off anything that gets on the table and to empty the spittoons. La Dama put in the cuspidors because the Mexicans can't stand our tobacco juice all over the floor. They think it ain't healthy."

They left the monte table and stood at the bar. "Dama won't serve Taos lightning or pulque," Mike said. "She thinks real highly of her Pass wine and brandy. It costs more to bring the good stuff up here from

El Paso, but it don't give you the fierce hangovers, *crudos* the Mexicans call them, like the local liquor does."

Mandolin-hipped women in sleeveless, low-cut blouses mixed with the men, chatting without diffidence and laughing loudly at their jokes. "She's a bold walker," McGuire said of one prostitute's swaying hips. "Hey, *dulce*, how about a cigarette." The woman, María Consuelo, turned and pulled a small leather tobacco pouch from between her breasts and, with sleight-of-hand speed, rolled a cigarette in a corn husk wrapper, twisted the ends, and handed it to him. Then, she lit a roll of twisted cotton with sparks from a flint she struck on a piece of steel. She put the glowing cotton to the cigarette and repeated the process for herself. Mike slipped a silver dollar into her hand and asked her to bring a jug of Pass wine.

"I've never seen American women smoke," Matt said.

"Most all the New Mexican women smoke this local tobacco, *punche*. It ain't near as good as what comes from Virginia or the Carolinas."

"What's that white stuff on their faces?" Matt asked.

"They put it on because they think dark skin is ugly, and the paste keeps the sun off. Some of them use it to hide smallpox scars. It's some kinda flour paste mixture."

"Looks like a death mask," Matt said.

"You get used to it, particularly if you haven't been with a woman for months. It don't look too bad until they sweat. Then, it looks like little goat trails all over their faces."

"They may cover their faces," Matt said when María Consuelo brought the wine, "but they sure don't cover their bodies."

"*Dulce,*" Mike said, "pour the mugs full." As María Consuelo bent to pour, her loose-fitting blouse exposed the purple nipples of her breasts and most of her belly.

"The only other time I've seen tits," Matt said, "was in a magazine I found in old man Banhofer's bedroom." María Consuelo stood beside Mike, trying to puzzle out the English words and to seem interested in their conversation.

"There's a lot more to see than that. Come on, *dulce*, let's go out back," Mike said, and they disappeared through a back door.

Matt went to the monte table. The men talked in loud voices, shouting when they won or lost a large sum, but La Dama made no noise, except for the clatter of her silver and turquoise jewelry when she shuffled and dealt the cards. She had an almost regal presence, an air of assurance and authority that commanded attention and, despite her profession, respect. Matt watched her hands and wondered how she could deal cards so deftly with a finger missing from her left hand. The *punche* tobacco had stained most Mexican women's fingers yellow, but, he noted, La Dama kept hers unblemished by using gold tweezers to hold her corn husk cigarettes.

"Can I fill your glass?" a woman asked Matt in heavily accented English. Her hazel eyes peered straight into his and made him slightly uncomfortable. He guessed that she was in her late twenties. Even with her white mask, he could see that she had attractive features, and her plumpness only made her look healthy. Since he was more than a foot taller than she was, he had a full view of the cleft between her tan breasts. She poured wine from a pottery jug and motioned for him to follow her into a small room that was curtained off by rawhide strips hanging to the floor.

Matt and Adelina Romero settled down on a buffalo robe under an open window and felt the cool night air. In the dimly lit room, Adelina laughed when Matt struggled with his Spanish, correcting him when it became unintelligible.

"My friend says that many ladies come to Santa Fe when the caravans arrive," Matt said. "Do you live here?"

"No, we live on a hacienda two days north of Santa Fe."

"We?"

"My husband and me."

Matt sat silently while Adelina explained that her peon husband, Leandro, worked on Don Ricardo Jaramillo y Naranjo's hacienda. In the summer, Adelina said, Don Ricardo rented Leandro six rams and two hundred ewes that he herded to the good grass in the high mountain pastures. At the end of the summer, Leandro returned the original herd together with rent of fifty lambs and two hundred pounds of wool. If there was anything left over, Leandro kept it as his profit. But if the coyotes or wolves killed a sheep, then Leandro suffered the loss. Last year, Adelina said, Leandro's flock got into a patch of poisoned weeds that killed twenty sheep. "So it is good that I work in here when the Americans are in Santa Fe," Adelina continued. "We use the money I make to pay down our debts to the *patrón*. If we ever get out of debt, we will buy a little rancho."

"With all this land in New Mexico, why not just go out and settle on some?"

"It is not that easy, Don Mateo. The government must grant you the land. And it takes money to get the officials to give it to you."

"Do you have children?"

"No, I am almost thirty, and I do not think that this will happen. My husband says that I am barren, but our priest says that it is God's will. We have talked about me, Don Mateo, so tell me about yourself. Where did you get that beautiful red hair?" Adelina said, putting her hand on the inside of his thigh.

"My mother and father died when I was a baby, and I do not remember them. People say my father was Irish, and that he had red hair. Could I have another glass of wine?"

"Of course."

When she got up to leave the room, Adelina's short skirt revealed her ankles, calves, and knees. *Even Banhofer's whores wore dresses that covered them to the floor,* Matt thought. He had listened to the teamsters touting the glories of poosey and he remembered Adelina's warm hand on his thigh. He wanted to know this mysterious, compelling world. *What should I do? How should I ask?*

Adelina came back with wine. She drank hers in two gulps, while Matt sipped his slowly. "Where were you born?" he asked.

"In Santa Fe. My parents moved up north when I was very young."

"Do you have brothers and sisters?"

"One brother. I had another, but he died of malaria when he was two. Two sisters."

"What does your brother do?"

"He is a farmer and has a few sheep."

"Wheat?"

"Mostly barley. I think I know why you are so nervous—asking me all these questions," she said. "You have never been with a woman, have you?"

"No."

"Come with me," she said. She led Matt by the hand out the back door and across a narrow alley. Matt almost bowed to his waist to get through the door to a darkened room. When he straightened, his head bumped a *viga* and sent a small cloud of dirt drifting down. Adelina lit a candle and drew a buffalo hide across the door, fastening it to wooden pegs in the adobe. Then she went to a corner and lit a votive candle in front of a *retablo* of a brown-skinned Virgin of Guadalupe. She motioned to Matt to lie down on a thick brown blanket made of wool so coarse that it scratched through his clothes. He was simultaneously terrified and so eager that he trembled; his mouth went dry and his tongue stuck to the roof of his mouth, while his penis throbbed into an aching hardness. He put his head on a log that served as a pillow, and Adelina rolled him on his side, lay down behind him, and nuzzled her body against his. Her billowing softness and the warmth of her body relaxed him, and he lay quietly, breathing as steadily and quietly as he could.

After some minutes Adelina rolled him on his back, hiked her skirt, threw her leg over his torso, and got on top of him. She kissed him full on the mouth, which made cracks in her paste mask. Startled by the kiss and the white flakes sprinkling on his face, Matt bobbed his head and thumped it hard on his log pillow. Adelina laughed and kissed him again, this time with her mouth open and her tongue running over his lips.

He grew more comfortable with the kissing and began responding. Adelina took his hand and placed it between her legs. Matt stroked her thighs and timidly put his hand under her blouse, leaving it on her lower ribs to see whether she would object. When she didn't, he slid his hand between her breasts and began touching them lightly. With his other hand, he tugged at her skirt, and she helped him raise it above her hips.

Several exploratory minutes passed. Suddenly Adelina sat upright. "Is anything wrong?" Matt asked. She said nothing while she slipped out of her skirt and blouse and helped him remove his shirt and pants. Still silent, she turned Matt on his side and lay back down. Adelina rolled to face him and began gently stroking his penis. In seconds, a stream of semen squirted on her hand. "I am sorry," he mumbled. "I am very sorry. I did not know."

"It is all right," Adelina said. "This is your first time. We do not have many customers tonight. We will stay here for a while. But do not worry—you will not have to pay twice."

"What will La Dama say?" he asked, feeling the scratchy, rough wool for the first time since their kissing had begun.

"She will not care, particularly when I tell her that you were a virgin. I will get us something to drink," she said, pulling her blouse over her head. While she wiggled into her skirt, Matt alternated between gawking at the black patch between her legs and trying to keep his eyes off of it. Minutes later, she returned with cups of Pass brandy. After he had taken three swallows, Matt felt a twinge in his groin, and he was erect. "I thought it might take an hour," Adelina said. "But I forgot how young you are. How old are you?"

"Seventeen."

Adelina drank half her brandy and covered his mouth with hers. Then, she mounted him. "Do not worry, *chico*, I will help you," she said with an almost motherly smile. She guided his penis inside her and began a slow, rotating movement. Matt reacted with two long strokes and ejaculated. A feeling swept over him that he would later describe to himself as a wonderful ache in his groin and brain, or as an exquisite pleasure, but, whatever the feeling, he liked it.

"It is all over, *mi bebé*," Adelina said, smiling and rolling off. She found a moist cloth and wiped him clean. Then, she squatted over a tin pan of water in the corner and washed herself. "That will be two pesos for me and one for the brandy," she said, a businesslike look on her face.

Matt fished in his pants pocket and paid. They dressed and she led him by the hand back into the main gambling room. "You still a virgin?" Mike shouted. Even the monte players looked up from the table.

"Adelina prefers veal," La Dama said, barely raising her eyes from her cards.

"Not only veal, but a redhead too," Adelina said, pleased.

Matt felt a strange sense of shame. His face flushed. He jerked his hand away from Adelina's and rushed out the door into Burro Alley. His head was fuzzy, but he wasn't sure whether it was from the brandy or the experience. Although it was June, the soft night air was cool and helped clear his head. He walked the few blocks down San Francisco Street to the plaza and went to his room in the *posada*, where he fell asleep immediately.

CHAPTER SEVEN

1803–1825

"I don't fancy spending my life lying under sweaty, stinking sheep herders. There might be another way. I have been thinking about gambling, playing monte."

JULIA BARELA WAS EIGHT YEARS OLD WHEN THE SPANISH GOVernment granted her father a tract of land after he retired from the royal army. Passing out land on the farthest outskirts of Spanish civilization served two of the vice regal government's purposes. It was long on land and short on gold to pay pensions and it wanted to populate the frontier with settlers who would absorb the first shock of Indian attacks.

When Luís Barela retired in 1803, he was a sergeant in the Santa Fe garrison, but he had saved nothing during his twenty years of service to kings Carlos III and IV. The quartermaster had paid him only when the annual supply train arrived from Mexico City, and, after a few months, when he had run out of money, Luís was forced borrow from his captain to buy food and clothes for his family. When the next caravan arrived with his wages, he paid back the loan, along with usurious interest.

Before Luís left military service, he borrowed against his unpaid salary to buy seed, supplies, and animals, and moved his family to his one-hundred-acre rancho north of Abiquiú. His land had two hundred *varas* of frontage on the Chama River, and his tract had enough slope for the *acequia* he and his sons dug to irrigate the entire tract. He planted apple and plum orchards and channeled water in narrow ditches to each tree's trunk. He set aside pasture to grow hay for his horse and two mules, and planted the rest in beans, squash, chili peppers, and onions.

Felicia Barela and her daughter built molds to make adobe bricks. With wooden hoes, they mixed red-brown river clay with water and straw, poured the mixture into the molds, and put the bricks into the summer sun to harden. Soon, they had enough to build the walls of a two-room house.

Luís took his mules high up in the mountains to haul back pine logs he had chopped down for *vigas*. Those beams, together with red willow branches the family cut for *latillas*, supported the earthen roof. When the structure was finished, Felicia and Julia smeared a thin layer of river silt over the adobe to dry and harden into a rainproof coating.

To keep warm in winter, there were no windows and an elk skin covered the only door. Felicia hung her kitchen utensils on pegs around a cookfire in a corner of the main room. Outside she built a domed adobe *horno* for baking. And Luís and his sons chopped piñon and cedar to make corrals for his mules and horse, and fences to keep the coyotes away from his chickens and goats.

The Spanish government carried Luís on its rolls as *puro español* and Felicia as mestiza, to indicate her mixed Spanish and Indian blood. Luís had immigrated to the New World in the 1780s from the Canary Islands, because staying home meant spending his life in debt peonage on an aristocrat's estate. And, he had heard, *puros españoles* got favored treatment in Mexico. Even though Luís had pure Spanish blood, he was illiterate, not overly intelligent, and had no friends or relatives in Mexico City to help him find a job. After six months without work, he signed on as a private in the king's army.

There were rumblings of revolution in the colonial capital, and Luís took part in several actions against liberals who were protesting against the autocratic kings and their viceroys. He had seen machete-wielding peons marching through the streets shouting "Death to the *gachupines*," the insult they applied to Spaniards. But, mostly, he spent his time in routine garrison duty in provincial Mexican towns.

In Puebla, Luís had met and married Felicia, the illegitimate daughter of a Spanish aristocrat and a half-Aztec girl who worked in the nobleman's household. The army transferred him to Guadalajara and then to Chihuahua. Bored with the inactivity, Luís volunteered to serve in Spain's most isolated province—New Mexico—where he knew he would see action against the Indians and where he would have a better chance at promotion.

The family made the trip to Santa Fe on the Camino Real with the 1798 trade caravan. At his new post, Luís fought bravely against the local Indians who were threatening the Spanish enclaves, and rose quickly to the rank of sergeant. He was used to fighting Indians, and he had no qualms when his captain suggested that he accept the government's offer to pension him off with free land near a village on the fringe of Spain's empire.

The Abiquiú plaza, which served as a defensive stronghold against Indian attacks, was on the west side of the Chama River, some fifty miles northwest of Santa Fe. Luís's rancho was less than a quarter mile upstream on the east side. In late May of 1804, Luís was pruning his fledgling fruit trees when he heard the church bell in the Abiquiú plaza clanging the alarm. He raced to his house and shouted for his wife, sons, and daughter to get on the mules and cross the Chama to the plaza's safety.

Inside the house, he grabbed his flintlock musket, powder horn, and pouch of lead balls. With the skill of an army veteran, he loaded the rickety old weapon his captain had given him when he retired and ran outside. His family was mounted bareback on the mules, waiting for him to get his horse from the pasture. Luís approached the gelding, but it trotted away and continued grazing on the fresh alfalfa. He followed the horse until he saw four Indians riding through a stand of cotton-wood trees less than fifty *varas* away. The Navajo warriors stopped and looked over the rancho and then charged. Luís fired his musket at the lead rider, and missed. With his family watching from the corral, two Navajo braves speared him with lances and a third hit him from behind with a stone-headed war club, sending blood and brains flying in a semicircle.

His horrified wife and children froze for several seconds, giving an-other group of Navajos time to reach the corral. Felicia screamed, and she and Julia kicked violently at their mule's flanks. Reluctantly, it walked through the corral gate toward the Chama, followed by the second mule carrying Felicia's two sons. An arrow struck the oldest boy's thigh, top-pling him to the ground, and a lance pierced his chest. Julia turned to look and saw her brother spitting up blood.

Arrows zinged through the air, frightening her youngest brother's mule. Just as the animal put its front foot in the river, two arrows hit the boy's back. He fell off and floated downstream, and his terrified mule rushed straight at Felicia and Julia. Their mount reared and whirled in a circle, giving the Navajo braves time to catch up to them.

A warrior jumped off his horse, pulled Felicia to the ground by her hair, and tried to tie her hands. She shouted, kicked, and then pulled a knife from her waist sash and slit the brave's cheek. The enraged Navajo crashed his war club into the back of her neck. Felicia's head flopped backward and her body went limp. Julia looked at her dead mother with a blank stare, and put up no fight as the Indians tied her hands behind her back and her feet under her mule's belly.

A Navajo chief gave the nine-year-old girl to a warrior who had won distinction in the raid. But a year later, when Spanish colonists killed the warrior during an attack on a rancho near the medicinal springs at Ojo Caliente, the Navajos sold her to a Ute band. At the Taos trade fair that autumn, the Utes sold Julia to a Comanche brave from the Water Horse band for eighteen buffalo skins, a musket, and six pounds of lead.

Julia's new owner, Buffalo Hump, had lost his wife to smallpox, but his older brother, Milky Way, a distinguished chief, had given Buffalo Hump his most cantankerous wife, the third of four. One evening, while Running Rabbit was serving Buffalo Hump his meal, he informed Julia that, "When you are older, you will be my second wife. Until then, I will bind you to me by blood."

During the first months of her captivity, Julia had been in a state of shock, but, gradually, she outwardly adapted to the ways of her captors. As part of the Comanche tribe, she accepted the blood ceremony as part of "normal" life. But she was still driven by a powerful urge to survive.

Buffalo Hump called several friends to his teepee to act as witnesses. He took Julia's hand and made an incision in the large vein on the back of her hand. Then, he rubbed her blood over her hand and named her Carrying Her Sunshade because of her habit of shading her green eyes with a piece of stiff rawhide.

Buffalo Hump turned Julia over to Running Rabbit for training.

"I do not like this white girl," his wife said.

"We have three Spaniards in our band, and they caused no trouble after they were properly taught our language and customs," Buffalo Hump said.

"This girl is not a baby, and she will be hard to teach. She will cause trouble."

"You are only jealous. Do your job with her, and we will have no problems."

Running Rabbit taught Julia to slice venison into thin filets and hang them over rawhide strings to dry in the sun. Julia also learned to skin buffalo with a stone knife and to scrape away the blood, fat, and flesh with a sharpened buffalo leg bone. At first, Julia was clumsy and cut through the skin, ruining it for making tepee covers or clothes. When she made mistakes, Running Rabbit slapped her hard across the face. The first time it happened, Julia cried and Running Rabbit slapped her until she stopped. After that, she never cried again. Instead, when disagreeable things happened, she either remained stoically silent or found humor in the situation.

In time, Julia became deft at balancing loads so that they would not fall off the horses. Buffalo Hump was pleased with his slave's skills in packing and handling horses, but Running Rabbit groused that the white girl was so stupid that she could not properly tie the tepee lodge poles together. Once, during a windstorm, the tent's walls shuddered so violently that the poles snapped apart and the tepee collapsed. After that, when Buffalo Hump wasn't around, Running Rabbit sneeringly called Julia "Breaks Something." Julia turned that into a joke, telling her friends that she would like to break a log over Running Rabbit's head.

During the spring and fall hunts, Julia helped butcher downed buffalo. She and the other women drank the warm blood and quarreled over who would get the brains, bone marrow, and tender liver. In the summer, Julia gathered wild persimmons, mulberries, plums, and grapes. For winter, she prepared pemmican: wild fruits that she dried in the sun and pounded with a stone before mixing them with dried meat and fat. She stored the pemmican by stuffing it in a buffalo's large intestine and sealing the ends airtight with melted tallow.

After two years with the Comanches, Julia was becoming a woman. She had noticed Buffalo Hump's eyes when she bent over to put more wood on the fire and the neck of her loose-fitting buckskin dress revealed her growing breasts. If Running Rabbit wasn't around, she would tease Buffalo Hump, "You will get cross-eyed if you stare so hard." She laughed broadly, and he chuckled sheepishly.

Her first menstrual period did not surprise her; she had seen it happen to two other girls in the band. "Breaks Something, you have to sleep and eat outside the tepee until your time of bleeding is over," Running Rabbit whispered to Julia. "Buffalo Hump is going with Milky Way on a raid against the Utes. If he gets too near you during this time, it will rob him of his power."

"I understand," Julia answered, gathering her buffalo robe and taking it to a willow grove next to the river. Lying on her robe, she heard a rustling in the willows. She sat up and saw the new mulatto slave the warriors had brought into camp.

"Come over here," Julia said to the girl in Spanish.

The girl, who had been sent to fetch water, was fearful. "Do not worry," Julia said, "I will not hurt you."

"Where did you learn Spanish," the girl asked.

"I am like you. I am Spanish. The Navajos captured me."

"And you are still alive?"

"Do not worry. They would probably kill you if you were a boy, but they do not usually hurt girls. Whose tepee are you in?"

"Horse Back. He is old and wrinkled. His wives are dead, and he needs somebody to take care of him."

"He is harmless," Julia said. "Just do as he says and you will not have any trouble. Horse Back spends his days making bows and arrows. The braves still respect him for his courage when he was young, and they will keep their hands off of you. If you need help, let me know and I will tell Buffalo Hump. What is your name?"

"Viola Ortega. I must go. Horse Back needs the water to soak his wood for the bows."

When her period ended, Julia moved back into the tepee. Since she had joined the Water Horse band, she had slept by the tent's opening and, one warm summer night, Buffalo Hump got up to urinate. He jabbed Julia's back with his toe. He motioned for her to follow him outside the tepee, and led her to a patch of high grass beside a playa lake. "You have breasts. You are becoming a woman," he said. "I need children, and Running Rabbit is too old."

Julia wasn't afraid, only uncertain. On many nights she had heard the alternating sounds of intensity and contentment that Buffalo Hump and Running Rabbit made on the other side of the tepee, and during full moons she had seen their twisting bodies in silhouette.

Julia stood in silence while Buffalo Hump raised her dress and eased it over her arms and head. He spread it on the ground and motioned to Julia to lie down. He pulled the front of his buckskin breechcloth from his belt and dropped it so that it hung behind his legs. He covered her and his greased braids lightly slapped each side of her face. When he had finished, he stood, looped his breechcloth under his belt, and helped her slide her dress back over her head. She pulled a handful of grass and brushed away the juices and blood that had dribbled on the front of her dress and tried to think of something funny to say. But nothing came. She laughed her broad laugh and kissed Buffalo Hump's cheek. When they reentered the tepee, Running Rabbit grunted and rolled over to face the wall.

After that night, Buffalo Hump changed Julia's name to Laughing Bear. But when he was away Running Rabbit punished Julia's mistakes even more severely and called her "Breaks Something" in front of everyone. Julia made no protest, but when Buffalo Hump announced that she was his wife she immediately took advantage of the Comanche custom that allowed her to send Running Rabbit back to Milky Way's lodge.

Chief Milky Way asked Buffalo Hump to ride to the Antelope band to spread the word that he was planning to raid a Spanish village called Las Truchas. Almost seventy Water Horse and Antelope warriors answered the call. When they gathered in front of Milky Way's tepee, he invited the men to feast with him before they discussed strategy. Milky Way's wives served the braves generous portions of a worn-out horse the women had butchered and roasted. As a special treat, his wives passed around grapes they had gathered near their campsite on the Canadian River.

After they ate, Milky Way filled his pipe, which was decorated with a blond scalp that hung below the bowl. He blew a puff of smoke toward the sun, the next toward the earth, and one in each of the four quadrants before passing it to the others.

When the pipe returned to Milky Way, he outlined his plan.

"Buffalo Hump has scouted Las Truchas. It is perched on the edge of a steep cliff that forms one side of a mountain valley. The Spaniards built the village in a square and it has only one entrance."

"I have tried to attack one of the Spanish towns," an Antelope band chief said. "Many of our men were killed trying to climb the walls. The putrid Spaniards poured boiling water on us."

"It will be difficult and dangerous," Milky Way said, "but the rewards will be great. We will harvest guns, tin pots to cook in, and metal to make arrow points."

"But there are only about seventy of us," the Antelope chief said, "and I have heard that more than three hundred Spaniards live in Las Truchas or on farms close by."

"To offset the Spaniards' numbers," Milky Way answered, "our Kiowa allies have agreed to send us thirty warriors. Besides, it is summer, and many of the Spaniards are herding their sheep and cattle high up in the mountain pastures."

"Are the Spaniards well-armed?"

"Buffalo Hump could not get close enough to find that out," Milky Way said. "But the Frenchman who came to our camp a few days ago has sold us six new muskets, ammunition, and flints."

"How do you plan to carry out the raid?" the Antelope chief asked.

"We will begin a surprise attack at dawn. We will catch many of the Spaniards asleep in their ranchos outside the fortress walls, and we will kill them first. We will not stop to count *coup* or to scalp. We can do that later. Instead, we will regroup and assault the village's west wall."

"To ensure our success," Milky Way continued, "I have summoned my *puha*—my power, my medicine—and it is strong. I had a vision, and my guardian spirit let me view our raid. We had great success. We captured many slaves and horses and we came home with fruit and honey, salt and tobacco. The spirit advises me to take extra horses so that we can haul away our riches. Now we will smoke again."

Milky Way took his ceremonial puffs and passed the pipe. The braves who smoked committed to the expedition, but the eight warriors who passed the pipe without puffing signaled that Milky Way had not convinced them. Milky Way waved a hand to indicate that the council was over and disappeared into his tepee to sing the chants that would assure victory.

Just before sundown, the war chief reappeared, his face blackened with charcoal. Three white stripes on his right cheek and four on his left reminded the warriors of the number of men Milky Way had killed in battle. A red "T" that ran across his forehead and down his nose recalled the blood that he had caused to flow from enemy wounds. His first wife brought him his war bonnet, a buffalo scalp with the horns attached and hawk feathers dangling from the back, and placed it firmly on his head.

The other braves, dressed and painted for war, gathered around a large fire in front of Milky Way's tepee. Julia joined the women and children in a circle around the dancing braves to sing the ritual verses that celebrated past valor. When they finished, the crowd split the desert air with war whoops, drum beating, gourd rattling, foot stamping, and hand clapping. Before sunup the warriors mounted their ponies and rode out of camp to meet their Kiowa allies.

Days later the warriors began straggling back into the Comanche camp. The campaign had been a disaster. The war party had stumbled across a herd of *churro* sheep a day's ride from Las Truchas. They killed many sheep and had a fine meal, but the shepherd escaped and warned the villagers that Indians were in the area. When Milky Way and his men reached Las Truchas, they found not only local farmers but a detachment of thirty soldiers from Santa Fe who had been patrolling the frontier. The Spaniards, barricaded inside the Las Truchas plaza, killed four Kiowas and twelve Comanches, including Buffalo Hump.

Julia and the wives of the other dead braves painted their faces black, piled ashes on their heads, screamed, and tore out plugs of their hair. With no show of fear, Julia cut off her left index finger and seared the wound with an ember to demonstrate her respect for Buffalo Hump.

"Laughing Bear, you must leave us," Milky Way told Julia. "If these were normal times, I would take my younger brother's woman as a wife. But, with so many of our men dead, we have too many women. At the next Taos fair, I am going to sell you."

"To whom?" Julia asked.

"To whomever pays the most."

"I beg you, Milky Way, do not sell me to another tribe. Sell me back to the white people."

"You have lain with a Comanche, and no Spanish man will have you. It is a stupid custom, but there it is. I can get more for you from another tribe."

"In your wisdom, Milky Way, you know the Spanish customs and you also know those of the weaklings—the Utes, the Navajos, and the others," she said, appealing to his Comanche sense of superiority. "I could not bear living with inferior men of little courage. If you cannot sell me to the Spanish, I plead with you to keep me with the Comanches."

"We do not have enough men to take care of the surplus women," Milky Way said. "You are healthy and your willingness to work will bring many horses and guns from another tribe."

"Unless you tell the Spaniards that I have lain with a Comanche, they will never know. It is not in either of our best interests to reveal this."

"I agree to keep your secret, Laughing Bear, and if a Spaniard wants to pay more for you then he can have you."

That fall, the Water Horse band road up the Cimarron River canyon.

During the trip, Julia pressed Chief Milky Way to promise that he would sell her only to a Spaniard. He answered with a slap and a harsh rebuke. "Do not bother me with this. I do not care what you want. I will do what is best for our tribe."

Julia changed tactics. She ran errands for Milky Way's first wife, Small Elk, gathering wood, butchering deer, and helping supervise the war chief's children. She did her tasks cheerfully, making jokes and teasing the children to keep them from crying. One evening when they were carrying water buckets to the camp, Julia told Small Elk of her fear of being sold to another tribe. "The Utes are animals," Small Elk said. "And the Navajos are worse. They killed my brother. I will speak to my husband."

After a meal of roasted venison and tiny, fresh raspberries, Small Elk called Julia aside. "Laughing Bear, my husband refused to speak with me about this. He threw a piece of firewood at me and threatened to beat me if I mention it again."

The Water Horse band crossed the Moreno Valley, stopping often to let their horses graze in the mountain pasture. As the horses labored up a set of switchbacks to the trail through the Sangre de Cristo Mountains, they snorted, wheezed, and passed gas. On the western slope, the animals carefully picked their way down a stony path that followed the Rio San Fernando into the Taos Valley.

The tribe marched through an almost-deserted Taos plaza to the Martínez hacienda, two miles south. Milky Way led his band to a campsite on the Rio del Pueblo just north of the hacienda. He ordered Julia and the six other women he planned to sell to put up a tepee. When they had lashed the lodge poles together and laid the buffalo skins in place, he put them in the tepee and posted a guard of warriors outside the door.

Milky Way took two braves with him to the hacienda's *zaguán*, the adobe fortress's main door. Americans, Frenchmen, Indians, and Spaniards were talking and trading, using a mixture of gestures and words from many languages. Inside, in the large patio, he saw whiskey barrels and monte tables where, the white traders said, the Martínez family made most of their money. With sign language, Milky Way found a Comanche-speaking *genízaro* to translate for him.

He explained to the *genízaro*, a Comanche who had been captured as a boy and raised as a servant in a Spanish household, what he wanted. "The Martínez family does not allow wild Indians to enter their hacienda," the *genízaro* said. "But they will let me in." He disappeared through the *zaguán* and returned a few minutes later. "They say that the slave sale will begin tomorrow at midmorning in that cottonwood grove over there," the *genízaro* said, pointing toward the river.

After a morning meal, Milky Way tied the women's hands with rawhide and Comanche warriors marched them from their camp past a line of staring trappers, farmers, and two priests. Under the cottonwood canopy, the cottonwood leaves clattered in the wind and buyers shouted and jostled one another to examine the human merchandise.

A Navajo chief forced Julia's mouth open, and looked at her teeth to see if they were strong enough to chew animal skins to soften them for clothing. Through a translator he asked her if she had borne children. She remembered enough of the Navajo language to understand the question, and answered "no." The chief was clearly pleased to find a slave who understood Navajo. Julia knew that she had made a mistake, and kept saying "no" in Navajo to whatever he said, as if it was the only word she knew.

"Here, girl, step up on this stump," the Navajo said. She waited until a translator relayed the command in Comanche. The chief pinched and felt her calves, thighs, and hips. "Raise your dress," he commanded.

"But—but," she stammered in Spanish.

"Raise your dress," Milky Way ordered.

The Navajo half squatted and looked at her vagina, probing with one finger. "Spread your legs, girl." He parted her labia with both hands, and turned to Milky Way.

"She has strong legs and she can carry heavy loads," the Comanche said.

"Yes, but she has a small vagina. She will have trouble bearing sons."

The Navajo moved on to the next slave, and a French-Canadian trapper asked Julia in stunted Spanish to raise her arms. He tugged at her buckskin dress, outlining her body's curves. His sleepy eyes surveyed her, looking for beauty hidden behind her greased braids and deeply darkened skin. Julia could tell from his shabby clothes and his ancient musket that he could never pay Milky Way's price. As the trapper ambled off a Spanish couple approached her.

"*Habla españal?*" the woman asked.

"*Si, señora,*" Julia answered.

"What is your name?"

"Julia Barela. The Comanches call me Laughing Bear."

"Barela? From where?"

"Abiquiú," Julia said.

"Was your father Luís Barela?"

"Yes," Julia answered, uncertain where the questions would lead.

"Then we have something in common."

"How?" Julia asked, peering at the woman cautiously.

"Luís Barela and my father were in the army together in Santa Fe."

"What is your name, señora?" Julia asked, her mind spinning to find a way to turn the coincidence to her favor.

"Delfinia Vigíl. My husband is Juan Pablo. The Navajos killed Don Luís, did they not?"

"Yes."

"And he was *puro español,* was he not?"

"Yes."

"And your mother was a mestiza? The daughter of a nobleman, if I remember correctly."

"Yes. She was three-quarters Spanish."

"How long have you lived with the savages?"

"Three years, I think. What year is this? I have lost track."

"Eighteen eight."

"Then it has been four years," Julia said after counting on her fingers.

"Did you have a husband?" Delfinia asked, rubbing her belly.

"I was a slave. Never a wife," she lied, looking straight at Delfinia.

"Did you mate with them?"

"No."

"An attractive girl like you? The sun has burned your skin to an ugly darkness, but you have lovely green eyes."

"The savages' idea of beauty is much different from ours, Señora Vigíl. They preferred Viola Ortega, the mulatta at the end of our line."

"We need a servant," Juan Pablo said. "My wife is having our fourth child, and she will need help."

"During my captivity, I cooked and tended to their children."

"Cook?" Delfinia chuckled. "Those red beasts do not know how to cook. They cannot make bread or *pozole.* But I can teach you to cook like a civilized person."

"It will be a matter of price," Juan Pablo said. "How much will your chief want?"

"I do not know," Julia said, masking her excitement with a slight smile.

"Because of our family ties, Julia," he said, "I will do my best to buy you. I have property, but it is limited. Are you sure you never bedded with those filthy animals?"

"Yes, Señor Vigíl, I assure you," she said, now comfortable with her dissembling.

"The heathens never violated you?"

"No, señor."

"I will speak with your chief. What is his name?"

"In Spanish it is Milky Way," Julia said, waving her hand across the sky.

Juan Pablo found Milky Way squatting by the river to drink. Through sign language and a *genízaro* translator, Juan Pablo asked, "What is the price of the Spanish girl?"

"Which one?"

"The one you call Laughing Bear."

"She will not be cheap. What is your offer?"

"Chief Milky Way, I am not a rich man. I can offer two fine mules. They are three years old, very strong, and they are broken to both the saddle and the pack."

Milky Way spun on his heel and walked away. "He is insulted by your offer," a subchief who spoke pidgin Spanish told Juan Pablo. "What is your real offer?"

"Bring him back," Juan Pablo said. "Tell him that I will give him the two mules and four Spanish knives that I bought in Santa Fe."

Milky Way walked toward Juan Pablo, glowering. While Juan Pablo was explaining his new offer, the Navajo chief who had examined Julia joined their circle.

"What is the Spaniard offering for the girl?" the Navajo asked. "We have had a good year. Our raids against the Utes and Apaches have produced many riches, and we can make a generous offer."

Milky Way described Juan Pablo's proposition, and the Navajo topped it with two horses and a female slave.

"We have too many women already," Milky Way answered. "I do not want your slave. I need animals and tools, not women."

"I understand," the Navajo said. "We will keep the woman, but she has a child, a boy, about four. You can have him."

Milky Way discussed the Navajo's proposal with his subchief until Juan Pablo reentered the negotiation. "I know their horses are more valuable than my mules, but I have no horses. I can offer one more mule, twelve *churro* sheep, the four knives, and three tin cooking pots."

"And you?" Milky Way asked, making signs to the Navajo.

"I will pay three horses, give you the boy, and I will add a musket."

"Let me see the gun," Milky Way demanded.

The Navajo produced the weapon and Milky Way looked at it carefully. "You offer me this musket? It is so old that it will explode in my face. And, if the boy is only four, he is useless to me for another six years. The girl goes to the Spaniard, but only after I have seen the mules and the sheep."

That afternoon, Juan Pablo and Delfinia brought the trade items to Milky Way's camp. The Comanche examined the sheep and had his braves ride the mules before he accepted them. Satisfied, he ordered a warrior to cut Julia's bindings and deliver her to her new owners.

Since the early 1700s, Juan Pablo Vigíl's family had bred mules and kept a herd of *churro* sheep in their pasture along the Rio del Pueblo, just west of the Taos plaza. But Juan Pablo had seen the Martínez family grow rich from their trading operations, so he decided to become a merchant. By 1808, when he bought Julia, Juan Pablo was one of Taos's most prosperous citizens. His wealth had grown, and Juan Pablo and Delfinia became increasingly proud of their *pureza de sangre*. As a light-skinned couple among a sea of mestizos and Indians, they were pleased to tell the census takers that their blood was *puro español*. And their wealth caused old friends and relatives to treat them with the deference due to *ricos*, but, behind their backs, they said that Juan Pablo and Delfinia had become "uppity."

To Julia the Vigíl's adobe house was a palace, after having lived in a tepee for four years. In the tepee, Julia had choked when the wind shifted and the smoke did not draw out of the top hole. But the Vigíl's kitchen fireplace drew perfectly, and Julia spent many hours in front of it, listening and watching as Delfinia taught her to cook proper Spanish stews of mutton, cabbage, chilis, corn, and tomatoes. And, instead of sitting cross-legged on the ground and dipping her hand in a common pot for food, she ate from the Vigíl's pottery plates and sat on a split-log bench at a table.

Delfinia taught Julia the rudiments of reading and arithmetic at night. But ink was so expensive that Delfinia would not let Julia use the supply she kept in a deer antler vial. Instead, Julia made ink by mixing water and crushed charcoal and spitting in the brew so that her saliva would bind it together.

One evening, Juan Pablo returned home from his store disconcerted. He asked Delfinia to walk with him by the river and they were gone for a long time. When they returned and sat down at the dinner table, the Vigíls would not look directly at Julia. That evening, the nightly reading and math lessons that had gone on for two years stopped. Several days passed before Juan Pablo confronted Julia in the kitchen while she was preparing breakfast.

"Julia, I have heard some disturbing things about you."

"What, Don Juan Pablo?"

"I have heard that you had relations of a sexual nature with the Comanches. Is this true?"

"Where have these lies come from?" Julia asked calmly.

"They came from my friend, Antonio Torres, a farmer who lives at Arroyo Seco. He was in the store last week and stayed after closing time. We shared a few glasses of wine from his vineyard and he told me that he bought a girl named Viola Ortega from the Comanches. Antonio says his oldest son approached Viola, and she accepted. When his son mentioned to Viola that she seemed to be experienced, she told him that she had lain with the Comanches. She said that all the female slaves lay with the Comanches. I am asking you if this is true?"

"It is a lie. Those barbarians never touched me," she said without blinking. "For whatever reason, Viola is not telling the truth. Perhaps, she is jealous that I work for an educated merchant, while she works for an ignorant farmer."

"At first, I did not believe the story," Juan Pablo said. "But my wife's family is very close to Padre Onofrio. He confirmed that the story is true."

"How would he know?"

"I cannot tell you, but he does," Juan Pablo said, keeping his promise not to reveal what Padre Onofrio had heard in the confessional. "Julia, we had hoped that you would work for us for a few more years, and then we would try to find a young man from a decent family to buy your freedom. But once the truth about your life with the savages spreads, nobody will have you. And my wife does not want you around the children. At best, you are disgraced. You must leave our house."

"What will I do? I have no family," she said, the initial fear in her eyes turning to anger. "My only choice is to marry a stinking shepherd with goat shit on his boots or to become the servant of some drunken farmer and spend my life cleaning the weeds out of his irrigation ditches."

"We have consulted with Padre Onofrio," Juan Pablo said without emotion, "and he agrees that a man of my position cannot have his name stained by permitting a woman like you to live in his house. I will give you ten silver pesos when you leave. Perhaps you can go to another town and start a new life."

"When must I leave?"

"I will give you two days."

That night, Julia lay awake, sucking in air in panicky breaths. Her mind was racing, recalling her life; watching the Navajos massacre her family and the indignities of the Taos slave market. She had survived all that, she told herself, and, one way or another—by guile or by determination—she would survive whatever was in front of her. After that, she slept.

Juan Pablo arranged for Julia to travel to Santa Fe with a burro train carrying wheat to the capital. Because highwaymen often robbed the pack trains, he suggested that she dress as a man. Before leaving, she bought a buckskin shirt and pants from a *cibolero*'s wife, and, with her hair tucked under a wide-brimmed straw hat, she looked like a man of medium stature. The train made the journey without incident, and its leader guided the burros to an alley west of the plaza, where the drovers tied them to hitching posts and headed to a cantina on San Francisco Street.

Juan Pablo had warned Julia that the capital's only *posada* was for men, but that she might find a family that would give her a place to sleep. In the plaza, she approached a guard lounging on a bench in front of the governor's palace. "The Chávez family might rent you a corner of their *sala*," he told her. "You cross the plaza and go by the *posada* over there. Then go straight until you come to the river. Turn right, and it is the third house along the alameda."

After she passed the *posada*, she took off her straw hat and her chestnut hair fell to her shoulders. Then she tied a rawhide rope around her waist to bring out her figure. At the third house she slapped her palm on the buffalo skin hanging across the doorway.

"Yes. How may I help you?" a short, dark woman said as she pulled the buffalo hide to the side.

"I am new to Santa Fe, and I need a place to eat and sleep. A guard at the palace sent me here."

"And you are who?"

"Julia Barela. From Abiquiú." She had already decided that saying that she was from Taos increased the risk that her history with the Comanches would be found out.

"Why are you here?" Anita Chavez asked.

"The husband of the family I lived with became ill. Something to do with his heart. He was too sick to work his farm, and they could not afford to keep me. I thought I could find work here in the capital, but I need a place to stay until I do. I can pay. In cash."

"Nazario and I have only one child. We could make room for you."

"There is a fandango next week to celebrate the coming of eighteen eleven," Anita Chávez told Julia. "Nazario and I are going, and you should come with us. The governor and his wife have promised to lead off the dancing. And the hacendados, the army officers, and the government officials will all be there. You might meet someone who needs a servant."

"I do not have anything respectable to wear. I cannot go in buckskins or these old clothes I brought from Abiquiú."

"Do not worry. I know a seamstress who fixes dresses that the *ricos* have discarded."

Julia found a red cotton dress that almost fit her. It had a plate-sized stain just above the hem line, but, the seamstress told her, "If you flip it just so, you can keep the spot covered most of the time. This lace on the bodice is torn and dirty. I can leave it on or take it off."

"Take it off."

"When I finish, with a few tucks here and there, it will reveal a bit of your fine figure and bosom."

On the afternoon of the fandango, the December air was cold. Julia and Anita found warmth on the west side of the house in the full sun, and they sat with their backs against the adobe wall picking lice from one another's hair. When they finished the delousing, Anita handed Julia a clay pot filled with bone marrow, wild rose petals, and rosemary. Julia smeared the pomade in her hair, and her friend braided and coiled it around her head. Anita went inside and brought out two pots, one containing white flour paste and the other a vermilion liquid. "Here, cover your face with the paste and highlight your lips with this juice from the *alegría* flower," Anita instructed.

Properly made up, Julia was watching a brilliant orange sunset when she heard loud noises coming from farther out on the alameda. She turned and saw the musicians who would play at the fandango, followed by a crowd of dancing, singing peons and their women. Between thumps of a bass guitar, they shouted that the dance was about to begin.

Nazario, Anita, and Julia followed the crowd to the *posada* and elbowed their way to a corner of the tap room. Looking over the crowd, Julia noticed an almost comical-looking old woman who was dressed in shiny emerald green satin accented by royal purple bows, her fingers and arms cluttered with rings and bracelets. As the woman smiled and chatted with friends, the candles on a sconce above her head gave away her wooden false teeth and black horsehair wig. Seated next to the woman was a plump but handsome young military officer in a dark blue coat with silver epaulets, who, when she stared at him, returned Julia's glance.

After an hour of smoking and socializing, the servants moved the crowd back and sprinkled water on the dirt floor. Through the haze of blue cigarette smoke, Julia watched as three guitarists and a violinist, drummer, and flautist mounted a platform at one end of the room. The crowd formed a circle, leaving the middle of the room open, and the governor and his wife danced a stately waltz.

For the second dance, men and women lined up randomly on opposite sides of the room. The band struck up a fast tune, and the men and women moved toward one another to dance with the partner directly in front of them. The heavily jeweled old woman flashed smile after smile with her false teeth while a barefooted peon whirled her around the floor. Anita pointed out a well-dressed *hacendado* who was dancing with a prostitute. And the robes of a short, fat Spanish priest flapped happily as he clutched a dark-skinned *genízara*.

Anita and Nazario joined in the next dance, the *batalla,* the "battle." Men and women, in no particular order, broke into two "armies," one at each end of the room. At one end, a hacendado's pallid son stepped forward and sang defiant words. When he finished, a chocolate-brown mestizo at the other end sang contemptuous verses in retaliation. After the singing, each side clapped violently and stamped their feet on the floor, raising a cloud of dust. The men and women in each "army" partnered and began whirling toward the "enemy," all the while yelling and shouting sounds of combat. When the dance ended, sweat had carved rivulets through the paste on the women's faces, and the men mopped themselves with bandannas.

As the warlike dance ended, Julia saw the candlelight flickering on the plump military officer's silver epaulets as he headed toward her. He waved his small, delicate hand toward the dance floor. Julia smiled and nodded in agreement.

"Have you danced before?" he asked, his voice, Julia noted, a smooth baritone.

"Not this kind of dancing."

"This dance is called the *cuna*. We put our arms at each other's waists and lean back to form a 'cradle.' Then, we rock slowly to put the baby to sleep," he laughed. "My name is Susano Baca, and yours is . . . ?"

"Julia Barela. Excuse me, Don Susano," she said when she stepped on his foot.

"No matter, Julia. May I call you Julia?"

"Yes."

"You are new in Santa Fe, are you not?"

"I arrived two weeks ago from Abiquiú."

"I know it well. I have been there on patrol. But I do not remember seeing you there," Susano said.

"I did not live in town," Julia answered, tensing, but quickly putting together her story. "We only went to the plaza if we needed something from the store, or when a priest came to the village to conduct services, which was not often."

"Is there any way that I can be of assistance to you here in Santa Fe?"

Until then Julia had kept her eyes from meeting his. Looking straight at him, she said, "Señor, I would appreciate your help. Other than Nazario and Anita, I have no friends in Santa Fe."

"Nazario? Nazario Chavez, who works as a clerk at the governor's place?"

"Yes."

The dance ended, and without asking Susano put his hand in the small of Julia's back and ushered her into the next room. "A *chupita* of some El Paso brandy?" he asked.

"I am not accustomed to liquor, Don Susano. I prefer water," she said, flipping the folds of her skirt to hide the stain.

"The water will 'boil your guts,' as we say in Santa Fe. Brandy or wine is safer."

"Mix a little wine with water then."

He returned with the drinks. "Who is that older woman you were sitting with?" Julia asked.

"My mother. She is visiting from our family hacienda near Albuquerque. She returns home next week."

"She is an elegant lady," Julia ventured.

"She is very old, but very lively. Very aggressive for a women." He leaned toward Julia and whispered, "Please come to my office in the palace. I may have an idea of how to help you." His breath tickled her neck.

"When?"

"I will not be working tomorrow, New Year's Day. But come by whenever you would like, at your convenience. Shall we dance the next waltz?"

"Of course, Don Susano."

So that she would not appear overly anxious, Julia waited three days before going to the palace. She put on a skirt and blouse that Anita loaned her and pulled a *rebozo* around her shoulders to ward off the January chill. At the front entrance she gave her name to the guard, and asked to see Susano Baca. "The captain is not in yet, but you may wait if you wish." Instead, Julia strolled along the *acequia* that ran in front of the palace, watching the magpies pick over the animal droppings and garbage in the plaza.

She hopped over the *acequia* and was walking down the east side of the plaza when she saw Susano entering a side door to the palace grounds. She crossed the plaza and told the guard, "I believe Captain Baca is now in his office." In a few minutes, Susano appeared and greeted her with an expectant smile. He guided her through the labyrinth of corridors to his office, a tiny room with only one small window and two candles on his desk to supplement the winter light. Susano closed the door and invited her to sit on the three-legged stool in front of his desk.

"Tell me about yourself, Julia."

"What do you mean?"

"Your family. Why did you come to the capital?"

"I came here to find work, or a husband, or some other means of support." She chuckled, and a saucy look animated her face.

"Have you found either one?" he asked, and gave her an appraising smile.

"I have spoken to a few families about becoming a servant, but I have received no offers."

"I am only a captain in His Majesty's army, but I may be able to help you. Your family name is Barela, you said. I think I remember a Barela family."

"Luís and Felicia Barela were my aunt and uncle," she said evenly, masking her lie.

"I seem to remember that the Navajos killed everyone in the family, except a girl."

"That was my cousin. Fortunately, I was in town when the Navajos attacked our rancho."

"Julia, I was a lieutenant at the time, and I investigated that raid. You have been lying to me," he said matter-of-factly. "There was no cousin. If your name is truly Barela, then the Navajos captured you and made you a slave."

For less than a second fear flitted across her face. Composed, she looked at Susano, "You are right, Don Susano. I am the girl. I have lied, but you know the reason why."

"Yes."

"If you disclose this, you know what effect it will have." She turned her eyes nervously away from his.

"Did you bed with them?" Susano asked.

"The Navajos traded me to the utes, who sold me to the Comanches. My owner, his name was Buffalo Hump, talked of making me his wife. But the king's soldiers killed him during a raid on Las Truchas."

"Are you lying to me again?" he asked. His face was composed. He tented his hands on the porch of his belly and tapped his index fingers together.

He had put her on the defensive, but she summoned a positive tone. "No," she said firmly.

"Then why would you worry about it." He ran his hand through his black, slicked-back hair.

"Everybody hates the Comanches, their viciousness, their paganism," she answered in a hard-edged voice. "Many people believe that living with the savages taints a person for life."

"I would bet a large sum that the Comanches bedded a lovely girl like you, either voluntarily or involuntarily."

"Then you would be wrong." She was alternating, she knew, between gaining and losing control. She paused for a moment, looked out the window, and gave him a bold smile.

"Perhaps so," he said. "But, if word spreads that you spent—how long were you with them?"

"Four years."

"Nobody would believe you."

"Perhaps so," Julia said, looking him in the eye.

"Well, that is enough of your background," Susano said. "Let us talk about your future. I have an idea for you to think over. Since you have no family and no dowry, the chances of finding a decent man to marry are slim."

"And what is your proposal?" she asked, almost sassily.

"That you come under my protection. I will rent a house for you, provide for your clothes and food, and give you an allowance to buy the things you might want."

"Let me think about this, Don Susano. I will need a few days."

"There is no rush."

That afternoon, Julia boiled a cup of coffee and went outside to warm herself in the sun and to weigh Susano's offer. For her, she knew, there were only three options: become a wife, a servant, or a whore. If her Comanche past became known, her chance of marrying a respectable man would be nil and good families would not hire her as a servant. *And I don't fancy spending my life lying under sweaty, stinking sheep herders. I would rather wallow with hogs.*

"You know Don Susano, do you not?" Julia asked Anita when she joined her.

"My husband knows him. They both work in the palace."

"What do people say about him?"

"His father was a *rico*, but he squandered most of the family money. The Bacas are no longer rich, but they are comfortable. Don Susano was the third son and he joined the royal army as a junior officer and worked his way up to captain. In addition to his army salary, he makes a little on the side by doing favors for people. He is ambitious, and some people say he is maneuvering to become a general or maybe governor. Why are you interested in Don Susano?"

"He has made me an offer."

"To become his mistress?"

"Yes."

"You would not be the first. His wife and children spend most of their time at his family's place near Albuquerque. She comes up here once or twice a year and he goes home occasionally."

"How does he deal with people?" Julia asked.

"Nazario says that he can be arrogant with the people beneath him. But he is a *lambiscón*, an ass kisser, with his superiors. He runs many errands for the governor, and the governor loves him. His colonel loves him too. The gossip is that he shared his last mistress with his colonel."

"Is there anything else about him?"

"As you know from your experience on New Year's Eve, Don Susano can be charming. But Nazario says that he can be slippery. Still, from your standpoint, he has many friends and he can be of great help to you."

Julia waited another week before contacting Susano. She stood on a corner of the plaza until she saw him leave the palace on his way home for lunch, and set a course to intercept him.

"Julia, how are you?"

"Very well."

"Have you thought about my proposition?"

"Yes."

"And?"

"I think that it is something we should discuss." Her flirting was so open that he looked to see that no one was watching them.

"We could meet later. There is an orchard behind the parish church."

That evening, when Susano found Julia sitting under a peach tree, a splendid sunset had turned the Sangre de Cristo Mountains a rosy red. She stood and dusted herself off and he embraced her and kissed her cheek. "I am delighted," he said.

"Can you tell me more about what you have in mind?"

"I believe that I can make you happy. Since my wife is seldom here, we can spend a great deal of time together. After we get to know each other, it would be my hope that we would develop an affection for one another."

"What kind of house do you have in mind?" Julia asked.

"The governor's chief clerk is returning to Mexico City. I was thinking of renting the house he is vacating. It has three rooms, all very commodious, and the roof does not leak."

"I will need a servant three times a week to wash and clean."

"I can arrange that."

"Do you plan to take your meals with me?"

"I would probably take lunch and dinner with you three or four days a week. I will give you two silver pesos a week for food."

"That is not enough. I will need at least three."

"Done."

"And the clothes? I will need new dresses, skirts, blouses, and several sets of underwear. I want new shoes, and my *rebozo* is dirty and has a tear in it."

"My sergeant will deliver twenty pesos to you."

"And my allowance? I will need ten pesos a month," Julia said firmly.

"After all the rest, that is too much," he said. "Five."

"Eight."

"Six."

"Seven."

"We are agreed," he said. "Come with me to my house. We can have wine and dinner and chat."

"Our first meeting will be in my new house," she said.

"If you are as good a lover as you are a businessman," Susano said, "we will have an exquisite relationship." She laughed uproariously—and, Susano thought, somewhat unladylike.

Over the years, Julia made friends with Santa Fe's demimonde, mostly gamblers and other kept women. Although the capital's elite did not invite her to the private balls at their homes, she was welcome at the public fandangos, where her looks and delicious figure made her the dance partner of the *ricos* and, once, of the governor himself. But she was twenty-nine, and she worried that the occasional gray hair and the wrinkles around her eyes and mouth would cool Susano's passion. She still loved the timbre of his baritone voice, but, she knew, they had been together for many years, and sooner or later he would find someone new.

She discussed her dilemma with Elena Montemayor, the mistress of a hacendado. "I have been a servant," Julia said, "and now Don Susano provides me with a servant. I could not go back to that."

"Maybe you will find somebody to take care of you when Colonel Baca tosses you out. But the pickings are slim. Very few men would want the colonel's castoff, and not many have the money."

"I will never be a common whore," Julia said, "with a pimp who steals my earnings. Whatever I earn, I keep. But there might be another way."

"And what is that?"

"I have been thinking about gambling, playing monte mostly. Both illiterate shepherds and *ricos*—and now the Americans—are fanatics about it."

"How are you going to handle cards with that finger missing? Besides, monte is a man's game."

"Up until now it has been," Julia said.

In the next weeks she had gambler friends for afternoon tea on the condition that they teach her to play monte. The game was simple, and she quickly learned that the banker had the odds in his favor. But to be a banker required a large cash stake. At first she had saved the allowance Susano gave her—until American traders began bringing tempting luxuries to Santa Fe.

"Susano, I am planning on running a monte bank," Julia told him one cold night while they were lying in her bed. She reached over and tickled the hair on his chest and abdomen. "I was thinking that, with all these Americans coming from Missouri, it would be a good time to start a gambling operation. There is a house on Burro Alley that I could rent. We could serve drinks. I have saved some money, but if the cards turn sour on me I would not have enough to keep going until they turn back my way."

"What makes you think you know how to play monte, *niña?*"

"I have been studying the game for weeks, playing with some friends, gamblers, and I can play as well or better than they can."

"How much are you thinking about?"

"If you could put up two hundred pesos, I could put up sixty. We would split the profits, half to me and half to you." She took his penis in a cold hand and he shivered until she released it.

"I would be putting up most of the money. Why not seventy percent to me and thirty to you?" he said, rolling over to face her.

"You do have a beautiful, slim Indian nose, Susano. Just like my mother's," she said, licking her finger and sliding it along the bridge of his nose. "I would be doing the work and I am the one who will sit there all night while you are at home asleep. I should get a larger share."

"You are a good negotiator, Julia, but I will not do it on those terms."

"Perhaps we could do it this way," she said, a teasing tone in her voice. "Seventy percent to you and thirty to me until you get your money back. Then we go fifty-fifty."

"I can do that. But no prostitutes. The liberals threw that son of a bitch Iturbide out as emperor, and my friends in Mexico City think that the new president will appoint me governor. Being a whoremaster would kill my chances. No whores! You must promise me that."

"We will make enough money off the gambling. I agree, no women."

When the American traders arrived in 1824 Julia was ready for them. To keep order, she had hired a short but heavily-muscled mulatto, who she nicknamed Payaso, "clown," because he had once worked in a circus. Two local girls were happy to serve drinks and *botanas* for a small salary and tips. By August, Julia had paid back Susano all of his capital, and they were sharing the fruits of the Americans' losses.

The Americans had taken to calling her "La Dama," for the most part out of respect. But Julia did not like the teamsters and drovers, who were almost uniformly loutish. They got obscenely drunk and vomited on her floor, grabbed at her barmaids' breasts, and fought over nothing. When they became too rowdy, she had Payaso pitch them into the street. But she liked, and felt comfortable with, the American proprietors. Instinctively, she knew that they did not care where she had come from or what she had done; all they cared about was who she was now.

And the Americans liked La Dama. She was a mature but still attractive woman who could conjure up an enigmatic look that put her at her most sensual, attracting men with more intensity than a buck rutting after a doe's musk. The look was composed of a crooked smile and green eyes that laughed, which, taken together, suggested that she knew deep, inner, visceral things about men that other women would never understand. But most of the time she was loud and bawdy—without being vulgar—and her humor made her good company for the proprietors, who were a thousand miles and many weeks away from friends and family.

In 1825 President Guadalupe Victoria appointed Susano Baca governor of New Mexico. Julia was pleased to have been invited to the formal dance, the *baile*, marking the occasion, even though she had had to make herself as unobtrusive as possible because Susano's wife was there. During most of the evening she sat in a corner and thought about her future, now that her lover was the province's chief executive.

She had accumulated a stash of silver dollars and pesos, gold dust and nuggets, and a small amount of American paper money. But, while her business was prospering, her relationship with Susano was slipping. Two weeks after Susano's wife returned to their hacienda, he paid his first visit.

"Julia, I have been thinking," he said, getting out of her bed and rolling them each a cigarette with expensive Virginia tobacco.

"About?"

"We have been together for fourteen years. Perhaps it is time that we separated. You know that I have great affection for you, but lately there seems to be more business than romance in our relationship."

"I have affection for you too, Susano. Without your support, I would have been somebody's maid. I will always be indebted to you. But I have sensed that you might have other interests. Do you have a new lover?"

"This town is so small that you would know it. The problem is that you spend more time at the monte table than you do with me. And all you talk about is how much you have won or lost."

"My work has produced good profits for both of us, Susano."

"That it has."

"And you are as acquisitive as I am."

"That is true too," he said with a smile.

"So tell me what the real problem is."

"We have had successful relationships, in business and in bed, so that is not the problem. But friends have advised me that our relationship could hurt my career. There is talk in Mexico City of a plot to overthrow President Victoria. If a new party takes office, they will use anything they can to throw me out."

"Perhaps I should step aside." She exhaled smoke through her nose and stretched. The blanket fell and exposed her to the waist. Susano, she knew, was still enchanted by her breasts. "We could still see one another every so often—in a discreet way."

"That would work, Julia. I would never want to lose your company permanently. But my friends feel that I should reduce our business ties, become a silent partner, or something like that."

"As your friend, Susano, I would advise you to completely separate our business affairs," she said, rolling on her side and propping her head on her hand. "I have been giving serious consideration to having prostitutes as one of the services we provide. The Americans are demanding it."

"Those goddamned Yankees. They meddle in our politics in Mexico City, and now they are trying to corrupt our Santa Fe business with whores."

"If I do not accommodate them, they will gamble elsewhere."

"There is no way that I can be involved in that business, Julia."

"I know that. How much do you want?" she asked, narrowing her eyes and then forcing a saucy smile.

"What is your offer?" he countered.

"I was thinking of three hundred silver pesos," she said as she got out of bed.

"That is less than you paid as my profit share last year," he said, his eyes wandering over her naked body.

"There is always risk," she said, warming to the excitement of bargaining. "I could lose money this year."

"Not the way La Dama plays monte," Susano said. "You have learned enough English to where you are getting the lion's share of the American business. When they are drunk, winning their money is like stealing, and the profits from liquor sales alone are worth more than three hundred pesos."

"They do drink. And that is good. But having to deal with drunks every night is not easy. That has to be worth something."

"Payaso handles the brawlers and the roughnecks."

"If I could pay you over two years, I might be able to offer more," she said.

"How about one thousand over eighteen months," he said. "No beaver pelts. No paper money. Only silver or gold."

"My God," she said, feigning a surprised gasp so obviously that they both laughed. "I could not pay that much over five years. What if the government stops the trade with the Americans? What if the Indians attack the caravans and shut down the Trail? Your price is too high. I would rather keep you as a partner," she said, knowing that that was not an option for Susano.

"I know La Dama's tricks," he said, smiling. "You are trying to get me to bid against myself. Give me an offer."

"I could perhaps pay you five hundred."

"Not acceptable."

"Do you like being governor? I hear that Lieutenant Zambrano is scheming for the appointment, and he has friends in Mexico City. While you were marking time up here in Santa Fe, Diego Zambrano was fighting against the Spanish in eighteen twenty-one."

"I have friends in Mexico City, too," Susano answered calmly. "I am not afraid of Zambrano."

"Maybe not. But I know—and you know—that a governor's opportunities for profit are substantial."

"I would accept nine hundred over two years," he said.

"Let us find the middle ground at eight hundred, payable over eighteen months. And do not forget that I hear many things at the monte table that might be useful and profitable for a governor to know."

"You have bested me in the bargaining, Julia. I accept. But do not come to me with stories about why you cannot pay. This must be a firm bargain."

"It is a firm bargain," she nodded and gave him her enigmatic smile.

CHAPTER EIGHT

1826–1827

"Jack, I've had all the trapping I need. The Santa Fe trade is a lot easier."

"May be easier, but in them mountains, there ain't no asses to kiss. No big shots."

AMOS VICK RENTED THE FRONT ROOM OF A BUILDING THAT Governor Baca owned on the west side of the plaza and hired Matt to help in the store. So that his clerk could save money, he let him sleep in a corner of the room on a stack of buffalo hides. After they closed the shop one night, Matt lit a candle and lay down to read.

"By the way," Vick said, "I have a hacendado acquaintance who has a good—good, that is, for New Mexico—library of Spanish books. Mendoza his name is."

The next morning, Moisés Mendoza came into the store and shook hands with Amos Vick. "Don Moisés, I want you to meet Mateo Collins. He was one of my scouts on this year's caravan, and he has been clerking for me since we arrived. His Spanish is good, but he wants to improve it, so I told him about your fine library."

"Yes, I see," Moisés said.

"What kind of things would you be interested in reading?"

"I like novels and history the most."

"Have you heard of Cervantes?"

"No."

"He is like your Shakespeare."

"I have read Shakespeare's plays and poems."

"Cervantes writes novels. You should read him. And I have some histories of Spain and Mexico. Come to my house this afternoon, after lunchtime—Spanish lunchtime, Señor Collins, not American."

Over the years, Matt would come to know that Moisés Mendoza was in many ways the prototype of a Spanish gentleman, a *rico*, a *hidalgo*—*un hijo de algo*, a son of somebody. He shared the aristocratic prejudice against manual labor, was passionate about the Mendoza clan, and believed deeply that his land had more than mere temporal value. His almost spiritual love of his land was in line with the other hacendados, but he differed with them on religion, his belief having been tempered by the time he spent around anticlerical radicals while a student in France. He did not lack for *pundonor,* honor, or for pride, dignity, and the stoic ability to bear his burdens with grace. And he had an abundance of politeness and hospitality, almost to a fault. From the way he carried himself, even a casual observer understood that Moisés Mendoza was supremely confident of exactly who he was.

What set Moisés apart from many of his fellow hacendados was that their perceptions were mired in medieval Spain. They approached the business of life with a closed conservatism that made them instinctively shy away from the new. At the Sorbonne, Moisés had immersed himself in Descartes and the other luminaries of the French Enlightenment. He was, for a New Mexican of his class and background, of a liberal frame of mind—curious, and receptive to the new. But there was something else, something that Moisés could not explain, that also set him apart from the other hacendados. On certain saints' days, the Mendozas observed a peculiar set of traditions and rituals that seemed bizarre to his friends.

Although he was not tall, most people would have sworn that he was. His backbone was always at rigid attention, even though he had a slight limp from a leg wound he had suffered as a young militia lieutenant fighting the Navajos. Moisés's deep-set mahogany eyes were set off against a thin, pallid complexion, punctuated by a hawkish nose, all reminiscent of a duke in an El Greco painting. Although he was nearing fifty, his snowy hair was thick and full. His white beard was groomed in the Spanish style of the 1600s. It ran down his sideburns, along his chin bone, over his full, sensual mouth, and jutted out in a sharply pointed goatee.

Matt had been impressed by his first meeting with a New Mexican *rico*, and he was looking forward to seeing how Spanish gentry lived. From the sun's angle, he guessed that it was four o'clock. He walked to the Mendoza house and clanged the long iron bar. A servant let him in and Matt followed the tiny man into a large, high-ceilinged dining room. He had been in Santa Fe for two months, and, he thought, he had not seen such luxury. On one wall, two oil paintings, one of a Mendoza ancestor and the other of San Francisco contemplating a skull, hung on either side of a large mirror in a baroque gilt frame. Behind a burnished table that still held the luncheon's porcelain and crystal, a boy a little younger than Matt sat beside his father.

Although David Mendoza was only sixteen, he had a self-possession that was unusual for a boy of his age. His face was a perfect oval and he had his mother's swarthy skin and his father's hawkish nose. His lips were so red that it appeared that they had been tinted. And his mother had seen to it that his hair was cut to a black stubble so that he would not pick up head lice from the servants' children.

"This is my son, David," the father said, rising and bowing gravely. The two young men shook hands, and Moisés nodded to Matt to take a seat. "So, you like reading and you wish to improve your Spanish?"

"My Spanish is getting better," Matt said. "But New Mexican Spanish is different from what I have studied in the grammar book Señor Vick loaned me."

"Some of our families have been here for centuries," Moisés said, "and sometimes we use words that were common in the sixteen hundreds. You must get used to our little *modismos*."

"Yes, sir."

"Let me show you my books."

Matt and David followed Moisés into the *sala*, where dark wooden bookcases covered one wall. Matt selected *Don Quixote* and Moisés helped him pick a history of Mexico.

"These books—leather bindings and gold lettering—must have cost a great deal of money," Matt said.

"That is not the point, Señor Collins," Moisés said, twisting his mouth in annoyance.

"Excuse me, sir," Matt said, knowing that he had somehow blundered, but not sure how.

"Will you be returning with Don Amos to Missouri?"

"No. I am going to Taos in September. The Comanches killed a friend on the way out here, and I am taking his money and supplies to his trapping partner. If his partner will let me, I want to go with him this winter."

"I am interested in your trapping expedition. Who is this man that you will be going with?"

"His name is Marentette. He partnered with my friend Bill Sartain for many years."

"There are few ways to make your fortune in New Mexico, Señor Collins, but this trapping business is becoming very profitable, particularly the beaver."

Amos Vick had not left his bed at the *posada* for two days. He had taken the herbal tinctures and laudanum he had brought with him, and they seemed to be helping. But, on the third day, malarial chills shuddered through Vick's body one minute, and in the next his bald head was covered with perspiration and his face turned a dangerous red. Matt went to find help.

"There ain't no medical doctors in Santa Fe," a proprietor told him. "But there's a fellow who came in with the last caravan who studied medicine for a year or so in Philadelphia." Matt found the almost-doctor at La Dama's and brought him to Vick's bed, a mat on the floor stuffed with corn shucks.

"You've got the ague real bad," Sam Murphey said after he examined Amos. "There's something wrong with your cardinal humors. Either your blood or your phlegm or your black or yellow bile is impure. Let's try bleeding to see if it gets the humors back in balance. Get a bowl," he instructed Matt.

"Get quinine," Vick mumbled. "That has pulled me out before."

"I don't believe in these new fads," Murphey said. "Besides, I doubt that there's any quinine in Santa Fe."

While Matt was wiping away the sweat, Murphey unsnapped his penknife from his waistcoat chain, took Vick's left arm, and cut a small incision in the vein. After a half pint of blood had trickled into the bowl, he bound the wound with his handkerchief. "Let's wait a day and see if that works."

The next day, Vick was worse. "An enema oughta do the trick," Murphey said, kneeling down to insert a rubber tube. That night, Amos Vick went into a coma. Panicked, Matt ran to Murphey's shop on Palace Street and found him sipping brandy with customers from Albuquerque. "Mr. Murphey, the captain's really sick. He needs your help," Matt said.

Murphey and Matt walked quickly back to the *posada*. "If he was conscious," Murphey said, "I'd prescribe an emetic to make him vomit. But, like he is, he might choke. Let's give him a good bleed this time." Murphey cut into the vein in Vick's right arm and held it over a bowl until a pint of blood had drained into it.

Matt spent the night at Vick's bedside, daubing his head with a moist rag and trying his best to make the Englishman comfortable when he pitched and rolled in pain. Matt dozed off and, when he awoke, Vick was dead.

At the orphanage, Matt had learned to distance himself from others. Making friends was emotionally dangerous, because people were always coming and going, being adopted, running away, or getting too old and being asked to leave. But his relationship with Amos Vick had been different. Other than Sister Marie Thérése, no one had ever gone out of their way to help him the way Vick had. At first Matt was in shock. He blew out the candle and sat in a silent stupor with his back against the cool adobe wall, until morning light crept into the room. Somehow, the light brought with it the reality of what had happened, and Matt sobbed without stop until a servant came into the room to take out the slop jar.

Matt collected himself and found a carpenter to build a pine coffin. He knew that the priests would not allow Vick's Baptist body to buried in the *campo santo*, but a proprietor told him about the new Protestant cemetery, and he arranged to have the grave dug. To conduct the service, he found a teamster who had been a backcountry tent revivalist before coming to Santa Fe. A crowd of Americans marched to the cemetery and Matt embarrassed himself by breaking down and crying in front of the mourners.

The next week, Matt sold the rest of Vick's goods at wholesale and gave Jay Birdsong four rawhide bags of silver and gold worth thirty thousand dollars to send to Vick's brother who Vick had said lived in Manchester.

With most of his caravan salary and two months pay for serving as Vick's clerk, Matt had ninety dollars in silver. He spent four dollars at La Dama's—one for drinks and three for a night with Adelina. Matt woke up the next morning naked, with an erection, and Adelina was standing over him with a cup of coffee. Matt blushed and covered his torso with a blanket. He drank the coffee and ate two slices of dark, heavy bread before going to the Mendoza's house.

"When you told me that you are going to the mountains this winter," Moisés said, "I began thinking that it might be good for David to learn something about the trapping business."

"I understand that there is great risk," Matt said.

"I know, Señor Collins," Moisés said. "But when I was a was a boy my father sent me to the mountains to herd sheep with the peons. I learned things about animals that I would never have learned otherwise. And there is another benefit. By speaking with you and Marentette, he will learn English. I hope to send him to school in your country, and, perhaps, he will enter the Missouri trade one day."

"I am honored, Don Moisés, that you would put this much trust in me. I would welcome David as a partner."

"Before he died, Don Amos told me that you are a responsible young man, Mateo. May I call you that?"

"Yes."

"I have checked up on this Marentette. When he comes down from the mountains, he drinks up his profits. But they say there is no better trapper and woodsman."

"Don Moisés, I must warn you that Marentette may not allow me or David to accompany him."

"Perhaps I can help Señor Marentette look upon you two with favor. Does he have a trapping license?"

"I do not know."

"I would guess that he does not," Moisés said. "Our law prohibits the issuance of licenses to foreigners. If the army catches you, they will confiscate any furs you and Marentette may have. I will speak with Governor Baca and have a license issued in David's name."

At dawn on the morning of their departure, Matt arrived at the Mendoza's house with a horse and burro. The high desert air was dead still and Matt caught whiffs of piñon smoke from Santa Fe's breakfast fires. Moisés showed him the trapping license with the governor's red wax seal at the bottom. After David embraced and kissed his father, he mounted his saddle horse and the young men headed up the slope north of town to the Taos road.

The horses spent most of the fourth day struggling up a steep track through the mountains. The climb and the thin air had worn them out, and with each step their heads bobbed up and down like gently rocking hobbyhorses. As they topped the pass into Taos Valley, Matt snapped his reins, splattering the white lather on his horse's neck.

The horses and burros zigzagged down the switchbacks, picking their way over fallen trees that a winter snowslide had knocked across the trail. About halfway down the western slope of the Sangre de Cristo Mountains, Matt and David found a stream and camped there.

The two boys left at sunup and arrived at the base of the mountains before noon. By late afternoon they were in the Taos plaza. Matt found a French-Canadian merchant who knew Marentette. "That sorry bastard," the merchant said in English. "He comes from good French stock. And now he lives like an animal with a *genízara* whore in a shack behind the church."

Matt and David rode to a low hut made of poles, roofed with chamisa branches. "Haloo in there," Matt called. A barefoot Indian woman threw back the deerskin door. "I am looking for Jack Marentette," Matt said.

"What for?" she asked.

"His old partner, Bill Sartain, asked me to find him."

The woman disappeared inside. Several minutes later, a very tall man wearing filthy woolen underwear emerged. Marentette's dark brown hair hung in gnarled tangles below his shoulders and his beard was a catchall for grease and food particles.

"I'm Marentette. Who wants to see me?" he asked, glaring suspiciously at his unexpected visitors.

"Bill Sartain asked me to look you up. Didn't you get my letter saying I was coming to Taos?"

"No. Where's Bill?" Marentette asked, coughing deeply and spitting.

"The Comanches killed him." Matt paused for a reply, then went on. "Bill raised five hundred dollars to stake you and him for this year's trapping season," Matt said, surprised that Marentette took the news of Bill's death with no show of emotion. "He asked me to bring it to you if something happened to him, along with six traps he bought in Missouri."

"Who's the Mexican kid?" Marentette asked, loading his mouth with chewing tobacco.

"I am Spanish," David said emphatically. "My father is Moisés Mendoza."

"I heard of him. Why's the kid here?" Marentette asked Matt.

"We're figuring on doing some trapping this winter," Matt answered.

"Get off your horses and have some coffee. It'll be good to talk some English. Does the kid speak good English?"

"A little bit," David said.

Matt and David dismounted, tied their horses to an olive tree that shaded the hut, and sat on the ground by the doorway. Marentette's woman brought them clay cups of coffee.

"The fella who told me where you live says that your grandpa was a governor of Louisiana."

"Yep. He was a count. Count de Abbeville. He was governor before the Spanish took Louisiana from the French."

"Why aren't you back home living easy?" Matt asked.

"My pa died young, from the yellow fever, and we had it rough. I came out to the Rockies when I was thirteen, and I never been back. Ain't never goin' back. Don't cotton to that life. Too many rules. You say you're goin' trappin' this season? Ever been before?"

"No, we haven't. That's why we were hoping to go with you. Sort of fill in for Bill."

"I been out by myself before. Bein' alone don't bother me none. You got any money?"

"I have over eighty dollars. And I'm a good shot. I was a hunter and scout for our caravan."

"What about the Spanish kid?"

"He's got a trapping license, signed by Governor Baca."

"I been workin' these mountains and sellin' pelts for years without a license."

"Governor Baca is madder than hell about all the foreigners harvesting pelts," Matt said. "He's going to send extra soldiers up to Taos next spring. If they catch an American with skins, they'll confiscate everything."

"A license might be worth somethin'," Jack admitted. "How much of a split you lookin' for?"

"I was thinking twenty percent for each of us."

"That's a damned good share to be asking when you two don't know your ass from a tin pot about trappin'."

"Could be. But we'll be doing our share of the work, and I'll buy another half dozen traps. That'll double our chances."

"Let's do it this way," Jack said, scratching his crusted beard. "You and me gets our money back first, Matt, and then we splits like you say."

"Fair enough. Is that okay with you. David?"

"I agree."

"Good. After the trade fair, we'll take off," Jack said. "I wanna get up to the mountains 'fore the snow starts."

"Where are we going?" David asked.

"I ain't tellin'," Jack said. "If I was to tell anybody about my secret valley, there'd be twenty trappers who'd go up there and pick it clean in a season."

During the next week, trappers, traders, and Indians drifted into Taos for the fair, more than doubling the village's population. They strolled around the plaza's perimeter to survey the merchandise laid out on blankets. Matt bought six steel traps, heavy iron chains, and spare parts from an aging trapper with a runny nose.

"What will happen to him?" Matt asked Jack. "He can't make a living without traps."

"He's old. Wore out." Jack shrugged, taking the old man's plight as a matter of course. "He always went out alone. Last season, he damned near died up there by hisself. He knows he can't make it through another winter, so he's sellin' off his equipment. He'll spend the money on whores and stay drunk till it runs out. If somebody don't take care of him, he'll just die. Come on. Let's ride out to the Martínez hacienda. There's usually some pretty good weapons for sale out there."

Below the hacienda, by the river, a crowd was watching a slave sale, but Jack pointed Matt and David toward a cluster of tents along the mud building's north wall. "I'm gonna depend on you two to kill some deer and elk," Jack told them. "Matt, get yourself a rifle with at least two extra ramrods. The damned things break all the time. You'll need skinnin' knives, and don't try to save money buyin' cheap knives—make sure the cuttin' end'll hold a sharp edge."

Matt wandered among the tents where traders were dickering over the prices of axes, cook pots, and deer sinew for sewing buckskin clothes.

"Come over here," Jack shouted. "Here's a Carolina rifle by Tim Vogler. A friend a mine's got a Vogler. You can drive a nail in a board at a hundred yards with one of 'em."

Matt bought the flintlock, along with powder, lead, and a bag of flints. For David, they found a Belgian-made musket. Another trader sold them skinning knives and whetstones. Marentette swapped a jug of Taos lightning to a Kiowa for buffalo horns that he would fashion into powder horns. "I got pots, a skillet, and cups for all of us," Jack said. "But you'll be needin' a tent and you'll wanna buy buffalo robes with the winter hair on 'em for your bedrolls."

The next day, they laid out their equipment in front of Jack's hut and started packing their burros and horses. Once they had loaded, they headed north. "Taos lightnin' comes from this village," Jack said when they entered Arroyo Hondo. "We'd better get a few gallons."

"Why do we need so much liquor?" Matt asked.

"You'll see."

From Arroyo Hondo, they followed a steep trail down to the Rio Hondo's junction with the Rio Grande and swam the burros and horses across. "Let's camp here. There's some hot springs a coupla hunnert yards up that way, if anybody wants a bath." Matt's eyes traveled up the six-hundred-foot cliffs of the Rio Grande gorge. That night, Matt and David bathed in the hot springs, and the next morning they broke camp. "Let the animals drink up good," Jack said, "it'll be a day or two 'fore we get to water." Jack took the lead and guided them up the switchbacks on the narrow rock trail.

At the top of the gorge they entered a high mountain desert so dry that it yielded little besides twisted, gray-green sagebrush and occasional clumps of tawny grass. They rode west for three days until they came to a small stream that wound its way through an outcrop of large rocks. On the plain to their right they saw a herd of antelope grazing lazily. "I'll shoot one," Matt offered.

"There's not one goddamned tree out there to hide behind," Jack said. "You get too close, and all you'll get is a look-see at their white butts runnin' away from you."

They turned north, passing a solitary mountain that rose up out of the flat desert. Autumn's first snow had capped its summit and sun dappled through the clouds to highlight gleaming yellow aspen leaves. After they passed San Antonio Mountain, they saw a column of smoke rising in the still air in front of them.

They took their weapons out of their saddle scabbards, laid them across their laps, and rode until they came on six Indians standing around a fire. Jack raised his right hand and shouted a few words. The Indians' leader motioned to them to ride toward the fire, and gave his men what sounded like commands. After communicating by hand signals and a few guttural words, Jack said, "They're Jicarilla Apaches—out meat huntin' 'fore the hard winter settles in. This here chief says he wants to do a little tradin'. I don't think they'll bother us, but don't get off your horses, and don't do anything to make 'em jittery."

Jack traded three jugs of Taos lightning for an elk hide and a braided horsehair rope. After the exchange, he led Matt and David at a trot toward a mountain range to the north. "Let's go as long as the horses'll hold up," he said. "Them Apaches ain't exactly teetotalacious. When they get that lightnin' in 'em, there's no tellin' what they'll do."

The three rode until after dark and stopped in a thick clump of cottonwoods beside a dry arroyo. "Don't unpack the animals, and make sure they're well picketed. We'll camp here without a fire," Jack ordered.

Well before dawn, Jack jabbed Matt and David with his rifle butt. "Get out of them bedrolls and let's get going. We can make four or five miles before sunup." They rode all day without stopping, sipping water from their canteens and eating the last stale bread they had in their saddlebags.

"Looks like them redskins ain't comin' after us. But just in case, let's bunk up in that line of trees along the river," Jack said.

The horses and burros had gone for two days without water. A strong north wind was blowing and the animals smelled the Rio de Los Piños more than a mile away. At first they broke into a shuffling trot, but when their riders relaxed the reins they hit a full gallop until they splashed into the clear stream.

"David, you get us some wood. And Matt, you help me unload these animals. I hope to hell they didn't get no sores after two days with them packs on."

When they awoke the next morning the grass was white with a thick frost. David pulled flint and steel out of a pouch hanging off his belt and started a fire. After coffee and slices of jerked buffalo meat, they packed their animals. Jack took the lead and found a trail heading northwest across the desert. At midday, they topped a rise and saw a line of cottonwoods in the distance. Two hours later they came to a wide river flowing out of a canyon. "Where are we?" Matt asked.

"The Mexicans call it the Rio Conejos, Rabbit River," Jack said. "You can follow it east till it dumps into the Rio Grande, but we're goin' *up* it. That's where the beavers is. And tonight we're gonna have somethin' different for dinner. There's some monstropolous trouts in there."

Jack tied hooks to lengths of string and attached them to slender willow branches. "You sonsabitches can help," he said, annoyed that Matt and David were sitting in the shade and watching him. "Use your hats to catch grasshoppers for bait." In minutes they had six trout. "David, Matt, you clean 'em. I'll cook 'em with some cornmeal. Throw them guts in the river so's they'll wash down and don't bring in the coyotes."

The next morning they rode up the Rio Conejos, following it along the valley floor. As they got deeper into the canyon its walls rose higher and higher. "These aspen changing color remind me of the oaks and maples at home," Matt said.

"What do oaks and maples look like?" David asked.

"There's nothing out here that I can compare them to," Matt said.

That evening they came to a large meadow. "This's it," Jack announced. "I always remember this place by that cliff. Looks like a monkey's face from this angle. There's a whole mess of deer up here, and the elk'll be comin' down from the high country for the winter."

"I'll see what I can do tomorrow," Matt said.

"Naw, we've got enough fixin's for a few days. Tomorrow, we'll set the traps. It's too early for the beavers to have their winter fur, but them beavers's tails is deliciferous."

The next morning, when they ran their traps, they found a female beaver that they roasted and heartily ate its tail. "The fur ain't prime yet," Jack said, "but we got plenty to do 'fore we start trappin' serious." They spent the next days making oval willow frames they would use to stretch and cure pelts. Then Jack took the elk skin he had gotten from the Jicarilla Apaches and laid it on flat ground. He drew patterns around their hands and feet with charcoal, and cut and sewed mittens and moccasins with a bone needle that he had honed to a fine point.

Matt killed a deer, fat from grazing on the valley's summer grass. The three men cut the meat into thin strips and hung it on tree branches to let the crisp air and sun dry it. "You boys listen up for bears tonight," Jack said. "If they get a whiff of this meat, they'll come for it. It'd be nice if we could kill us a bear. She'd be fattened up for hibernation, and we could harvest enough oil to keep us in fryin' grease for the winter."

No bear came, and as the days passed the weather grew colder. An afternoon hailstorm sent them running for cover under the willow bushes by the Rio Conejos, and snow dusted the valley floor almost daily, until, one morning, they woke to find six inches of snow on the ground. That afternoon a bull elk's bugle call echoed off the canyon walls, breaking the valley's usual silence. Jack went in one direction, and Matt and David the other, making a wide sweep around an elk herd. They crawled through the snow and waist-high grass, keeping track of the herd by listening to the cows' catlike meowing.

When they were in range of the grazing animals, Matt propped his Vogler rifle on a low cottonwood branch, aimed, and fired a one-ounce lead bullet that crippled a young bull. Matt and David followed the blood stains and found the elk penned by a thick stand of willows. The bull, its front legs splayed in exhaustion, stared wide-eyed at the two men approaching him, but did not move. "We're close enough for your musket," Matt whispered. "Aim for his shoulder." The ball crashed into the animal, snapping his thigh bone. He stumbled and fell. They rushed toward him, and Matt slit his throat with his skinning knife.

"I'm guessing he weighs six or seven hundred pounds," Matt said.

"How much is that?" David asked.

"About three hundred kilos. We need to gut him and get that musk gland out before it ruins the meat. Then we'll get the horses and burros to haul him back to camp."

When they returned with Jack and the pack animals, a wolf was ripping flesh off a hind quarter. The gray wolf stopped eating, flicked its tail nonchalantly, and trained its yellow eyes on the creatures who had interrupted its meal. Jack walked toward the wolf, waving his hat and shouting. The wolf walked slowly, almost insolently, into the willows and disappeared.

Jack skinned the bull with deft strokes of his long-bladed knife. Using their hatchets, the three hacked the elk into large pieces of beet-red meat. "Let's work on the bones," Jack said. "The marrow's the best part."

They loaded the mules and led them back to camp. "When we finish unloading, Matt, you take them pack animals into the river and clean that blood off 'em so's we don't have every mountain lion in the valley trying to get at 'em." While Matt was at the river, Jack washed half-digested grass out of the elk's intestines. He stuffed them with the fresh meat and put the entrail containers in the cold river and covered them with rocks to keep the odor from scavengers.

"I hate to move some place else in this heavy snow," Jack said, his frosted breath stringing out in the dry, freezing air. "But we've about trapped out this lower stretch, and our animals have about eat out all the grass."

The next morning they struck their tents and stuffed their panniers and saddlebags with supplies and pelts. "David," Jack said, "you go on upriver ahead of us. We're gettin' a little short on meat, and you might come across a deer or elk. We'll finish the packin' and catch up with you tonight."

Matt and Jack carefully balanced the loads so that the packs wouldn't slide off the animals' backs, and led the horses and burros up to a ridge where the snow was only knee-deep. "Where'd that damned kid go?" Jack growled. "I thought we'd see his tracks somewheres up here. Well, to hell with it, we'll catch up to him."

As the sun was going down behind a large mountain, Jack called a halt. "This is a good spot. The sun and wind done hit that knoll over there and melted enough snow so's the animals can get at the grass. We better get our tents up and a fire goin'. As clear as it is, it's gonna be colder 'an a whore's heart tonight."

"What about David?" Matt asked.

"He can't be too far away. Shoot off that rifle."

Matt fired the gun and listened to the sound ricocheting off the canyon walls. When the sound evaporated in the snow and trees, there was only the snapping of Jack's fire.

"Where the hell could he be?"

"He'll turn up," Jack said. "There's no place to go but up or down this canyon. If he don't see or smell our smoke, he's got his blanket and buffalo robe."

"There will be hell to pay with Moisés Mendoza if we don't bring his boy back," Matt said.

"Don't worry about it," Jack said, shrugging with disinterest. "Cook some beans and jerky and let's get some sleep. We'll find him tomorrow."

The sun was up when Jack and Matt crawled out of their tents the next morning. While Jack rekindled the fire, Matt walked to the top of the knoll and fired two shots. Nothing.

"Goddamn dumb kid!" Jack said, irritated that David had gotten himself lost. "Matt, you double back to where we started yesterday. We never seen David's tracks, so the only thing that makes sense is that he went further up the side of the canyon than we thought. If it don't snow today, it'll be easy to pick up his tracks."

Matt rode back down the trail until he was even with their old camp site. He coaxed his horse up the canyon's north side and soon saw hoof-prints in the snow. "Why the hell did he come way up here?" he asked himself. Matt clucked at his horse and followed a narrow game trail that skirted the canyon wall. "Be careful on this narrow son of a bitch," he said to the animal, and thought to himself that he was beginning to curse as much as Jack did. "One wrong step and we both go straight down that dropoff."

He rode for an hour and came to a boulder jutting out of the canyon wall, making the trail no wider than two feet. He got off his horse to lead it around the rock, and, as he inched along with his back to the boulder, he looked down and saw a wide gash in the snow. Farther down, he saw David's horse lying motionless, its body wrapped around a blue spruce that had stopped its slide. Matt shouted, but there was no answer.

After he got around the rock, he tied his horse to an aspen sapling and skidded downhill, losing control until he rolled into David's horse. In an aspen grove twenty yards on the downhill side of the dead animal, he saw a mound of snow that looked like a fresh grave. Matt worked his way down, clutching at white aspen trunks to slow himself.

When he got to the mound, Matt scraped off the snow and pulled back David's blanket. His friend's normally red-pink lips were white, tending to blue. "What the hell happened?" Matt asked.

"When I came around that boulder," David said, his voice weak, "the horse's left front foot slipped off the trail. He pitched forward and I jumped off. I was sliding down right beside him when my leg got twisted funny. It snapped. I couldn't walk, but I crawled over to the horse and got my blanket and robe and then got down into these trees."

"Let's see the leg."

In the middle of David's calf, his leg veered off at an angle. "You busted it all right. Is your hatchet on your saddle?"

"Yes."

"I'll chop some aspen branches for a splint. Even though they're green, they'll do till we find something better."

Matt picked up the leg gingerly, and tried to recall how Mike McGuire had set his arm. "I don't think I can do it easy. I'll give have to give it a jerk." David's scream rocketed off the canyon walls. "I'll bind it up, and then we'll figure out how we're going to get back up to the trail."

He put his arm around his friend's waist and helped him up the slope, stopping every few feet to chop foot holes with the hatchet. After climbing to David's dead horse, Matt was sweating and heaving to catch his breath. "I have a better idea," he said. "It's at least fifty yards up to the trail. I'll go up there and get my horse and circle around below you. Then, I'll come back up and help you down." He draped David's blanket in a tree so he could find him later.

Matt scrambled up the canyon wall, got his horse, and finally reached the flat ground below David. Matt climbed up to David's dead horse, retrieved his friend's saddle and musket, and threw them down the steep slope. When he slid back down to David, the snow was coming down so heavily that he could see only a few feet.

"Hang on to me," he said, getting David up. They slipped and slid down the vertical slope, David groaning when the splint hit a tree or caught in the snow. They landed on the flat ground and Matt heard his horse whinny. He half-dragged David in the direction of the sound. The horse stamped its hooves and twitched nervously while Matt slung David crosswise on its rump, piled the saddle, muskets, and blankets on top, and tied them to his saddle. When Matt mounted, his horse swayed and adjusted itself to the unaccustomed extra weight.

After riding almost a mile in the driving snow, Matt steered his horse into a stand of cottonwoods. "We're staying here tonight," he said. "The sun will be down in a few minutes, and I can't see a damned thing. I have a little jerky in my saddlebags, and we can start a fire."

Matt helped David off the horse and gave him his canteen and a stick. To the music of David's taps on the canteen, he circled the camp site looking for firewood, but he was sinking to his hips in the powdery snow and gave up his search. "We're going to get real friendly tonight," Matt said. As Marentette had taught him, he dug a square in the snow with his hands, arranged their blankets and robes into a bedroll for both of them, and covered that with snow to seal in their body heat.

By the next morning, the storm had blown over. They sky was sapphire blue and, with no wind, it was almost warm in the sun. They rode up the river, and when Matt thought he was near the new camp site he fired his rifle. Instead of a shot in return, he heard Jack shouting and banging on a skillet.

David remained in camp while his leg healed, and Jack and Matt tended to the trapping, making their rounds in the mornings to pick up dead beaver. When they removed a carcass, they moved the trap to another location in the river's shallows. Matt chopped away the ice with his hatchet and Jack anchored the trap with a heavy chain tied to a stake on shore. Jack rigged a willow branch so that it was directly over the submerged trap and smeared it with drops of vile-smelling oil from a beaver's scent glands. When a beaver stood on its hind legs to sniff the aphrodisiac oil, it stepped on the trip and a powerful spring snapped the trap's iron jaws around the beaver's leg.

Matt's feet became numb and ice covered his mittens. "Jesús," he said, "let's get back to the fire. My goddamned moccasins and pants are frozen to my skin."

In camp, David skinned the beavers and scraped off the flesh before stretching their hides on the willow frames to dry. When it was too cold or the snow was too deep, they stayed in their tents and sewed leather shirts and pants to replace their rapidly disintegrating woolen clothes.

By March 1827 the days were becoming warmer, and David was getting around without a crutch. "We've had a bodacious season," Jack said exuberantly. "I bet we got at least six or seven hundred pounds of beaver. And thirty-five or more coyote and wolf skins."

"When will we be heading back?" Matt asked.

"I'd say another week," Jack answered. "We gotta get outa here 'fore the snow melt starts and turns these rivers into torrents. A couple'a years back, I waited too late and got caught on the wrong side of a river. Had to go thirty miles outa my way 'fore I found a crossing. Real goddamned pain in the ass."

Deep snow in the mountains and heavy loads on the animals had slowed their trip back to Taos. After they unpacked in front of Jack's hut, Matt found a family that had a tin washtub. Without bothering to negotiate, he paid the wife two silver dollars to heat water for the tub and another twenty cents for a square of bear tallow soap.

"Six months without a wash," he said to himself, sinking to his nose in the tub. "God, is this wonderful." When the water began to cool, Matt stepped out and put his shiny buckskin shirt and pants into the soapy water. He scrubbed them until the water turned black, and put them on wet to keep them from stiffening as they dried. Clean, he found Jack and David.

"We'll wait till there's more buyers come into town 'fore we sell," Jack counseled. "There's not enough of 'em to get the best prices. And don't never sell to that thievin' son of a bitch that works for John Jacob Astor. He'll beat you down to the last penny."

As more fur buyers came into Taos, the prices began to firm. "Matt, you do the sellin'," Jack said. "I don't count too good. These is splendiferous winter pelts with thick hair, so don't let them traders give you a loada crap about how beavers from the southern Rockies ain't as good as the ones from up north."

Matt haggled with three buyers and sold the beaver pelts for four dollars and ten cents a pound and the wolf and coyote skins for three hundred and ten silver pesos. "My sweet Jesús," Jack said, "that's more 'an

I ever made. You're my lucky charm, Matt. First thing I'm gonna do is rent me a little house and get a few jugs of lightnin'. Then I'm gonna buy me an angeliferous little slave girl."

"What are you going to do with your other woman?" Matt asked.

"Her? She's a whore. She knows how to make a livin'. You comin' back next season?"

"Jack, I think I've had all the trapping I need. My profits are enough to get in the Santa Fe trade, and it's a hell of a lot easier than trapping."

"May be easier," Jack said, "but in them mountains there ain't no asses to kiss. Ain't nobody to lord it over you. No big shots. You don't owe nobody no money and you don't pay no taxes. Out there, you do whatever you damned well please."

CHAPTER NINE

1827

Tenorio rammed his lance into the buffalo's side and retrieved it with the skill of a French fencing master.

MATT AND DAVID LEFT TAOS BEFORE EASTER, TAKING THE road through Talpa and Vadito. They arrived in the village of Peñasco in the early afternoon of Holy Thursday and went to the hacienda of David's cousin, Rubén Mondragón. Rubén, in a state of high excitement, told them about the *penitente* ceremonies that would be performed in remembrance of Christ's execution. Out of politeness, Matt expressed interest and Rubén immediately arranged for him and David to witness the rituals.

"New Mexico is very poor," Rubén explained, "and we have very few priests. None have visited Peñasco for two years, and the faithful are forced to conduct our own religious ceremonies." What Matt would see, Rubén said, was a combination of the Passion Play and a rite of penitence. That night, the *penitente* brothers gathered in the candle-lit interior of their *morada* and watched while a *sangrador* scourged initiates with a whip until blood splattered the altar.

After the ceremony, Matt was nauseous from the bloodletting and the intensity of the moment. "I'm not sure I want to go tomorrow," he told David.

"For the brothers it is not so bad. They firmly believe that such penance purges the evil hiding in their flesh."

On Good Friday morning, a young man carefully chosen to portray the Savior came out of the *morada*. Barefooted and crowned with wild rose thorns, he sagged under the weight of a cross. While the believers along his route beat him with cactus-spine-tipped whips and spit on him until saliva ran down his face, he continued to look heavenward with such ecstasy that Matt was both repelled and caught up in the reenactment. The procession continued along a dirt and rock path, and Jesús left a trail of bloody footprints. He climbed a hill designated as Calvary, and at the top he dropped the cross and lay down on it. A team of brothers tied his hands and feet to the cross, raised it, and lowered it into a hole. The women dropped to their knees and shouted, "I have sinned. I have sinned."

On the cross, Christ's body turned a sickening blue and his belly distended. His head slumped on his chest until he jerked it up, but his eyes had rolled back in his head and only the whites showed, denying him further glimpses of Heaven. "Will they let him die?" Matt whispered to Rubén. His stomach was churning and he was afraid he would be sick.

"No," Rubén growled. "The brothers are skilled at knowing when it is time to take him down."

After the brothers took Jesús off the cross and revived him, the three returned to Rubén's hacienda. Matt's revulsion had clearly angered David's cousin. "The Church has long accepted such penance," he said. "Our Jesús didn't feel the pain. You did not hear him scream, did you?"

"That was awful," Matt blurted out.

"Not for him," Rubén snapped, resentment in his voice. "Being chosen to be Our Lord is a great honor. You are a foreigner. You will never understand our spirit."

He is right about that, Matt told himself.

The next day Matt and David left Peñasco. They rode in silence and Matt tried to sort out his feelings. He was confused by the disgust the *penitente* ceremony made him feel. In the last year he had seen men scalp other men and animals tear at men's flesh. But somehow the morbidity of a man allowing himself to be brutalized and humiliated had shocked him more than any of those things. *How*, he thought, *could a people that produced* Don Quijote *seem to revel in scourging themselves? I don't understand it.*

Matt and David passed through Las Trampas and spent the night in Las Truchas. Riding hard the next day, they went through Chimayó without stopping. Before nightfall, they reined in their horses on the crest of a low hill and listened to La Castrense's bells tolling vespers. It was chilly when they arrived at Moisés Mendoza's house. In the *sala*, David embraced his father and Matt shook his hand. "Please stay, Mateo, my family was just about to sit down to dinner."

"It would be my pleasure, Don Moisés." Matt realized the significance of being asked to dine with the Mendozas, and was flattered.

Moisés ushered them into the dining room. "May I present my wife and my daughter, Celestina."

"Señora Mendoza, Señorita Celestina," Matt said with an awkward bow toward the women.

"Let us be seated," Moisés said. Celestina, he saw, had flustered Matt. *She is indeed beautiful*, her father thought.

Matt watched to see what his hosts did, and then covered his lap with a large linen napkin. He sat in silence while the family asked David about his adventure. He heard none of their conversation and had to deliberately think to keep his eyes from staring at Celestina. Her delicate features, a softer version of her father's aristocratic appearance, were striking, and she carried herself with a dignity that made her seem tall. Her gestures were graceful and natural, and her face open and lively. The only thing that marred her face was a tiny scar on her chin, a mark from being thrown off a horse when she was seven. She was still a girl of fifteen and had a healthy, slim figure that would fill out as she matured. Her skin was of a light hue, but dark enough that it might never wrinkle. And her thick black hair gleamed in the candlelight, as did her blue-black eyes. She was dressed casually, but, as her mother insisted, primly, in a red skirt that revealed nothing of her legs or ankles, and a lace-fronted white blouse that buttoned halfway up her long neck.

Matt turned his attention back to the conversation in time to hear David tell his family, "Mateo saved my life when I broke my leg. He found me and fixed it himself."

"Without David, I would never have finished reading *Don Quijote*," Matt said in an attempt to equalize what they had done for each other.

Barefooted servants silently brought the first course, cactus fruit stewed with *chilies colorados*, from a marble-topped sideboard. Matt fumbled with the silverware and finally picked up a small spoon. "Mateo," David whispered, "you may wish to use the larger spoon." Matt flushed and tried to cover his gaffe, joking that dinner would have taken all evening if he had continued with the small spoon. Moisés squeezed out a smile, "We thank you for what you did for David."

"Don Moisés, David would have done the same for me," Matt said. His eyes fixed on Celestina. She caught his glance, and he ducked his head and turned to Sara Mendoza. "You have a very fine son, Señora Mendoza."

"Thank you," Sara said without looking up from her plate.

Sara Concepcíon Toledano y Espinoza de Mendoza was dressed simply for a woman of her station. She wore a black dress of fine wool that had large cuffs to accommodate the frilly handkerchiefs she fancied. Around her neck, a single, large, out-of-round pearl that Moisés had given her for a wedding present hung by a gold chain over her almost invisible bosom. Despite this modest aspect, she had tied a wildly colored Chinese silk sash around her narrow waist.

Sara was ten years younger than her husband, and her hair was only just beginning to show a few strands of gray. Her sole vice was smoking *punche* cigarettes, which she did often, and the tobacco had stained her thumb and index finger a sickly yellow. Her overall appearance was that of a sparrow. She had small bones that carried no extra flesh. Her chicory-brown irises almost filled her eye sockets, and her eyes darted back and forth constantly, seeming to not miss anything. She moved with quick, nervous twitches, and when she ate she bobbed her head jerkily, like a bird pecking at bread crumbs. But when angered Sara's face could become a mask of formality and reserve, and her posture stiff and unyielding.

A paternal ancestor, a captain in Cortés's army, had settled in Puebla, and her family still resided on land granted to them by Carlos V. She was raised in the tradition of Spanish patricians. Her father had arranged her marriage to Moisés when she was eighteen, but for six years their couplings failed to produce children. Then David was born, followed the next year by Celestina. After that Sara had three miscarriages, and she developed a protectiveness for her surviving children that would have smothered them if Moisés had not intervened from time to time.

"Papá," David said, "Mateo and I have had a very profitable season. My share is close to four hundred pesos."

"This can wait, son," Moisés said. "Your mother and sister have no interest in business affairs."

"Excuse me, Papá, but I was getting to another point. Mateo and I have been talking about my going back to Independence with him."

"You are not going anywhere," Sara Mendoza said. "You have been gone for months."

"Sara," Moisés said gently.

"David is not going on that dangerous trail with only"—she glared at Matt—"this—this, young man to look after him."

"Sara, that is enough," Moisés said, raising his voice. "So you want to go to America?" he asked David.

"My English is much better, Papá, thanks to Mateo."

"I can only imagine what he learned from that filthy trapper," Sara muttered to herself.

"If I go to Missouri I will learn the Americans' ways," David said.

"That is not necessarily good," Sara said so that only Celestina heard her.

"Mamá, let them be," Celestina whispered.

"My son," Moisés said, "I would like for you to learn the mercantile trade. But we must be prudent. The Indians are attacking small parties on the Santa Fe Trail. I do not want you and Mateo crossing the prairie alone."

"Don Moisés, I could not agree with you more," Matt said. "But we need to get back to Missouri as soon as we can, so that we can return with the first or second caravan this season. If we do not get to Santa Fe early, we might have to sell our goods at distress prices, or take them to Chihuahua."

"What a nice word. Chee—wah—wah," he continued. Matt reddened, realizing that his clumsy observation had nothing to do with their conversation.

Moisés ignored Matt's blunder. "The governor tells me that a party of *ciboleros* is leaving in two or three days," Moisés said. "And he is sending a detachment of troops to escort them."

"Papá, can you talk to them for us?"

"Of course, my son."

"Moisés," Sara said. "Is it not enough that David spent months with an ignorant trapper. Now, you want him to travel with *ciboleros*. That scum are as wild as the Comanches."

"Sara, do not argue with me," he said, cutting her off.

After dinner they moved to the patio. Sara and Celestina took seats on adobe *bancos* by the fountain; Sara picked an early blooming white rose, snapped off the thorns with her thumbnail, and brushed back Celestina's hair and tucked it behind her daughter's ear. Matt sucked in his breath and held it, struck by the intimacy of someone touching Celestina's face and hair. He exhaled loudly enough that the girl turned to look at him, and he cut his eyes to the quarter moon rising over the mountains.

"Would you like a cigar, Mateo?"

"No thank you, Don Moisés."

"An iced wine and apple juice punch?"

"Ice? I have not had an iced drink since I left Missouri."

"I send my peons to a pond in the mountains to chop and haul it back in the early spring." Moisés clapped his hands twice and a servant appeared from the *portal*'s shadows. "Iced wine punch for the men."

"Your daughter is lovely, Don Moisés."

"She celebrated her *quinceañera* last month."

"It is when girls turn fifteen," David said, seeing that Matt did not understand the word. "Their parents give them a party. It tells everyone that they are no longer a little girl."

After they finished their wine punch, Moisés stood and took his wife's hand. "I am getting chilled. Sara, please come inside with me. David, you stay here with Mateo and Celestina."

"Your father is an interesting man," Matt said when Moisés and Sara left. "Somehow, he does not seem to be so—so Spanish."

"He is different," Celestina said, looking directly at Matt. "He has many modern ideas. His parents sent him to study in Mexico City when he was thirteen. And he was attending the University of Paris when the French Revolution broke out. He has read Thomas Paine and James Madison."

"Surely, you are not interested in politics," Matt said.

"Surely I am," she said evenly. "I have heard speculation that your president, John Quincy Adams, will not be reelected. I would have thought that, with his family's connections, he would have been stronger."

"You know more than I do, Señorita Celestina," he said, keeping his eyes on the moon so that they would not reveal his thoughts about her. "I have been out of touch with my country for more than a year."

"Girls don't need to know about politics," David said rapidly in English so that Celestina would not understand. He switched to Spanish and monopolized the conversation with stories about Jack Marentette until Sara returned and made it clear that the evening was over.

Matt and David left Santa Fe with twelve soldiers and twenty-three *ciboleros*. The buffalo hunters' horses were fresh and the men were excited to be on the year's first hunt. They followed the Santa Fe Trail and covered fifty miles a day by changing horses every few hours. They made camp on the Rio Sapello so that their slow-moving supply wagons could catch up with them. The *cibolero* captain, Tenorio Reyes, sent out scouts, who returned to report that they had found day-old Comanche campfires and that the Indians were headed north. Despite the danger, Matt and David were anxious to go on.

"Stay with us at least until we have killed a few buffalo so that you will have fresh meat," Tenorio said. "With the good water and pasture here on the Rio Sapello, your animals will be in good shape to cross the *jornada*."

"Maybe we should stay a few days," Matt said, remembering his dry trip over the *jornada*.

The next day a scout located buffalo five miles to the east. "You are welcome to join the hunt," Tenorio said. The young men rode beside the *cibolero* captain over the spring-green buffalo grass, until they stopped to get directions from a scout who had been tracking the herd. Tenorio sent half of the *ciboleros* to ride east in a wide loop, while he took the other half to the west.

They rode to the top of a high ridge and saw a dense mass of animals that looked like bees on a honey-soaked hive. The herd was strung out on a north–south axis for two miles and was a quarter-mile wide. The buffalo were losing their thick winter coats, and the scraggly patches of hair that were waiting to fall off gave them a bedraggled look. New calves were poking their noses at milk-bloated udders and bulls were rolling in wallows and pawing the ground, kicking up a dust cloud that floated in a tan haze over the herd.

A scout reported to Tenorio that he had found a dry creek bed that they could follow to get close to the buffalo unobserved. "Don Mateo," Tenorio said, "you and Don David can watch, but do not get too close. The beasts do not hear well and they do not have good eyes. But they can smell danger a long way off." When the hunters were in position, the *cibolero* captain ordered a scout to fire a shot to signal the men to the east to begin moving toward the buffalo.

Tenorio told his *ciboleros* to prepare their weapons. Two men, the only ones with muskets, poured powder in their firing pans and checked to see that their flints were screwed down tightly. Others pulled eight-foot lances out of scabbards hanging from their saddle pommels, and the rest tested the tautness of their bow strings. Tenorio nodded to the men. They leaned forward on their horses' necks and charged out of the arroyo, surrounding a cluster of buffalo that had separated from the main herd.

The captain spurred his horse at the animals, cutting out a cow. The terrified female, slowed by her sagging udder, ran until she was exhausted. She stopped, gasping for air. Saliva drooled down her lolling tongue and foam outlined her mouth as she eyed Tenorio. He maneuvered to get a safe angle of attack, and when he was ten yards away he shouted and jammed his spurs into his horse's flanks.

Before the cow could move, Tenorio rammed his lance into her side and retrieved it with the skill of a French fencing master. The animal roared a bellow, tossed her horns furiously, and lunged at her tormentor. Patiently, Tenorio guided his horse out of harm's way by pressing his knees gently into one side or the other. When the cow stopped he charged again. This time, the lance found her liver. She spouted blood, stumbled to her knees, rolled her eyes, and fell, panting. Before she was dead, two *ciboleros* were on the cow with their knives, and, in minutes, they skinned and butchered her. In all, the *ciboleros* killed fourteen buffalo that day.

"In another ten days, we will be going to the Arkansas River," Tenorio told Matt that night after a meal of fresh buffalo. "You should wait and go with us, just to be safe."

"What do you think, Mateo?" David asked.

"The first caravans make the best money. I am willing to gamble that the Comanches are more interested in stocking their larders after a hard winter than in worrying about us."

"That is a risky decision, Don Mateo," Tenorio said. "If I may say so, you have little experience in dealing with the Indians."

"There is chance in everything," Matt said. "If I had not taken chances, I would have been a store clerk forever. David, are you in agreement?"

"Yes."

Matt and David made Independence so easily that, over lunch at their boarding house, they made fun of the warnings people had given them about the Santa Fe Trail's dangers. After they ate, they walked to the town square. Ancient oaks and hickories were in full spring foliage, and yellow dandelions and pink buttercups dotted the shaded green lawn. "Let's go over to Stanfield's store," Matt said. "He's got a good selection."

"What are we going to do for wagons and teams?" David asked.

"We'll work something out."

Matt stooped to avoid the low-hanging, hand-lettered sign reading TRAIL OUTFITTERS, NICHOLAS R. STANFIELD, PROP. Matt looked over the merchandise in the log building. "Captain Vick bought some costume jewelry last year that he had to mark down by more than half, and even then he couldn't get rid of it."

"What about this light-weight cotton?" David asked a store clerk.

"Batiste. Good for making underwear."

"Matt, this batiste will sell fast," David said. "Most everybody uses homespun wool for underpants. It keeps your privates warm, but it scratches so bad you think there's ants in there."

"How much?" Matt asked the clerk.

"Seventy-five cents a yard."

"Give us a hundred. Where's your calico?" Matt asked.

"Over there, behind the boxes of boots."

"What about this, David?" Matt asked, fingering the end of a bolt of brown cloth.

"Too dull. Your American women might like those browns, but Spanish women like colors. A good, strong red will sell a lot better."

After the clerk cut their the cloth and rolled it on spindles, Matt crossed the room to a neat stack of boxes. "Here's some leather work gloves."

"They won't sell in New Mexico," David said. "The peons' hands are tougher than leather, and their *patrones* won't pay for gloves."

They ruled out iron pots and skillets because the freight costs for the heavy items would be too high. Instead, they bought shaving brushes made with Chinese hog bristles, needles, spools of thread, and silver thimbles.

"I saw some cotton stockings that might work," Matt said.

"We don't need stockings. Spanish ladies knit woolen stockings that are plenty good. Look here, Matt. This Belgian lace will sell in a heartbeat. Most of our women haven't seen, much less owned, such frillery."

Matt turned to the clerk. "We've spent over seven hundred dollars with you. Give us a good price."

"Seven hundred dollars don't entitle you to no discounts," the clerk said. "We got customers spending thousands."

"Look here," Matt demanded, "some of these ribbons have dust on them. I worked in a dry goods store in Kaskaskia, and I can tell that this is last year's merchandise."

"I could make you a deal on some of the older ribbons, but there's no price breaks on anything else."

"What about credit?" Matt asked.

"I'll talk to Mr. Stanfield, but I can tell you that you ain't gonna get no credit. Never seen you before, and you both look like you're about thirteen."

"I'm almost eighteen," Matt said.

To round out their stock, Matt and David bought a barrel of aged Kentucky whiskey, five pounds of hard candy, and two whale-bone corsets. "La Dama has gotten a little thick in the waist," Matt said. "Maybe she'll buy them."

Matt and David helped the clerk stack their merchandise in back of the store and cover it with an oilcloth tarp. "Let's find somebody to partner with on the freighting," Matt said as they crossed the square. "Stanfield's clerk gave me the name of a proprietor who is taking four wagons down the trail. Somebody by the name of Waterman. He's staying at Mrs. Mong's boarding house."

A maid at the Mong boarding house told them that Edward Waterman was at Chism's Tavern. "It's the log building on the far side of the blacksmith's," she said.

"They're almost *all* log," Matt said.

"We're gettin' a few brick and clapboard buildings," the maid sniffed. "We're beginnin' to civilize."

It took Matt's eyes a few seconds to adjust to the tavern's darkness, and his nose took in the heavy smell of stale tobacco smoke. "Give us two beers," Matt told the barman. "We're looking for Mr. Waterman."

"Over there," he said, handing them the glasses and pointing to the room's only window.

"Mr. Waterman," Matt said to a ruddy-faced man in his midtwenties. Edward Waterman had a shock of crinkly hair that he had carefully combed to cover a receeding hairline. He had a well-trimmed mustache that he waxed and twirled to a point. He shaved the rest of his face, but his beard was so heavy that it looked as if someone had smeared charcoal on his jaw and cheeks. He was neatly dressed in a midnight-blue suit with understated pinstripes and a waterfall of white lace flowed from his throat down the front of his shirt. When Waterman turned in his chair to see who had addressed him, Matt saw a pistol butt at his waist.

"Yesss?" Edward said, stretching out the word with a Southern drawl.

"I'm Matt Collins, and this is David Mendoza."

"Yesss."

"The clerk at Stanfield's gave us your name."

"Yesss," he drawled again, and took a sip of wine.

"He said you might have some extra space in your wagons."

"How much merchandise you got?"

"I'd say it'd take up about a quarter, maybe a third, of a freight wagon."

"Where did pups like you get enough money for merchandise?"

"Trapping last season. David and me did pretty good."

"Is he related to Moisés Mendoza?" Waterman asked.

"He's my father," David said.

"Sit down. Let's talk. I've got enough room for you, but I'll need thirteen cents a pound."

"That's a little high, Mr. Waterman," Matt said. "Last year, the going rate was eight cents."

"If you've got a third of a load, that should weigh in at about two thousand pounds," Waterman said, savoring his wine and stretching out his short legs under the table. "At thirteen cents, that comes to two hundred and sixty dollars. You boys got that kind of money?"

"No."

"Then, what are we going to do?"

"I guess we can turn back some of the goods to Stanfield," Matt said.

"Hate to see you do that. How much cash you got?"

"Close to two hundred, but we need to buy food and supplies for the trip."

"I'll do this. I'll cut the rate to ten cents. Pay me a hundred now, and I'll hire you both as mule skinners at thirty a month. You can pay me the rest after we get to Santa Fe and you sell your merchandise."

"What do you think, David?"

"It's fair enough."

"It's a deal," Matt said. "Can we buy you another wine, Mr. Waterman?"

"If you'll join me."

Matt went to the bar and got glasses of beer and wine. As he walked back, a teamster slumped off a packing crate he was using for a chair, flopped onto the plank floor, and began vomiting. "Roll him on his side so he won't choke," one of his tablemates said, and turned to resume his conversation. Matt stepped around the watery mess and went back to his table. He and David finished their beers, shook hands with Edward Waterman, and left.

They went down the street to Big-nosed Kate's establishment, which she discreetly called a boarding house, and listened to the metallic sounds of a cheap piano. "I've never heard a piano before," David said. Teamsters and proprietors, anxious to enjoy their last female company until they reached Santa Fe, crowded around the bar, waiting their turn for the woman of their choice to free up.

Kate, a frail woman with a gray complexion, sat on a high stool in a corner, gowned in pink satin. Her eyes, black in the dim light, shrewdly surveyed the room, while a scruffy parrot with nervous black eyes hopped between her shoulder and a perch behind her. In between puffs on a cigar, Kate drank white wine.

"Kate has her dresses made with two hidden pockets," a teamster told Matt. "One to stash her money in, and the other to hold her derringer."

A prostitute brought Matt and David glasses of beer, and they stood watching the players at the poker table. "Do you think Mr. Waterman is an American?" David asked. Like many persons who learn a foreign language, he was sensitive to accents.

"I'd say so. Why do you ask?"

"I thought I picked up a little bit of an accent."

"He's from the South. That's what you hear."

"Once in a while, he mispronounces a 'v' or a 'w,'" David said.

A prostitute was sitting at a table in the middle of the room, drunk and wobbling on her chair. Her hair was matted and food and wine stains dotted the front of her shabby gown. She stopped rubbing a proprietor's crotch, flashed a smile at Matt, and moved toward him.

"I'm not desperate enough to take on the gals in here," Matt said, nudging David toward the door. "If this is the best Kate has to offer, let's go somewhere else."

"Son," a card player who overheard him said, "the beauties ain't out here on the frontier. If you want the best, you gotta go back to St. Louis."

CHAPTER TEN

1827

"Flashing a little money is vulgar, but flashing a lot of money is in the greatest of taste."

AT COUNCIL GROVE THE PROPRIETORS ELECTED EDWARD WA-
terman captain and he appointed Matt as his chief scout. In late June
their caravan reached San Miguel del Vado. When the caravan's first
wagon drew up in the San Miguel plaza, Matt, Edward, and David dismounted and greeted the customs inspector, who told them that Susano
Baca was still governor.

"Really?" Edward said. "We heard there was a coup d'etat that un-
seated the president. I am surprised that Don Susano was able to stay in
office."

"Don Susano has ties to General Santa Anna through his mother's
family," Bonifacio Chacón, the whispy customs chief, explained. Matt
listened carefully to the first Spanish he had heard in months, enjoying
its soft consonants and the predictability of its vowel sounds. "Mexico
City politics are in such a mess that anything is possible," Chacón continued. "More important, gentlemen, we need to discuss your import
duties. I would like to meet with you in an hour."

The three walked down the hill from the San Miguel plaza to the
west bank of the Pecos River to watch the wagons cross. "It's a good
thing we cached that merchandise yesterday," Edward said. "Don Bonifacio doesn't often come to San Miguel. He usually collects the taxes in
Santa Fe."

As the last wagon rattled over the river rocks, Matt, Edward, and
David returned to the plaza and went to the small customs house where

Bonifacio Chacón was waiting for them. "Don Bonifacio, allow me to pour you a glass of this champagne," Edward said. "It is not as cold as I would like, but you will enjoy its flavor. We have also brought you half a case of smoked oysters."

"Champagne and oysters are my favorites, Don Eduardo."

While Matt and David sat silently on the floor with their backs against the wall, Edward and Bonifacio chatted about the price of beaver pelts and the possibility of Andrew Jackson being elected president.

"Enough of that, Don Eduardo. As you Americans like to say, let us get to the point. Governor Baca is reforming our taxes on imported goods. The Mexico City government has not sent us money for the soldiers or priests, and there is nothing in the Santa Fe treasury."

"We certainly understand the need, Don Bonifacio, and we are sympathetic with the governor's predicament," Edward responded. "His responsibilities are heavy."

"Indeed they are. The new customs duties will be based on the value of your merchandise."

"What happened to the old system of charging a certain amount for each wagon?" Edward asked.

"Because of this sudden change, the governor has granted me some flexibility." Chacón smiled a sly smile that exposed large gaps between his upper teeth.

"Don Bonifacio, I have no concern. You have always been a reasonable man."

"Don Eduardo, may I speak to you in confidence?"

"Of course. And Matt and David will respect your need for privacy."

"You are the second caravan this season, and your profits will be high," Chacón said with a musical whistle through the gaps in his teeth. "The governor and I wish to participate in your good fortune."

"You are certainly entitled to a portion, Don Bonifacio, assuming that you give due consideration to the amount of taxes."

Within minutes, the two men agreed on three thousand pesos in taxes and six hundred to be split between the customs chief, Governor Baca, and Captain Zambrano.

The caravan arrived in Santa Fe at midmorning, and, after Matt and Edward arranged for their merchandise to be unpacked and for the rental of a store, Edward paid a duty call on Governor Baca. Later, Edward took lunch with Matt at Florinda Maesta's house. "Governor Baca is sponsoring a dance to celebrate our caravan's arrival," Edward said.

"A fandango?"

"No. It's a *baile*. At the *posada*. By invitation only. And he wants you and me and the other proprietors to come."

"Fine by me," Matt said, chewing a piece of gristly pork. "When does the *baile* start?"

"About nine o'clock, he said."

Matt switched to Spanish, "Florinda, would you be kind enough to heat some water. Here is the money to buy extra firewood. And get me some mint from the garden to freshen my breath. I will not be needing soap. I have some from England."

"God did not intend for us to take as many baths as you do, Don Mateo," Florinda said. "God intended for us to have the *olor de sanctidad.*"

At nine-thirty, Edward and Matt went to the *posada*. Peons, surly because it was a *baile* that they could not attend, stood across the street watching the government officials, army officers, American proprietors, and *ricos* enter the hotel.

"Welcome, welcome," Governor Baca said, greeting them jovially at the door. "I must be nice to the men who pay our taxes. Come in, come in. I think you know my military commander, Captain Zambrano."

"Of course," Edward said, giving the Captain a hearty *abrazo*. "My congratulations, Diego."

"Thank you," Diego Zambrano said, pleased that Edward acknowledged his promotion from lieutenant to captain.

"We will chat later," Edward said, and he and Matt went to the bar. "Diego is unusually graceful in his loss."

"Loss?"

"Bonifacio Chacón told me that Diego tried to get himself appointed governor, but Susano's contacts were too strong. In addition to his connections with Santa Anna, Susano's cousin knows Countess Regla, President Victoria's mistress. Diego's military friends threw him a sop and got him appointed captain."

Across the room, Matt saw La Dama with a cluster of men and women around her. "I wouldn't have thought that the gentry would have welcomed La Dama to their *bailes*," Matt said.

"She goes to most of them," Edward said. "The hacendados' wives would slit their wrists before letting Doña Julia in their houses, but they chat with her at the *bailes* because they know who loaned their husbands the money for their silk dresses."

"How's that?"

"Dama has more gold and silver than anybody in Santa Fe. She makes loans to the *rico* families when they're short on cash."

"But Don Moisés's house is full of silver, books, paintings," Matt said.

"They have probably been in the Mendoza family for generations. Don Moisés, like the rest of the hacendados, is rich in land but poor in cash. That's why he wants David involved in the Santa Fe–Missouri trade. So he can make real money—silver dollars and gold pesos—that the Mendozas can use to pay off the lenders in Chihuahua and Durango."

Matt and Edward wove their way through the dancers to where La Dama was seated on a wooden bench, splendid in a lime green ball gown that revealed a substantial portion of her bosom. "You are exquisite tonight, Doña Julia," Matt said with a deferential bow.

"Thank you, Don Mateo."

La Dama rolled Edward a *punche* cigarette, and when Matt stepped aside to make room for La Dama to light it something slammed into his back, almost knocking him to his knees. He wheeled around with fists clinched until he saw a girl sprawled on the floor.

"Excuse me," Celestina Mendoza said, flashing a smile as she struggled to get up. "This waltz was a little too fast and Filberto is a little too clumsy."

"Please forgive me, Mateo," Filberto Baca said, "but we were whirling so fast that I could not stop."

Matt stood frozen, saying nothing. He had not seen Celestina for weeks, and he had forgotten how lovely she was. Moments passed before he composed himself. "You are indeed clumsy, Filberto," she said. "You need dancing lessons."

"Do you know Señorita Mendoza?" Filberto asked Matt.

"Yes. It is a pleasure to see you again," Matt said and bowed formally.

Governor Baca's eldest son told them about his trip to America. He had planned to travel up the Santa Fe Trail with Amos Vick, but, after the Englishman's death, Filberto arranged to go to Missouri with another proprietor and had returned with the first caravan of 1827. At a break in Filberto's monologue, Celestina curtsied and went back to her family circle.

"Aren't you related to her?" Matt asked.

"We are distant cousins," Filberto said, "and my father and her father have known one another for some time. Moisés Mendoza is a good person to know. He has over fifty thousand sheep. And he is very enterprising. Don Moisés has bought American looms to weave his wool into *rebozos* and *ponchos*, rather than ship the raw wool to those Chihuahua rascals to process and send back with a huge markup."

"Whatever Don Moisés has done," Matt said, "he has certainly produced a spectacular daughter."

"That he has," Filberto said. "You do not see girls in Santa Fe with that combination of honey-colored skin, blue-black eyes, and dark, dark hair."

"She should not put that white paste on her face," Matt said. "It hides her features."

"She is no longer a girl," Filberto said, "and women wear the paste."

"Are there rules for asking her to dance?"

"At a fandango, anybody, even a peon, can ask. But, at a *baile*, you must seek her father's permission. Come on, I will go with you."

"Don Moisés, Doña Sara, I believe you know my American friend, Mateo Collins."

"Yes, we do," Moisés said, "he is a good friend to our son."

"I have heard that you are sending David to school in the United States," Filberto said.

"Yes, we—"

"*You*," Sara said, butting in.

"I am sending David to a Jesuit school in St. Louis. The modern world demands more education of our sons."

"Why not Mexico City?" Filberto asked.

"Santa Fe is closer to Missouri than to Mexico City, and this cross-border trade is growing. It will be important for David to understand the Yankee barbarians," Moisés said, smiling and looking at Matt to make sure that he took it as a joke. Matt grinned to show that he wasn't offended.

"I am not here to ask about David, Don Moisés," Matt said, "but to ask if I might dance with your daughter."

"Of course," Moisés answered. Sara Mendoza stared sourly across the room, refusing to look at Matt.

After servants sprinkled water and fresh straw on the dirt floor, the flautist announced a *cuna* and Matt led Celestina to the center of the room. They placed their arms on each other's waists and began the easy motions that imitated a rocking cradle. "Where is your home in America?" Celestina asked.

"I was born in Illinois, but the closest thing I have to a home is in Missouri."

"You Americans move around so much."

"We are always trying to reinvent ourselves," he said.

"If Americans were happy with their families and their homes they would not have this need to change all the time. But, tell me, where does your family live?"

"The Sisters of Charity raised me."

"No family? Do you know who your parents were?"

Ashamed, he lied. "No. I was a baby when they died. I understand that *your* family is well-known in New Mexico."

"My ancestors came here shortly after Pedro de Peralta founded Santa Fe in sixteen ten. We have been here ever since, except when we went into exile in sixteen eighty."

"You left?"

"The Pueblo Indians revolted, and my family fled to El Paso del Norte until Diego de Vargas regained our rights in sixteen ninety-two."

"Your family has been here for more than two hundred years?"

"Yes. And on the same land that King Felipe III granted to us."

"How nice that you can trace your family for generations. It must be very comforting."

"We are descended from the Great Cardinal, Pedro de Mendoza, who was an advisor to King Fernando and Queen Isabel," Celestina said with obvious pride. "And in fifteen thirty-five, Emperor Carlos V appointed a Mendoza to serve as the first Spanish viceroy to Mexico. My father can recite every detail by heart."

"That is very impressive," Matt said. He tried to appear nonchalant, but, in the face her centuries of genealogy he felt awkward and inadequate.

"You, too, have a lineage," she said, sensing his discomfort, "you are just not sure what it is. Tell me about America. My brother likes it very much, but he says it is very different."

"The music has ended, and you must go back to your family. If we could meet again," Matt said, "I could tell you about America."

"I will arrange for you to come to our house."

"Edward, she is angeliferous," Matt said the next morning while they were arranging merchandise in their shop.

"You won't get anywhere with a hacendado's daughter if you talk like those ignorant trappers. But you won't get anywhere with Celestina

Mendoza in any event. The Mendozas don't trust someone like you. To them you're a Yankee who's too boorish to understand that you come from a certain class—and they come from a class that you will never be a part of."

At first Edward's remark angered Matt. Then he worried that his friend might be right. "How do you know so much about them?" Matt challenged.

Edward became secretive and mumbled several sentences that Matt could not understand. Finally, he said, "I've been around aristocrats. It doesn't matter where or how. But I can tell you that they're the same all over the world. The Mendozas smile and nod and have nice manners. But they would sell their son to the Comanches before they would let somebody like you marry their daughter."

"Don Moisés doesn't seem to be that way," Matt said defensively.

"The Mendozas will always be courteous. But in their view you're an ill-bred American who spends his life grubbing for money—a man who is consumed with materialism and a man who has no spiritual sensibility. If you've got a hankering for a wife, find yourself a nice farm girl or a doctor's daughter back in Missouri."

At home Matt had been around people who had more money than he, who had more education, who had been more places than he. Yet, he had never felt uncomfortable around them. Now Edward was telling him that there was another level. Another social rank that he might never join and might never understand. He didn't want to think about it, so he changed the subject. "We're making good profits so far," Matt said.

"I'm going to take mine and make a down payment on a farm," Edward said.

"Not me. I'm putting it all back into goods."

Edward refused to drop the unpleasant subject. "No matter what you do, the Mendozas will think you're a 'self-made man.' To us Americans, that's a compliment, but to the *ricos* it's an epithet. To them it means an ambitious charlatan who has clawed his way out of the gutter, but who still has the gutter's stink. You'll have to make more money than John Jacob Astor to satisfy the Mendozas."

"But David says that flashing money around is rude."

"That, my friend, is bullshit," Edward said emphatically. "Flashing a little money is vulgar, but flashing a lot of money is in the greatest of taste. Stop talking and help me unpack these boxes. The faster we sell this stuff, the sooner we can go back home where we belong."

Edward's vehemence startled Matt. He suspected that Sara Mendoza might have some of the prejudices that Edward described, but Don Moisés appeared to be more open. Or, perhaps like Edward said, he was just good at hiding his real feelings with politeness.

"I sold my merchandise to a friend of my father's in Chimayó," David said as he finished his whiskey and appraised the new girl in La Dama's saloon. "How did you do in Taos?"

Matt had gone to Taos to buy pelts with his gold and silver profits. "Very well," Matt said. "I bought two *carretas* of first-quality skins. Another drink?"

"Yes. What about the price?"

"I was one of the few buyers with hard cash, so it was easy for the trappers to see sweet reason," Matt said. "I'll be able to sell the furs for at least a dollar a pound more in Missouri. What's been going on in Santa Fe?"

"We had a stabbing right here at La Dama's. A Yankee teamster was sloppy drunk and started cursing Mexico and Mexicans. Then he launched into a diatribe of how filthy Mexico is, and how corrupt and undemocratic. I guess he didn't know that Captain Zambrano fought in the revolution. Don Diego jumped up and said that no falling-down drunk American was going to talk about Mexico that way. That's when the knives came out. The captain cut up the Yankee pretty badly. They say he's going to die. Some teamsters were talking about lynching Don Diego, and a bunch of drunks tore down the Mexican flag over the palace and raised an American flag."

"But there are more pleasant topics," David continued. "Celestina wants you to come to a *tertulia* at our house tomorrow afternoon. There'll be plenty of food and drink. Some cards, music, lots of conversation, and a chance for—what's a good English word for it—gallantry?"

"Flirting," Matt said.

"Tossing out *rimbombantes*, sweet words, to let someone know that you care for them," David said. "But don't let my mother catch you flirting."

On his way to the Mendoza's house the next day, Matt paused to sniff the air's freshness. He was excited by the prospect of seeing Celestina again, but Edward's diatribe about aristocrats still troubled him. He shook off the disturbing thoughts and looked at a pristine sky that had been washed by showers earlier that afternoon. To the east, the afternoon sun played on the Sangre de Cristo Mountains, and to the west the desert stretched beyond the Rio Grande to the blue Jemez Mountains. Matt clanged the iron bar by the *zaguán* and a servant came to show him in.

Governor Baca, who was standing just outside the *sala* door, crushed out a cigarette with his heel and shook Matt's hand before they entered the brightly lit room. Moisés Mendoza broke off his conversation with a group of ladies and hurried to greet the newcomers. "Your Excellency, Mateo, it is an honor to have you in my home."

"It is always a pleasure to visit the most elegant house in Santa Fe," Matt said.

"It is nothing to compare with the fine homes I have seen in St. Louis. We are so isolated here, but you Americans are changing that," Moisés said, and moved off to greet Diego Zambrano, who was standing at the door by himself, his right hand tucked between the buttons of his vest.

"Excuse me, Don Susano," Matt said, "but I see Señorita Celestina."

Celestina was sitting beside her mother on an adobe *banco*, wearing a loose-fitting blouse embroidered with Zuñi Indian designs, a sky blue skirt to the floor, and deerskin moccasins. Her black hair was braided and coiled on top of her head and her cheeks and lips shined red with *alegria* flower juice. *Fortunately,* Matt thought, *she had not smeared her face with flour paste.*

"Señorita Celestina, Señora Mendoza, it is a pleasure to see you again," Matt said, trying with only moderate success to imitate the deep bow that he had seen New Mexican gentleman make to ladies.

"I am happy that you returned safely from Taos," Celestina said. "I hope your trip was successful.

"Very much so."

"Tell me about your country," Sara Mendoza commanded. "My husband has been there, but I have not. Do you have plays? The opera? When I was a girl in Puebla we had music and theater, but up here all we have is an occasional traveling circus."

"Once in a while acting companies came to Kaskaskia," Matt said, "but I seldom had the money to go. I was an apprentice."

"A what?"

"An apprentice. I was bound to a store owner."

"You worked in servitude?" she asked with a blank expression.

"Well, Señora, it is not like the peonage system you have here, which can last all of a man's life. I was under contract until I was eighteen."

"How old are you now?"

"Eighteen."

"How did you get here if you were bound by contract?"

"I ran away."

"Ran away?" Sara Mendoza said. She pulled a lace handkerchief from her sleeve, daubed her nose, and turned her back to talk to her sister-in-law.

"Could you show me your garden, Señorita Celestina?" Matt asked. In the patio, the late afternoon sun had softened the brilliant colors of the roses and bougainvillea to warm pastels. "I am afraid that I always say the wrong thing to your mother. I get flustered and I stumble over what I am trying to say."

"Do not worry," Celestina said, taking his hand and holding it, but only briefly. "When will you return to the United States?"

"In a few days. I have had a profitable year, and I will make even more money when I sell my pelts in Missouri."

"You are very interested in money," Celestina said.

"You do not approve?"

"My father says that gentlemen should not discuss their fortunes, because it is unkind to those people who have less money than you do."

"I do not have enough money to boast about," Matt snapped, "so I could not offend anyone. Perhaps when I become rich I will have the luxury of being as thoughtful of other people's feelings as your father is." He was instantly mad at himself for the sarcastic remark. "Until then, I plan to work hard and get ahead and become a gentleman like your father," he said, trying to rehabilitate himself. He reached into a bougainvillea vine to pick a flower for her and closed his fingers on a thorn. "Dammit," he said in English.

"Little stickers should not bother an ambitious man," Celestina said, laughing and taking his hand to wipe the blood on his finger with her handkerchief. "We should return to the *sala*. Mother will be wondering where I am."

"But this is the most perfect time of day. Do we have time to finish our walk around the patio?" he asked, taking her elbow and ushering her along the *portal*. They passed the open door of a room that blazed with light.

"This is our family chapel," Celestina said. "Let's go inside."

"You have your own chapel?"

"My mother prays often. Look at the carving on the door. St. Peter's keys."

Two candelabra with twelve candles each made the narrow room hot and close. A pink silk cloth stitched with a gold cross and lilies covered the altar. Above it an ivory Christ hung on a black marble cross, his face twisted in pain.

"That carving is more finely done than the religious statues, the *bultos*, that you see out here," Matt said. "I am sure that it is very valuable."

"More important, it is very beautiful. Queen Isabel gave that crucifix to Cardinal Mendoza in 1495, when he was on his death bed."

"That was over three hundred years ago."

"We keep careful records of our family history."

Votive candles burned in front of a crudely carved *bulto* that was sitting on a wall sconce. "Who is that?" Matt asked.

"San Isidro, the patron saint of farmers," she said, and turned to a painting of the Virgin of Guadalupe. "My mother brought this with her from Guadalajara when she married my father." Celestina genuflected and made the sign of the cross. "My grandparents thought that my mother was going to the end of the earth, so they wanted her to have a painting of Our Lady. That *retablo* over there is Santiago Matamoros. They say he can work miracles. Look! Our cook has pinned this drawing of an arm on Santiago's portrait so that her son's broken arm will heal straight."

"Do you believe in such things?"

"I am not sure. Shall we go back?"

On the patio, people coming out of the *sala* were crowding around tables of food. Matt guided Celestina back to her mother and joined a knot of men. The focus of their attention stood with his back to the adobe wall.

"Tell us what is happening in Mexico City, Don Armando," Susano Baca said.

"The capital is a dangerous place," Armando Salazar, the Grand Master of Santa Fe's York Rite Masons, said. "The aftermath of Vice President Bravo's attempted revolt against President Victoria has created a malignant atmosphere."

"I will never understand Nicolás Bravo," Moisés Mendoza said. "He fought with Morelos and Hidalgo, and he helped force the dictator Iturbide into exile. Now he is siding with the reactionaries."

"Gentlemen," Governor Baca said, "let us not get into the wrangling that is consuming Mexico City. Let us just hope that the politicians will leave us alone to float quietly in our little backwater."

BOOK II

1831–1844

CHAPTER ELEVEN

1831

"Ahorita, somos verdaderos hombres de confianza."

WHEN EDWARD WATERMAN GAVE MATT HIS LECTURE ON ARISTO-cratic behavior, he had not explained how he had come to understand the patrician class. Born Solomon Wassermann, the son of a kosher butcher, he had grown up in Vienna's Jewish quarter. When he came of age, Solomon became a yeshiva student, and on the Sabbath he draped a prayer shawl over his shoulders and accompanied his devout father to the synagogue.

Solomon's encounters with Christians outside the quarter made him increasingly self-conscious. He was aware that his black skullcap and the ringlets of dark hair that covered his ears set him apart from those who lived in the wider world of Vienna. Though he excelled as a student, particularly in Aramaic and Hebrew, the long days at the yeshiva and the endless exegesis of Talmud and Torah made him restless. He developed a keen interest, however, in what separated Jews and Christians, and why Jews had to suffer insults and indignities when they strayed into the Christian world. He found a few passages in the holy texts that skirted the edges of his question and he discussed them with his teacher. Still, the rabbi's explanations did not yield satisfactory answers.

After the defeat of Archduke Charles of Austria by Napoleon at Wagram, the French forced revolutionary reforms on the Austrians, including giving full citizenship rights to Jews. Emperor Franz's ministers issued a decree that directed the School of St. Ignatius to recruit Jews, and Solomon's teacher recommended him to the authorities. His father, Jacob, opposed it, fearful that the Jesuits would lead his son away from his Jewish faith. But Solomon passed the entrance examinations with such an outstanding score that a high official of the Ministry of Education, together with Solomon's pleas that he wanted to study something beyond the Torah, pressured Jacob into relenting.

Solomon did well at St. Ignatius, excelling in German grammar and Latin. At the daily chapel he was required to attend he found Catholic ritual and doctrine interesting in aesthetic and intellectual ways, but he felt no impulse to convert. He had few friends among his aristocratic classmates, and, although no one called him a Christ killer, the boys' hostility confused him. Christ, he had learned, was born and died a Jew, and his teachings drew from the same prophets the rabbis talked about. *How can they hate Jews?* he asked himself. *Without us, there wouldn't be them.*

On occasion he got into fights when another boy insulted his Jewishness. At first he lost these battles, but as he grew taller and stronger he began to prevail, and the bullies left him alone. And he never forgot his anger when he applied to join a liberal political club and the members snubbed him by not even responding. Solomon was never quite comfortable, even around the few sons of barons and counts who acted civilly towards him. If they made a kindly gesture, he still felt vaguely anxious that an anti-Semitic remark would follow. And, when the remarks did come, they never failed to make his face flush and his heart stop for an instant.

When it came time to make good use of his splendid education, Solomon, ever the realist, decided that the tide of a revolution that had carried him into St. Ignatius had not knocked down the barriers that blocked him from a career in something like law or medicine. He admired the French revolution's principles, but not its bloody results. The revolution that fired his imagination was the one that had taken place in America. There, he had read, a man was free to go as far as he could, without reference to his background or religion. But America was a distant dream, in part because his father would oppose it and because he had no money. He wrote to one of his mother's relatives in Amsterdam.

Dear Cousin Ruben,

I know that this letter may come as a surprise to you. We met only once, when you were in Vienna four years ago, and you may not remember me well. I am now fourteen, and I have studied in a very fine school, which, I think, would make me a helpful addition to your fur business. I have indicated to my father that I do not wish to become a butcher, and I am writing you to inquire whether you might have a position open for me. When you respond, please do not send your letter to my house. Instead, send it care of my friend, Israel Vogelson, Gold-strasse 26, Vienna.

Your cousin,

Solomon Wassermann

P.S. If you have a place for me, please send me 25 crowns to pay for my trip to Amsterdam. Of course, you will deduct this amount from my wages.

The fur trade was booming. Pelts were flooding in from America and Russia, and Ruben Weinberger needed help desperately. In early 1810 Solomon, over his parents' protests, left for Amsterdam. He worked at Ruben's fur shop, living in his cousin's attic to save money. He was good at languages, and soon he was speaking passable Dutch.

In Amsterdam's tolerant atmosphere, Jews had lived comfortably since the Spanish and Portuguese had expelled them in the late 1400s. Solomon met men with Sephardic names who had integrated themselves into Dutch society so seamlessly that they mingled on an equal basis with bishops and noblemen. Solomon decided that, when he crossed the Atlantic he would go even farther—he would bury his old Jewish self in America's virgin society.

Solomon studied English every night and read every American newspaper he could get his hands on. After working almost two years for Ruben, Solomon took his savings and bought a ticket to America, landing at New Orleans.

"What's your name?" a customs officer asked.

"Waterman. Edward Waterman," Solomon answered.

"Sounds like an English name, but your accent don't sound like no Englishman. Where was you born?"

"Hamburg, sir."

"Fine. If it's Edward Waterman you want to be, then that's who you'll be." He entered Edward's new name and place of birth on the immigration rolls.

Edward's English was still halting, but his burly frame induced a barge captain to hire him as a deckhand for a trip up the Mississippi. When his friends had asked about his background, he invented a story about his being the third son of minor German nobility who wanted to escape being drafted into the Prussian army to fight Napoleon. And, in his newly minted persona, he was a Lutheran, although he barely knew what being a Lutheran meant. Solomon worked hard at both his English and his job, and his captain promoted him to chief deck officer. A year later he found a job as captain of a barge.

In late 1814 he was in Natchez, waiting to join a party that was going up the Natchez Trace to Nashville, when General Andrew Jackson put out a call for men to defend New Orleans from the British. Edward answered the call and, because he could read and write, his colonel made him a sergeant. Colonel Clarence Stewart gave him a copy of the *Manual of Arms,* and Edward began drilling the privates under his command in grammatically flawless but still accented English. Edward's insistence on constant practice and meticulous attention to detail soon had his men firing two shots per minute and performing close-order drills so well that they earned a commendation from the colonel.

After General Jackson's forces defeated the British in 1815, Colonel Stewart offered Edward a job as a slave overseer on his cotton plantation south of Vicksburg. "It pays ninety dollars a month," Stewart said, "plus you get a two-room cabin, food, and a nigger gal to cook and clean for you."

It was more than double Edward's pay as a barge captain, and, with his room and board included, he saved most of his pay until he had accumulated twelve hundred dollars. He was hearing stories of Missouri merchants who were making fortunes from their investments in the fur trade, and on his occasional trips to Vicksburg to visit Miss Betsy's Boarding House, he questioned travelers and businessmen about opportunities on the frontier. In the whorehouse's front parlor, the men told him about a progressive new town in central Missouri that the town fathers had named for Benjamin Franklin. After the 1817 cotton crop was harvested, he gave Colonel Stewart notice that he was leaving.

On his way to Franklin, Missouri, Edward stopped in Kaskaskia and bought a stock of goods at Hans Banhofer's store. "Where are you from?" Banhofer asked. "Sounds like you're from middle Tennessee."

Edward was pleased that another German speaker detected no trace of a German accent. "I'm from up and down the Mississippi, mostly, and I've spent some time just outside of Vicksburg," he answered vaguely.

Edward booked passage for himself and his merchandise on a barge that was headed up the Mississippi and Missouri rivers, and left Kaskaskia the next morning. It was late autumn and the rivers were running low. With only a gentle current, the boatmen made good time poling upriver. In Franklin, Edward sold his stock for a handsome profit within three weeks.

At the Waterfront Tavern, he met two French-Canadian trappers who had gambled and drunk up their earnings from the last season. At first he was suspicious that they might be too irresponsible to invest with. But between their pidgin English and Edward's few words of French, he decided that he could trust them, at least until they got back to civilization's saloons. Edward bought the gear his new partners needed for the trapping season and booked passage for them to the Dakota country.

The two trappers returned to Franklin in the spring of 1818 with bales of beaver and fox skins, and Edward convinced them that his cousin in Amsterdam would give them a better price than they could get in Missouri. When the Planters & Merchants Bank in St. Louis notified Edward that the funds from Amsterdam were in his account, he deducted his advances and paid each trapper their shares. With more than five thousand dollars left in his account, Edward was a man of financial substance.

He continued his mercantile and outfitting operations in Franklin, and, on one bitter cold night in February of 1822, Edward joined a table of men at the Waterfront Tavern. At the end of the table closest to the fire, Captain William Becknell was holding court, telling the others of his western adventure. The previous September, Becknell said, he and a small party of men had headed west with a pack train of goods to trade to the plains Indians.

"We were in Indian country," he continued, "but we didn't find many Indians to trade with. We come across a squadron of what we thought was Spanish soldiers."

"Did they put you in jail, Billy, like they did Zeb Pike?"

"We thought we might wind up in jail. But it turns out that the Mexicans done thrown out the Spanish and declared themselves independent. This Mexican captain says that the new government welcomes foreign trade, now that they are out from under the *gachupines*. That's what Mexicans call Spaniards—kind of like we'd say 'mick' or 'kike.'"

Edward's face flushed and his throat tightened.

"The Mexican soldiers escorted us across Comanche country and all the way into Santa Fe. You never seen anything like it. When them Mexicans found out we had calico, whiskey, beads, and so on, they crowded around us in the plaza, begging to see our merchandise. We sold out in three days, mostly for gold and silver, and made over six hundred percent."

"Six hundred?" Edward asked.

"At least that," Becknell said. "I'm going back this spring."

Edward invested nine hundred dollars in Becknell's 1822 venture and got back four thousand dollars when the trader returned. "I've made good money in the fur trade," Edward told Becknell, "but Mr. Astor's company has almost monopolized the pelt business, and he's getting greedier than ever. Maybe I ought to think about something different."

Edward continued investing in the Santa Fe trade, and in 1824 he stocked three wagons and went down the trail himself as a proprietor.

After their trip together down the Santa Fe Trail in 1827, Matthew Collins and Edward Waterman became partners. *"Ahorita, somos verdaderos hombres de confianza,"* Matt said. Although Matt, with less capital to invest, was the junior partner, they drew straws to decide their firm's name, and he won. By 1831, Collins & Waterman was a major participant in the Santa Fe trade, outfitting twenty or more wagons a year. The two had succeeded because they trusted each other and because they had developed a strategy that allowed Matt, who was fascinated with New Mexico, to work in Santa Fe, while Edward spent most of his time in America.

"I believe you love the United States more than I do," Matt said one evening over dinner at Florinda Maestas'.

"I do," Edward replied. "If you'd been brought up where I was, you'd have more appreciation for America. But you're used to it. You take it for granted. In Europe, the aristocrats sit on top of the pile and everybody's afraid to stick their head up, scared that it might offend the nabobs or the Church. Everywhere you turn, there are limits."

"Limits on what?"

"On everything. On trying out new ideas. On initiative."

Each year Edward returned to Missouri to do the buying and to arrange the next season's shipments while Matt wintered in Santa Fe. Rather than sell all their merchandise in the summer, Matt held back seasonal goods and sold them during Santa Fe's cold months. Heavy wool coats, blankets, and felt hats brought good prices between December and February, and he sold Kentucky whiskey to La Dama at a premium when the summer's supply was gone.

The partners owed part of their success to a bit of luck that grew out of tragedy on the Santa Fe Trail. In 1828 Indians attacked a caravan, stampeding over six hundred horses and mules and killing two men. Later, in September, Comanches raided a four-wagon party and killed its captain and stole their animals, forcing the traders to abandon most of their silver and gold and walk to Missouri. Word of the atrocities spread and, instead of the one hundred wagons that went to Santa Fe in 1828, only thirty wagons ventured out on the trail the next year.

Despite the fear that tempered many proprietors' ambitions, Edward concluded that the others' timidity gave him an opportunity. His gumption—and getting word early from political friends that President Andrew Jackson had ordered the Sixth Infantry at Fort Leavenworth to escort the caravans to the United States–Mexican border on the Arkansas River—convinced him to take the risk.

Edward took all of Collins & Waterman's capital and borrowed an additional fifteen thousand dollars to outfit a fleet of wagons. Captained by Edward, the Collins & Waterman wagons made the trip without incident and were the first to arrive in 1829.

With scant merchandise in Santa Fe that summer, the partners made a profit of just under one thousand percent. Edward returned home in the fall and invested part of his money in Missouri River bottom land, while Matt reinvested all his profits in merchandise for the next year's caravan.

Matt was spending an increasing amount of time visiting the Mendozas. Moisés, missing David, who was in school in St. Louis, invited Matt to go with him on one of his monthly trips to inspect his hacienda forty miles west of Santa Fe. With good horses, they were able to make the trip in a day. The next morning, they rode along the Rio Grande under an umbrella of cottonwood leaves that the fall's first cold snap had turned a rich yellow.

They came to a cluster of one-room adobe huts where four peon families lived, and Moisés asked for Eloy Suárez. His wife, too awed by Moisés to speak, pointed toward a field where peons were clearing weeds out of the irrigation ditches. When Eloy saw who was riding toward him, he ran to Moisés. The peon was short and thin, with wizened, stubble-covered cheeks that had survived somewhere in excess of fifty winter's storms and summer's suns. Eloy smiled a toothless smile that swept back almost to his ears. Then, he took the cuff of his *patrón's* pant leg in his hand as if it were an altar cloth and kissed it.

With a deference that Matt had not seen in Santa Fe, the other peons whisked off their hats and bowed their heads, never raising their eyes to look directly at Moisés. Their voices were strong from yelling at straying sheep and reluctant plow mules, but when they greeted their *patrón* their tones softened to reverent whispers. Matt blanched at the peons' subservience and pursed his lips in displeasure.

"Don Moisés, you could not have come at a better time," Eloy said. "I am in trouble. Your *mayordomo* has raised my interest rate so high that I cannot buy clothes for my little ones. He knows what my wages are, and he knows I cannot pay thirty percent."

Eloy was the fourth generation of Suárezes to work for the Mendozas and he was entitled to special consideration. "I will speak with him," Moisés said. After an effusion of thanks and "God bless yous," Eloy answered his *patrón's* questions about the year's harvest and the prospects for the spring planting season.

Matt and Moisés left and rode in silence for several miles. As they cantered along, Matt remembered Edward's warnings about how different aristocrats were from ordinary folk. In Santa Fe, Matt had sensed that the Mendozas—and particularly Sara—viewed the world differently than he did. But, until he came to the hacienda, the obsequiousness to which Moisés' position entitled him had not been so evident. Anybody who was treated with that servility, Matt told himself, couldn't help thinking he was a superior being. Thank God I'm an American—a white American at any rate.

Moisés sensed that the peons' submissiveness had affected Matt, and he broke their silence to explain that he loaned money to his peons, and most of them would be indebted to him all their lives, but he would continue to grant credit and would forgive most of it at their death. Although the law prohibited the peons from leaving as long as they were in debt, he had never punished a man who ran away. "It is a better system than your slavery," Moisés said. "At least there is a chance—perhaps not a great one—that they can pay off their debts and leave to do whatever they want."

During the next day's ride around the Mendoza estate, Matt and Moisés kept the conversation away from debt peonage. Instead, they talked about whether to plant wheat or barley and the better quality wool that a hard winter would produce. And Moisés, a man curious about all things, peppered Matt with questions about the Santa Fe trade.

During their inspection tour, Matt suggested that Moisés might want to invest with Collins & Waterman. "Perhaps I might make a small investment," Moisés said. "Just enough to learn about the risks and rewards."

Matt gave Moisés favorable terms. He would charge only ten percent for buying and handling the goods and the Spaniard would pay his share of freight, bribes, and other expenses. *If Edward thinks the terms are too easy*, Matt thought, *I can work something out that will keep him happy.*

The next day Matt and Moisés rode back to Santa Fe. "Will you stay for dinner?" Moisés asked when they arrived at his house. Matt had not seen Celestina for weeks and accepted immediately—in Moisés' opinion, a little too enthusiastically.

When Celestina came into the dining room Matt gulped in air as quietly as he could to quell a dizzy feeling. Moisés saw the reaction and held a seconds-long debate with himself. He liked Matt a great deal. He was a bright young man who was developing a pleasing set of manners. Still, he was a rough-hewn American, and, as much as Moisés admired that country, Matt was a foreigner in New Mexico. *But things could change*, Moisés thought as he sat down. Sara Mendoza did not return Matt's smile. "We need more candles," she said, clapping her hands sharply to summon a servant.

Matt suppressed his excitement, and he and Moisés engaged in a long discussion of irrigation techniques that had been passed down from Arab to Spaniard to New Mexican farmer. Matt peered through the candlelight at Celestina, hoping that Sara would not catch him admiring her daughter. "That is enough about irrigation," Moisés said. "How is your English coming, Celestina?"

"It is improving, but slowly," she answered.

Moisés turned to Matt. "Perhaps you would have time to help Celestina with her English this winter."

Before Matt could answer, Sara went rigid in her chair, the muscles in her arms flexing as she clenched her fists and flashed a withering look at her husband. "I would be most pleased, Don Moisés," Matt said before Sara could protest.

Two years passed, during which Matt's courtship of Celestina Mendoza progressed in fits and starts. He saw her from time to time, but he suspected that her mother invented reasons why the couple could not see one another. Sara had arranged for young men from good families in Mexico City and Guadalajara to visit Santa Fe, but Celestina had not been interested. And in 1830 she sent Celestina to spend six months in Puebla with her Toledano y Espinoza cousins, but, to Sara's chagrin, her daughter returned without a *prometido*.

Meanwhile, Collins & Waterman's fortunes increased steadily. Edward depended heavily on Matt's advice about what their Mexican customers would buy; but, because his partner had not been home in three years, Edward feared that Matt was losing touch with the new kinds and styles of merchandise. He also worried that his partner was becoming more and more Mexican. It seemed to him that Matt actually enjoyed the drawn-out preliminaries to business—the long, detailed conversations about the progress of Governor Baca's children and the severity of Señora Baca's gout. Worse yet, Edward felt that Matt was becoming less practical. Edward had been to dinners at the Mendoza's where Matt and Moisés and sometimes Celestina bored him with their lofty and lengthy discussions of human spirituality and theological relevance. And Matt and Celestina often took turns reading the romantic poems of Lord Byron and John Keats, while the guests sipped their after-dinner coffee. *This is no way for an American to spend his time,* Edward said to himself.

Despite Edward's concerns about Matt, 1831 was shaping up to be the biggest year ever on the Santa Fe Trail. By the time he got to Santa Fe on a July morning, the customs house had already counted more than a hundred wagons, and, Edward reported, there were still more out on the Trail. "With all this merchandise flooding in," Matt said while they were stacking the goods in their store late that afternoon, "we're going to play hell getting rid of all our goods this year."

The partners calculated that if they couldn't sell their goods before Edward left for Missouri in the fall, Matt could dispose of them during the winter, or ship them to Chihuahua and Durango. Sending their merchandise south would cost them more in freight and bribes, and would expose their goods to raids by the Mescalero Apaches along the *jornada del muerto*, but, they decided, rather than see their profit margins shrink to nothing in Santa Fe, they were better off taking the risk.

Matt listened to the church bells strike seven o'clock, lit a lantern, and poured them each a cup of wine to celebrate Edward's arrival in Santa Fe. "Isn't Miss Celestina about marriageable age?" Edward asked with a blank expression that he hoped masked his curiosity.

"She's nineteen."

"How do you figure your chances?"

"They've improved. But her mother wouldn't shed a tear if the Comanches barbecued me," Matt answered dryly.

"She might get her wish. Diego Zambrano told me that the Comanches are furious over the slaughter of some of their braves by a gang of white men. If the savages get bold enough, they might ride into Santa Fe and roast us all."

Matt took a long drink of wine and changed the subject to Susano Baca's ouster as New Mexico's governor. In Mexico City, he told Edward, an arch conservative had revolted and made himself dictator. Within weeks, he fired Baca and appointed Filemón Rodríguez to New Mexico's highest post.

Edward listened to the story, amused by how fascinated his partner was with Mexico's confusing political scene. Trying to keep up with the power struggles between liberals and conservatives, and which side the opportunistic schemer Santa Anna had taken, was almost impossible. The only thing about Mexican politics that interested Edward was how it affected the business of Collins & Waterman.

"I don't think we'll have any trouble with Rodríguez," Matt said with a sly smile. "I've taken care of Don Filemón. Philosophically, he's a passionate conservative and he doesn't care much for the United States, but he knows he needs to go along to get along. I agreed to give him two percent of our sales proceeds."

"Who's doing the counting?" Edward asked, returning Matt's sly smile with one of his own.

"We are," Matt said. "If Don Filemón gets eight hundred or a thousand, he'll be happy."

"What's our friend Baca doing?" Edward asked.

"He spends most of his time at his hacienda down by Albuquerque. It's about double the size that it was before he was governor," Matt said, his eyes crinkling with pleasure at his insider's knowledge.

"What about Celestina?" Edward asked, moving to the topic that he knew most interested Matt.

"I saw her at the fandango Governor Rodríguez gave to celebrate his arrival in Santa Fe. And Don Moisés invited me to a family dinner, but I didn't get much chance to talk to her."

"Maybe Moisés Mendoza is thinking about adding a rich young American to his family," Edward said. "The aristocrats don't ask outsiders to family dinners casually. If you're not a cousin, or a childhood friend, it's hard to get invited to the sanctum sanctorum."

"Could be," Matt said. "Before I forget it, Edward, the Mendozas have invited us to a party on Saturday."

"It'll be something to help pass the time," Edward said. "A few days in this damned dried-out desert, and all I want to do is get back to sweet, green Missouri."

On Saturday morning, Matt had Florinda Maestas heat buckets of water for the copper bathtub Edward had brought him from Missouri. "You'll smell so good that Miss Celestina won't be able to resist you," Edward teased.

"To hell with you, Don Eduardo," Matt said, sinking to his neck in the water. He stepped out and walked to the fireplace in the corner, leaving wet footprints on the dirt floor. He dried himself with a piece of brown muslin and slipped into his gray wool pants. He buttoned a white, ruffled shirt that he had sent to St. Louis for washing and ironing, tied a black cravat, and slipped on a coat with a collar that went up to his ears.

He and Edward walked up the hill to the Mendoza's house. Moisés greeted them on the patio and steered them to a group of men who were discussing politics. Matt glanced around the patio until he saw Sara Mendoza, her sparrowlike eyes canvassing the crowd. When their eyes met, she squinted and grimaced. Matt turned back to the men and concentrated on the discussion of the conservative usurper who had seized the presidency in Mexico City.

"That son of a bitch Bustamante," Moisés said with an uncharacteristic show of passion, "he murdered one of our only honest politicians. Vicente Guerrero was one of the few liberal heroes that we had left."

"There is no proof that Bustamante was behind it," Diego Zambrano said.

"Don Diego, you know as well as I do that Bustamante staged Guerrero's show trial for treason and executed him," Moisés replied, unsuccessfully trying to lower his voice. "This is not government by law. This is government by gun barrel."

"Don Moisés," Zambrano said, the sleek and hungry look that Matt had noted before coming over the captain, "show some loyalty to your class. Vicente Guerrero was the son of an ignorant peon. He claimed he was half white, but, if he was a quarter white I would give you my three best stallions."

"Bustamante has turned the Republic into a dictatorship." Moisés was almost shouting. "That is not what the country needs—or wants. The Eighteen Twenty-four Constitution. That is what we need."

"That constitution stinks of America," Zambrano said, his normally pale cheeks turning scarlet with anger. "There is not one damned thing those American radicals can teach us. The Yankees concocted their government for Protestant Anglos, and their ideas will never work in Catholic Mexico. You have seen these vulgar Americans, Don Moisés. Drunk and carousing through our streets. That is what happens when the mob is free to do whatever it wants. Is that what you want for Mexico?"

"I have been to the United States, and there are good people there," Moisés countered.

"Anyone who believes the Americans' democratic drivel are idiots, fools," Zambrano said. His fists were balled in knots and his face was beet red. "The people are louts. The truth is that you can only govern people from above."

"The Yankee ideas are dangerous," Bonifacio Chacón, the customs chief, added. "They are trying to spread their manure, and if we are not careful they will cover us up with it."

"The Americans only want what they can use, and this New Mexico land is so poor that they will never covet it," Moisés said after remembering that he was the host and regaining his sense of humor. "On the other hand, I would bet that if the Mexico City politicians could saw off the Republic just north of Chihuahua, they would do it. To them, we are like baby birds in the nest, always begging for money to pay soldiers and bureaucrats and priests."

Matt, standing at the group's edge, wrestled with himself. Should he defend the United States? Should he support Mexico? Should he keep quiet? The argument was winding down and he elected the latter.

"Don Moisés, you seem to have a *querencia* for the Yankees," Zambrano said. His better judgment reminded him that he was arguing with one of New Mexico's most powerful hacendados, but, even though tempers were cooling, he could not resist a last jab. "Are you saying that we should be more like them?"

"No. There are things we can learn from the Americans, but our cultures are too different. There are some Americans who understand us," Moisés said, "but most of them never will. You must excuse us, Mateo and Eduardo, but emotions sometimes run high. We certainty do not include you when we speak of the less-attractive types of Americans."

"Thank you, Don Moisés," Matt said, "but I share some of your concerns about my countrymen. You mentioned that Mexicans can learn from Americans, but I can assure you that there are many things that Americans can learn from Mexicans."

"Well said, Don Mateo," a hacendado from Española said.

"Please excuse us," Matt said, using a break in the conversation for him and Edward to exit the group of men. Edward joined an American business associate who was standing in a corner by himself. Matt got another glass of wine and leaned against a *portal* post, hoping to catch a glimpse of Celestina. Instead, he saw Sara Mendoza sitting alone on a bench. *Now,* he thought, *might be the time to let her know that I am not like the other Americans she so intensely dislikes.* Matt walked across the patio and bowed respectfully. "Señora Mendoza, allow me to present you with a gift," he said, fumbling to pull out a package that barely fit in his coat pocket.

"You are too kind, Don Mateo," she said, a flicker of suspicion darting across her face.

Matt handed her the package. Sara untied the thick twine and unwrapped the oiled paper protecting it. "Ah, the poems of Sor Juana Inés de la Cruz," she said, still wary. "My mother read these to me when I was a girl. Sor Juana expresses feelings of love with a unique delicacy. What did you think of Sor Juana, young man?"

"I admire great poetry, Señora," Matt said. "I have read the sonnets of our English master, Shakespeare. But I must say that the poetry of Sor Juana is the equal of Shakespeare."

"I am surprised. Many men do not like Sor Juana's work."

"Why is that, madam?"

"Because she attacked the idea that women are subservient to men. Sor Juana wrote in the late sixteen hundreds, when the Inquisition was in full bloom. The Church fathers accused her of heresy and she recanted and never wrote again."

"That is a shame," Matt said, delighted to be having his first real conversation with Celestina's mother. "I do not think that those ideas would be heresy today."

"There are many who would argue that women are subordinate to men."

"My country has many shortcomings, Señora Mendoza," he said, "but we are beginning to recognize the value of women."

"Do they vote?" she asked in an arch tone. "Do they go into business?"

"No."

"Then things are no different in Mexico and the United States."

"Perhaps not, Doña Sara," he said, trying to recoup lost ground. "But it seems to me that Mexican life revolves around the home, and that women are the glue that binds a strong family."

"It is our bastion against the outside world. Our protective womb. If somebody hurts you. Or cheats you. Or will not help you. When all else fails, you can depend on your family."

"It creates a sense of belonging to something that is ongoing," Matt said, feeling for the first time that he had found common ground with Sara. "I have always regretted that I was not part of a family."

"A man without a family is nobody," she said harshly. "It is the place where you learn discipline and respect and manners. It is who protects you when you are old." When Matt's lips pursed, Sara softened her voice. "Our Spanish customs and our families are, indeed, a great comfort, Don Mateo. But I am surprised at your interest in family. To me, Americans seem to be adrift, and they seem to like it that way. When I ask your countrymen where they come from, they answer that they wandered from some place called Carolina to the Mississippi River and then on west. They are rootless. They have no loyalty to place."

"Perhaps my background with the nuns causes me to think differently, Señora," he said.

The conversation stopped while Sara took the silver scissors Matt gave her and carefully cut the ends of the pages to free them for reading. "Sor Juana was illegitimate, and perhaps that made her more sensitive to human beings' need for loving families," Sara Mendoza said.

"I am not illegitimate. I am not a bastard," he snapped in a defensive, but hostile tone. Immediately, he was furious with himself for losing his temper and for letting his chance to win Sara's favor slip away.

"Perhaps you are too sensitive, Don Mateo. That is not what I meant," she said, straightening her back and giving him a frigid smile that said that their conversation was over.

You stupid son of a bitch, he said to himself. *How could you have been that dumb? You almost had her, and you let her get away. You half-wit.* Matt walked to where Edward and Celestina were standing by the fountain. "You look elegant in white, Señorita Celestina," Matt said in an overly hearty voice, still trying to steady himself after his failure with Sara.

"My dressmaker copied it from an American magazine."

"You see, Miss Celestina," Edward said in English, "the Mexican saying that *'Todo malo viene del norte'* is not necessarily true."

"There are, indeed, many good things that come from the north," Celestina said, her blue-black eyes looking directly—and seriously—at Matt. She blushed at her own assertiveness and quickly added, "And from the south too."

"I gave your mother a book of poems by Sor Juana," Matt said, switching to Spanish.

"It will be my pleasure to read them," Celestina said. "She is Mexico's greatest poet. My mother says that Sor Juana was the first writer to develop a truly Mexican style."

Matt and Celestina walked on a gravel path through hollyhocks and bushes heavy with pink and red roses. "I find it strange that you are interested in Mexican poetry. My mother believes that Yankees think of nothing but business."

"I admit to tending to my business, just as your father tends to his hacienda. But there must be room for other things."

"Other things?"

"Poetry. Friendships. Eduardo and I are business partners, but we are also good friends. I was thinking, Señorita Celestina, that we might go on a picnic tomorrow after mass."

"I will ask my mother. Look, Padre Domingo just came in. Do you know him?" she asked, pointing at a tonsured Franciscan in a coarse brown robe.

"I have seen him at mass."

"Papá says that because of the political mess in Mexico City there are only fifteen priests to minister to all of New Mexico. And the *penitentes* have grown even stronger."

"For a woman, you know a lot about politics and religion."

"My father and I discuss many things."

Because Padre Domingo was in Santa Fe that weekend to say mass, La Castrense was full. Spanish paintings decorated the military chapel's whitewashed walls, and, behind the gilded altar, a statue of Santiago Matamoros, Spain's patron saint, brandished his mighty broadsword to slay Christianity's enemies.

In the pews, barefooted peons sat next to ladies in silk gowns on rough-hewn benches that gave up splinters to the bottoms of wiggly children. La Dama positioned herself two rows behind her former lover, Susano Baca, and his wife and children. The Mendozas and their servants filled the first two rows on the right. When La Castrense's bell stopped ringing, Padre Domingo emerged from a small door beside the altar, his cloth-of-gold robe drawn close so that the precious garment would not snag on the narrow door frame. To the side of the altar a guitarist, drummer, and flautist provided music.

Matt arrived late and stood against the back wall at an angle that gave him a view of Celestina's profile. As her head nodded and bobbed under her white lace mantilla and her lips moved to form "amen"s, his stomach felt suddenly empty and his head became light, until he put his cheek against the cool adobe wall. Her long neck, the color of smoked buckskin, enchanted him. She had done her black hair in braids and pinned it up around the back of her head. Whisps of hair, as soft as gosling down, curled down her neck, and Matt longed to nip at them with his lips.

Padre Domingo concluded the services with an announcement that he would hear confessions that afternoon and that he would conduct seventeen weddings and forty-three baptisms on Monday. Matt waited in the middle of the plaza by the sundial until the Mendozas filed out. He edged through the crowd toward them, bowed to Sara, and shook Moisés's hand before turning to Celestina. "Are you ready? We have a fine day for our picnic. The air is light and clear, and the sky is so blue that it hurts your eyes to look at it."

Celestina removed her mantilla, folded it carefully, and handed it to her mother. "I am ready, and Cousin Rebeca is ready. Father is letting us use his buggy."

"I thought we might go to that hill just south of town," he said. "It has not rained for more than a week, so your buggy will make it to the top easily. The view is spectacular."

Matt mounted his saddle mule and rode beside the buggy that Cousin Rebeca, Celestina's chaperon, was driving. A mile south of town, he turned off the Santa Fe Trail and piloted them along a goat path to the foot of the hill. He dismounted and took their horse's reins, then guided it through the piñons and junipers to a spot on the summit where a break in the trees gave them a view of Santa Fe. "May I offer you ladies a glass of champagne?"

"Of course, of course," Cousin Rebeca said, laying her *rebozo* on the ground and lowering her bulk awkwardly onto it. "This is a great treat,

Don Mateo. When I was a girl, before the trail to Missouri opened, we never had champagne."

"The Trail has brought many good things to New Mexico," Matt said to Celestina almost in a whisper.

"That is true, Don Mateo," Celestina said, kneading her hands in her lap and her keeping her eyes fixed on them.

"Please call me Mateo," he said.

"What are you two talking about?" Rebeca asked.

"The subtleties of the Spanish language," Matt answered and filled Rebeca's glass again. "Would you like some canned sardines, Cousin Rebeca? They are excellent. Señorita Celestina and I may take a little walk."

"Fine. Just stay close," Rebeca said, raising a sardine to her upturned mouth and dropping it in.

Matt and Celestina strolled around a fat juniper bush. "I hope you did not have trouble getting your mother's permission to come on the picnic," Matt said.

"I was surprised. She did not seem happy about it. All she said was that I should arrange for Cousin Rebeca to come with us."

"Good. Maybe she does not think I am such an ogre," he said, laughing. "With this newfound acceptance, may I call you Celestina?"

"Please do."

"Look through there," he said. He put one hand around her waist and pointed with the other. At first Celestina stiffened. Other than dancing, it was their first touch. After what seemed to Matt to be a time without end, she relaxed and moved closer to him. "You can still see snow on top of the Sangre de Cristos," Matt continued.

This was the first time that Matt had dealt with a woman—other than a prostitute—and, he thought, it was difficult to know how to act, to know what to say. He had never been on such unfamiliar ground. "Have you had a chance to read Sor Juana's poems?" he asked, struggling to find a topic.

"Some. And they are as beautiful as Mamá said they were. What did you think about Sor Juana's suggestion that women should not be too submissive to men?"

"Since I have not spent much time with women, I have not had reason to think about it."

"But you have had time to read Sor Juana," Celestina said. Unconsciously, she slipped into using the familiar—the *tú*—form of "you," a form they would thereafter always use with one another.

"I always make time to read. How are you doing with the story by Edgar Allen Poe that I gave you?"

"I can understand almost every word. You are a good teacher," Celestina said.

"What does Doña Sara say about our lessons?"

"When we started, she and I had a fight. But Papá told Mamá that speaking English will be important to us in New Mexico, and that settled it."

"I saw a guitar in the buggy," Matt said. "Will you play for me." He took her hand and led her back to their picnic site, where Rebeca was napping.

CHAPTER TWELVE

1832

"Mother is opposed to my marrying a foreigner. She fears that you might disappear to America and never come back, like other Americans with Mexican wives have done."

"Thank you for receiving me," Matt said, slapping snow off his greatcoat.

"Come in, come in," Moisés Mendoza said. "We will go into the kitchen. There is a good fire and the cook will warm us some wine. Have you come to see Celestina?"

"I hope to see Señorita Celestina, but I have come to visit with you about a matter of business."

"How can I be of service?" Moisés asked, stepping aside to let Matt enter the kitchen first.

"Don Moisés, I have sold most of my goods, but it is already March, and I have close to four-thousand-pesos-worth of merchandise left. When the first caravan gets here in June, my old stock will not sell. I know that you own part of a store in Chihuahua, and I was wondering whether we could work out an arrangement to send my goods south."

"What do you have left, Mateo?"

"A dozen pairs of brogans, thirty *varas* of velvet, some batiste and calico, a few other items."

"How would you want to work, Mateo?"

"I am very flexible, Don Moisés."

"Is it in good condition?"

"Some of the cloth is stained, but nothing serious."

"Let us do it this way, Mateo. I will pay half the wholesale price and we will share expenses and split the profits."

"We have an agreement," Matt said with a wide smile. It was significant, he knew, that Moisés had consented to go into business with him, something the Mendoza patriarch would not have done if he had not trusted him. Even better, it brought him a step closer to Celestina. "When will your *carretas* be leaving for Chihuahua?"

"I am sending David next week."

When they shook hands, Moisés clapped his other hand over Matt's. *"Comos hombres de confianza,"* Moises said.

"I would like to pay my respects to Señorita Celestina if it is convenient."

"Certainly. Celestina tells me that your English lessons are very helpful."

"She is intelligent and she learns quickly, Don Moisés. I gave her the American newspapers that Eduardo brought down the Trail, and she can read them almost perfectly."

Moisés clapped his hands and a servant appeared at the kitchen door. "Ask Celestina to join us."

Matt picked up his damp greatcoat and pulled a bottle of champagne from an oversized pocket. He had chilled the wine in the snow before coming to the Mendozas and it was sweating in the warm kitchen. Moisés looked through several cabinets before he found crystal glasses.

"A toast to our new partnership," Matt said, "and to the arrival of an excellent student."

"Celestina is a bright girl. I knew that I was taking a risk when I decided to educate her. Looking back, though, I am glad I did it. There are not many women in Santa Fe who can carry on an intelligent conversation. She has her own ideas and opinions, and that will make it difficult for me to find her a husband."

"That should be the least of your worries, Don Moisés," Matt said. He stood when Celestina entered the kitchen and pulled a stool beside her father in front of the fire.

"Celestina, get a glass. Mateo has brought champagne." Moisés quickly finished his glass and excused himself.

"Matt, you've only had one glass of wine, and your face is almost as red as your hair," Celestina said in English.

"The champagne and the fire and you have heated me," he said, looking straight into the blue-black eyes that never failed to startle him. "Could we go out to the patio. I feel light-headed."

"What is 'light-headed'?"

"*Mareado.*"

Outside, the dry, cold air cleared his head, and he watched snowflakes float down on her hair and catch on her eyelashes. "Matt, you look so serious," she said.

"I am serious, Celestina. We've known one another for several years, and I think you know how I feel about you. And I think I know how you feel about me."

"I would like to continue this discussion in Spanish, Mateo, so that everything is completely clear."

"As you wish. But, in either Spanish or English, I think you know where this conversation is going," he said, leaning forward and kissing her for the first time. "I am asking you to be my wife."

"I have been considering it for some time," she said, somewhat formally.

"I have spoken with my father," she continued, "and he is sympathetic. But mother is opposed to marriage with a foreigner. She only has David and me, and she worries about us more than she would if she had six or eight children. She fears that you might disappear to America and never come back, like other Americans with Mexican wives have done."

"I plan to live in Santa Fe with you, *mi amor,*" he said, looking at her carefully to see how she reacted to the endearment. Celestina smiled and wiped snow off her eyelashes.

"Mamá says that no Yankee can ever adapt to our Spanish customs."

"It is true that I will never be fully Spanish, Celestina. There are some things here that are difficult to adjust to, but there are things about America that I do not like. If I could organize my life the way I wanted, I would work like a Yankee but live like a Spaniard. Americans take themselves and their business so seriously that they don't know how to enjoy themselves. Among Spaniards, there is a passion, a spontaneity, a joy that Anglos don't have. It is the difference between a dried peach and a fresh, juicy, ripe peach."

"That is not the only thing that Mamá frets about."

"Then what?"

"It is difficult to say." It would have been rude to bring up his birth and orphan background, but he read her thoughts.

"I can't change the fact that I'm an orphan who worked his way up," Matt said, switching to English and speaking with a hardness that she had not heard before. "I've heard New Mexican aristocrats sneering at Americans. We're upstarts. Ill-mannered. Ungentlemanly."

"Matt, it's not me who is saying those things. It's Mamá. She feels strongly."

"You have not accepted my proposal," Matt said, suddenly calm, his voice softening.

Celestina had listened to her mother's objections to Matt and, out of respect, she had considered each one carefully, but she had rejected them. Instead, she had catalogued the reasons favoring a marriage. He would not try to dominate her the way a Hispanic man would. They both enjoyed reading and discussing, something that she could say about few men, American or New Mexican. With his jugged ears and a nose her mother said was so large and so sharp that he could cut down a tree with it, he was not overly handsome, but she loved his red hair and blue eyes and his extraordinary height and, besides, marrying a foreigner was exotic, adventurous.

"Of course I accept. I have been in love with you for a long time," she said, kissing him and stroking his hair to brush away the snow.

"Would it help if I went to your mother directly?"

"That would be the worst way," Celestina said. "Let me speak to her. Before now, Mamá and I have only spoken in theoretical terms. But now that you have proposed and I have accepted, there is something concrete."

"Mother, put down your embroidery," Celestina said.

"Yes, daughter?"

"Mamá, Mateo has asked me to marry him, and I have accepted. But only if you agree."

"And your father?"

"He has given his consent, but Papá also wants your agreement. Mamá, I love this man, and I feel that I know his heart."

"His heart is pure American."

"He is part American and part Spanish, Mamá. He came here when he was only a boy of sixteen, and you have seen for yourself that he has developed manners and habits that are unusual for a Yankee."

"You may think you understand him, but inside he is no different from those other loud-mouthed boors. This Mateo tries to speak of things other than business, but he cannot keep his mind off of money for more than a few minutes."

"Mamá, I am not as good at divining a person's character as you are.

But I have spent time with this man. Father has agreed to do business with him, and he saved David's life when they were trapping together."

"Does he plan to live in America?"

"No. We have discussed this. He wants to live here."

"This man has no family," Sara said. "He claims that he is not a bastard, but that may or may not be true. I want to speak with your father."

Celestina found Moisés in the back patio giving instructions to an itinerant blacksmith. "Papá, Mamá wishes to speak with you about Matt," Celestina said. "She is resisting."

"Let me see what I can do with your mother. Go to your room."

Moisés found his wife sitting in the *sala,* her embroidery needle flashing in and out of a white lily that she was stitching on a silk altar cloth. When he entered the room, she refused to look up. "Sara," he said to the top of her head, "I know your feelings about this foreigner, but I do not understand them. He goes out of his way to please you."

"I will admit that he is courteous," she said. "Still, there are profound differences that will guarantee our Celestina an unhappy life. Now, he is just a romantic boy who is trying to please us, but when he gets older he will be just like the rest of them."

"Let us look at some of his good points, *querida.* He does not have the nasty habit of chewing tobacco and he keeps himself clean."

"In that respect, I agree that he is not like most of his countrymen."

Moisés knew men who beat their wives if they violated the powerful weight of law and custom, but he had always used a subtler approach, preferring to persuade her to his point of view.

"Another thing we must consider are Celestina's alternatives," he said in his most reasonable voice. "I do not know of any New Mexican of marriagable age with pure European blood. You have brought her young men from Mexico City and Puebla, and she has rejected them. And, if she married someone from so far away, we would never see our grandchildren. Think of this, *mi alma,* Matt might give us a blue-eyed grandchild."

"We can try again to get a Spanish husband to move to Santa Fe," Sara said, her eyes leaving her needlework to give him a cold stare. "You have enough property to attract a man of quality."

"Mateo has his own property," Moisés said, his voice still soothing. "He will not need a large dowry."

"Like all the rest of the Yankees, he will only be interested in material things," Sara said. She tried to compose herself, but her eyes filled with tears.

"I am sure that Matt can be hard in his dealings with others," Moisés said, sitting on a footstool at her feet and taking her hand. "But I can also be tough when I deal with outsiders. Mateo has always been overly fair with me, and he understands the benefits that a Spanish family offers. And he is terribly in love with Celestina."

"I overheard his partner, Waterman," Sara said, pronouncing the foreign name with almost a snarl, "saying that our Church is nothing more than superstitions that the rich use to exploit the poor. Fools like him do not understand that it was our Holy Catholic Church that brought civilization to Mexico. Without Christ's mercy, the Aztecs would still be ripping out human hearts and performing blood sacrifices."

"Mateo and I have discussed his becoming a Mexican citizen," Moisés said, stroking her hand softly. "He was born a Catholic, although he has not taken it seriously. But he assures me that he will reaffirm his vows of loyalty to the Church."

"Moisés, if you scratch a Yankee, you find a Puritan, a Protestant, or whatever they call themselves. Heretics," Sara said, her already-high voice reaching an even higher pitch.

"Sara, think of this. You agreed with my decision to educate Celestina, and her independent nature may make it impossible for her to be happy with a Spanish husband. If she marries a man who tries to rule over her, that will never work. This American will be more liberal with her."

"Someone needs to rule, Moisés. Too much liberality can ruin a family. Women need to know when to give in for the sake of harmony in the family."

"Celestina," Moisés said, "has enough intelligence to know when her opinions are no longer welcome. She learned that from you, *querida*."

As she had done hundreds of times during their life together, she accommodated herself to his wishes. "I understand my duty. I will consent to the marriage," Sara said in a flat voice that held no emotion.

"Once again, *mi amor*, you have acted wisely," Moisés said, rising and kissing her lightly on the lips.

Before he could leave the room, in a final act of dignity-saving defiance, Sara laid down conditions. "He must first become a Mexican. He must agree to raise our grandchildren in the true faith. My last condition is that they wait another year. Padre Domingo has told me that Bishop Zubiría will visit Santa Fe next year. I will arrange for him to officiate."

"I am certain that I can persuade Mateo and Celestina to agree to your wishes," he said.

"The Mendozas have accepted me," an exultant Matt announced to his partner when he returned to their store after breakfasting with his future in-laws. "We'll be married in the summer of eighteen thirty-three—by the Bishop of Durango, no less. I'm meeting with Don Moisés tomorrow to discuss the dowry arrangements. Will you come with me as my witness?"

"I'm flattered," Edward said.

The next afternoon the partners walked to the Mendoza's house. Moisés ushered the two Americans into the *sala* and introduced them to Fidelio Vargas, a Chihuahua notary public.

Spanish law required that Notary Fidelio Vargas keep the public records for marriage contracts, wills, and other legal documents, and, by happenstance, Notary Vargas was making his annual visit to Santa Fe. Despite the seriousness of his work, he was a comical figure. He had no neck, and he was short—more than a foot shorter than Matt—and his head and torso formed almost perfect circles of well-fed flesh. But Fidelio Vargas offset his dwarfish appearance with a sober demeanor and an air of self-importance that befitted his rank in society.

Moisés was dressed in a gray Spanish-cut suit of fine wool that accented the *gravitas* that he had assumed for the occasion. "Mateo, I want to officially welcome you into our family. I know that you will be a good husband for my Celestina, and I am certain that, as Celestina Mendoza de Collins, she will be a good wife to you."

"Thank you, Don Moisés," Matt said, straining to read the nuances of Moisés's words and gestures so that he could meet the standards of etiquette that he knew were expected of him.

"Fortunately," Moisés said, his voice gravelly with formality, "Notary Vargas is here to attend to our legal needs. I would appreciate your speaking slowly so that he can copy down your statements. For the record, you and Don Eduardo will give Don Fidelio the information he needs to authenticate your identity."

"Mateo Collins, American citizen, born in Kaskaskia, Illinois in eighteen oh nine—the groom." The notary gave Matt a quizzical look and sounded out "Coleens." Matt spelled his last name slowly and the notary inscribed it in his protocol book.

"Eduardo Waterman, naturalized American citizen, born Hamburg, Germany, seventeen ninety-six, witness on behalf of said groom, Mateo Collins."

When the notary finished his entries, Moisés proclaimed the purpose of the legal instrument. "We are here to confirm the terms of a marriage contract, and, more specifically, the details of the herein below described property that I am giving to my daughter, Celestina María Elena Mendoza de Toledano y Espinoza and the aforenamed groom, Don Mateo Collins."

Fidelio Vargas looked up from his writing and asked for time to sharpen a new quill. Moisés was annoyed by the interruption of his carefully organized thoughts. "Don Mateo," he continued after the notary had brushed the sharpenings off his black suit, "I have carefully weighed what I should offer as a dowry. Since you know nothing of farming and ranching, I was at first reluctant to suggest land. But I have concluded that managing a small hacienda will be an excellent way to introduce you to our Spanish—strike that, Notary Vargas—Mexican way of life. For centuries, our family's wealth has come from the land. I love New Mexico's beauty—even its bleakness. It is the stage on which God determined that we should live."

"That is very different from the way Americans look at land, Don Moisés," Edward butted in, not understanding the solemnity required for a transfer of Mendoza family land.

Moisés' sour look at Edward and the sharpening of his already sharp features silenced Edward. "The following is not on the record, Notary Vargas," Moisés said archly. "I suppose that it may sound strange to an American that someone would fall in love with dirt and rocks."

"We are back on the record, Notary Vargas," Moisés continued. "I am deeding, assigning, conveying, and transferring in perpetuity to my aforementioned daughter, Celestina, as her sole and separate property a tract of land that is known as 'Rincón de los Álamos.'" Moisés paused for several seconds, took a deep breath, and continued. "The name comes from its being on a bend of the Río Grande, and it is further marked by a thick stand of very tall cottonwoods. It is almost due west of Santa Fe, about forty miles. The tract has two thousand *varas* fronting on the Río Grande. There is an irrigated orchard that produces excellent apricots, pears, plums, and apples. Another five hundred acres of wheat and barley are irrigated. There is good grazing on the rest of the land. And there are four thousand sheep, some cattle, and twelve peon families."

"You are too generous," Matt said when Moisés indicated with a wave of his hand that he was finished. "Thank you, Don Moisés."

"I understand," Mendoza said, "that in America, married women cannot hold property in their own names. But under our law women can own land. Therefore, I have transferred Rincón de los Álamos to Celestina." What Moisés did not say was that Sara's warning—that Matt might some day abandon his New Mexican family—had convinced him to give the land to his daughter, eliminating any chance that it would pass out of Mendoza hands. "But, of course, it will be for the benefit of the two of you and our grandchildren. I hope this does not offend you."

"Of course not, Don Moisés," Matt said. He understood the true reason for deeding Rincón de los Álamos to Celestina. *It's the practical thing,* he thought. *If I were in his shoes, I would have done the same.*

"We must attend to the final formalities," Fidelio Vargas said. "Señorita Celestina appeared before me earlier and signed the necessary documents. Will you gentlemen please affix your names at the bottom." Matt signed first and Edward witnessed his signature. Then, Moisés wrote his name in his illegible scribble and Fidelio Vargas served as his witness, signing with a flourish developed over years of putting his name to important documents.

Moisés clapped loudly and a servant who had been waiting outside the *sala* door came immediately. "Tell the cook to set two extra places for dinner. Tonight we have a special meal. We are celebrating the feast day of Santa Ester, after whom my mother was named. Let us go outside. It is time for Patricio to slaughter the lamb, and I want to make sure that he does it right."

Matt and Edward watched as Patricio tied the lamb by its hind legs, threw the rope over a tree limb, hauled the squirming animal up, and slit its jugular vein. The dark blood ran fast at first, slowed to a trickle, and then stopped. "Well done," Moisés told Patricio. "There is not a drop of blood left in him." The peon dressed the animal with professional skill and tossed the carcass into a vat of salt water.

After sundown, a servant trotted around the patio ringing a small silver bell to call the Mendozas to their family chapel. Matt and Edward followed Moisés inside and watched while Sara removed a box of candles from under the altar. "These are special candles that we burn only when we have Friday services," she said. She put the candles in a seven-branched holder and lit them.

"Celestina, would you close the door," Moisés said, putting a square cloth on his head. "Since this is the day of Santa Ester, I will read from the One hundred and twenty-ninth Psalm:

> "May Israel now say:
> Many a time have they afflicted me from my
> youth; yet they have not prevailed against me . . .
> The Lord is righteous: He hath cut asunder
> the cords of the wicked.
> Let them all be confounded and turned back
> that hate Zion."

Matt caught Edward out of the corner of his eye. His partner's face went from amazement to deep sadness; he choked and wiped moisture from his eyes before it turned to tears.

"Now, let us go to dinner," Sara said. "Our family will not eat again until the sun sets on Saturday, but we can look forward to a Saturday of no work. Mateo, you sit next to Moisés, and Eduardo, you sit next to me."

Sara handed Edward a basket of flat bread that resembled crackers. "Please have some and pass it along."

"Where did you learn to make this bread, Doña Sara?" Edward asked.

"It is an old recipe from my family. It is an unleavened bread that we call *pan galleta*. I have taught our cook to follow a little ritual that brings good luck. She pinches off a bit of dough, throws it in the fire, and says, 'Blessed are you, Adonai.'"

"Do you ever have pork?" Edward asked.

"We never eat it on our special Fridays," Moisés answered. "We have it occasionally, but it tends to upset my stomach."

"I see," Edward said. "This lamb is very good. I was interested in your Santa Ester services, Doña Sara. I am not a Catholic, so you must excuse what may seem to be stupid questions."

"No question that clarifies our faith is stupid."

"What is special about Santa Ester's day?"

"It is a celebration of the saving of God's people from suffering."

"Have you ever heard the word 'Hadassah,' Doña Sara?"

"Is it an Arabic word? How do you pronounce it?"

"Ha—dass—ah."

"It is a new word to me," Sara said. "Have you read the story of Santa Ester, Don Eduardo?"

"Years ago, when I was a boy."

"Then you will recall that Santa Ester starts out as a rather meek woman. But she asks God for help against a plot to destroy the Jews, and her prayers save God's people."

"Do you know the origin of the Santa Ester services?" Edward asked.

"Those are very old traditions," Moisés answered. "They have been passed down in our families for generations. My grandfather read that same passage from Psalms."

"Did he use the word Adonai?"

"He said that it is another way to refer to God. Why are you so curious about all of this, Don Eduardo?" Moisés asked, feeling that Edward's probing was bordering on rudeness.

"It was a lovely ceremony, and it made me think of my family in Germany."

"What in the hell were all those questions about Santa Ester's day," Matt asked Edward when they were walking back to their store. "Couldn't you feel Don Moisés's annoyance?"

"I couldn't believe it," Edward said, paying no attention to his partner's displeasure. "The Mendoza's customs are almost exactly like some that I saw in Vienna—in Hamburg."

"Like what?"

"Lighting seven candles on Friday night. Slaughtering the lamb in the kosher way. And fasting on Saturday."

"So."

"It is all Jewish," Edward said. "Do you know about Jews?"

"I'm sure I've met one or two," Matt said. "And the priests mention them every now and then. Are they one of those splinter groups like the Mormons?"

"It's a whole religion."

"How do you know about Jews?" Matt asked.

"I went to school with some," Edward answered. "I had meals with them. The woman that the Mendozas call Santa Ester is one of the great Jewish heroines. They call her Hadassah."

"But the Mendozas are Catholics. They go to mass as regularly as a clock."

"Maybe Jews and Catholics have some of the same customs," Edward said. "I don't know my history too well, Matt, but I remember something about the Spanish forcing the Jews to either become Christians or get out of Spain. Lots of Jews converted in public, but in private they kept their traditions. Maybe some Mendoza ancestor was a Jew."

"Could be, but who cares," Matt said.

"You're right. Who cares. But it is curious."

CHAPTER THIRTEEN

1833

The fire in the corner fireplace was down to ashes and her warmth kindled his own. Now he would never be alone again.

"Welcome back to santa fe," Matt said, walking beside Edward's mules as he led his caravan into the plaza.

After meeting with the customs collector, Edward joined Matt at a table in La Dama's bar. "We haven't had any American news since last fall."

"I brought you the St. Louis and New Orleans papers," Edward said. "There's some good news: we reelected Andy Jackson." But, Edward continued, the New York financiers hated Jackson and his opposition to the Second Bank of the United States. Westerners claimed that the bank gave control of the American economy to Nicholas Biddle, the bank's president, and a coterie of eastern money men. Bitter over Jackson's reelection, Biddle had used the bank to screw down credit so tightly that he had created a financial panic.

"People are going broke left and right," Edward said.

"Did we get hurt?" Matt asked.

"I had enough cash on hand to buy eighteen wagon loads. Nobody can borrow a nickel, so that'll keep the number of wagons down this year. I hope you didn't take too many beaver pelts in trade this spring."

"I've got a about one hundred pounds."

"That's good. John Jacob Astor was right. He predicted that the style in men's hats would switch from beaver to silk. Beaver prices are down from six dollars to two in St. Louis."

"What books did you bring me?"

"There's a new book, *Domestic Manners of the Americans*, by some English woman, Frances Trollope. I read it on the way down the Trail. Just to give you a flavor, in one place she says, 'I do not like Americans. I do not like their principles. I do not like their manners. I do not like their opinions.' Some limeys can't get over the 1812 War and the Revolution."

"She sounds like some Mexicans I've met," Matt said, chuckling.

"And how is Celestina?"

"She's wonderful. We're counting the days until the wedding. Edward, I was going to ask David Mendoza to be my best man if you hadn't made it in time. But, now that you're here, I want you to stand up for me."

"Of course I will. What's been happening in Mexico since I left?"

"The politicos in Mexico City got rid of Bustamante and General Santa Anna is in power," Matt said. "Let's get the merchandise in the store before sundown."

"Mateo, this is Bishop Zubiría," Moisés said, pulling the bishop from a group of men. "Your Excellency, this is Mateo Collins."

"Yes, yes," the Bishop said. "You are the young man who is marrying Don Moisés's daughter. I want to talk to you about your conversion to our holy faith, my son."

"It is more of a restoration, Your Excellency, than a conversion," Matt said, stooping to kiss the ring on Bishop Zubiría's extended hand. "I was raised a Catholic by the Sisters of Charity, and I want to reaffirm my allegiance to the Church. How was your trip from Durango?"

"Long. Disagreeable. Uncomfortable. I see why no bishop has visited Santa Fe for more than seventy years. That trip across the *jornada del muerto* was particularly tedious. No water for days. Fortunately, the savages left us alone."

The bishop reached up and put his arm around Matt's shoulder and drew him into the group of hacendados. "How goes it with the *penitentes?*" Zubiría asked Moisés.

"They are getting more powerful all the time, Your Excellency," he replied. "The government's banishment of Spanish priests and the deaths of older ones has left us with few padres to minister to the people."

"I am working to send you more priests, but the government refuses to pay them, and they would starve on the small fees that your New

Mexican peons can pay. My sources tell me that the *penitentes* are undermining the Church."

"In my village, Peñasco, many of the devout cannot attend mass because the priests come so seldom," Rubén Mondragón, a Mendoza cousin, said. "Hundreds of couples live in sin with bastard children because there are no priests to perform weddings and baptisms. The Brotherhood provides many people with the only religious comfort they can find."

"You must not forget, Don Rubén, that you are at the end of civilization up here in New Mexico," Bishop Zubiría said. "Clearly, the people need religious guidance, but I have heard that the *penitentes* have run amok."

"The Brotherhood is filling a void,"Rubén answered.

"The *penitentes* have done some good, Rubén," Moisés said, "but I agree with His Excellency that they have gone too far."

"The Brotherhood helps the poor buy coffins," Rubén said, ignoring the bishop's warning signs. "They support the needy and pray for souls in purgatory."

"Don Rubén, you are overly sympathetic to these blasphemers," Bishop Zubiría said, has face assuming a harsh look.

Rubén continued his protest. "But, Your Excellency, with all respect, I must tell you that some priests live openly with their mistresses and their illegitimate children. I challenged a priest about this and he only laughed. He told me that he had abandoned celibacy so that he could better understand the nature of sin."

"Are you a Brotherhood member?" Bishop Zubiría snapped.

"The brothers are sworn to secrecy," Rubén said.

The bishop was furious at the challenge to his authority. In angry, but carefully measured tones, he said, "Because of your position in society, Señor Mondragón, I will not press this issue. But I caution you that there is no defense for people who engage in the morbid practice of flagellation. The so-called brothers are brothers of butchery, and, before I return to Durango, I will be issuing an edict outlawing the Brotherhood."

Rubén left the group and the others stood in silence until the Bishop lightened the mood with a joke. Matt and Edward also left and found a servant carrying a tray of wine.

"A lot of this Christian stuff doesn't make sense," Edward said.

"I thought you were a Lutheran."

"I'm not much of anything, Matt. My parents were religious, but I've been too busy making a living to pay much attention to it."

"Let's go talk to Celestina," Matt said.

Three days before the wedding, Moisés Mendoza presented Matt with a suit of clothes that he had commissioned from a Mexico City tailor. With Moisés looking on, Matt stood on an empty packing case in the Mendoza's tack room while a local tailor did the final fitting of a white silk shirt with ivory buttons. The tailor helped Matt slip into a red velvet waist-length jacket embroidered with silver rosettes, and marked the alterations with chalk. Then he fitted a pair of grey trousers with black pinstripes. From ankle to knee, white linen ruffles fluffed out of slits in the pants and rows of silver buttons decorated the outer leg seams.

To finish the costume, Moisés gave Matt a pair of boots made of soft Cordoban leather, a green silk waist sash, and a black, broad-brimmed felt hat with a flat crown. "I cannot thank you enough, Don Moisés. But, with this red hair of mine, nobody will mistake me for a Mexican gentleman," Matt said and laughed nervously.

"The clothes are a present to welcome you into our family and our Republic," Moisés said.

After Matt was sworn in as a Mexican citizen at a ceremony in the governor's palace the next morning, Matt and Edward crossed the plaza to their store. "You look like an authentic hacendado in that getup," Edward said, somewhat sharply.

"I'm beginning to feel like one," Matt said.

Edward's voice became heavy with sarcasm. "Maybe what you like is the children who'll never learn to read and write because there's no teachers. Or the people dying because there's no medicine."

Matt was surprised by his partner's attack on Mexico. *It may be*, Matt thought quickly, *that Edward is afraid that Celestina might come between us.* In the past, when they had had disputes it was usually Matt who sought an accommodation. But the unexpectedness of Edward's words had caught him off guard and he struck back.

"The New Mexicans may lack some things, but one thing is certain: Spaniards have a dignity that Americans will never have."

"Among the grandees, maybe. But the ones that don't have anything to eat but tortillas and beans aren't so dignified."

"The peons," Matt flared, "have learned to accept their lot with a cheerfulness that Americans can't begin to understand. Americans are a bunch of troublemakers who don't know their place. They're too busy clawing their way through life to enjoy it."

"Your beloved peons are busy clawing their way out from under a Church that keeps them mired in poverty and ignorance."

"For them, the Church is the best thing in their lives," Matt countered.

"The spiritual life they're so proud of keeps them wallowing in their backward-looking past. In America, a man can do anything he's big enough to do. Look at me! When I got off the boat in New Orleans I didn't have a damned thing and didn't know a damned soul."

"That's what infuriates me," Matt shot back, "that sanctimonious, condescending, Puritan certitude that everything American is superior."

Matt kicked over keg of whiskey, slammed his fist on a box of sugar candy, crushing it, and stormed out of the shop. It was the first serious argument they had had. The next day they treated one another with exaggerated politeness.

Matt had always known that his partner did not share his fascination with New Mexico, but, until their outburst the day before he had not realized that Edward felt so bitterly about his new country. Edward, Matt knew, had the immigrant's fervent belief in America's democracy, and perhaps he had overreacted to Mexico as a symbol of the Old World that he had left behind. Or Edward might resent his marriage into one of New Mexico's grandest families, which would automatically raise Matt to the level of society that Edward hated. *Whatever the reasons*, Matt thought, *I'm not going to let this come between us.*

That night at a small party arranged by a group of American proprietors, Matt cornered Edward by himself. "Look, old friend," Matt said, "we've always been able to hash out our differences. What's the problem?"

"I'm afraid you'll get lost in all that high-falutin' Mexican bullshit." Edward was much drunker than Matt.

"Edward, we've been friends and partners for six years. And I'm telling you true, in teamster patois, 'I ain't gonna get lost in nothin'.'"

"Damnit, Matt, listen to me!" Edward said, agitated. Everyone at the party had fallen silent and turned to listen to Edward. "You don't appreciate the country you were born into. You don't know what it's like to have your life decided for you on the day you're born."

"I was born a Yankee," Matt said, surprised by his partner's vehemence, "and in spirit I'll always be one." He took a sip of brandy and swirled it in his mouth, giving himself time to think.

It was the evening before his wedding and he wasn't going to get caught up in an argument that if continued could lead to a permanent break. Matt whistled the first few bars of "Yankee Doodle" and did a jig step. Edward smiled slightly. Matt continued in a teasing tone. "You're just jealous that you're still a balding bachelor and that I'm marring the most elegant, the most gorgeous woman in New Mexico."

Edward, too, realized that they had been on the brink of ending their friendship. He gave Matt a hearty *abrazo* and risked one last comment. "Trying to perform that balancing act between being an American and a Mexican isn't going to be easy, my friend. Some day you might have to walk a fine line, but, if there's anybody in New Mexico who could do it better than you, I'd like to meet him. I apologize for my remarks, Matt. You and I will always be friends, no matter what."

The next morning Matt and Edward climbed into a carriage loaded with crates of presents and drove to the Mendoza's house. Edward stopped the carriage and Matt dismounted and banged on the *zaguán* door. A servant peeped out a small window in the door, waved, and flashed a smile of genuine joy.

When the massive double doors swung open, a crowd of squealing children rushed out and threw flower petals at the groom. He walked into the patio, where Moisés Mendoza took him in a warm and lengthy *abrazo*. Over Moisés's shoulder, Matt saw Celestina dash across the patio, followed by a covey of female cousins and friends, and disappear through a door.

In Celestina's bedroom, a servant used a maul and wedge to pry open the wooden crates that contained Matt's wedding gifts. "Give me the nails," Celestina told the servant, "so that I can give them to father." Her friends unpacked the presents—green and red silk; a Chinese shawl that Matt had specially picked because it was as blue-black as Celestina's eyes; two Persian rugs; four silver place settings; and six dresses that St. Louis's finest seamstress had made from Parisian patterns.

"Your foreigner must be very rich, Celestina," her cousin Rosaria said.

"He has been successful in his business," Celestina answered, managing not to gloat. "But he is not a foreigner. When you get to know him, cousin, you will see that he has adopted our ways."

"Still, he is a Yankee," Rosaria said.

———

The Mendozas had transformed their house into a festival palace for their only daughter's wedding. Fresh piñon and ponderosa pine branches twined around pillars and scented the patio. Four dozen tin lanterns from Guadalajara would spread a warm glow into the night. Celestina's cousins had hung white paper streamers embossed in gold with images of the Virgin of Guadalupe. And the garden flowers were in full, early summer bloom.

Mendoza relatives and friends from up and down the Rio Grande filled the patio. The ladies drank thick hot chocolate made from Sara's special recipe, and the men crowded around casks of El Paso wine and American whiskey. From tables under the *portales*, guests used blue corn tortillas to scoop chilis and beans from Zuñi bowls decorated with black-and-white geometric designs.

The servants had cleaned the soot off the fireplace's mantle tiles, revealing the Mendoza coat of arms. They had whitewashed the *sala* walls with a fresh coat of *tierra blanca*, and, for dancing, they had rolled back the black-and-white-checked *jerga* rugs and burnished the dirt floor with smooth, round river rocks until it shined like rich mahogany.

The maids had spent hours with feather dusters clearing cobwebs from the *latillas* and *vigas*, and had hung billowing muslin sheets to catch any dirt that might sift down from the ceiling. Sara had taken her finest Oaxaca wool blankets, woven so tightly that they could hold water, out of their storage trunks and covered the chairs of honor, where Matt and Celestina would sit at one end of the *sala*. Next to the chairs, an ebony table inlaid with mother-of-pearl held Sara's silver and crystal, which the bride and groom would use for the wedding feast.

That afternoon Celestina and her parents rode to the plaza in their four-horse carriage. It had rained the day before, and they had to hold tightly to the awning posts when the wheels listed into deep ruts. Behind the carriage, a train of walking and riding relatives and friends followed musicians playing religious and popular tunes. When the procession passed in front of the palace door, the governor joined in the walk across the plaza to La Castrense.

Moisés and Sara Mendoza stepped out of the carriage first and helped Celestina keep her bulky wedding gown from dragging in the filth and mud. When the guests were seated, Bishop Zubiría emerged from the small door beside the altar. The bishop motioned for Matt and Celestina to move closer to one another. Moisés passed Celestina's hand to Matt's and said in archaic Spanish, "Here is she whom you sought."

Four huge candles on the altar made the silver embroidery on Matt's jacket glisten as he held Celestina's hand and turned toward the Bishop of Durango. José Antonio Zubiría adjusted his foot-tall miter and tugged at his splendid robes until they hung straight, and began the ceremony. After the nuptial mass, the couple turned and faced the crowd. While Celestina's maid of honor knelt to arrange the train of her white satin gown, Matt and Celestina kissed lightly and made their way down the aisle into the afternoon sun.

"I can't tell you how much I love you," Matt whispered in English as they waited for the carriage, which the servants had garlanded with flowers. "We shall have an excellent life, my husband," she answered in Spanish.

"The most excellent."

When the carriage stopped in front of the Mendoza's *zaguán*, the doors swung open and musicians came out to lead the wedding party inside. On the patio, the guests danced the *jarabe tapatío* and stamped their heels to the thundering rhythm of the *raspa*. During the next tune, Celestina's uncle from Albuquerque stood beside her and made up verses praising her beauty and noble ancestry. The crowd cheered, inspiring Rubén Mondragòn to improvise a poem he dedicated to Matt:

> "Not so many years ago, there were no Yankees to
> be seen.
> But now they are everywhere, and their dollars are
> turning this dry country green.
> Some say that they are only interested in greed.
> But that is not true; they also like to plant their seed.
> Some say that they are colossal boors and louts; that
> they are vulgar and crude.
> But I would never say that publicly, because that would
> be very rude."

The crowd fell silent. "You are the lout," Moisés shouted, grabbing his cousin Rubén's arm and pulling him away. Two other guests hustled

Rubén to the back patio. "Mateo, please accept my apologies for Rubén," Moisés said. "He is drunk."

"No offense is taken, Don Moisés," Matt said stiffly, and turned to dance with Celestina.

When the sun went down, the soft air went chill and the dancing moved into the *sala*. In the candlelight, mica flecks in the new white-wash sparkled. The white paste on the women's faces made them look ghostly and the heat turned the men's faces red.

For those who didn't care to dance, Moisés had allowed a monte dealer to set up a table in the back patio, and he had contributed four of his best birds for the cockfights that were a traditional part of wedding festivities. Celestina had disappeared for some unknown reason, and Matt ducked his head and went down the long, low passageway to the back patio.

Matt stood at the back of a crowd that had formed around two trainers and their caged roosters. He had seen cockfights before, but he had never warmed to the sport. Each trainer reached in his cage and caught a bird, flipped it on its back, and strapped iron spikes to its legs. Then the trainers jerked out two tail feathers to infuriate the gamecocks and tossed them on the ground.

The birds circled for a few seconds and then flew at one another in a flurry of feathers and squawking that roused the crowd. The birds rolled on the ground, sending up clouds of dust. Their legs flailed until Moisés's rooster's spike landed squarely in the eye of his opponent. Matt winced when the wounded gamecock jumped up with the spike in his eye and ran in a circle, dragging the other bird, which was flapping helplessly behind it. After quick snaps of his head, the injured rooster dislodged the spike and blood spurted from the empty eye socket. His trainer tried to snag the one-eyed gamecock, but, in its pain and fright, it ran in a circle until it fell dead.

"*Hijo de puta!*" a losing bettor shouted.

"I won," Susano Baca said, chuckling and turning to collect his winnings from a man behind him.

"I am going back to the dancing," Matt said to Baca. "Good luck with the other fights."

"I always have good luck, Don Mateo."

Near midnight, Celestina disappeared from the *sala*. Shortly, she reappeared from her bedroom wearing the first of the new dresses Matt had given her; repeating this until she had displayed them all. After she had modeled the last dress, a gray silk that was cut to emphasize her bosom,

Matt waited several minutes and slipped into Celestina's bedroom. Without speaking, her godmother, Gabriela Oñate y Rael, stopped brushing the bride's hair and left.

Celestina stood by the bed, her figure silhouetted by two candles behind her. The blue-black Chinese shawl Matt had given her hung to her knees and underneath she wore a white cotton nightgown with tiny pink roses stitched across the bodice. Matt drew her to him awkwardly, and they both laughed when her face landed in the middle of his chest. "Would you rather wait until another day?" he asked.

"I am twenty-one, and I have waited a long time for this moment," she said.

"This has been an exhausting day for you. If you'd rather wait, I'll understand."

"Let's begin, and we will see," she said.

She pushed him until he sat on the bed. She sat beside him, and they kissed and listened to the deep bass thump of the *guitarrón* coming from the patio. He reached under her shawl and stroked her shoulders, his fingers sliding over the smooth cotton nightgown. He trembled slightly and fumbled with the small buttons at the back of her neck.

"Let's stand up and I'll turn around," she said.

He undid the buttons, kissed the strands of hair at the nape of her neck, and stood back and watched as she pulled the gown over her shoulders. "I told you at the church that I couldn't tell you how much I love you," he said, his throat constricting so that he could not swallow. "Now I can tell you. I ache when I'm away from you. The sight of you stops me in my tracks."

"We'll always be happy," she said. "I love you too."

He fumbled with his own buttons until he stood naked by the fireplace, where a pan of water was warming on the coals. He bathed himself carefully and tiptoed across the room and slid under the sheets.

"You're all wet," Celestina said. "And cold. Roll on your side." She wrapped her body around his back, put an arm over his waist, and pillowed her head on his shoulder. For a moment he thought of the mother he had never had. "What are these dark splotches on your shoulders?" she asked.

"Freckles."

"Freckles? What's the Spanish word?"

"I don't know." The fire in the corner fireplace was down to ashes, and her warmth kindled his own. Now he would never be alone again.

CHAPTER FOURTEEN

1833

"In our world, being a friend to Americans is not always desirable, and being shrewd is not feminine. And the King of Spain will not make me a duchess for being in business."

MATT HAD GONE TO THE MOUNTAINS HIMSELF TO SELECT THE straightest spruce logs for the *vigas* in his and Celestina's new house, a house that he built in the classic Spanish *U* shape. The west wing was the bedroom, with enough space for Celestina to put the desk she sat at to administer her household. The east wing housed the three servant girls that Sara insisted that Celestina needed, and in the middle there were rooms for the *sala,* dining room, and kitchen. For the central patio, Celestina had taken cuttings from her mother's garden and planted bougainvillea and, in a spot that got sun all day, thyme, bay leaf, and sage. Their house was not as grand as the Mendoza's, but when they had children they planned to add more rooms.

The house, with its two-foot-thick adobe walls, faced south so that the sun coming through the doors and windows would warm it in winter. Matt imported glass panes from Missouri at great expense, and, because nobody in Santa Fe knew how to work with the precious material, he taught himself to cut and install it. No other house in Santa Fe had nine glass windows, and on weekends men took their curious families to inspect the phenomena.

One of their first guests—after they had held a family house warming—was an American couple. Jim and Margaret Perryman arrived exactly at the specified time, seven o'clock. Margaret was just over thirty. She had dull blond hair and a plain face that a beautiful, toothy Irish smile rescued. She had been a school teacher when she met and wed

Jim in Memphis. And, even though it was against school rules for expectant women to teach, she kept her pregnancy a secret until her belly swelled. Then, the school trustees fired her.

Jim was a slender man with a massive jaw that stuck out like the blade of a shovel. People who had just met him couldn't take their eyes off it, and his friends teased him about it, wondering how he could hold his head up with all the extra weight. Jim had clerked in hotels up and down the frontier, and had gotten lucky speculating in western land. A wanderer, he invested his profits in merchandise and came down the Santa Fe Trail. When Jim got to the capital, he visited the Collins & Waterman store and met Matt. Matt wanted Celestina to meet an American woman and immediately invited the Perrymans to dinner.

"Welcome to our home," Celestina said in English. She guided the Perrymans to a *banco* beside an outdoor fireplace under the *portal*. "We have found this to be our favorite place to sit," she said. Celestina clapped her hands and a servant appeared and curtseyed. "María Dolores, bring the drinks. Now, Mrs. Perryman, you must tell us what brought you to Santa Fe."

"My husband thought it would be interesting," Margaret answered. "But, we'll see. Mr. Collins tells me that you have only been married a few weeks."

"We are still getting used to our new house," Celestina said.

"Enough lady talk," Matt said. "Jim, tell us what's been happening in the States."

"Credit is starting to ease a little, but everybody's still afraid of paper money. It looks like President Jackson will be able to put a lid on Nicholas Biddle and his East Coast crowd."

"I read that the British are about to outlaw slavery," Matt said.

"Who cares what the English do," Jim bristled. "Slavery's the bedrock of our country—the South at least. And it'll continue."

"Let's don't talk about slavery," Celestina said. "It's poisonous. Tell me, Mrs. Perryman, did you bring any dress patterns with you? Matt gave me some beautiful fabrics as a wedding gift and I'd like to have them made into dresses."

"I did," Margaret said. "Why don't you come by our room at our hotel—you call it *posada* I think—in the next day or so and we'll have tea and look at the patterns. They're from Philadelphia and New York."

"I would love to," Celestina said.

María Dolores announced that dinner was ready.

Celestina and Margaret Perryman ordered tea from a *posada* servant. Margaret gave Celestina the hotel room's only chair and she cleared away the dress patterns they had been looking at and sat on the bed. "Jim's thinking about buying this *posada*," Margaret told Celestina. "The current manager, Señor Flores, is leaving and Jim and I want to stay here for a few years."

"What made you decide to stay?"

"Jim thinks he can make good money here. And back in Tennessee our daughter Betsy had terrible trouble breathing," Margaret said, picking up the little girl who was trying to crawl under Celestina's chair. "Twice, we thought she'd die for sure. But since we've been out West that brassy cough and heaving to catch her breath have cleared up. I'm convinced that the muggy air back home was what was hurting her. If we give her a few years in this dry air, her lungs will get stronger."

"There are many people who come to Santa Fe to cure consumption," Celestina said.

"The doctor said Betsy had some kind of croup, but it could have been consumption. Whatever it was, it's gone. In addition to your healthful climate, Mrs. Collins, I'm dazzled by your sunsets, particularly when the clouds are low enough to reflect the light. If anybody ever doubted there was a God, watching the sun go down across the desert would make them believers."

"Try some of these cookies, Mrs. Collins," Margaret continued. "I bought them from a girl on the plaza this morning. They have those wonderful toasted piñon nuts in them." She smiled and nodded at Celestina and then at Betsy, and invited Celestina to hold the child. Celestina took the girl on her lap, kissed her, and fed her a small bite of cookie.

"The cookies are good and Betsy thinks so too," Celestina said. "They remind me of my mother's cook. When I was a child, she made the best *pan dulce* you ever tasted. When I would smell the sugar and cinnamon baking in the *horno*, I'd run outside and stand there until it was done, and she'd give me a bun that was so hot I had to toss it from hand to hand till it cooled. But, enough about New Mexico, Mrs. Perryman, tell me about America."

"What do you want to know?"

"Maybe you could just tell me about yourself."

Margaret related the story of her family. Her mother and father had married in Virginia, moved to Georgia, then to Alabama, and then to Mississippi, where she was born—and then on to Tennessee. Her father was a farmer, and she and her eight siblings had lived mostly in one-room log cabins. Although her father was illiterate, her mother taught the children to read and write. When she was twenty she met Jim, the son of a wealthy doctor who owned a grist mill. "Before Doctor Perryman went bust during a financial panic," Margaret said, "folks said that Jim was a pretty good catch, even though you could use that big jaw of his to plow with."

"All that moving around seems so strange," Celestina said.

"Sometimes we moved because the land played out. Or because Pa thought there was more opportunity out West. Or, in Jim's case, because it's more exciting. Maybe there's something in our blood. I don't really know."

"How can we make you feel more at home in Santa Fe?" Celestina asked.

"Mrs. Collins, I'll make a deal with you. If Jim buys the hotel, I'll need to speak Spanish so's I can help him run it. If you'll teach me Spanish, you can practice your English. Not that you need much help."

"I would appreciate that, Mrs. Perryman. Matt has taught me a lot, but he teaches me about men things. I don't have a vocabulary for sewing or cooking or taking care of babies. And I don't know any of the words for a woman's body parts."

"I know what you mean, Mrs. Collins. Being on that Trail with nothing but men for ten weeks reminded me that there's some things that you can only talk about with another woman."

"Would you do me a favor?" Celestina asked.

"Of course."

"Could I touch your hair. Until I met you, I'd never seen a woman with blonde hair."

"Nacho Flores doesn't own the *posada*," Matt told Jim Perryman while they were sipping wine at La Dama's. "La Dama owns it. People joke that half the Santa Fe Trail's profits wind up in Doña Julia's strongbox. In any event, she's bought up a pot full of property."

"Well, she ain't getting my profits," Jim Perryman said. "I'd rather sink it into the *posada*. The ones that makes the money on the frontier are the ones that supplies the services. I'll let the teamsters and proprietors sweat it out on that goddamned dusty Trail. For me, I'd rather be the one that sells whiskey and rents hotel rooms. How much do you think La Dama would want for it?"

"You won't be buying it," Matt said.

"How come?"

"Once La Dama buys something, she never sells it. She's like the *hacendados*. If they were down to their last cent in cash, they still wouldn't sell a square foot of their property. Besides, you're a foreigner, and Mexican law says you can't own land."

"Maybe we could work out something else," Jim said. "Nacho Flores says he's moving to Chihuahua next month to try his hand at mining. I'd like to talk to La Dama and see what she'll do."

Matt went to the back of La Dama's chair at the monte table and whispered in her ear. After she finished the hand, she stood and Matt followed her out the back door. They turned right and stepped around puddles of water that had collected in hard-packed potholes. "What is all this water?" Matt asked. "It has not rained for more than a week."

"I have twelve girls working for me now," Julia Barela said, giving him a jovial smile, "and they have to douche once in a while. Here, through this door."

Her office was a small room with one window on each wall, and she had planked its floor. Matt stopped and looked curiously at the wood, planks from dismantled freight wagons. "It's the only planked floor in Santa Fe," La Dama told Matt, proud of her new acquisition. "Now, what can I do for you, Don Mateo?"

Matt told her that Nacho Flores was leaving and that Jim Perryman was interested in leasing her *posada* on the southeast corner of the plaza. "Jim," Matt said, "has brought his wife and daughter with him, and Señora Perryman will work in the hotel."

"I have seen her in the plaza," La Dama said. "Thin lips. Eyes the color of a jaybird. Dirty blond. Isn't she the first American woman to come down the Santa Fe Trail?"

"As far as I know, she is," Matt answered. "She and her husband are serious, hardworking people, Doña Julia. They will run a reputable establishment."

"There are no reputable establishments in this town, Don Mateo." La Dama slapped her belly and laughed loudly, not the least insulted by the implication of Matt's remark.

"You know what I mean, Doña Julia. They will not allow the wild ones and the drunks to tear up your property."

"At one time or another, Don Mateo, all Yankees are wild and drunk. Señor Perryman will not have any business if he keeps them out."

"That may be true," Matt said, grinning to show that he was amused by her jab at his former countrymen.

"Bring him to my office and we will talk. And say hello to Adelina Romero on your way out. She misses you."

"You know that I am out of that, Doña Julia."

"You are not a monk just because you got married."

While Matt was guiding Jim to La Dama's office, Jim asked, "Should I call her La Dama or Doña Julia or Señorita Barela?"

"In the saloon, you can call her Dama. But when you're doing business call her Doña Julia. It's more dignified, and she likes that," Matt said.

"Doña Julia, let me present Jaime Perryman. His Spanish is not very good." Matt switched to English: "Jim, would you rather that I stay to translate?"

"Please do. Doña Julia, it is a great pleasure to meet the most famous woman in Santa Fe," Jim said.

"The most famous woman?" she said, swelling with mock anger. "What do you think it is that makes me famous? Is it because I am the best monte dealer? Because I have the most attractive girls?"

"Doña Julia, I did not mean to offend you," Jim said. He glanced toward Matt in hope of salvation and missed La Dama's mischievous smile. "I meant that as a complement. Your admirers—and there are many—say that you are the best businessman, the shrewdest person in New Mexico, and that you like dealing with Americans."

"In our world, being a friend to Americans is not always desirable, and being shrewd is not feminine," La Dama said with false gravity. Matt knew that she was enjoying dangling Jim on a string. "And the King of Spain will not make me a duchess for being in business. Do you have any other complements?"

"Doña Julia—La Dama, I do not mean . . ." Jim stammered. "Matt, can you clarify what I mean?"

"I cannot be offended," La Dama said, laughing so hard that her bosom and belly shook. "Many people have tried, but I have stared down murderous drunks and lost thousands at monte in one night. Nothing ruffles me. You are right, though. I am a good businessman and I am damned shrewd. So, let us talk about the *posada*. What do you have in mind?"

"I was thinking of leasing the property."

"What experience do you have running a hotel?" she asked.

"I have worked in them for many years and I managed hotels in Memphis and Independence, Missouri. My wife helped me part of the time. Margaret is a very clean woman. Everyone commented on how clean she kept the hotel. Of course, we had slaves to do the heavy work."

"General Santa Anna could send you an army division, Señor Perryman, but even they could not clean up after your Yankee teamsters," she said.

"I will oversee the operation," he said, missing her joke. "We will serve food and have a bar. And Mrs. Perryman and I have talked of putting in a bathhouse and a barber shop."

"From the smell of them, most of your countrymen have never heard of soap and water. What kind of rent do you have in mind?"

"I was thinking of forty pesos a month."

"Just a minute ago you said that I was shrewd. But your offer looks like you think I am stupid," she said in rapid-fire Spanish. "Do you think I am a *pinche* idiot? Nacho Flores paid me sixty silver pesos every month."

"Matt, I didn't catch everything she said. Maybe I don't want to know," Jim said, smiling weakly.

"She says your offer is too low," Matt said blandly.

"Doña Julia, my wife and I have inspected the hotel, and we found a number of problems with the building. Nacho Flores has let it run down badly. The roof leaks, tobacco smoke has stained the whitewash yellow, and vermin parade across the mattresses like Napoleon's armies."

"It is true that Nacho Flores is a terrible manager," La Dama said. "It is also true that he is a slovenly man. But for four years he paid me sixty pesos a month."

"Perhaps," Jim said, "Señor Flores paid too much rent and did not have the money to maintain your property as you would like it to be kept."

"I must have sixty."

"Doña Julia," Matt said. "Perhaps I could suggest another way."

"And that is?"

"Señor Perryman would pay you a percentage of his income."

"What percent? And would it be before or after deducting expenses?" she asked, squinting her eyes.

"After," Jim said, giving Matt a grateful look for keeping the negotiations open.

"Who would count the expenses?" she asked, and answered: "You would, Señor Perryman."

"Make it four percent before taking out expenses," Jim said, "and I will give you a monthly accounting."

"Six."

"Done at six," Jim said. "Doña Julia, shrewdness is not an adequate word to describe your business skills."

"I have learned from you Americans," she said, and waved both hands regally to indicate that the meeting was over.

CHAPTER FIFTEEN

1836–1838

"We saw what happens when Yankee subversives worm their way into our Republic. The Texians lied when they swore loyalty to Mexico. Then, Mister Collins, your fellow Anglo-Saxons stole our territory."

THE WINTER OF 1836 HAD BEEN HARSH WITH COLD, BUT THERE was little snow, and the lack of spring rains had left the high mountain desert around Santa Fe drier than it had been for years. Dispirited by the drought and by the rumors of their new governor's arrogance, few had bothered to turn out for the *baile* celebrating his arrival from Mexico City.

Governor Albino Pérez had kept a small crowd of Santa Fe's elite waiting for almost two hours in the *posada*'s ballroom, and they were restless. "What is the government doing?" Moisés Mendoza groused to a group of friends. "Sending us this Mexico City dandy who doesn't know a damned thing about New Mexico or New Mexicans."

"Pipe down, Don Moisés, here he comes," Matt said, turning to shake hands with New Mexico's new governor.

Albino Pérez was a slight man, small in height, in bone structure, and in flesh. His face was almost cadaverously pale, and, to anyone who mentioned it, he proudly proclaimed that not so much as a drop of negro or Indian blood had tainted his lineage. Although his outfit had been out of fashion for many years, on formal occasions such as the *baile* he wore a powdered wig, satin knee britches and stockings, and a purple silk tailcoat.

Wags claimed that he wore this Spanish court dress as testimony to his royalist leanings, and, in fact, an ancestor five generations earlier had been a disenfranchised marquis who the King had banished to the New World. Although Pérez had no legal claim to a coat of arms, he had designed his own and had it monogrammed on his shirts and, some said, his underwear.

"Gentlemen, let us toast to New Mexico's prosperity during my administration," Governor Pérez said, taking a glass of wine. "How kind of you to invite me to this *baile*. It seems that you do more dancing in Santa Fe than we do in the capital."

"Other than going to church, Governor, it is our only entertainment," Matt said.

"You are an American, are you not?" Pérez asked. "But you have no accent. When most Yankees pronounce 'd' in Spanish, it sounds like the thud of a boot being thrown on the floor."

"I *was* an American, Your Excellency, but now I am a Mexican citizen," Matt said.

Pérez excused himself and worked his way around the ballroom until he came to Sara Mendoza. He took her hand and led her to the center of the room to begin the festivities. After a fast-paced waltz that he danced with gentlemanly grace, he took Sara back to her lady friends and joined a group of men. The talk turned to General Santa Anna, who was then in Washington waiting for a chance to return to Mexico. Although the Texians had humiliated the general at the San Jacinto Battle, Santa Anna's switch to the conservative cause had made Pérez a supporter.

"Santa Anna has finally seen the light," Pérez said, carefully adjusting the red-white-and-green sash across his cloth-of-gold waistcoat. "At one time, Santa Anna flirted with those absurd liberals. But he too is fed up with the lack of order that those radicals have created. Obedience to authority. That is what the country needs. Not that democratic drivel that has seduced a few romantic fools."

Pérez reached into his coat pocket and took out a silver snuff box from Taxco that the new president had given him on the occasion of his swearing-in ceremony at the Palacio Nacional. He sniffed tobacco up each nostril, sneezed, and drew a lace handkerchief from his sleeve and daintily daubed the excess tobacco from his mustache.

"But concentrating power in Mexico City is what caused the Texians to revolt," Moisés said. He tried, unsuccessfully, to keep his loathing of the conservative government out of his voice, but Pérez, arching an eyebrow, did not fail to notice it.

"There are stories that the government wants us to send our taxes to Mexico City," a Bernalillo hacendado said. "If history repeats itself, we will get nothing in return. If we cannot keep the taxes we collect from the Americans, we cannot protect ourselves from the Indians."

"The president understands all this," Pérez said. "He realizes that Santa Fe is too dependent on the trade with the Anglo-Saxons. That is why he sent me here—to guide New Mexico back to its traditional trading patterns. Before I finish, this province will once again be firmly in the Mexican fold."

"How is the government going to raise money?" Moisés asked.

"I have not announced it yet, but Congress has created new taxes—and I intend to collect them."

"People are joking that they will levy taxes on men for sleeping with their wives," Matt said, smiling.

"Remarks like that could get you into trouble, Mister Collins," the governor said, deliberately using the American form of address and pronouncing it "Meester."

Pérez had been in Santa Fe for only three months when Captain Diego Zambrano led a mounted procession into the plaza. The squad of soldiers and their two prisoners stopped in front of the palace's main door and dismounted. On the governor's orders, Zambrano had arrested Moisés and Matt earlier that morning.

"Gentlemen," he motioned to them, "follow me."

Zambrano guided them through the labyrinth of passages to the palace's east wing. "Governor Pérez has remodeled a suite of rooms for his needs," the captain said, showing them into a reception room. On one wall, carved cherubs cavorted on a large gilded frame that set off a mirror that reflected candlelight from a crystal chandelier. "Take a seat," Zambrano said, pointing to a plush sofa. "I will tell his secretary that you are here."

"My God, Don Moisés, so much elegance," Matt said. "He must have brought these things from Mexico City."

"All except the chandelier," Moisés said. "When Don Albino came through Albuquerque on the way up here, he visited my cousin's house. He suggested that the chandelier might better serve the Mexican Republic if it hung in the governor's palace. It was a family heirloom, and she refused to give it up. When he threatened to requisition her horses for the army, she gave him the chandelier. He said it was just a loan, but you wait; when he goes back to Mexico City, the chandelier will go with him."

"Follow me," said the secretary, a short man dressed in knee britches and a powder blue tailcoat with red piping and a collar that was up to his ears.

"He looks like a lackey for Louis XV," Matt whispered in English.

"Or Iturbide," Moisés said, referring to the creole army officer who had made himself emperor after Mexico became independent in 1821.

The governor's secretary preceded Matt and Moisés into a large room and announced, "Your Excellency, Don Moisés Mendoza and Don Mateo Collins are at your disposal." Then he bowed to the waist and backed out of the room. A deep-pile Chinese carpet covered most of the dirt floor. On the walls, polychromed sconces held statutes of saints, and behind Pérez hung a life-size painting of Matías de Gálvez, a Spanish viceroy in the 1700s.

Governor Pérez remained seated behind his desk. His eyes, Matt noted, looked like a goat's, so pale that the blue was only hinted at, and so expressionless that it seemed that there were no feelings behind them. "Come forward, gentlemen," he said without asking them to sit in the chairs beside his desk.

"I see that you are partial to the Spanish viceroys," Moisés said. "You may know that Emperor Charles V appointed my ancestor, Antonio de Mendoza, the first Spanish viceroy in fifteen thirty-five."

"Perhaps we share a *querencia* for the old ways," Pérez said. The striking of the hour by a bronze desk clock with a well-muscled nude statue of Apollo, the god of male beauty, distracted Matt's attention for a second.

"But, Don Albino—" Moisés said.

"Excellency," Pérez interjected.

"Excellency," Moisés said, "with all due respect, it was not necessary to have armed guards bring us to your office."

"We felt that it was necessary because of what appears to be criminal activity," Pérez said.

"I do not understand," Moisés said.

"Our sources tell us that you and Don Mateo have understated the number of sheep you own by ten thousand head. With our new tax of twenty-five cents per head, that means that you have cheated the New Mexican treasury."

"Your Excellency, let me explain," Matt said.

"We do not need an explanation," Pérez snapped. His pallid face reddened in anger, but his eyes were incapable of expression.

"Your Excellency," Matt said, "the people are very unhappy with these new taxes. And it was unjust taxes that made the Americans revolt against England."

"Mister Collins," Pérez said, pronouncing "meester" slowly and deliberately, "last March we saw what happens when Yankee subversives worm their way into our Republic. Mister Esteban Austin and the other Texians lied when they swore loyalty to Mexico. Then, Mister Collins, your fellow Anglo-Saxons stole our territory. Your Texian swine even claim that they own all the land up to the east bank of the Rio Grande."

"But, Your Excellency," Matt said, "New Mexicans have never been required to pay this kind of tax."

"You gentlemen owe the government twenty-five hundred pesos, plus fines. Because of your delinquency, I am unable to buy new muskets or boots for our soldiers so that they can properly defend our Republic from the Indians."

"We are loyal patriots," Matt said, "and we are prepared to do whatever is necessary to support the Republic."

"Perhaps you are. But we know that you and Don Moisés read treasonous material. The rantings of that idiot Rousseau and that trash by Mister Madison. We do not want a rabble-ocracy like you have in America."

"But—" Matt said.

Pérez cut him off. "Excuse me, gentlemen. Let us stop this emotional discussion. We need twenty-five hundred pesos in taxes immediately. We will forgive the fines."

"Many of the sheep you are talking about are owned by our shepherds," Moisés said.

"We do not have time to send out tax collectors to the mountains to find a bunch of shepherds. You two will pay the tax, and then you can collect from them."

"But they have little or no money, Your Excellency," Matt said.

"That is not our problem."

"We cannot raise twenty-five hundred pesos in cash overnight," Moisés said.

"Guard," the governor shouted. A sergeant and five privates entered the room. "Jail them. Chain their feet. If they try to escape, shoot them."

The guards marched Matt and Moisés to a small cell near the back of the palace's west wing. The sergeant ordered them to strip, searched their clothes, and took their pocket watches and the few coins they had. The room had no furniture, and a small window with wooden bars provided the only light. At sundown a guard brought them a plate of fried corn meal cakes and a pitcher of water.

"A French claret would go nicely with this elegant meal," Matt joked when the guard left.

"I am sure that His Excellency is enjoying a good wine with his dinner," Moisés said with no trace of humor. "He knows that every hacendado in New Mexico undercounts his herds. That *hijo de puta*." Matt was shocked. His father-in-law almost never used profanity.

"Your mistake is having an American son-in-law," Matt said.

"Our biggest crime is going against the conservatives," Moisés said. "They are terrified that too much democracy will send the peons on a rampage."

"I need to relieve myself," Matt said. "Guard!"

"Yes, señor."

"Can you take me to the latrine?"

"No, señor."

"What is it you want? A payment?"

"Señor, if the governor found out that I let you use the latrine, he would have my head."

"Can you bring me a bucket?"

"No, señor. Use the corner."

"How do we clean it out?"

"You do not, señor. We have orders to give you no amenities."

Governor Pérez allowed Celestina and Sara to visit their husbands after their fifth day in prison. When they opened the door, sunlight cut across the room and raised the flies swarming over the pile of excrement in the corner.

"Guard," Moisés yelled, "will you permit us to meet outside, in the courtyard?"

"You cannot leave your cell. The ladies can stand at the door."

"You have no beds, no blankets. And the filth," Celestina said. She raised her skirt and untied her petticoat. "Use this to cover the droppings."

"Is there any news about our trial?" Matt asked. "We have heard nothing."

"Governor Pérez will try your case himself," Celestina said. "He is the judge and jury, and he will decide the punishment. David was at La Dama's last night, and Pérez was there drunk. He says he is going to keep you in jail to show everyone that even the hacendados must pay their taxes."

"Pérez wants to use our trial to take people's minds off his failure to stop the Navajo attacks up north," Moisés said. "The guard says that the Navajos killed three soldiers near Abiquiú."

The guard returned. "Time to go, ladies."

Days later, Diego Zambrano unlocked the cell door and motioned for the prisoners to follow him. In his office, Governor Pérez waved his hand to indicate that they should stand in front of his desk. "You may leave, Captain. Now, gentlemen, tell us about your stay in the palace." Matt and Moisés did not answer. "By your silence, we assume that it has not been pleasant. There is a way you can remedy your situation."

"Yes?" Matt said.

"We would release you immediately if you agree to pay your taxes in full, plus a fine of five hundred pesos, plus one thousand for me."

Matt and Moisés told him they had little cash on hand, and Matt asked for a reduction of the taxes. "That is impossible," Pérez said, "a government auditor is on his way from Mexico City to check our income and expenses." Both sides said nothing until the governor broke the silence—the law, he said calmly, permitted him to jail them in the nearest prison at Durango for seven years. And Durango was three months travel time from Santa Fe. They would, he said, never see their families.

Matt and Moisés asked for time to confer. Pérez allowed them to speak in whispers at the far end of his office, and when they finished Matt proposed reducing the fine to one hundred pesos and letting Pérez select one thousand dollars worth of merchandise from the Collins & Waterman store. They would pay half the taxes in cash immediately and secure the second payment with wool that they would deposit in the customs house until final payment.

"Never let it be said that we are not reasonable," Pérez said. "We agree."

Although Albino Pérez thought he was reasonable, other New Mexicans were furious over the taxes, and over the 1836 Constitution that concentrated power in the hands of the conservative forces: the Church, the military, and the rich land owners. In a low-ceilinged cantina in Chimayó, Cesario Vega, a bearish man with arms almost as large as his thighs, shouted over the din.

"That *pinche cabrón* governor can take the eighteen thirty-six Constitution and ram it up his ass! These taxes fall on our poorest, the woodcutters and the shepherds, and they even want to tax fandangos. The Mexico City politicians want to pick our bones like the scavengers they are. And they sent that prissy, effeminate bastard from Mexico City to force us to pay. It is time for action!"

A small farmer from Taos argued that New Mexicans should set up an independent government the way the Texians had. "No! No!" Cesario Vega bellowed. "We are loyal Mexicans. We are not like those *hijos de puta,* those Anglo-Saxon Texians. We will stay with our culture, our language. All we want is to be left alone."

The men cheered Vega's patriotism and drank more Taos lightning. By unanimous vote they adopted a plan that Padre Lucero had written, calling for a return to the liberal 1824 Constitution and rescinding the taxes.

Ricardo Treviño, dressed as a peon, slipped out the cantina door unnoticed. The next morning he reported to Governor Pérez that there were well over two hundred rebels, mostly Indians from San Juan, Taos, and Picuris Pueblos, and peons and *rancheros* so poor that their armament was mostly sticks and farm tools. The rabble's leaders, Treviño said, were Cesario Vega, a *cibolero* from Taos, and Padre Lucero, one of the few who was literate and who had written the insurrectionists' treasonous *pronunciamiento.*

Governor Pérez gave his spy a small leather bag of gold dust and summoned Captain Zambrano. Of his contingent of thirty-three regular army troops, Zambrano said, only twenty-four were able-bodied. Of their twenty muskets, only twelve were in working order, but, he said, the men were trained to fight with bows and arrows and lances.

Pérez ordered his military chief to raise a militia, and, three days later, he had drafted a ragtag army of still-loyal Pueblo Indians and Santa Fe peons. To officer them, Zambrano enlisted the gentry, including Matt, who he appointed a lieutenant. The army mustered in the plaza, and Matt began teaching his company of Indians the Spanish words for left and right. But when he attempted "about face" and "oblique right,"

Cochití Indians were bumping into Sandías and two Santo Domingans almost marched out of the plaza until Matt grabbed them and led them back to their places.

After lunch, Governor Pérez, a perfumed handkerchief under his nose to cover the soldiers' stench, reviewed his hundred-man army.

"Your Excellency," Zambrano said, "trying to teach European battle maneuvers to these ignorant militiamen is hopeless."

"You drill the bastards until they drop," Pérez said. "Go to it, Captain. And we want Mister Collins out of there. We will not have known tax cheats—particularly American tax cheats—in our army."

Matt returned home, somewhat embarrassed at his dismissal, but Celestina was delighted. Her husband would not be involved in a fight that, she worried, might become a bloodbath.

At sunup the next day, the army formed in front of the palace and marched north through the pink hills above Santa Fe. The governor was splendid in a green velvet coat, red vest, and white satin trousers. Two *carretas* carried his tent, candelabra, camp bed, silver dining service, extra uniforms, and linens. Two days later, Pérez ordered his army to make camp on a mesa near Santa Cruz de la Cañada. While the soldiers were huddled around breakfast fires early the next morning, the rebels emerged out of the gray desert gloom and, without a fight, many militiamen deserted and joined the enemy ranks. Surrounded, two rebels took Pérez's arms and twisted them behind his back.

"Scalp the *hijo de puta*," a peon screamed.

"No," Cesario Vega commanded, "we are not going to do this the Indian way. We are going to do this the proper European way." Vega snatched the governor's sword from its scabbard, looked into Pérez's pale blue goat eyes, and forced his head down. Then, with his powerful arms, he slammed the sword into the back of the governor's neck.

Captain Zambrano managed to escape, and led the remnants of his army into Santa Fe, where word of Pérez's defeat spread quickly. The next day, the rebels were carousing in the plaza, drinking the wine and brandy that they had liberated from the cantinas.

Matt and Edward had gone to the plaza to secure their store. When they were about to unlock the door, they heard a hoarse cry from the crowd. A cloud of dust hung in the still air as the men pushed and shoved and finally broke into two teams. "Jesús Christ," Matt said, "they're using the governor's head to play some kind of kick-ball game."

"We'd better get our butts out of here," Edward said.

"They're not paying attention to us," Matt said. "Let's go." As they fast-walked down San Francisco Street, Matt heard the rebels shouting Cesario Vega's name, proclaiming him governor.

Some days later, Moisés Mendoza brought Matt and Celestina the news that Susano Baca had issued a *pronunciamiento* against the rebels. He read: "We must decide to die with arms in our hands or to be cold victims of the fury of a disorderly insurrection that has no other goal than killing and robbing."

"Eduardo is in touch with Diego Zambrano," Matt added. "The captain is rallying troops and will join with Don Susano. Eduardo and I are donating money and supplies. And La Dama has sent Susano two thousand pesos. She says the rebels are an 'inhuman and unbridled mob.' Pretty fancy language for La Dama. Maybe she still has feelings for her old lover."

"She is about as sentimental as an Apache war chief," Moisés said. "Her only fear is that Cesario Vega and his thugs will steal her money and use her girls for target practice."

The next day, Susano Baca and Diego Zambrano led their troops into Santa Fe and met little resistance. They put down a disturbance north of Santa Fe and took four rebel leaders as hostages to secure the peace. Baca declared himself governor. Informants told Baca that rebels were organizing in Santa Cruz to retake power. But by then—January 1838—the central government had sent him dragoons and infantry from Zacatecas and Chihuahua. When the rebels refused to comply with Baca's order to disband, he beheaded the four hostages and marched on the insurgent forces, routing them. The loyalists captured Cesario Vega and Governor Baca executed him without trial.

CHAPTER SIXTEEN

1838

"Every day of my life I have seen the mountains. This prairie is so flat that—it makes you think you're inside a compass with a three hundred and sixty degree view."

MATT STOPPED ROCKING AND LOWERED THE BOOK HE WAS reading to admire his wife, who was sitting by the *sala* window, sewing. Celestina's blue-black eyes and the elegance of her almost swanlike neck still startled him, making him ache inside even more strongly than he had before their marriage. She bent down to get a thimble from her sewing basket and caught him staring at her. At first she smiled, and then she stuck out her tongue and crossed her eyes. They both laughed so loudly that a servant poked her head in from the kitchen to see what was causing the ruckus.

When they stopped laughing, Matt turned serious. "I've been thinking. Miguel is almost five and Ana María is three. They ought to know something about America. And it would be a good experience for you, too."

"Sometimes it isn't a good idea for women to know too much," she said in a mocking tone.

Even before they had married, Matt had alternated between teasing and praising her for her an intellect that, he told her, set her apart from other women. "You're already corrupted, my dear," he said. "You've got a head full of ideas."

"I'll be a practical *americana* for a minute," Celestina said, looking up from her needlework. "Who would take care of the store and the hacienda."

"Edward has agreed to stay in Santa Fe. I talked with David about the hacienda, and he'll look after it."

Matt, she realized, had been planning the trip for some time and had not discussed it with her. She got up abruptly, poked the fire back to life, and turned to look straight at him. "When are you thinking about going?"

"In September," Matt answered.

"And when were you going to tell me about this?"

After five years together, the chill in her voice told him that she was more than a little annoyed. Still, he tried to maintain a matter-of-fact exterior. "There's a caravan going back through Ratón Pass. The Comanches haven't been raiding that far west this year, so it will be safe."

"How long would we be gone?"

"Two, maybe three years," he said tentatively, waiting for her reaction. Her back was to the fire and her face was in shadow. He heard her take in a deep breath; then there was silence. After several long moments he continued, hoping that the opportunity for their son to study in a formal— and Catholic—school would soothe her anger. "Edward says there's an excellent Jesuit school in St. Louis that will take Miguel."

"But he barely speaks English."

"He would have until the spring term to improve his English. I didn't learn Spanish until I was sixteen, and younger children catch on even faster. I've exchanged letters with Jim Perryman. He and Margaret have four children now, and Ana María can spend time with them."

"Why didn't you discuss this with me," she said. Her eyes brimmed, but she did not cry. "You've planned the whole thing without saying one damned word to me about it."

"Well, *mi amor,* I wanted to have the answers to all your questions before I brought it up. It's a big step, and—"

"Three years in America might turn them into Yankees," Celestina said. "When Miguel grows up, he might take off on some crazy money-making scheme, like your former countrymen are prone to do." Matt leaned forward in his rocking chair to better see her expression, and saw worry. "I don't want them to turn into Americans," she said. "They live in New Mexico."

"I know, *corazón.* But, since Albino Pérez was killed and Don Susano returned, everybody is concentrating on the Missouri trade, and Miguel needs to understand Americans."

"He is Spanish."

Matt stood and led her back to her chair. He knelt in front of her and drew her to him. With her head buried on his shoulder, she said: "You keep telling our friends that you are New Mexican, but sometimes I doubt it."

"I am New Mexican because of you, *mi vida*," he said. "Let's not make a decision this minute. Talk to your father about it, and think it over yourself."

That evening, the Collinses arrived early for a dinner party that the Mendozas were giving for Celestina's favorite cousin, Fernando Esquivál y Mendoza, who was visiting from Albuquerque. Celestina drew her father aside and asked his opinion. Without hesitation, he said, "I went to school in France, and David's studies in the United States have made his business on the Santa Fe Trail a success."

Later, while the guests were finishing their desert of hot *sopapillas* covered with honey and toasted Missouri pecans, Moisés raised the possibility of Miguel and Ana María being schooled in St. Louis. "It is important that we understand the Americans," Fernando said. "The Missouri trade will keep growing, and those who speak English and know how to deal with the Yankees will prosper." Other guests agreed, and even Sara Mendoza seemed to favor the project.

At home in their bedroom that night, Matt debated with himself whether to bring up St. Louis again. Celestina seemed to be in good humor, but to buy more time he went to the kitchen and got them each a glass of wine. They sat sipping their wine in front of the fire until their glasses were half empty. When he brought up the trip, to his surprise Celestina responded positively. She had thought it over carefully, she said, and, although she didn't think that three years was necessary, overall it would be good for their children. "But after that we're coming home for good," she said with emphasis. He nodded in agreement, kissed her, and silently blessed Sara Mendoza for teaching her daughter the value of yielding with dignity.

Matt, like most Santa Fe traders, regularly smuggled gold and silver out of Mexico to avoid the export tax. The night before he was to leave for Missouri, Matt checked his carriage, one of only two in Santa Fe with springs and padded seats, the other belonging to La Dama. Earlier, behind their store, Matt and Edward had drilled holes in the carriage's front and rear axles and filled them with ten-thousand-dollars-worth of gold dust. For their silver, they had lined a secret compartment under the front seat with felt to keep their stacks of coins from jangling.

When Matt had first come to Santa Fe in 1826, breaking the law had made him uneasy. But over time he had rationalized his extralegal actions. All the American and Mexican traders, he told himself, skirted what they regarded as arbitrary laws, arbitrarily applied. Since much of his tax money wound up in the private pockets of government officials, wasn't he justified in cheating the tax collectors? And he knew if he got caught he could bribe his way out of trouble, or the Mendoza family would intervene to save him.

Matt finished loading the carriage and went back into his store. "Edward, thanks for staying in Santa Fe this winter," Matt said.

"It'll be good for your family to get to know the States. Sooner or later, Texas or America is going to take over this godforsaken place."

"New Mexico's not all that bad," Matt said defensively.

"Say all you want, but you know as well as I do that Santa Fe is fifty years behind the United States."

"I agree that the people in Mexico City don't know we exist," Matt said.

"New Mexico is nothing more than a backwash. You haven't been home in years, but you'll see the difference when you get back. But that's enough of my diatribe." The two partners shook hands and Matt drove to his house.

Before sunup the next morning, the Collins family climbed into their carriage and Matt tapped the two mules' rumps with his whip until they broke into a trot. In the plaza, Matt took the lead position in the caravan, and when all was ready it left the capital and headed up the Santa Fe Trail. During the hot September days, the wind whipped the caravan's dust cloud two hundred feet in the air. But at night it was still, and the desert became cool. Celestina and Ana María slept in a tent, while Miguel and his father spread their bedrolls outside and marveled at the shooting stars until they fell asleep.

The caravan made good time between Santa Fe and the point where Ratón Pass dropped off to a plain hundreds of feet below. Matt had shot two rabbits that day, and his peon Timoteo stewed the meat for dinner, flavoring it with fresh sage he had gathered along the trail.

They had had a hard day, covering almost twenty miles, and went to bed early. In the rising sun's dim light the next morning, Celestina almost tripped over her sleeping son when she ran to a weed patch by a creek. Matt heard her sputtering and coughing and, when he sat up he saw her shoulders heaving before she knelt and disappeared into the weeds. She came back to the campsite and he wrapped his arms around her, feeling the cold water on her face and smelling the vomit on her breath. "Are you all right? Do you have fever?"

"No, *mi vida*. I think I have a baby. I missed my last two periods, and I have the same nauseous feeling I had with Ana María." Celestina had suspected that she was pregnant before she left Santa Fe. But she wasn't certain, and, anyway, she had had no problems with her first two children, so she saw no reason to worry her family.

"He'll be born in St. Louis, so we'll have a little Yankee," Matt said, pleasure in his voice.

They breakfasted on the rest of the rabbit stew and walked to the rim to look at the trail to the bottom of Ratón Pass. "I haven't been on it before," Matt said. "It looks rough."

"It's steep," Celestina said matter-of-factly.

"Lots of wagons have made it before us, *mi amor*. It'll be all right," he said, knowing that she was nervous but was trying not to show it. Matt backed his mules into the carriage harnesses and Timoteo loaded their trunks on the back. "You better tie 'em down tight, Mr. Collins," Wilbur Berry, an experienced proprietor, said. "It's gonna be a bumpeleferous ride. If I was you, I'd get out and lead them mules. And watch out for their hooves. Them rocks'll chew 'em up quicker than a blacksmith's rasp."

"Thanks for the advice, Wilbur," Matt said. "Celestina, you and the kids go ahead and get in."

"I want to walk with you, Papá," Miguel said.

As Matt and Miguel led them down the trail, the spindly carriage wheels groaned when they rolled over large rocks. "It gets real steep the next couple 'a hundred yards," Wilbur warned. "Them wooden brakes prob'ly won't hold. You might wanta unhitch them mules and let us ease the carriage down with ropes."

Celestina tried to climb down by herself. "Wait!" Matt commanded. "I'll help you."

"My God, it's almost straight down," Celestina said, looking at the slope in front of them. "Can the men get wagons down that?"

"We've got several proprietors who've made the trip. We'll make it."

Matt and his servants Timoteo and Pablo unharnessed the mules and unloaded the trunks. They double-wrapped a rope around a pine tree and tied the other end to the carriage's tongue. Six men held the end of the rope and played it out a few inches at a time, while others slid down the incline with the carriage to keep it from turning over.

When they reached flat ground, Matt hitched the mules to the carriage and Celestina and the children climbed aboard. That afternoon, they came to a creek that was running high and fast with muddy, yellow-brown runoff from a rainstorm high in the mountains. The mules were skittish, fearful of entering the stream when they could not see the bottom. Matt gave them the whip, and they started across. In midstream, the carriage's right front wheel dropped into a hole and pitched Celestina and the children into the icy water.

Miguel and Ana María splashed to the bank unhurt, but Celestina's chest had hit on a boulder that lay just under the water's surface. Matt waded to her and helped her to the bank. She was heaving and gasping for breath and he held her upright while she refilled her lungs. "Are you all right?"

"I don't think I broke anything. Are the children all right?"

"They're fine. The carriage got banged up, but we can still use it," Matt said.

They camped that night at the bottom of Ratón Pass. To ease Celestina's pain, Matt smeared a poultice of mud and mule urine on her chest and applied warm stones wrapped in muslin. When they got back on the Trail the next day, every jolt of the carriage made Celestina wince. To cushion the bumps, Matt made her a bed of woolly buffalo hides and blankets in a freight wagon.

In five days, the caravan reached the Arkansas River and had an easy crossing. "Welcome to America," Matt said when Celestina got out of the wagon on the north bank. "How do you feel?"

"My ribs still hurt and my left breast is as purple as a ripe plum. And I feel a little queasy."

"Maybe there'll be a doctor at Bent's Fort."

The mules and oxen pulled the wagons up out of the floodplain toward an adobe fortress some three hundred yards from the river. Because there were no trees around it and it sat on high ground, it seemed even larger than it was. On two corners, circular turrets with gun ports provided clear fields of fire in case of Indian attack. Second-story apartments housed hunters and trappers and the fort's owner. The exterior walls were twenty-four feet high and the side walls ran for two hundred forty feet. There were no windows; the only access being a massive *zaguán* that could accommodate the largest freight wagons. Above it, a guard sat in a watchtower. "It's the largest building I've ever seen," Celestina said.

They paused for a minute and watched the Europeans, Mexicans,

Americans, Indians, and Canadians coming and going through the *za-guán*. Matt parked their carriage between a Mexican *carreta* and an American freight wagon. When he helped Celestina down, she doubled over in pain. "What is it, *mi amor*?"

"My stomach. I need to lie down," she said.

Matt went inside and a trapper pointed out William Bent, the Fort's manager. Bent wore a black broadcloth suit, white shirt, and black string tie and combed his neatly trimmed hair forward to cover a receding hairline. Matt shook his hand. "I understand you're William Bent," he said.

"That's right. And you are?"

"Matthew Collins. Collins and Waterman."

"I know your partner. Met him in Independence," Bent said.

"My wife had a fall coming down Ratón Pass and she feels pretty bad. Is there a doctor at the Fort?"

"No. But Jessica our cook knows a little medicine."

"Is there a private room we could have?"

"We don't have many women out here. There's a billiard room on the second floor. You can have that. Do you have beds?"

"We've got bedrolls but no proper bed."

"I've got an extra single bed. You can put a thick blanket over the mattress so the straw doesn't stick her," Bent said.

"Any bedbugs in it?"

"Shouldn't be. I'll get Jessica to bring your wife something to settle her stomach."

"Much obliged, Mr. Bent."

Matt helped Celestina up the steps to their second-story room and made her comfortable. After a late supper, her pain eased and the family went to sleep.

Just before midnight, Celestina whispered, "Matt, wake up! Something's happening."

"What?"

"I'm bleeding—down there."

Matt crawled out of his bedroll on the pool table, lit a candle, and pulled her blankets back. He froze for a moment, startled by the size of the blood stain on her nightgown and bedclothes.

"Be quiet. Don't wake the children. But get that cook," Celestina said.

In the dark, Matt took the stairs two at a time and pounded on Jessica's door. "You drunken son of a bitch, you leave me alone," she said. "Not tonight."

"Jessica, it's Matthew Collins," he said, his voice heavy with fear. "My wife's in a bad way. I need help."

The black cook opened her door carefully and peeped out. "What's the problem?"

"She's bleeding from her female parts." Matt was on the verge of panic.

"It's just her monthlies."

"It's something else, Jessica. She's about two months pregnant."

"You get back up there, Mr. Matthew. I'll bring hot water and candles. You got some clean rags?"

"Yes."

By the time Jessica arrived, Celestina was motionless. Matt was sitting on her bed, his mouth to her ear, whispering to her in Spanish. Jessica pulled back the blankets and held a candle close. Matt stood, his jaws flexing rapidly as he stared at the blood and a small pod of flesh attached to a cord. "She's miscarried," Jessica said quietly. "Good thing it's so early on. Is your knife sharp, Mr. Matthew?"

"Yes."

Miguel and Ana María, who had been sleeping next to their father on the pool table, sat up and blinked their eyes at the large black woman who was leaning over their mother. "Mr. Matthew, you done woke them kids."

"You two roll over and go back to sleep," Matt said. The children whined and mewed until he patted them and pulled their covers up to block their view.

"Get your knife and pass the blade over that candle a few times," Jessica commanded. She watched impatiently while Matt, his hands trembling, held the knife over the flame. "And calm down. I been around the birthin' of plenty of Indian, and black, and white babies." Matt took deep breaths and managed to choke down his fear and stop his hands from shaking.

When she had finished her work Jessica changed the bed clothes and, turning so that Matt could not see, rolled the umbilical cord and fetus in a strip of muslin. Matt walked her back to her room. "I can't thank you enough," he said, handing her ten silver pesos. Back in his room, Celestina was lying on her side, holding her stomach. He lay down behind her on the narrow bed and wrapped his body around hers. Warm, she fell asleep.

"Will Mamá be all right?" Miguel whispered from the pool table.

"She will be fine," Matt said.

"I have never seen a black woman," Miguel said with a child's facility to switch between unrelated subjects.

"Go to sleep, *mi hijo*," Matt said.

As the sun was breaking over the plains to the east, William Bent knocked lightly on the billiard room door. Matt got out of bed and opened it. "Mr. Collins, come have breakfast with me in my apartment," Bent said. "We've got fresh buffalo liver and eggs. Jessica's going to make pancakes."

"I'll be there after I've taken care of my wife," Matt said and closed the door. He turned to Celestina. "How do you feel?"

"Much better. The bleeding has stopped."

"I'll have Jessica bring you something to eat. They have real China tea here."

"That would be wonderful."

Matt and William Bent sat down at a small table.

"My caravan's leaving in a couple of days," Matt said, "and I was hoping to get off not too much later so I can catch up with them. But I need to get my carriage repaired."

"We've got the only blacksmith and wheelwright between Missouri and California. They're fixing my wagons, but I won't need them till next spring. I'll tell the boys to put your carriage first in line."

"I'd appreciate that."

"Let's go downstairs," Bent said. "I'll introduce you to Goddamn and Son of a Bitch."

"Who?"

"Goddamn and Son of a Bitch. Goddamn is the blacksmith. Son of a Bitch is the wheelwright. The Indians started calling them by those names because they say those words all the time. Then the whites picked it up."

In the blacksmith's shop, files, hammers and tongs hung from the wooden ceiling beams. The bellows whooshed and Matt's eyes burned from the charcoal smoke swirling through the unventilated room. At the anvil, Goddamn sent yellow-orange sparks flying off the horseshoe he was beating into shape. "In Santa Fe, we only have itinerant blacksmiths," Matt said. "There's not enough iron in the whole province to keep a smith busy full time."

"Goddamn, this is Mr. Collins. He busted up his carriage. Needs it fixed in a hurry," Bent said.

"Nice to meet you, Mr. Collins."

"Nice to meet you. You think it'll take much time?"

"I saw your carriage out front, and it looks like the steel tires on your right-side wheels are bent. It's not much to fix. But some of those wood spokes are broke all to hell. Son of a Bitch," Goddamn yelled at the shop next to his, "get your goddamn ass in here."

"You think it'll take long, Son of a Bitch?" Matt asked, trying to keep from laughing.

"I'll need the better part of three days to let my wood dry out good," Son of a Bitch said.

Matt gave them each five dollars and he and Bent went back into the courtyard. "If you've got a minute," Bent said, "I'll give you a tour of our mud castle. Over there's the tailor's shop. He's a Frenchman from New Orleans. He used to work with silk and wool, but now he can sew a set of buckskin clothes better than anybody on the frontier. I've got a special treat for you. Let's go out back to the corral," Bent said, kicking at one of the fort's peacocks. The bird shrieked and flapped. "The Indians hate the damned things. But they're good watchdogs. If anything strange happens at night, they screech like Satan's banshees."

Matt bent almost to his waist to get through a low passageway from the courtyard to the adobe corral on the fort's west side. "I traded the Kiowas a pistol for four mustangs," Bent said. He nodded toward a tall, thin mestizo who was walking toward a hitching post in the middle of the corral. "Beneficio's gonna break them. You've never seen a rider like him. Do you have a silver peso?"

"Yes," Matt said, pulling one out of his pocket. Bent took the peso and flipped it to Beneficio, who snatched it with such speed that Matt barely saw his brown hand move. Beneficio sauntered to the hitching post where his assistant had saddled, blindfolded, and snubbed a paint mustang. "This one's so hard to handle," Bent said, "that we've named him 'El Chignón.'"

When Beneficio put his foot in the stirrup, the stallion sucked in air and his chest and stomach swelled until it seemed that the girth would break. The animal calmed, and Beneficio pulled himself into the saddle and smiled nonchalantly while the paint did a nervous dance with his back hooves. Beneficio leaned down and put the silver peso between his moccasined foot and the left stirrup and signaled his assistant to untie the rope and remove the blindfold.

Sighted, the horse ran as fast as it could toward the adobe corral wall and, just before a collision, cut to the right. Beneficio swayed slightly. The mustang realized that the tactic wouldn't work and began bucking, swirling first to the left and then to the right. But Beneficio's balance was so true that only once did the mustang force him to grab the saddle horn. He reduced the horse to trotting and then to standing still with its sides heaving. Beneficio smiled and leaned to his left, raised his foot, and plucked the silver peso off the stirrup. Matt applauded and shouted for him to keep the peso.

When Goddamn and Son of a Bitch had repaired the carriage wheels, the Collinses prepared to leave. "Miguel, hold this mule's rope while I hitch him up," Matt said.

"Will it take us long to find the caravan, Papá?"

"They are only three days in front of us, son. The freight wagons are so slow that we'll catch up to them."

"I am a little afraid to be out on the prairie by ourselves," Miguel said.

Matt squatted to his son's level. "Pablo and Timoteo are with us, and I have plenty of ammunition."

"But they are peons, Papá."

"Timoteo can shoot better than I can, *mi hijo*. He was a *comanchero* when he was younger, and he knows how to deal with the Indians. Besides, this is the fall hunting season, and the Comanches are more interested in killing buffalo than they are in killing white men. If I were you, son, I would worry more about choking on trail dust or getting eaten up by mosquitoes than about having Indian trouble."

Matt and Miguel led the carriage to the *zaguán*. Inside the Fort, Matt saw Ana María saying good-bye to the pet buffalo calf she had befriended.

"Come along, sweetie," Matt said. She ran to him and he lifted her into the carriage.

Jessica brought Celestina a hamper filled with fresh apples that had arrived from Taos the day before and handed Matt a chest packed with venison. "Complements of Mr. Bent," she said. "That fresh meat'll replace the blood Miss Celestina lost."

"Jessica, thank you for taking care of Mrs. Collins," Matt said and boosted Celestina into the carriage.

On the afternoon of their second day, Matt saw the caravan's tracks in the sandy soil. "They can't be more than a half day in front of us, Celestina," he said. "But you look tired. We'll stop here, and catch up with them tomorrow." Matt guided the carriage to a grove of cottonwoods close to the Arkansas River.

While Timoteo and Pablo were gathering driftwood, Matt heard a rumbling sound coming from the north. He and Celestina walked to the top of a ridge and saw the afternoon sun playing on an enormous dust cloud. Within minutes, a buffalo herd's vanguard topped a small hill. The lead bulls paused for a moment and sniffed for water before lurching into their awkward, rocking chair lope toward the river. At the bank, the shaggy bulls sank in sand to their knees and lowered their massive heads to drink.

Matt and Celestina watched the buffalo pour over the hill, lowing and bellowing as they came. "Children, come see this," Celestina shouted, "there are thousands of them." They stood for an hour watching the unending parade of bulls, cows, and calves cross the river. During dinner the rumbling continued, and a haze of dust floated over their camp and coated everything and everyone with fine grit.

"Timoteo, you and Pablo make sure the picket stakes are hammered down deep," Matt told his peons. "If the buffalo get too close to camp tonight, it might spook the mules into running off."

The next morning Matt awoke to the grinding sound of mules' teeth nibbling on the short buffalo grass. He stretched his stiffened muscles and rolled out of the sandwich of buffalo robes and blankets that he shared with Celestina and the children. It had been hot the previous day, but, during the night, a cool front had come through and created a thick fog that rolled off the Arkansas.

"This deadwood makes a lot better fire than buffalo chips," Timoteo said as he knelt down to fry bacon, potatoes, and onions in a skillet so black with soot that it was crusting off. Matt and Celestina sipped boiled coffee and warmed their hands on the tin cups, while Miguel and Ana María toasted bread stuck on the ends of springy willow branches.

"We will catch the caravan sometime this afternoon," Matt said.

"I hope so, Don Mateo," Timoteo said. "There will be Indians following that buffalo herd."

"Take the mules to the river to drink," Matt said. "They got plenty to eat last night, so we should make good time today."

They traveled on the high ground above the river, where the sun had burned off the fog. As they rolled along, the fog by the river lifted and revealed three Indians sitting motionless on their horses.

"Just remain calm," Matt whispered to Celestina, "and keep Ana María and Miguel in your lap. They're Comanches, but they aren't wearing war bonnets or carrying shields."

Matt and Timoteo walked slowly toward the Indians and stopped a safe distance away. Except for breechcloths and moccasins, the Indians were naked. Their leader had silver and glass beads woven into his heavily-greased braids and a red circle with a slash across it was tattooed on his cheek. He sat in his saddle with an almost regal disdain, and the sun glinted off the barrel of a new rifle that was propped between his legs.

Timoteo, the old *comanchero*, raised his right hand in the peace sign and spoke in halting Comanche. "What do they want?" Matt asked.

"Their leader is Fast Antelope. They are from the Buffalo Eaters band and they are hunting. They only want honey and tobacco," Timoteo said.

"Tell them I can give them honey," Matt said, "but I do not have any tobacco."

Timoteo relayed the message. Fast Antelope gestured back angrily and the Indian ponies flicked their ears and twitched nervously.

"Don Mateo, excuse me, but he says he thinks you are lying."

"Tell him that my wife and I do not smoke or chew tobacco," Matt said.

"Don Mateo, Pablo and I have some *punche* tobacco that we can give him."

"Thank you, Timoteo. Tell him we will give him the tobacco and two cups of honey."

Timoteo translated and the chief agreed. Matt pulled a cask of honey from his box of food supplies and poured two cups into a buffalo intestine pouch the Indian leader had given him. The hunting chief accepted his gifts, nodded to his men, and they crossed to the south bank of the Arkansas River. "Let's get moving," Matt said. "They might come back and want something else. Celestina, take Ana María to that tall grass and relieve yourselves so that we do not have to stop."

They did not stop for lunch and, in the late afternoon, they caught up with the caravan.

The train traveled along the Arkansas River to where the Cimarron and Mountain routes joined, and two weeks later they came the great bend of the Arkansas. Matt stopped the carriage on the high ground above the river.

"Every day of my life," Celestina said, "I have seen the mountains. This prairie is so flat that it makes me uncomfortable."

"I know what you mean, *querida*," Matt said. "It makes you think you're inside a compass with a three-hundred-and-sixty-degree view."

"You sound like Sor Juana."

"I wish I could write poetry like she did," he said. "How about this:

> "The silky grass, tall and thick, glistens like gold in the
> midday sun.
> It rolls back and forth with each puff of air like the undulating,
> heaving waves and ripples of an unending ocean."

"Sor Juana would have loved that," Celestina said, "particularly coming from a Yankee businessman."

He laughed, clicked his tongue at the mules, and pulled his hat brim down to shield his eyes from the sun. Then he continued,

> "The sky, almost cloudless, and
> punctuated only by an occasional hawk or crow,
> Adds to the feeling of loneliness and solitude and the
> smallness of humanity."

"That's enough poetry for today," he said, happy.

Matt tapped the carriage mules lightly with his buggy whip and drove to the front of the caravan. "It's too bad that this Great American Desert is so worthless," he said. "Nobody but the Indians can use it. You will love it when we get back home, Celestina."

"Home?"

"Missouri."

CHAPTER SEVENTEEN

1838–1839

"Damn it, Matt, I can't stand that Yankee smugness. Americans think they have everything figured out."

THE CARAVAN STOPPED TO CAMP TEN MILES WEST OF INDEPEN-dence. Even though it was late afternoon, Matt sent Timoteo into town to buy food. For supper Celestina prepared what she and her family hoped would be their last meal of beans and jerked buffalo, the same food they had eaten for two weeks. The children, excited that they would soon be in a new country, peppered their parents with questions until after dark. Timoteo woke them the next morning with a breakfast of fresh eggs and clotted buttermilk, lean bacon, and a fresh loaf of bread.

Celestina sat by the breakfast fire, stirring coals with a poker and staring absently at the flames. Matt knew that something was bothering her and he guessed at what it was. Before they had left Santa Fe, Celestina had hinted at being anxious about whether she would feel comfortable in America, but her comment had been so understated that he did not take it seriously at the time. "Don't worry. You're smart. Your English is good. And you're beautiful," he had said and gone back to reading.

The closer they got to Independence, however, the more he noticed her uneasiness, and he had assured her: "In a month or two you'll feel completely at home." Still, she knew, that in her twenty-six years she had never been farther away from her parents than an occasional trip to visit relatives in Albuquerque. And she had led a sheltered and—for Santa Fe—a pampered life. During her five years of marriage, she had met many Americans, from the gracious and polite to the raw and vulgar. But knowing them on her home ground was one thing. Being surrounded by foreigners with strange habits and customs would be different.

She worried that her English would fail her at just the wrong moment. That the American ladies would think her dowdy and provincial. Or that she would make some social blunder that would embarrass her and Matt. But what agonized her most was that for the first time in her life she might confront prejudice. At fandangos, she had overheard Americans who didn't know she spoke English, ridiculing "lazy pepper bellies" and "ignorant papists."

She tried her best to dismiss the remarks as the product of America's underclasses. Surely, she thought, Matt's social position would shield her from meeting people like that. And, she told herself, the United States wasn't completely unfamiliar. When the caravans brought American newspapers and novels each year, she had read them eagerly and had tried to imagine what being an American was like. But she recalled her mother saying that "literature doesn't always portray reality."

Having Matt there to guide her through any difficulty was comforting, and she was determined to be optimistic about the new life she would be leading. *I'll be damned,* she thought, *if I'm going to be like those Yankees who come to Santa Fe and spend their time criticizing everything and everybody.* "What will Independence be like?" she asked Matt in her most matter-of-fact voice.

"Independence is a raw town," he said. "Lots of teamsters and plainsmen. They get drunk. They fight."

"Just like they do in Santa Fe." Her attempt at a joke somehow fell flat.

"It's the frontier, *corazón.* The edge of civilization. It's a tough life, and it takes tough characters to make do. Out here, there's a premium on the physical, and very little credit given to any form of refinement."

"I can't wait to get to Independence so I can take a bath," Celestina said. "It's been ten days since we washed in the Neosho."

"It did feel good, sugar."

" 'Sugar sounds funny in Spanish," she said. "*Como estás, azúcar.*"

"Do you like honey or sweetheart?"

"*Miel o dulce de corazón?* I like '*querida*' better." In America, she knew, she would miss the sound of Spanish. Its musicality. Its emotion.

"*Querida* it will be," he smiled.

Timoteo came around the carriage with his hands behind his back. "I have a surprise," he said, and produced a pumpkin pie he had bought in

Independence. They savored the flavors of cinnamon, nutmeg, and cloves, and when they finished it, Matt and Celestina left the children with Timoteo and Pablo and set out on saddle mules. At the Blue River, they turned off the Trail, rounded a bend, and rode into a thick grove of elms and sycamores. They stripped off their clothes and splashed into a calm pool created by an uprooted elm tree that had fallen halfway across the stream.

"Where do those disgusting lice come from?" she said. "They're in my hair and between my legs and under my arms." Matt and Celestina sank under the water for as long as they could hold their breaths. After several dunkings, the bedbugs and lice floated out of their hair. Matt ran to the mules and came back waving a trophy. "Here," he said. "I had Timoteo get this soap in Independence. It's French and it's scented with sandalwood." They took turns scrubbing one another, and she laughed when he strung a film of suds on a Y-shaped twig and blew bubbles.

Matt ducked his head under the chest-high water, surfaced, flipped his long red hair out of his eyes, and stood, squishing his toes in the muddy bottom. From behind, he felt Celestina's arms and legs lock around his chest and waist, and he shivered with pleasure when her breath tickled the hair on the back of his neck. The delicious contrast between the cool water and her warm body excited him, and she heightened it as she slipped around his body until she was staring him straight in the face. She slid down and, with a wiggle, they joined. They smiled at one another for a long moment and slowly undulated until the water lapped on the bank. After, they lay naked on a blanket by the river. "With all that thrashing around, I'm surprised we didn't draw a crowd," Matt laughed.

"The worst thing about being on the Trail," Celestina said, "is the proprietors and teamsters swarming around all the time. It's funny. You're out on that solitary plain, but there's no privacy."

They arrived in Independence and, the day after they had settled in Mrs. Lynn's boarding house, Matt announced, "I'm going the barber to get a trim and have this beard shaved off. After that, I'll be at Lokey's Tavern catching up on the news. If you want to do some shopping, there's a ladies outfitter just north of the courthouse. I'll be back for supper at six."

"Six?" she said, and thought to herself: *At home, we don't eat until nine or ten.*

"I'll see you then," Matt said, putting on the new stovepipe hat he had bought that morning.

"You look silly in that thing," Celestina said.

"It's the latest fashion."

"Not in New Mexico."

"It will be soon," he said.

Matt took the steps of Mrs. Lynn's boarding house two at a time and walked to the barber shop. Clean-shaven and smelling of lavender water, he went to Lokey's Tavern on the square. Inside, it was dim and a low beam knocked his hat off. He stood still for a minute and shrugged his nose at the stale odor of tobacco smoke that had soaked into the log walls. When his eyes adjusted, he made out three well-dressed men sitting at a table. One of them was motioning to him to join them. When he got to the table, he recognized Luke Dodge, a proprietor he had done business with over the years.

"This is John Rucker," Dodge said, "and this is Christopher Lagarde."

"He owns the newspaper," Rucker said. "He's a Frenchman, but he's okay." Christopher Lagarde grimaced and ground his teeth. It annoyed him when people said he was French. His great-grandfather had immigrated to Louisiana, and the only French he knew were the obscene words he had learned from an octoroon mistress in New Orleans. "What's happening in Mexico, Mr. Collins?"

"There's the usual chaos in Mexico City—"

"What are those crazy Mexicans doin'?" John Rucker broke in.

"There are a few Mexican politicians who want an American-style democracy," Matt said, "but most of them don't understand it—or don't like it. I've been gone a long time, so tell me what's going on here."

"This damned depression won't go away," Lagarde said. "Lots of bankruptcies. Back East they're closing mills left and right."

"And people are mad about those goddamned Mormons," John Rucker said, shooting a string of tobacco juice toward a spittoon, and missing. "They favor coddling the red niggers, but they love the black niggers even more. If we don't get rid of 'em, they'll be voting to turn Missouri into a free state."

"They're a screwy religious sect," Luke Dodge added. "They think they're God's chosen people—and they even call themselves 'saints.' 'Course, our Baptist and Methodist preachers are all pissy-eyed."

Lagarde pulled a sheet of paper out of his coat pocket and read a proclamation by Missouri's governor: "The Mormons must be treated as enemies and must be exterminated or driven from Missouri for the public good."

"Exterminate or expel—my God," Matt said, astonished at the harshness. "I need to get back to my boarding house," he said, and left without having a drink.

Matt circled the log county courthouse in the middle of the square and walked slowly toward Mrs. Lynn's, passing a new split-rail corral crowded with oxen that would pull wagons down the Santa Fe Trail in the spring of 1839. At the boarding house the stairs creaked when he went up to his room. "No dirt floors here," he said to himself.

"What's going to happen?" Celestina asked when Matt told her about the Mormons.

"Things have settled down," Matt said. "Most of them are already packing up and heading for Illinois."

"The Spanish Inquisition expelled Jews and Moors," Celestina said. "The Americans are doing the same thing to the Mormons."

"The Inquisition was not a piece of cake, my dear," Matt said, irritated by her challenge. "And what goes on in Mexico City between the factions—the hangings, the firing squads—is not exactly child's play."

"Damn it, Matt, I can't stand that Yankee smugness," she said, her eyes widening and filling with tears. "Americans think that they have everything figured out. How to think. How to do. And they look down their noses at us Spaniards. But the Americans don't have all the answers."

"Calm down, Celestina," Matt snapped. "Let the governor worry about the Mormons. I've booked steamboat passage for the day after tomorrow. Perhaps you'll find St. Louis more to your liking."

"I'm looking forward to seeing Jim and Margaret Perryman," Celestina said quietly. The storm had passed. She had made her point and she sat staring at her lap, casually flipping her skirt to straighten the pleats. "It's been two years since they left Santa Fe."

It was early November and the Missouri River was running low. At night, the *Celestial Belle*'s cautious captain tied up to trees along the shore, and Matt rigged netting around his family's bunks to keep the swarms of mosquitoes away. During the day, even with a lookout sitting on the bow, the sidewheeler's paddle tangled in sunken tree branches that were hidden under the muddy water. And when the flat-bottomed *Belle* ran aground on sandbars Matt joined the passengers and crew, stripping to his underwear and jumping in the river to help pull it off. The ship passed the site where the town of Franklin had stood before it had been washed away by floods, and Matt told Miguel the story of his escape from his apprenticeship twelve years before.

"Were you a criminal, Papá?"

"Kind of, but not exactly."

"When will we get to St. Louis, Papá?"

"A few more days, son. Let's get a pole and fish off the back of the boat."

Four days later, the *Celestial Belle* glided around a bend into the Mississippi River and headed south. The captain ordered full steam, and in hours the ship scooted up on the slick mud bank at St. Louis. Matt hired a wagon for their baggage, and he and his family and servants walked to Perryman's Excelsior Hotel on the corner of Third and Locust.

Margaret and Jim showed them to their suite on the fourth floor, facing the Mississippi. "Margaret, this is exciting," Celestina said. "I've never been this high up before."

"I think you'll be comfortable. There's plenty of room for you and the children."

"Let's sit by the window where we can watch the boats coming and going," Margaret said. "My Spanish has gotten terrible, Celestina. Maybe you can help me brush up."

"Of course," Celestina said. "What is Miguel's school like?"

"The Jesuits run it. Most of the priests are Belgian and French, but there are two from Italy and one from Poland. People think it's the best school in St. Louis. If you're here long enough, there's a good girls' school for Ana María."

"Matt is planning on staying until eighteen forty-one so that Ana María can get some formal schooling, too."

"I guess things haven't changed in Santa Fe," Margaret said.

"There's still no school," Celestina said. "The best we can do is hire an itinerant teacher who only stays a year or two. Some of them don't know as much as Miguel does. Enough of that. How are you and Jim doing?"

"St. Louis is booming and the hotel is making a nice profit."

"Your place is wonderful," Celestina said. "I noticed that you have water closets instead of slop jars. And your furniture and drapes are beautiful."

"You'll like our new chef too. We lured him away from a New Orleans restaurant. He makes crepes with ice cream and flambeed cherries that are the best things I've ever eaten."

"What is a crepe?" Celestina asked.

"It's kind of like a flour tortilla," Margaret answered.

Matt joined Jim for a drink in the hotel's taproom. Jim was proud of it and was pleased to divulge how much he had spent to outfit it. The zinc-covered oak bar that ran the length of one wall had cost eight hundred dollars. He had paid two thousand dollars for a large mirror and a frame with bas relief portraits of busty Roman goddesses. Matt gave the decor appropriate compliments and they settled back in stuffed armchairs to enjoy their whiskey.

"Matt, I wouldn't put my money in these damned banks," Jim Perryman said. "The bankers will look you in the eye and swear that they are solvent. But almost all of them are tottering on the brink. If you want, you can put your cash in my office strongbox."

"That's good counsel, Jim. I hate to lose interest on my money, but I'd sure hate to lose it all," Matt said.

Jim changed the subject. "Tomorrow night I want you and Celestina to join us and some friends for dinner. Our chef is fixing a seven-course meal and I'm uncorking our best wine."

The next evening Matt brushed his blue wool suit and tied his red silk cravat. "My God," he said when Celestina came into the sitting room. He had heard the swish of Celestina's silk dress and turned to face her.

"I know the dress out of style in America," she said, fumbling with the buttons at her throat.

"It's not the dress. It's the makeup. Wash that paste off your face," he ordered.

"Parisian ladies whiten their faces," Celestina said.

"I don't give a damn what Parisian ladies do. American ladies will think you are a freak—wearing a flour-paste mask."

"You don't have to get so mad. It will make us late, but I'll wash it off."

"You face is beautiful without the paste, *mi amor*," Matt said when Celestina came back into the sitting room. "You should never hide it.

I'm sorry I raised my voice, *querida*, but I didn't want us to be embarrassed. Let's go downstairs."

"Matt, rescue me if I get stuck with somebody who talks too fast or swallows his words," Celestina said.

"No need to be nervous, your English is fine."

Matt and Celestina went down three flights of stairs and into the Perryman's private drawing room. "Matt, will you have a whiskey?" Jim asked.

"No thanks, I'll wait for that fine wine."

"Let me introduce you," Jim said, taking Celestina's and Matt's arms. "Meet Seth and Mary Kramer. Seth's in the shipping business. How many boats you got working the rivers, Seth?'

"Six."

"Where do your ships go, Mr. Kramer?" Celestina asked.

"All over. The Mississippi. The Ohio. The Missouri. The Arkansas. Wherever somebody wants to send cargo."

"You've probably handled some of Matt's merchandise," Jim said. "He's one of the biggest traders on the Santa Fe Trail."

"Probably have. We make regular runs to Independence."

"Seth, Mary, excuse us," Jim said. He steered them across the room to a man seated on a leather sofa. "Matt, Celestina, meet Henry Hawley. Henry has built himself a good business making wagons. He was a pioneer in adapting the old Conestoga wagons for the Santa Fe Trail, and he was the first to paint their beds sky blue and their wheels red."

"I know Mr. Hawley's wagons," Matt said. "My partner and I have bought quite a few over the years."

"Matt's probably made as much or more money than anyone out in Santa Fe," Jim said.

"I've heard of Collins and Waterman," Henry Hawley said without standing. "I met Waterman. Didn't care much for him."

Jim tugged Matt's arm and they crossed the room quickly. "You'll have to excuse Henry," he whispered to Matt and Celestina. "He's a little on the coarse side. Worked his way up from the bottom. Started out as a hod carrier and he can barely write his name. His workmen are scared to death of him. The story is that he killed somebody in a brawl in Baltimore, and that's why he came out here."

After meeting the other guests, Matt and Celestina stepped outside on the verandah. "My dress is completely out of date," she said.

"It looked fine in Santa Fe, *corazón*, and it looks fine here."

"It looks like a sack here."

"Margaret will know a dressmaker, and you can buy whatever fabrics you like," Matt said.

"Did you notice that every time Jim introduced us he told us what the man's business was and how successful he was and how rich you are?"

"A few years ago," Matt said, "I wouldn't have thought about it, but, I know what you mean. It's the American way. In Mexico, people know that you're somebody because they call you 'Don Fulano.' The Americans don't have titles and it's hard to know who's important, so they don't shy from telling you how much money they've got."

"Whatever the reason," Celestina said, "it's boorish."

"Let's go inside, *querida*," Matt said, and followed her to the dining table. While he drank wine and ate his soup and salad and fish courses, Matt was silent and seemingly calm, but inside he was warring with himself. He had been away from America for the better part of twelve years and he had conjured in his mind an almost flawless vision of his boyhood home. In the past, he had never questioned the things Americans said and did. But Celestina's sharp eye had caught a number of Yankee peculiarities, and he had noticed several himself. Taken separately, he told himself, they were of minor importance, but the little things were beginning to grate.

"More wine?" a tall slave dressed in livery asked.

"No thank you," Matt said, turning to Celestina. "I've already had three glasses."

"Tell me about Messico," Henry Hawley said, his slurry voice booming across the table. "Jim says you're a Messkin, Mr. Collins."

"I am," he answered stiffly.

"Why would you wanna be a Messkin?" he asked, stuffing his mouth with gravy-covered cornbread and not bothering to wipe the dribbles off his beard.

"It's where my family is." Matt's fists and arms tensed, but he forced them to relax.

"Seems to me, them Messkins can't take care of themselves," Hawley said, his open mouth exposing the mush of cornbread and gravy. "Their governments are like dominos. You line 'em up and they all fall down. And their economy's a wreck."

"America's economy doesn't look so good right now," Matt said.

"Boom and bust. That's the way it is in a free country. Everything's free to go up and free to go down. But in them dictatorships like you got, it's the rich stealin' from the poor."

"Isn't that what Mr. Nicholas Biddle's rich friends are doing with the Bank of the United States?" Matt asked, succeeding in keeping his composure.

"Andy Jackson whacked 'em across the knuckles and Marty Van Buren's gonna take care of them thieves," Hawley said, his veined cheeks glowing purple-red. "But your people—her people," he said, pointing at Celestina with his fork, "don't have the slightest damned notion of what a free country's all about. I got friends who've done business in Messico. Everybody down there's corrupt."

"Let's talk about something else," Jim Perryman said.

"Your wife don't look like no Messkin," Hawley insisted. "Almost white skin. Is she a real Messkin, Mr. Collins?"

"Henry, that's enough," Jim said.

"Enough of what?" Hawley shouted. "All I'm askin' is how come a nice redheaded Irish boy is married to a greaser."

"You bastard," Matt shouted and jumped out of his chair, his face flushing crimson in the candlelight.

"Let's go, Henry," Jim said as he and Seth Kramer pushed Hawley out of the dining room. "I'm sorry," Jim said when he came back. "Henry can be a jackass, particularly when he's drunk. I apologize for his rudeness. Matt, sit down and enjoy the desert. The chef has named it 'crepes a la Celestina.'" Matt and Celestina finished in silence, while the other diners chatted nervously and tried not to look in their direction.

Later, Matt sat on their bed and unlaced his shoes. "That bigoted son of a bitch. I could have killed him. He knows as much about Mexico and Mexicans as I do about Queen Victoria's palace."

"I must admit that I was shocked by his vulgarity," she said, taking his chin in her hands and kissing him. "Help me with these buttons on my chemise."

"Most Americans don't know where Mexico is and don't care," he said. "But there are ignorant bastards like Henry Hawley who hate anything that isn't American. I'm sorry you had to hear that, *mi alma*," he said, and kissed her neck.

"Senator Benton, this is Matthew Collins," Jim Perryman said. "He's struck it rich on the Santa Fe Trail."

"Have a seat, Mr. Collins," Thomas Hart Benton said, waving a beefy hand toward a cluster of chairs in the hotel drawing room. "Jim, bring us some brandy to toast in the new year. I'm particularly interested in the New Mexico trade, Mr. Collins. When there was a run on the Bank of Missouri, your fellow proprietors saved it by depositing their gold and silver. So I'm always interested in knowing how the Santa Fe trade is going." Jim brought them brandy and sat down with Matt and Benton.

"Well, Senator, we had a good year in eighteen thirty-seven, about eighty wagons going down the trail. But that dropped off to fifty in 'thirty-eight because of Mr. Biddle's depression."

"That son of a bitch," Benton said. "If we don't get rid of him and that goddamned Second Bank of the United States, he and his Eastern pals will ruin the country."

"My proprietor friends are proud of the way you have fought the Bank, Senator. Here's to a prosperous eighteen thirty-nine," Matt said, raising his glass.

"The Second Bank frames the issue of whether the people or the propertied classes will govern. We can't let a small coterie of financiers who produce nothing run this nation like it's their personal clubhouse. We'll get rid of that damned Bank sooner or later. But, I've talked enough. Jim tells me you became a Mexican citizen, Mr. Collins."

"I did. It makes doing business a lot easier. And my wife is Mexican."

"Very sensible, very practical," Benton said. "But Mexico seems to be a mess."

"We've got a class war going on," Matt said. "The privileged groups have banded together to put down the people and the people are so ignorant they don't know how to fight back."

"I met General Santa Anna after Sam Houston whipped him and he came to Washington," Benton said. "He says Mexico will take Texas back."

"We'll see," Matt said. "What's all this talk I've heard that the United States might expand to California? My New Mexican friends aren't too happy about that."

"There's talk that America is destined to expand to the west. But the question is all tied up with slavery—whether any new territory would be slave or free. And, sure as hell, our trying to move west would put us toe-to-toe with Mexico. Where would you come down, Mr. Collins, if we went to war with Mexico?"

"First, sir, I have a hard time imagining why anybody would want to fight over that desert. But if the two countries went to war, I'd be in an awkward position. It's hard to forget that I was born poor—an orphan—and that America gave me the freedom to improve my lot. That's something that wouldn't have happened if I'd been born poor in Mexico City."

"What about Henry Hawley, Matt," Jim said "He was born poor and moved up. Is that good?"

"Not in his case," Matt laughed.

"Why did you bring your family to St. Louis, Mr. Collins?" Benton asked.

"I want my children to understand the United States. And, if the chaos gets worse in Mexico, we might have to live here some day."

"Mr. Collins, this tie between Missouri and Santa Fe is extremely important to my constituents. I would be greatly in your debt if you would keep me informed about what's happening in New Mexico and how the trade is faring. Would you do that?"

"I am flattered, Senator. Of course, I would be pleased to correspond with you."

"Another brandy, gentlemen?" Jim said. "It's twelve o'clock. Happy New Year!"

CHAPTER EIGHTEEN

1841

"If these infidel Texians conquer our beloved New Mexico, they will stamp out our Holy Mother Church and bludgeon us into becoming Protestants—force our babies to speak English—steal our land and impose their slave system on us."

AFTER THREE YEARS IN ST. LOUIS, THE COLLINSES TRAVELED back down the Santa Fe Trail and tried to resume their former life, but there was something disturbing, something different. Still, they had settled back into their familiar routines, and had planned a welcoming home party for family and close friends. In her bedroom, Celestina quietly went about dressing for the evening. Matt, already dressed, sat by the fire and watched her without speaking. He was happy to be back in his own home, sipping Pass wine and listening to the quiet "slap, slap" of their servant's moccasined feet on the hard-packed dirt floor.

He swirled the wine in his glass and let his mind wander. Missouri had nothing to compare to the Santa Fe sunsets that lighted the sky with an artist's palette. And the crisp, dry Sangre de Cristo air—as light and soft as Celestina's breath on his neck after they were both spent—reminded him of how much he had disliked St. Louis's muggy summers, the soggy heat that made him feel greasy and sticky.

When they had ridden into the Santa Fe plaza at the end of their trip, onlookers assumed that Matt was drunk when, in his exuberance, he burst into an aria from the *Marriage of Figaro*, which he and Celestina had seen just before they left St. Louis. All in all, he thought their stay in the United States had been successful, but that part of their life had ended and it was time to readjust to New Mexico.

Celestina, too, was happy to be home, but she felt a strange ache for St. Louis's bustle, its steamboats and travelers coming and going, its plays and operas and restaurants, and its air of unbridled optimism. She remembered that her first months in the American city had been difficult. She had worried that her children would forget New Mexico and had insisted that she and Matt speak only Spanish to Miguel and Ana María. And there were times when she had sat at their hotel window overlooking the Mississippi and longed for the taste of crunchy, toasted piñon nuts and juicy Rio Grande plums.

At first, Celestina had missed Santa Fe, but because talking about it made Matt uncomfortable, she rarely mentioned her yearning for New Mexico's stark beauty. Soon, however, she assimilated. After a lifetime of intimacy with mostly family and childhood friends, she surprised herself by becoming close to several wives of St. Louis's merchants and lawyers. And her English became so fluent that the few people who picked up her accent thought she was French or Italian.

Fortunately, there were no more episodes like the one she had had with Henry Hawley, where the word "greaser" had charged the atmosphere. Occasionally, someone made a sarcastic remark about Mexico's instability. And, at a dinner at the mayor's house, a ship's captain just back from Mexico had told the macabre tale of Santa Anna forcing his cabinet officers to attend a funeral for a leg the General had lost in battle. When Celestina had first arrived in Missouri, the telling of such stories offended her. Still, they made her wonder whether Spaniards were unable to govern themselves without the iron fist of a king or a military strongman. But as time passed her American friends' gossip about corrupt Indian agents and scandalous bank frauds confirmed her suspicion that her countrymen were probably no worse than the Americans.

Celestina's maid left the room after helping her mistress button a blue-black gown that matched her eyes. She took a silver and turquoise collar from her jewelry box and Matt stood and clipped it around her beautiful neck. She blushed when he stared at her low bodice and whispered a flowery Spanish ode to her breasts and hinted at what they might do when the party ended.

The guests began arriving just before sundown, and after chatting and drinking in the patio they entered the dining room at ten thirty. Matt looked over the table and saw that Celestina had had the cook prepare his favorite dishes: *pozole, carne adobado,* and *sopapillas.* He signaled to the guests to sit, and Edward Waterman took his place on Matt's right. "Edward, how is our chubby friend Susano Baca?" Matt asked, leaning toward his partner.

"He is as corrupt as Santa Anna," Edward answered, his voice heavy with contempt. Edward went on to detail how Baca had granted a million and a half acres of land to Guadalupe Miranda and Carlos Beaubien. "The King of Spain doesn't own that much land!" The beneficiaries of the governor's largess had given Baca a bribe, a secret ownership interest in the land. Edward calmed himself and asked Matt for American news.

"They finally got rid of Nicholas Biddle and the Second Bank of the United States, and John Tyler became President after Harrison died."

"I read some confusing things in the newspapers that Mateo brought with him," Moisés Mendoza said. "The *New Orleans Picayune* says Texas is sending an army to Santa Fe to lay claim to eastern New Mexico up to the Rio Grande. But the St. Louis paper says the Texians are only cutting a commercial trail from Austin to Santa Fe."

"Before we left Independence in May," Celestina said, "a Texian cotton broker told Matt that the Texian President, Lamar, intends to conquer New Mexico and that the expedition is only posing as a business venture."

"Governor Baca has arrested a spy he says is conspiring with the Texians," Moisés said.

"Nobody quite knows what is going on," Edward said. "But Baca is suspicious of all Americans. I saw him at a fandango last week and he refused to talk to me. When I left, one of his soldiers followed me home and stood across the street all night."

Matt kept trying to turn the conversation to less controversial subjects, but it inevitably returned to the Texian threat. The diners left early, just after midnight, and Celestina stayed in the kitchen helping her servants until she was sure that Matt would be asleep.

Over the summer of 1841, tension between Americans and New Mexicans continued to build. A mob marched on the American consul's home, where a group of proprietors had barricaded themselves, and shouted anti-Texian slogans. And there were individual incidents, fights in La Dama's and other cantinas. Even in the security of their patio, Matt and Celestina felt the fear and apprehension in the air.

"Things aren't the same as before we left," Matt said to his wife. "With this talk of a Texian invasion, there's a certain chill, and even some old friends give me suspicious looks. The Spanish think I'm American and the Americans think I'm Spanish."

A servant came from the front of the house. "Don Mateo, Governor Baca's messenger is at the door. The governor wants to see you immediately."

Matt put on a buckskin jacket and his stovepipe hat and followed the messenger to the plaza. Two *comancheros* lounging in front of La Castrense snickered when he grabbed awkwardly at his strange looking hat to keep a wind gust from blowing it off. Matt stopped and glared the men into a surly silence.

At the palace's main door, he doffed his hat to Diego Zambrano and congratulated him. The government had promoted Zambrano from captain to colonel, despite, Matt knew, Susano Baca's behind-the-scenes protests. "Don Mateo, we have captured two soldiers from the Texian invasion force, and the governor wants you to translate for him."

"The last time I saw Don Susano, he seemed to be distracted," Matt said, looking directly at Zambrano for any telltale expression.

"He is upset by these stories about Texian intentions," Zambrano said blankly, "and the underhanded game that some American proprietors in Santa Fe are playing."

In his office, Susano Baca sat behind his desk, outfitted in a sky blue uniform garnished with gold epaulets and yellow piping. Baca puffed heavily when he raised his bulky frame out of his chair to shake Matt's hand. He was smiling broadly, but his eyes were unreadable. "I want to interrogate the prisoners," the governor said when they sat down, "but they do not speak Spanish. Will you help?"

"Of course, Your Excellency."

"Bring the bastards in," Baca said, motioning to Zambrano.

The governor slumped in his chair and his head drooped forward so that the lower of his multiple chins rested on his chest. In measured tones, he told Matt of the Mexican government's weakness. "Here I am, trying to defend our Republic's northern frontier from those *hijos de puta* Texians, with no help from Mexico City. Then they add insult by elevating that back-stabber Zambrano to a colonelcy."

Baca became more animated and his jowls shook in anger as he stormed at the Texians' claim that the eastern part of New Mexico belonged to Texas. Santa Anna, the Texians said, signed a treaty after the Battle of San Jacinto that brought Santa Fe, Taos, and Albuquerque under the Texas flag. In a booming baritone, the governor denounced the treaty's validity. "Everyone knows that Santa Anna was a prisoner and that that traitor Houston put a gun to the president's head and forced him to sign that treaty. And everyone knows that these fucking Texians are all Yankees in disguise. And that the Yankees are behind this invasion too."

Matt paused a second to form a diplomatic response. "It is true that most of the Texians came from the United States, Don Susano. But they revolted against the same Mexico City politicians who want to put their hands around our throats and control us in New Mexico. Even worse, they want to levy new taxes. Our fellow New Mexicans are making the same complaints that the Texians did."

Before Baca could respond, the office door opened and guards pushed two men into the room. The prisoners stood in front of Baca's desk, licking chapped and split lips. Their hair, matted with dust and sweat, had turned a whitesh tan, and their odor filled the room.

Matt asked them, in English, for their names. "Koppman and Bennett." The prisoners looked at him closely, unable to understand why someone with blue eyes and red hair was helping the Mexicans. "Your Excellency," Matt said, "could we open the windows? These Texians stink."

"Open them," Baca ordered a guard.

"The prisoners say their compatriots sent them ahead to ask for help," Matt translated.

"Help?" Baca said, his eyes wide in disbelief. "For invaders?"

Matt listened to the prisoners' story. Their expedition had gotten lost because they did not have a map, and at one point their caravan had marched in a circle. They left Austin too late in the summer and the heat had burned up most of the grass and there was no water in the creeks. To make it worse, Comanches had killed a few stragglers and a prairie fire destroyed some supply wagons. Both men and animals are were badly beaten down, and they were living on snakes, horned toads, and skunks.

Matt started to ask another question, "Mr. Koppman—"

"Prisoner Koppman," Baca snapped. "Ask them why they are marching on New Mexico."

Koppman explained that the Texian commanders had told their men that the New Mexicans were fed up with the "corruption and tyranny" in Mexico City. When they got to Santa Fe, the commanders had claimed, the oppressed New Mexicans would welcome them with open arms, delighted to become a province of the Republic of Texas.

Diego Zambrano, enraged at the insulting words that Matt had translated, clubbed Koppman from behind with the butt of his pistol. "No *pinche cabrón* foreigner will talk about our Republic like that." The prisoner slumped to his knees, bewildered by the blow and by the Spanish shouted in his ear. His friend pulled him up and, before thinking, Matt gave Koppman a handkerchief to staunch the blood running down his neck. Matt glanced at Zambrano, and caught a smug look that said: "Collins is still a Yankee."

"Gentlemen," Baca said, after the guards marched the prisoners out, "we need to raise an army. Colonel Zambrano, you talk to Padre Domingo."

"About?"

"Tell him to scare the shit out of people so that they will volunteer."

During the next days, the foreign merchants stayed in their stores, and some abandoned their merchandise and left Santa Fe for Missouri. Matt followed Celestina's advice and stayed home until Sunday, when they decided it was safe to attend church.

"Mexico needs you. Your governor needs you. And Colonel Zambrano needs you," Padre Domingo pleaded from the pulpit in a low, growling voice that forced those in back to strain to hear. "If these infidel Texians conquer our beloved New Mexico, they will stamp out our Holy Mother Church and bludgeon us into becoming Protestants."

With every sentence, the priest's voice grew louder and he became more passionate, jabbing his finger at the heavens as he made each point. "The Anglo-Saxons will force our babies to speak English, and mothers will not be able to talk to their own children. They will steal our land and impose their slave system on us. They will sell us in the plaza like mules because our skin is not white."

"Even the wealthiest among us is not safe," Padre Domingo continued in a state of high excitement. "They will relegate us to a class beneath that of the lowest *genízaro*. You have seen for yourselves how the Anglo-Saxons insult our women. And these wanton Texians have been on the march for weeks. When they get to Santa Fe, there will be rape, and worse. Now, let us pray to God the Father, His Son, and the Holy Spirit to deliver us from these barbarians."

From his seat in the Mendoza family's second-row pew, Matt could feel the eyes behind him staring at his red hair and fair skin. After the last hymn, the crowd stood to leave and Moisés Mendoza made a point of giving Matt a hearty *abrazo* and Sara tugged on his sleeve for him to lower his head so that she could kiss his cheek. The other parishioners turned and left, whispering to one another that Matt's neck and face had flushed crimson during Padre Domingo's sermon.

On Monday morning, Matt went to the palace and volunteered to serve in the militia.

"Are you saying you want to fight the Anglos?" the governor asked, his eyes studying Matt intensely.

"Your Excellency, I am a Mexican."

At dawn the next day, Matt joined a thousand-man army in the plaza and fell into line behind Susano Baca's staff. The governor led them down the Santa Fe Trail and over Glorieta Pass to the village of San Miguel del Vado, where the *alcalde* told Baca that he had captured five Texians.

"Governor Baca," a man waiting outside the *alcalde*'s office said in heavily accented Spanish, "I am an American, not a Texian. I am married to a Mexican woman and I have lived in San Miguel for four years. A mob stormed my store and looted it."

"A calamity of war. The people are frightened of foreigners—and with good reason. If your Anglo brethren had not marched on New Mexico, this turmoil would not exist," Baca said, dismissing the American and turning to Matt. "I want to question the prisoners. Come with me."

Inside an adobe house that the *alcalde* was using for a jail, the captives sat on the floor with their hands tied. Matt translated the governor's questions, but the men refused to answer. Furious, Baca ordered Colonel Zambrano to take them outside.

Matt joined the soldiers surrounding the prisoners in the plaza. Baca pointed at a blond young man named Sebastian and told Zambrano to take him to an adobe wall in plain view of the other prisoners. A soldier kicked the back of Sebastian's knees until he sank to the ground. The soldier backed off ten feet and pulled the trigger on his rifle. A heavy lead bullet slammed into Sebastian's left shoulder. He keeled over, his writhing stirring up dust. Zambrano ordered a corporal to administer a heart shot at close range. Flames spewed from the pistol barrel and caught Sebastian's shirt on fire, burning his skin until his blood snuffed it out.

When the remaining prisoners finished telling what they knew about the Texian army and its location, Baca picked out one. "What's his name?" he asked Matt.

"Mayberry, Excellency."

"Tell prisoner Mayberry to ride back to his compatriots and tell them that we have an army of four thousand trained men ready to destroy them." Baca managed to stifle the smile that would have given away his lie.

The bedraggled Texian army surrendered and Governor Baca instructed Matt to interrogate the prisoners. Baca made it clear that he wanted Matt to develop evidence that the Texians' true mission was to conquer New Mexico. A battle report, Susano knew, chronicling his glorious defeat of a ruthless invading army would resonate more loudly in the Palacio Nacional than would a tale of rounding up a few half-starved merchants.

Matt first questioned General Staley, the Texian leader. Next, he went to a windowless adobe house where an American journalist was being held. Joe Lyon was a loquacious man, prone to the high-flown vocabulary that he felt befitted a man who dealt in words. He spoke with a cultured Louisiana drawl, and, although he was short, he was stunningly handsome. Matt gave the prisoner a Havana cigar and he puffed it slowly and lovingly.

Joe Lyon told Matt that he was an American citizen—not a Texian—and that he worked for the *New Orleans Picayune*. He described the trip across the *comanchería:* "It was worse than Napoleon's march from Moscow. The only difference was that the Russian Steppes and the snow defeated Napoleon. For us, that damnable desert and an appalling and oppressive heat were our nemeses. The Texians were pitiable, subsumed by weakness and too demoralized to fight." Lyon's story, Matt knew, would do nothing to bolster Susano Baca's reputation as a warrior.

Lyon smiled lazily and puffed. "You have interviewed General Staley. What are his observations about what has transpired?"

Matt had warmed to Lyon's rhetorical charm. "Staley is defiant. With a man as proud as Governor Baca, that won't go down very well."

"I fully comprehend what you mean about General Staley's arrogance. Does it appear likely that he could nettle the governor's ire to the point that he would execute us."

"I don't think so," Matt answered. "His Excellency is treating this like a great military victory. He wants to send a report to Mexico City that will make him look like Napoleon at Austerlitz, and he doesn't want to do anything that'll make him look bad. Shooting Texian prisoners falls into that category. Still, if he decided to treat you as traitors—"

"Traitors?" Lyon broke in, his easy manner deserting him momentarily.

"Some Mexicans claim that Texas is still part of Mexico and that the Texian invasion was a treasonous act."

"That means they could shoot us," Lyon said calmly. "I say, could you speak to the American consul and see if he can seek clemency for me as a noncombatant?"

"It wouldn't do any good. Don Susano is convinced that the consul is conniving to set up New Mexico for an American takeover."

Matt left and went to Baca's headquarters in the San Miguel *alcalde*'s home. Along the *sala*'s walls, Diego Zambrano and other officers squatted on blankets, while the governor issued orders from the *alcalde*'s scruffy sofa, the room's only furniture.

"What will you do with the prisoners, Your Excellency?" Matt asked.

"Don Mateo, you know that I am not stupid enough to get caught in a political mess. I have decided to march them to Mexico City, where the politicians can decide what to do with them."

"Your prudence and good judgment have never been in question, Don Susano. But should they be forced to walk fifteen hundred miles in the condition they are in?"

"I did not invite them here, and I do not have the money to furnish our guests with mules and wagons. You are not questioning my decision?"

"No, Your Excellency."

Although he knew that tempers were stretched almost to the breaking point, Moisés Mendoza hoped that he could ease the rancor between Americans and New Mexicans. He invited Padre Domingo, Edward Waterman, and Matt to dinner, and after they finished the men moved outside to the patio to smoke and drink brandy.

"Padre Domingo, I am worried about the anti-American climate," Matt said. "It is getting worse. I went to a play at the church and one of the character's lines was: 'Whenever you hear New Mexicans bark at foreigners, they always bite them.'"

"That play was written," Padre Domingo said, "with the knowledge that Bent's Fort is an American outpost for spying and that the Bent brothers are supplying guns to our Indian enemies."

"But the American government has nothing to do with the Bent brother's business," Matt said.

"Anyone who reads an American newspaper," Padre Domingo said, "knows that the United States is just waiting for an excuse to steal

Mexican territory. That ill-fated—and, I might say, stupid—Texian invasion is only one example of the Yankees' intentions. Our Republic has done nothing to provoke such aggression, and President Santa Anna even went so far as to treat the Texian invaders as prisoners of war and let them go home."

"But only after fifty died on the march," Edward said.

"That is all propaganda," Padre Domingo said.

"There is a great deal of tension," Moisés Mendoza said. "Riots in Santa Fe and Americans murdered in Taos."

"I do not condone violence," Padre Domingo said, "but every time an American suffers a bit of bad luck, the United States Consul and the foreign proprietors bombard Governor Baca with pleas and petitions."

"But their petitions do no good," Edward said angrily. "When those two Mexicans murdered an American in cold blood last month, His Excellency did nothing until the Americans threatened to take justice into their own hands. And after he arrested the killers, he turned them loose. How is that fair?"

"Fairness has nothing to do with it," Padre Domingo said. "We are involved in a struggle to preserve our nation, Don Eduardo."

"Gentlemen," Matt interrupted, "we could argue whether Mexicans or Americans are wrong or right all night long, and we would get nowhere. Let us have another glass of brandy. My wheat crop is coming up nicely this year, but my *mayordomo* tells me that that the coyotes and bobcats are killing our sheep and goats."

CHAPTER NINETEEN

1843–1844

They discussed Javier Otero's murder and the strong reaction it had received in Santa Fe . . . . the Americans in New Mexico feared for their lives. There was talk that President Santa Anna would shut down the Santa Fe Trail.

IN THE FIFTEEN YEARS THEY HAD BEEN PARTNERS, MATT AND Edward had always rented store space, mostly from Susano Baca. But they were tired of paying rent for cramped and often leaky quarters. Matt purchased a property on the plaza's east side and tore down a building that had been used as a ten-cent-a-night dormitory for teamsters. In its place he built an adobe building with glass windows across the front and a deep *portal* to block the west sun. He hung a sign with brass lettering from the *portal* that announced COLLINS & WATERMAN'S GENERAL MERCHANDISE. Above the store he built storage space, an office, and a suite of rooms to house Edward when he was in Santa Fe.

In early 1843, Edward returned from a trip to Chihuahua, where he had disposed of the goods that they had not sold in Santa Fe. The partners shuttered their store on a cold January night and went to the upstairs office to close out their 1842 books. Matt tried to use the firelight to read the notes and numbers written in his own scrawl and in Edward's neat hand, but gave up and lit an oil lantern. When they finished, they celebrated the year's one-hundred-seventy-thousand-dollar profit with a bottle of snow-chilled champagne. "Even with the slow sales, we did well," Edward said.

Champagne and good profits normally made the partners happy. Instead, they were glum. Joe Lyon, the New Orleans journalist, had returned home and written a book that had inflamed American public opinion. Even the East Coast newspapers, which had little interest in the western frontier, were writing stinging anti-Mexican editorials.

Lyon's book catalogued a string of Mexican atrocities during the Texian prisoners' 1841 march to Mexico City. One vivid story told how the Mexicans forced their captives to march across the *jornada del muerto* for forty hours without food or water. When a prisoner fell behind, a Mexican soldier wheeled his horse around and trampled the exhausted Texian. Then, he rammed his lance through the straggler's hamstring muscle and left him to die.

The book, Matt and Edward knew, would hurt the Santa Fe–Missouri trade. An express rider had already brought them letters from their wholesalers and suppliers, who were frightened that a war would cripple the Santa Fe Trail and make it impossible for Collins & Waterman to meet their obligations. In another letter, their insurance company tripled their premiums.

After dinner that night, Matt told Celestina about Joe Lyon's book. He also told her that he and Edward had decided that he needed to go to the United States to calm down their suppliers and insurers.

"Why doesn't Edward go?" Celestina asked, surprised by Matt's announcement.

"The people we do business with back East know Edward, but they don't know me. With this jittery situation, it's time our suppliers put a face to my name. We think my giving them a firsthand picture of what's happening in New Mexico will help."

"But the trouble is between Mexico and Texas."

"I know. But the people in St. Louis and Boston and New York are frightened that this could boil over into war with the United States."

"There are stories that the Texian *banditti* are planning to attack Mexicans on the Trail," Celestina said.

"We've heard these stories for months and nothing has happened. Susano Baca has been floating those rumors to get the government to send him more money and soldiers."

Celestina was angry, as much with Matt's decision to go as with his failure to seek her advice in advance. When he told her that he was going with Javier Otero in February, her anger turned to concern. "Javier's so young, and it's been a horrible winter," she said. "And a *curandera* told me that the comet we saw last month is a bad omen."

"Don't tell me you believe her," Matt said, laughing.

"Not really. But she might be right."

Matt had laughed at the *curandera*'s prediction, but a certain feeling—it wasn't fear, but more an uneasiness—had kept him from a restful sleep for several nights before he left. Despite his apprehension, the four-wagon caravan made an uneventful trip across New Mexico, down the Arkansas River to its great bend, and then due east to Cow Creek. Matt's peon, Timoteo, had scouted ahead of them and found that a large buffalo herd had come through the area and had left a supply of buffalo chips, *bois de vache*, the French called them.

At Cow Creek, the wagons crossed easily, and Matt rode upstream to find a campsite. "Flat. Flat. Flat. There isn't a pimple on this prairie for two hundred miles in any direction," he muttered to himself. He settled on a spot just below a ridge that would help block the north wind, rode back to the wagons, and guided them to the site.

The only other proprietor in their caravan, Javier Otero, had never made a trip on the Santa Fe Trail and was of little help. But Matt liked the young man and spent hours patiently explaining how things were done on the Trail. Although Javier Otero was only twenty, his hair had receded halfway back across his scalp. To compensate, he had let his thick black beard grow to the middle of his chest. He had the characteristic amber eyes of the Otero clan and dark olive skin that he had inherited from a great-grandfather who had adopted his illegitimate children by a Taos Pueblo woman. Javier had exquisite manners and his mother's friends uniformly said that he was "a sweet boy." His father was among the most prominent of the *hacendados* who had been successful on the Santa Fe Trail, and he had powerful contacts, not only in Santa Fe but in Mexico City and Washington as well.

Before they set up camp, Matt looked at the sky, unhappy at the sight of a large blue cloud rolling towards them from the north. "You boys get plenty of *bois de vache* and whatever wood you can find," Matt told the peons. "It is going to get cold tonight. Drive those tent stakes in extra deep and double the guy ropes." Later, Matt and Javier inspected the mules and horses to make sure that the peons had tied buffalo robes, with the hairy sides down for warmth, over the animals' backs.

After a dinner of boiled beans flavored with hot peppers, Javier produced a clay jug of brandy and he and Matt each took long drinks.

"You may want to have a couple of your peons sleep in your tent tonight," Matt counseled. Javier gave him a quizzical look. "For the warmth. If you put one of them on each side of you, they will keep you from freezing your butt off."

"Those peons? They stink like mares in heat," Javier said. Nevertheless, he followed Matt's advice.

After midnight, sleet began a lazy tap-tap on their tents. Soon, it turned into a steady drumbeat. The wind slapped the tent sides, and the stakes on the north side of Javier's tent jerked out of the ground. It flapped furiously for a few seconds, then collapsed, and Javier and his two servants crawled into Matt's tent. *"Mi casa es su casa,"* Matt said and laughed. "The more people we can crowd in here, the warmer it will be."

After daybreak, the sleet tapered off and snow fell in curtains. Matt opened his tent flap and could barely make out the silhouette of a wagon parked ten yards away. He closed the flap and settled in for a dull day, trapped in his tent with five other men. That afternoon, the snow slackened and they crawled out to stretch and start a fire. Matt instructed Timoteo to make sure the snow was shoveled ten feet back from the fire pit so that it would not melt and create a mud puddle.

Timoteo Suárez was at least 80 percent Indian. He stood just over five feet and had dark brown skin and black eyes and hair. His father had been a *comanchero,* and at the age of six Timoteo had first gone with Alejandro Suárez to trade with the Comanches. When Timoteo was fourteen, a Comanche band, certain that Alejandro had cheated them, killed him. His mother had a nephew who worked for the Mendozas, and managed to find her son a position as a house servant. When he was eighteen, Moisés Mendoza assigned Timoteo to work for Matt and Celestina after they had married.

He was now in his twenties and he was Matt's senior peon. Instead of shoveling the snow himself, Timoteo handed out the shovels to the other peons and shouted orders with a command voice that a sergeant major would envy. When the other peons finished shoveling, Timoteo assumed his role as chief cook, issuing precise instructions on building his cook fire.

Rather than lowering himself to the menial task of chopping onions and peppers, he supervised Pablo. Timoteo took over the work only when experience and talent became important. He sprinkled just the right amount of herbs on his rice, onion, and pepper dish and boiled it until the rice was soft but not too mushy.

Matt and Javier stood apart from their men, who were squatting by the fire. "Even the peons fit themselves into a hierarchy," Matt said. "After all these years in Mexico, it still surprises me."

"Knowing your place—where you fit in—is very comforting," Javier said. "You always know who you are and how you are supposed to act. You always know who is *usted* and who is *tú*. Americans are not quite sure who they are, and they waste a lot of time searching for their place."

They crawled into the tent and lighted two candles. On the solitary prairie, the candle glow made their tent look like a Chinese lantern. Snow fell all night and the wind blew in gusts, causing the tent's sides to collapse and expand like bellows. When there was enough light the next morning, Matt poked his friend. "Javier, your breath formed icicles in your beard. Don't bend your head down or you will stab yourself."

"I am happy that you can find humor in this, Mateo."

Timoteo supervised the boiling of coffee and the men warmed their hands on their tin cups and chewed mutton jerky for breakfast. When they finished, the peons began shoveling snow so the mules and horses could get at the dry brown nubbins of grass below, and Javier and his two peons went to the creek with axes and chopped holes in the ice so the animals could drink. On the north side of their wagons, the snow had banked to the top of the canvass bonnets. "Those are the biggest mountains you will see until you get back to New Mexico," Matt said to Javier.

That night the sky cleared, and the frigid air made the stars even more brilliant. "They look like crystal chandeliers stretching from horizon to horizon," Matt said. When the sun rose the next morning in a cloudless sky, Matt squinted at the light reflecting off the snow. Most of the horses and mules had wandered in search of food, and Matt sent Timoteo and Pablo to round them up.

When the two peons rode back into camp two hours later, they were so stiff with cold that the other men had to help them off their horses. "Most of the animals are in a cottonwood grove about two miles upstream" Timoteo said. "They gnawed plenty of bark for breakfast, so they are all right. But four mules and a horse did not find the trees. They are dead. Frozen."

After two days, the sun and a steady wind melted the snow enough for them to see the Trail's ruts. The small caravan left the next day and slogged through the mud until they made camp by Owl Creek. "With the wind blowing like this, the Trail will be a lot drier tomorrow," Matt said.

While the servants were loading the wagons the next morning, Matt heard the thwack, thwack of branches slapping on leather. He looked toward the sound and saw a white cap bobbing above the willows along Owl Creek. The white cap stopped for several seconds, turned slowly, and disappeared to a staccato of thwacking branches.

The peons, with Matt hurrying them, finished loading the wagons and the caravan got under way. It had gone less than two hundred yards when mounted men, led by the one in the white cap, rode out of the creek bottom. At their leader's signal, fourteen riders with rifles and pistols drawn split into two columns and surrounded the wagons.

"What brings you gentlemen out on the great plains so early this year?" the white cap asked.

"We've come from Santa Fe," Matt said. "We're traders. Are you gentlemen out for an early buffalo hunt?"

"Among other things."

"I'm Matt Collins. And you are?"

"McNulty. Captain Lloyd McNulty."

"Captain? In the Missouri militia?"

"The Republic of Texas army. I want you to turn them fuckin' wagons south and follow me."

"Captain, we want to get an early jump on our competitors this year, so we're anxious to get back to Missouri," Matt said.

"I ain't givin' you no choices, Mr. Collins."

"Let me speak to my friend."

"You can talk all you want, mister, but the order's the same," McNulty said, waving his hand to indicate that Matt could talk to Javier.

"What do they want?" Javier asked.

"They must be one of those Texian pirate bands we heard about. My guess is they will take our valuables and let us go."

"Quit speakin' that greaser language," McNulty said.

"Take what you need, Captain, and let us be on our way," Matt said. "We've got some extra jerky and coffee we could share with you, but we're pretty low on the rest of our supplies."

"You come with us," McNulty said. "We won't be takin' much of your time."

They followed the Texian soldiers to their camp, where they dismounted and collected Matt's and Javier's weapons. McNulty was much shorter than he had appeared on horseback. He had narrow shoulders and a sunken chest and legs as thin as cedar fence posts. A scar on his left cheek had twisted his mouth into a permanent scowl and a scanty beard partially disguised his youth.

McNulty motioned for Matt to follow him to their fire, but held up his other hand to indicate that Javier and the peons should stay by the wagons. "What's a white man doin' with them pepper bellies, Mr. Collins?"

"The well-dressed one is Javier Otero and the others are our servants. Mr. Otero comes from one of New Mexico's most respected families, and his father has close ties to Senator Benton."

"You know, Mr. Collins, I don't give a shit who their friends are." McNulty's smile made him look like a malevolent boy about to stick hot pins in a captive frog. "Nobody's forgot what them greasers done to the Texians they marched down to Mexico City in 'forty-one. An' I done heard about you, Mr. Collins, you and your partner."

"I thought you were from Texas, Captain McNulty. How do you know about Collins & Waterman?"

"We're from Missouri. Around Independence."

"How is it that you're a captain in the Texian army?"

"Colonel Robert Smith done give me my commission. And he got his directly from President Sam Houston. I seen the papers."

"We're north of the Arkansas River, Captain. Why is a Republic of Texas army operating on United States soil?"

"Our commission says we're part of the Invincible Battalion. An' Texas is at war with them spic bastards. An' we got the right to take Mexican property wherever we find it. We ain't gonna take your property, Mr. Collins, you bein' an American."

Matt thought for a second about correcting McNulty's assumption, but felt no guilt when he didn't say he was Mexican. *If McNulty thinks I'm an American,* he thought, *that might be our way out of this.* "Look, Captain, we've got some buffalo robes in the wagons. You can take them, mine included, if that'll expedite your letting us go on our way."

"We'll take the greaser's robes, but that ain't all we want," McNulty said.

"Before you take any precipitous action—"

"What's that?"

"Before you do anything rash, you should know that, if you hurt Mr. Otero, you will create real problems for yourself and your men."

"You may think I don't know much, Mr. Collins, but there's a couple of things I do know. This Señor Otero's a by God prisoner o' war and we're entitled to the spoils o' war." McNulty's eyes narrowed. "Whose side you on?"

Matt took a deep breath and curbed his anger, but didn't answer. McNulty ordered Matt and Javier to get under a wagon, and posted guards at all four wheels.

"What is McNulty going to do?" Javier whispered in Spanish.

"He will take our valuables, but I do not think that he will do violence to you and me. He hates Mexicans and he might do something to the peons."

"Does he know that you are a Mexican?"

"He has not asked," Matt answered. He was embarrassed and kept his eyes trained on his boots.

That night, Matt asked McNulty if they could set up a tent. Unexpectedly, the Texian captain agreed. Matt had a hard time going to sleep, but he slept until the dawn's light created an ominous gray in the tent. He remained quiet, listening to their guard clearing the phlegm from his throat and urinating by their tent flap. Javier rolled over and silently looked at Matt. Soon, they heard the other men rustling, a fire popping, and a spoon stirring coffee in a metal pot.

"You assholes get outa there," McNulty's voice commanded.

Matt and Javier stood with their backs to the fire and sidled up to the only well-dressed man among their captors. Dr. Philippe Agier, they learned, had lost his money in land speculation and his drinking had led the government to fire him from a job vaccinating Indians against smallpox. And his creditors had forced his wife and eight children out of their house. "They even took my medical library," he said. He had met McNulty in a tavern in Independence, and he had seen the Texian commission that authorized McNulty and his men to keep half of what they confiscated from Mexicans. "It seemed like a quick way to lay my hands on some cash."

Agier also told them that McNulty was hell-bent on shooting all the captives so there would be no witnesses. "But some men are arguing that they can't shoot you, Mr. Collins," Agier said, "because you're an American and this is American territory. That would be murder."

Javier looked at his feet and kicked a red coal back into the fire, waiting to see if Matt would confess his Mexican citizenship. For a second, Matt thought of telling the truth, but just as quickly he let the thought pass.

"My guess is they're going to send the pepper bellies—minus Mr. Otero—back to New Mexico on foot."

"That's a death sentence," Matt said. "Either they'll starve or the Comanches'll kill them."

"That's understood," Agier said.

"And me?" Javier asked.

"I'm not hopeful, Mr. Otero."

"Dr. Agier," Javier said, "would you be kind enough to ask Captain McNulty if I might have a private word with him?"

Agier found McNulty squatting behind a stand of brush. With the message delivered, the captain walked around the brush pulling up his pants and tucking in his shirt. He stopped within inches of Javier. "His doctorship says you wanna see me."

"Matt, would you come with Captain McNulty and me?" Javier said. "I want to make sure there's no misunderstanding if my English isn't good enough."

"Sure."

Javier led Matt and McNulty several paces away from the fire. "Captain, before you come to a final decision about me, I want to mention that I have a considerable amount of gold dust in a money belt around my waist. I'm offering this to you, separate and apart from what your friends and the Texian Republic get."

"I ain't sharin' nothin' with the Republic of Texas noways, Mr. Messkin," McNulty said.

"In addition, Captain, when I get to Missouri, I will arrange for my bank to pay you one thousand dollars. Mr. Collins can verify that I'm good for it."

"Lemme mull it some."

After breakfast, McNulty's men held a conference. Matt could not make out what they were saying, but heard shouted curses and rifle butts being hammered on the ground to punctuate the disputes. McNulty, sitting by himself by the fire, motioned to Javier to join him. "Mr. Messkin, I won't be goin' back to Independence any time soon to claim the money you offered. But you say you got gold strapped to your waist. Lemme have it."

Javier raised his shirt, took off the money belt, and handed it to the captain. "You got any more money hidden in them wagons?"

"No," Javier said.

McNulty ordered two of his men to search the wagons. Minutes later, the men returned with three rawhide sacks of silver pesos. "You lyin' son of a bitch," McNulty shouted in Javier's face. "I give you a chance, and you lied to me." He turned to his men: "Strip that fuckin' Messkin. We're gonna give him a whuppin', an' there ain't no use ruinin' a good set 'a clothes."

After the lashing, McNulty and two men took Javier over a small rise. Matt heard two shots and saw Javier running naked over the rise, followed by McNulty and the others. McNulty stopped, aimed his rifle, and fired. Javier dropped, but got up and ran, clutching his leg. McNulty caught him from behind and knocked his legs from under him with his rifle butt. Standing where Javier could watch him, McNulty slowly and deliberately reloaded his rifle, pointed it at the Mexican's face, and fired.

Matt's guards had forgotten about him and went to examine the corpse. He jumped on a saddled mare that was grazing close to the camp, grabbed the reins of another horse, and galloped out of the camp. He raced the horses until he was beyond rifle range and continued riding hard, changing mounts every hour, until well after dark. During the night, the chilled ground woke him and he forced the mare to her knees and onto her side. He tied her fore and hind legs with the bridle and, with the saddle blanket around his shoulders, snuggled up to the animal on the lee side of the wind.

Before dawn, Matt mounted and pushed the horses to a lope until he reached Lost Spring, stopping for a half hour to let the animals drink and forage. He slept a few hours at Diamond Spring, and the next morning he arrived at Council Grove. Matt headed for a pod of wagons parked on the west bank of the Neosho River and waved to the men milling around a large fire. "Why was you out on that godawful desert by yourself?" Don Blackburn, the caravan's captain, asked.

Matt quickly told Blackburn what had happened, sopped bread in bacon grease for breakfast, and got back on his horse. In Independence, he met with the sheriff and gave a detailed account of the murder before traveling east to meet with his business associates.

By May 1843 Matt had been to New York and Boston and had satisfied his suppliers and insurance carriers that Collins & Waterman would remain solvent, no matter what happened between Texas and Mexico. Then he took a steamboat down the Ohio and up the Mississippi to St. Louis to make his final arrangements for the spring caravan. Although Henry Hawley was the biggest wagon maker, Matt refused to do business with him. After a day negotiating to buy new wagons, he joined Jim Perryman in his hotel bar.

They discussed Javier Otero's murder and the strong reaction it had received in Santa Fe. It had created an explosive situation, and the Americans in New Mexico feared for their lives. There was also talk that President Santa Anna would shut down the Santa Fe Trail. While the two friends were exchanging news, Senator Thomas Hart Benton pulled up a chair and sat down at their table.

"We caught that son of a bitch McNulty, and he is going to get his due," Senator Benton said, his bulldog jowls trembling. "His defense is that he's a Texian privateer operating under color of law, but, for my money, they can't hang the murdering thief soon enough."

Matt had already signed a sworn statement describing the details of the murder. The prosecutor, the senator assured him, would introduce his statement into evidence and Matt would not be required to wait for the trial. But the state wanted the four peons who had been rescued to stay and testify in person. With Matt's and the peons' testimony, they all agreed, it was certain that the Texian captain would be convicted.

"We'll resolve this McNulty mess to my good friend Francisco Otero's satisfaction," Benton said. "But I'm more worried about what's going on in Mexico generally. How do you read it, Matt?"

"I'm not sure I know what you mean, Senator."

"Our last ambassador to Mexico told me that the country is in disarray." As Benton told of the sad state of Mexican politics, his voice took on the oratorical timbre that he usually reserved for the Senate floor. "We broke away from a king and so did they. We have problems in America, but Mexico is a disaster. You understand them, Matt. What's their problem?"

"There's no easy answer, Senator. But there are huge differences. Language. Culture. Religion. Outlook. Jim, can I have another mint julep?" Matt asked, uneasy and wanting to change the subject.

Benton, a veteran debater, refused let Matt divert him. "It must be frustrating, living down there," he said.

"Having a Mexican wife makes it easier. And I went to Santa Fe when I was only sixteen. I guess I was young enough to adjust."

Benton lit a cigar, carefully rolling it over a match. "There's no rule of law down there," he said.

"It's true that things get done on more of a personal basis," Matt said.

"There's some of that that goes on here," Jim said. "I had to contribute a barrel of beer to Alfie Griffith's campaign for mayor. No beer, and I'd get a visit from the city health inspector."

"Those things happen everywhere," Benton said with the air of a politician who had seen vice in all of its forms.

"But in Mexico it's institutionalized," Matt said. "If you don't play the game, you get spanked on the knuckles—or worse." Matt had already been more negative about Mexico than he had intended, and his strong feelings surprised even him. *Maybe I've had too many mint juleps,* he thought. Or maybe his doubts about his home country had been building up and had merely gone unsaid.

"Why," Benton asked, "can't their politicians unite on at least a few things? We've got this fight over slavery. But we've always compromised the nigger question, and on other issues we find ways to get along."

"I don't understand why people get so upset over niggers," Jim said. "I've got six darkies working for me and we don't have any problems."

"The Mexican Constitution outlaws slavery," Matt said. For reasons he couldn't define, he was unable to stop his criticism. "But New Mexico is so remote that nobody enforces it. And our debt peonage is nothing more than feudal serfdom dressed up in new clothes."

"I've read some of the Mexican liberals' writings," Benton said. "They sound like Thomas Jefferson or James Madison."

"To you, Senator," Matt said, "their words sound like beautiful music from a Mozart opera. But when the ruling class hears those same words, all they hear is the death knell of their system."

"What is it they hate about us?" Benton asked. Matt looked at the Senator carefully, thinking that he could not be so naive that he did not understand why Mexicans were skeptical of America.

"I'm not so sure it's hate," Jim said. "It's more suspicion and jealousy. When I was there in the thirties, you could feel it. The way they said 'Anglo-Saxon' with that certain tone."

"They're afraid that Americans are agents of change," Matt said. "It's the same thing as the slave owners not wanting abolitionists in South Carolina. And they're scared that the Americans are bound and determined to snatch New Mexico and California."

"Well, gentlemen, their suspicions are well grounded," Senator Benton said without hesitation. "I must go. My daughter has invited me for dinner."

"The senator's daughter is married to John C. Frémont," Jim said. "The fellow who mapped the Oregon Trail in 'forty-two."

After Senator Benton left, Matt sat quietly with his mint julep; his thoughts alternating between feeling guilty for criticizing Mexico and anger at being squeezed between the two cultures. "You know, Jim, every time the tension between Mexicans and Anglos increases, it gets harder. In St. Louis I feel like I'm pandering to the Americans if I say something bad about New Mexico. In Santa Fe it's the other way around. Some day soon this might explode like an overheated steamship boiler."

"I didn't think you were pandering."

"Jim, you lived in Santa Fe and you know that there are a lot of good things about New Mexico that I didn't bring up to Senator Benton. I don't like this—having a foot in two camps."

After Susano Baca's triumph over the Texians in 1841, it appeared that he could remain as New Mexico's governor for as long as he wanted. But his heroism lasted only until his next entry onto the battlefield. In 1843, gangs of armed men commissioned by the Republic of Texas—who the Mexicans called *banditti* and the Texians called soldiers of fortune—had been operating on both sides of the Arkansas River.

They attacked the village of Mora and killed five men, and were threatening to rob every Mexican merchant on the Santa Fe Trail. Governor Baca and Colonel Diego Zambrano put together an army and marched north toward the Arkansas. The Texians surrounded the New Mexican's advance guard and killed twenty-three without suffering a loss. Two New Mexicans escaped and rode south to warn Baca, who was leading the army's main body. The governor immediately ordered a retreat to Santa Fe. To punish Baca's cowardice, the central government sent a general from Mexico City to replace him.

Although Baca was once again out of office, he still had hopes of a return and schemed to regain his office. But his fainthearted military leadership had earned him the contempt of most New Mexicans, and his arbitrary treatment of American merchants had fouled his relations with them. Now that he was an ordinary citizen, Susano Baca wanted to mend fences. He asked La Dama to organize a *tertulia* at her private home and to invite Santa Fe's more prominent *ricos* and proprietors. Doña Julia, he knew, was always pleased to help repair relationships that would further the traffic on the Santa Fe Trail. "Santa Fe's future depends on the Missouri trade," she had told him.

"Julia, you look at things as cold-bloodedly as those damned Yankees do," Baca said.

"When we were younger, Susano, you thought I was hot-blooded," La Dama said, laughing. Instead of clapping for a servant in the Mexican style, she rang a small silver bell that an American admirer had brought her and ordered drinks to be brought to the *sala*.

La Castrense's bells struck nine and a servant ushered Matt, Edward, and three other Americans into the *sala*. "Welcome to my *tertulia*, gentlemen," she said in English.

"Thank you for inviting us, madam," Matt said, taking her hand and raising it to his lips. "There's no more elegant parlor in Santa Fe."

"Thank you, Matt."

"Could you please speak Spanish?" Baca asked.

"Of course," Matt said. "Please excuse us, Your Excellency."

"No need for titles any more," Baca said in an effort at joviality. He forced a chuckle.

"I slipped, Don Susano. I am sorry that the president chose to replace you with this Mexico City fellow," Matt said.

"This new chap," Baca sniped, "is not much better than Albino Pérez, constantly carping about New Mexico's backwardness."

"We may be in for difficult times," Matt said. "I was at the *posada* bar yesterday, and the gossip was that Governor Tafoya is going to raise the import taxes."

"These taxes, and Santa Anna's closing the border last year, are going to hurt," Edward Waterman said.

"But Santa Anna reopened the border in time for the eighteen forty-four caravans," La Dama said.

"Still, it is frightening to have a single man in Mexico City who can decree the destruction of your business," Edward said.

"But, Don Eduardo, you must admit that Governor Tafoya has done a few good things," La Dama said sarcastically. "At last, somebody has planted trees in the plaza so that it no longer looks like the Arabian Desert."

"Yes, yes," Baca said. "But he should listen to local people when it comes to local issues."

"You mean he should listen to you, Don Susano," La Dama said, snickering behind her fan. "Have another drink, gentlemen."

The door opened and Colonel Diego Zambrano entered the *sala*. "Welcome to our *tertulia* for out-of-work governors," Susano Baca joked.

More hacendados and proprietors filtered in and listened to the conversation, which centered on making fun of Governor Mariano Tafoya's fopperies. "That *hijo de puta*," Zambrano said, "is going to fall on his face up here."

"But he has Santa Anna's ear," Baca said. "Until someone else whispers in his other ear, we will have to live with Don Mariano."

When Moisés Mendoza entered the *sala*, Matt stood to give his father-in-law an *abrazo*. "I apologize for my lateness, Doña Julia," Moisés said.

"You, Don Moisés, may arrive at whatever time you like," La Dama said graciously. "Gentlemen, let us adjourn to the dining room." She rang her silver bell and instructed a servant: "María Concepcíon, tell the chef to send in our first course."

Edward helped La Dama into her chair at the head of the table. During the soup and tamale courses, she kept the conversation on the price of wheat and lambs, and arranged a pool bet on when the first caravan would arrive from Missouri. But the talk inevitably turned to Javier Otero's murder and Captain McNulty's death by hanging.

"I was surprised to see so much outrage in the American newspapers," Moisés said.

"My countrymen are still astonished by the brutality," Edward said. "But I am proud of the swift justice meted out by the American courts. And Mateo's testimony helped execute that *cabrón*."

"It could be that your American friends do not really give a damn about Javier Otero," said Zambrano, who had downed four glasses of wine. "It could be that they were only worried that Javier's murder might hurt the Santa Fe trade."

"That is not fair, Don Diego," Baca said. "Even the Americans are not that crass."

"Perhaps you are right, Don Susano, but they are not particularly generous," Zambrano said. "To them, everything is business."

"There is some truth in what you say, Don Diego," Matt said, "but I believe that the Americans felt genuine sympathy over Javier's death."

"Sympathy?" Zambrano said, rolling his eyes to the ceiling. "Like when the Yankees shot those five men at Mora last year?"

"It was not Americans, Colonel, it was Texians," Matt said. "And they were only reacting to the seventeen Texians that the Mexicans executed after the Mier Expedition."

"Americans and Texians are all the same," Zambrano said, "and they are all part of the conspiracy to steal Mexican territory."

"Gentlemen, all that happened months ago," La Dama broke in.

"If the Texians are right about their treaty with Santa Anna, everybody in Santa Fe are Texians," Moisés said. He had intended for the remark to be taken as a joke, and La Dama and most of the men had laughed.

"That is not funny, Don Moisés," Zambrano said angrily. "The Texians are full of shit. Santa Fe is not, and never will be, Texian or Yankee."

"But the Texians destroyed your advance guard last year," John Weber, a proprietor, said.

"God damn you, Weber," Zambrano shouted, standing and putting his hand on his saber.

"This is getting out of hand," La Dama said. "Calm yourselves."

"Let me explain why I ordered our forces to return to Santa Fe," Susano Baca said in his smooth baritone. "My spies told me that the Texians were numerous and that the enemy had the new revolver pistols and the latest percussion cap muskets and rifles, while my troops had worn-out flintlocks and bows and arrows. I decided to return to Santa Fe in order to save lives."

"I understand your logic," Matt said, hoping to end the conversation.

"Gentlemen, you all know that I am not afraid to meet the Anglos," Baca said. "You were here in 'forty-one when I demolished that Texian expedition."

"Nobody accuses you of anything, Don Susano," Matt said. "You have served our country and New Mexico well."

"I will not have any more of this heated talk at my table," La Dama said. "The Americans have their case and the Mexicans theirs. We will not discuss it further."

Shortly after the new governor, Mariano Tafoya, had arrived from Mexico City in 1844, he sent the Mexican army in search of a Navajo band that had been raiding frontier villages. The soldiers mistook a Ute encampment for a Navajo, and slaughtered braves, women, and children. The Utes, who thought they were under the protection of a peace treaty they had signed, were enraged. To quiet them, the governor invited three chiefs to meet with him in Santa Fe. Instead, hundreds of armed Utes made camp in a field just outside the capital.

Matt moved his household to the Mendoza's fortresslike compound and joined Edward in their store. They barricaded themselves inside, stacking buffalo hides and pushing shelving in front of their doors and windows.

"The government has to stop sending incompetents like Tafoya up here," Matt said. "Undoubtedly, he was good at ballroom politics in Mexico City, but he doesn't have a glimmer of how to deal with Indians."

Matt and Edward got almost no sleep. All night, gunshots from Ute braves firing in the air punctuated their drumming and chanting. In the morning, the two partners moved a stack of buffalo robes from in front of a window and watched the Indians, in full war paint, shout curses at two Mexican soldiers who were guarding the palace's entrance. Suddenly the palace doors flew open and Mexican soldiers ran into the plaza. They fired randomly into the crowd, and the Utes panicked, broke, and ran west down Palace Street to their camp. Before the Mexican officers could reorganize their forces, the Utes mounted their horses and rode west toward the Rio Grande.

"Is the army going to follow them?" someone asked Colonel Zambrano.

"Governor Tafoya does not want to take any action. He says there are too many of them," Zambrano answered.

"But they will take revenge on our villages and *ranchos*," another man said.

"That may be," Zambrano said, a look of disgust on his face, "but those are his orders."

Several days after the Ute incident, Diego Zambrano and La Dama were enjoying her best brandy in the office behind her cantina. "Why can't Mexico City give us a governor with *cojones?*" the colonel said. "This coward Tafoya refuses to punish the Utes."

"I heard that the Indians slaughtered two families outside of Ojo Caliente," La Dama said. "They murdered everyone."

"President Santa Anna's emissary paid me a visit last week," Zambrano said. "The government is thinking about replacing Tafoya with Baca. I told him that Baca has proven over and over that he is totally unfit to be governor."

"Susano has his faults, but he understands the savages."

"He sells himself to whomever pays the most. He would even sell out to the Yankees if the price was right."

"It is no secret," La Dama said, "that Don Susano is, shall we say, a little on the acquisitive side."

"Acquisitive? That fat *hijo de puta* is a thief."

"Who else would you have as governor, Diego?"

"I could do a better job than that incompetent."

"You would undoubtedly make an excellent governor, Diego, but now I want you to meet a splendid new American girl."

"What is she like?"

"She is tall. Statuesque. A mound of beautiful red hair. And her bosom and her figure are exquisite. Do you think you can set aside your patriotism for an hour or two?"

"What is her name."

"Dixie Ledford."

BOOK III

1846

CHAPTER TWENTY

1846

"All we want to do is lift the New Mexicans out of squalor. What they need is a good dose of American optimism and get-up-and-go."

AFTER HIS WHITE HOUSE MEETING WITH PRESIDENT POLK AND Senator Benton, Matthew Collins walked down Pennsylvania Avenue to the City Hotel. He had lunch by himself in the quiet comfort of the hotel's oak paneled restaurant and went to his room to lie down and think. A cold wind blew in through the open window and Matt sat up, pulled a blanket to his chest, and lay back with his arm over his eyes to blot out the light.

In a way, Matt thought, *I'm flattered that Senator Benton recommended me for this mission. But Polk was uncertain.* "I'm worried about your loyalty to the United States," *the president had said.*

At first, the president's bluntness had offended Matt, but, as he thought about it, it wasn't unreasonable for Polk to put him to the test. If the president sent an untrustworthy agent to Santa Fe he might jeopardize the Mexican–American war.

But the question for Matt was whether he wanted to work against Mexico. He got up from the bed and sat down at a small desk in front of the window and looked out at the White House. For a moment, he listened to the street clatter and watched the military officers and government workers hurrying from building to building. He took a quill pen and City Hotel stationary out of the desk and listed the pros and cons. "I'll treat it like any other business proposition," he muttered to himself.

"Mexico has been good to me," he included in his list of pros. "For the first time in my life I have a family; even Sara Mendoza treats me like a family member." Among the items favoring his siding with the United States, he wrote: "I'll never forget the insulting poem that Celestina's cousin recited at our wedding; I'll always be a foreigner in many people's eyes. Do I want my children and grandchildren to grow up in a forgotten backwash, a province that nobody cares about?"

Frustrated with his indecision, he threw the quill on the desk, splattering ink on his balance sheet. He went downstairs to the bar, where he saw Senator Benton's beefy hand waving to him from a corner table.

"Matt, this is Silas Thayer from Massachusetts, one of our finest congressmen," Benton said, "and this is Matt Collins, one of Santa Fe's most successful businessmen. Sit down and have a drink with us, Matt. Congressman Thayer is on the War Committee, and I was just telling him about the mission we have in mind for you."

Thayer came from a New England family that included Cotton Mather in its genealogy. He had the sharp, craggy good looks of a patrician, and he carried himself with an air of complete self-confidence. He was thin and almost as tall as Matt, and he combed his snow white hair straight back.

"What do you make of what's happening between us and Mexico?" Thayer asked.

"Things are moving pretty fast," Matt said. "Texas being annexed into the Union. General Taylor marching to the Rio Grande. Battles around Matamoros."

"President Polk only ordered Zack to march after Mexico turned down our offer to buy their northern territory," Senator Benton said. "I thought they'd take it. Twenty-five million is a lot for a bankrupt country."

"Don't you think it was a bit presumptuous, Senator—offering to buy a part of a sovereign nation?" Thayer asked.

"Why, hell, everything's for sale down there," Benton answered.

"The battle reports say the fighting was vicious at Palo Alto and Resaca de la Palma," Thayer said.

"The Mexicans attacked first," Benton said. "Came across the Rio Grande."

"Senator, you know as well as I do that there are varying versions of who provoked whom," Thayer said. "Some would argue that when General Taylor blocked the mouth of the Rio Grande it was an act of war."

"Mexico was clearly the aggressor, and the president had to preserve our honor," Benton said, annoyed with what he considered Thayer's effete timidity.

"I worry," Thayer said, "that our expansion will spread slavery."

"Why, hell, man," Benton said, "even with slavery, the New Mexicans'll be better off with us."

"You talk like it's a sure thing we'll win," Thayer said.

"Those goddamned Mexicans—excuse me Matt—can't pour piss out of a boot," Benton said. "A bunch of Texian militiamen whipped Santa Anna's regulars at San Jacinto and that New Mexican governor ran away from a fight in 'forty-three."

"Gentlemen," Thayer said, pulling himself up from his chair, "I have a committee meeting." He shook hands and left.

"The president has decisions he needs to make," Benton said. "Things are in motion. Zack Taylor is advancing on Monterrey and Winfield Scott is planning his attack on Veracruz. General Scott says we have enough men and supplies to fight a two-front war, but it would be rough going if we had to fight on three fronts. His plan calls for taking New Mexico without a fight."

"I understand," Matt said.

"Confidentially, President Polk has already ordered General Kearny to march to New Mexico. What kind of an army could Governor Baca raise?"

"I would guess that he could muster four or five thousand men. Militiamen mostly."

"I know you're having a difficult time deciding whether to help us," Senator Benton said, his deep voice assuming a warm and reassuring tone. "If you don't mind, Matt, I'd like to share some things that have come to mind."

Before Matt could answer, Benton began pleading his case. He enjoyed the combat of debate, at which he considered himself a virtuoso, and leaned forward until his large, square face was inches from Matt's. "Since the day Cortés conquered Mexico, it has been mired in ignorance and despotism," Benton said.

"I'm afraid, Senator, that you have fallen victim to the Black Legend—that old shibboleth that everything Spanish is bad or cruel." Matt's muscles tensed, but he willed them to relax.

"You once told me that you were an orphan. If you'd grown up in Mexico, you'd have been a peon with no chance of working your way out of that hole," Benton said. His mastiff-like jowls began trembling, whether with rage or righteousness Matt couldn't tell. "The Mexicans need to be conquered because they can't govern themselves. It's a republic without citizens."

To that point, Matt had controlled his anger at Benton's simplistic view of Mexico. But, he decided, the senator had gone far enough. "With all due respect, sir, that condescending attitude—that Americans have all the answers—is dead wrong."

"Well, son, the Mexicans damned sure don't have the answers," Benton said. He shifted his argument from denunciation to seizing the high moral ground. "You yourself told me there's no sawmill, no blacksmith, no doctors, no tannery. We'll bring them schools and newspapers. All we want to do is lift the New Mexicans out of squalor. We'll be rescuing them from themselves. And we'll bring them democracy."

Matt's face and neck were crimson. "If what the Americans bring is their bombastic jingoism and vulgarity and bad manners, then New Mexico may be better off the way it is."

"The way it is now—is broken," Benton said, adopting a prosecutor's intimidating tone and jabbing his finger at Matt's nose. "They can't even protect New Mexico from Stone Age savages like the Comanches. They've had nothing but civil war since they broke away from Spain. What New Mexicans need is a good dose of American optimism and get-up-and-go."

"But there's a trade-off, Senator. You Yankees are so serious about getting up and going all the time that there's no time for life's pleasures."

"I guess you're right, my boy," Benton said, and turned to sarcasm. "Perhaps the Mexicans have plenty of time to enjoy life's pleasures because the Church and the government do their thinking for them. What's the old saying about Spaniards: 'The King commands their bodies and the Pope commands their souls.' That's what stifles their initiative, their get-aheadedness."

"Do you think those American trappers and teamsters who come to Santa Fe are tying to get ahead?" Matt asked. His voice was so loud that the men at the bar turned to stare. "For the most part, they're drunks or criminals running away from the law."

"That's enough, son," Benton said.

"Don't call me 'son.'"

"Excuse me, Matt, but I feel strongly about this, and so does the president. Let me put another thought to you. You can save thousands of lives if you convince Baca and Zambrano to stay in the barracks with their arms stacked. You have a decision to make, Matt."

"I know. I guess we'll see whether I'm Mexican or American."

"I guess we will. I'll pick you up at nine-thirty tomorrow morning to go to the White House."

In his room after Senator Benton left, Matt sat at the desk and gazed out the window for more than an hour before going back downstairs to the bar. While he was finishing his second whiskey nog, Congressman Thayer sat down on a stool next to him. The conversation moved from the Irish potato famine to Beethoven's opera *Fidelio*, which was playing in Washington, and, then, to the Mexican war. "It has to be difficult," Thayer said. "Born American, but a Mexican citizen. And the two at war."

"Senator Benton and I had a very difficult discussion about that."

"The good senator can be a bully when he's after something," Thayer said, chuckling.

"He was heavy-handed and insulting," Matt blurted out.

"Strong words for the distinguished Senator from Missouri, Mr. Collins, but no doubt well deserved. There are not many things that Thomas Hart Benton and I would agree upon, but I do agree with him on this Mexico situation. The Mexican Republic is so weak that it is very possible that a European power will take control of the Pacific Coast. We're already squabbling with England over Oregon."

"I take your point, Congressman," Matt said.

Thayer spoke slowly and deliberately, "To me, it is an inexorable fact that the United States is going to acquire new territory. I rather agree with an editorial I read the other day. The thrust of it was that it is our manifest destiny to expand to the Pacific Ocean."

"I'm having one more drink and then I'm going to bed," Matt said.

"Good luck, Mr. Collins. I don't envy you the decision you have to make," Thayer said, and left.

In his room, Matt relaxed for the first time since his polemic with Benton. The senator had come at him like a pugilist, punching and pounding home his arguments. That in turn had fired Matt's instinct to resist. But as he went over the pluses and minuses again, he found himself leaning toward Congressman Thayer's view that an American conquest of the West was inevitable.

The next morning a hall porter opened Matt's door. "It's after eight, Mr. Collins. You'd better get a move on. Senator Benton'll be pickin' you up shortly, and he don't like to be kept waitin'. You looks a little woozy. I'll bring you some coffee.'"

Matt ordered two pitchers of water to give himself a spit bath. He put on fresh underclothes and a white shirt that the City Hotel's laundress had boiled and starched, brushed his charcoal gray wool suit, and picked out a black silk vest and tie.

"Well, what's it going to be," Senator Benton asked as their carriage passed the Treasury Department.

"You'll know when I tell the president," Matt said, annoyance in his voice.

"I may have been a little rough last night, Matt, and I apologize. Sometimes, my emotions run away with me. But it's our God-given right to protect our western flank. Next to the Revolution, this is the most important question our republic has faced."

They rode in silence the rest of the way along Pennsylvania Avenue and into the presidential mansion's gravel drive. "You're early, Senator," the White House butler said, "but the president told me to bring you and Mr. Collins in as soon as you got here."

"Sit down, gentlemen, and have some coffee," James Polk said in his drawling Tennessee accent. "Well, Mr. Collins?"

"This is very difficult for me, Mr. President."

"I'm sure it is."

"If I help, and if the United States doesn't take over New Mexico, I could lose everything."

Polk's eyes locked on Matt's. "In politics, and war, and business, Mr. Collins, there are uncertainties. But there is one thing that I am certain of: we are going to own New Mexico and California. It's only a matter of time until General Scott grabs those Mexican politicians by their throats and shakes them until that dictator they call president gives us what we want."

"Mr. Collins," Polk continued, "let me put this on a personal level. I read you to be an ambitious man. So am I. I would have never been content to be a bump on a log in a million-tree forest, and I think you're the same. You've done well and become a man of substance. But what you've done so far won't mean a damned thing to history. On the other hand, if you're an instrument in bringing millions of square miles under the American flag, then you'll have made your mark."

"Mr. President, may I have a few minutes to go outside and think about this?" Matt asked.

"Yes," Polk said.

"What the hell is going on, Tom?" Polk asked Benton when Matt left. "You said there wouldn't be any problem getting this Collins on board."

"I may have riled him yesterday, Jim. I may have come down on him too hard. We'd had a few drinks," Benton said.

Matt nervously paced the greening lawn. All manner of thoughts were racing through his mind, and he struggled to clear it. *This is the most agonizing decision I've ever faced.* His mouth went dry and a sour taste coated his tongue. He had never been afraid to gamble and had taken pride in his ability to calculate the odds and to keep emotion from clouding his judgment. But those earlier decisions, to run away from his apprenticeship and to face danger on the Santa Fe Trail had only involved himself. This decision would affect Celestina, Miguel, and Ana María—and the Mendoza clan. Never had he been forced to confront something that was so personal, so visceral. If he acted for the United States and it failed to conquer New Mexico, things could spin out of control. The mob might murder his family and Susano Baca would surely confiscate all of his property. One last time, he ran through the list of arguments for and against helping the United States. Then he made his decision. He went inside, knocked, and opened the president's office door. "Mr. President?"

"What did you conclude?"

"How can I help?"

"You have made a wise choice," Polk said. "Mr. Collins, I'm authorizing you to do what it takes to convince Governor Baca and Colonel Zambrano that it is not in their best interests to fight. You can tell them whatever you like, but the main point to drive home is that history is on our side—and, as certain as it is that God created this earth, it is certain that the United States will own New Mexico."

"Governor Baca is a very acquisitive man," Matt said.

"You can guarantee him up to three hundred thousand in gold, deposited wherever he wishes," Polk said.

"My God, sir, there's nobody in New Mexico who has that much cash."

"I don't mean for you to offer the whole amount. Negotiate. Get the best deal you can. But go all the way if you have to. It'll be cheaper than fighting a war."

"And for Colonel Zambrano?" Matt asked.

"What will it take?"

"He's not averse to money, but money alone won't move him."

"Senator Benton tells me you're a clever man, Mr. Collins. I can come up with two hundred thousand for the Colonel, but it will be up to you to find a way to sway him."

"I want to involve my partner, Edward Waterman," Matt said. "He has a better relationship with Colonel Zambrano than I do."

"I don't give a damn how you do it, Mr. Collins. Just get it done. If you need to take liberties with the truth, then so be it. Within reason, I'll back you up. Now, if you'll excuse me, Mr. Collins—Senator, can you stay for a moment?" Matt left the president's office.

"Collins didn't ask for a dime," Polk said. "I was waiting for that shoe to drop."

"He has convinced me that he genuinely likes many things about Mexico," Benton said, "but he's also practical. I suspect that knows that New Mexico joining the Union will increase his fortune tenfold."

Matt traveled from Washington to St. Louis by the quickest means, and checked into the Perryman Hotel. After he unpacked, he went downstairs and found Edward Waterman on the wide porch that faced the Mississippi River. Edward was sitting in a wicker rocking chair reading a book when Matt walked up. The two partners embraced and clapped one another on the back in the Mexican style, drawing a look of puzzlement from a well-dressed American seated a few feet away.

Edward had left Santa Fe shortly after Matt so that he could organize an early caravan, but, he reported General Kearny's march down the Santa Fe Trail had cut the trade link with New Mexico.

Matt turned and told a slave who was standing silently behind their chairs to bring rum punch. When the drinks came, Matt told Edward about his visit with President Polk and Senator Benton. "I agreed to help the Americans."

"What do they want you to do?" Edward asked, rocking his chair gently.

"They want Baca and Zambrano to surrender," Matt said. He stopped when a steamboat whistle drowned out his voice and then continued. "Polk doesn't want to fight a major battle in New Mexico."

"I'm not so sure that Baca and Zambrano will roll over and play dead," Edward said.

"My instructions from the president allow me to bring you in—if you want to get involved." Edward, Matt knew, was as passionate in his love of the United States as Colonel Zambrano was in his of the Mexican Republic. "I think I can convince Baca," Matt continued, "but if anyone can persuade Zambrano that it's foolish to resist, it's you. Between the two of us we can get it done."

"Zambrano's touchy as hell about anything he thinks insults Mexico's honor," Edward said. "Trying to get him to surrender might spark his flash pan. I'm not so sure I want to get involved in this. I need some time to think."

Edward's caution caught Matt short. But they had been partners for almost twenty years, and Matt knew that Edward didn't like to be pressured. Still, Edward's good relationship with Zambrano made his partner's involvement crucial. "I agree with you that it won't be easy to bring Zambrano along," Matt said. "I can't share the details, but President Polk gave me plenty of latitude to offer attractive packages."

"The only package you'll need for Zambrano is a blond or a redhead," Edward said, laughing and taking a deep swallow of his rum punch. "He's crazy about a new gal—Dixie Ledford—that La Dama imported. He's set her up with her own house and servants. Dama is mad as hell, because Dixie was her top earner."

"The *Missouri Queen* leaves for Independence tomorrow," Matt said.

"Explain something, old friend. Why in the hell did you get mixed up in this? This is rolling the dice for everything you've got."

"Edward, you've known me long enough to know that I don't take foolish risks. I've thought this through, and I don't think there's a chance in hell that the Americans will fail."

"If Baca and Zambrano raise enough men, they might whip Kearny's ass," Edward said.

"I've looked Polk in the eye, and I can tell you that he's determined to do whatever is necessary to get to win this war."

"What about Celestina? How is she going to feel about you helping deliver New Mexico to the Philistines?"

"She likes the United States. Not everything, but most everything."

"And her father?"

"He used to think Mexico could sort things out. But he's disenchanted with the *cuartelazos*, the anarchy. And he worries that Mexico's weakness is an open invitation for France or England to conquer it. He'd rather be an American than part of some European kingdom."

"I'll go with you as far as Independence," Edward said.

———

In the *Missouri Queen*'s lounge, Edward listened while Matt talked him through the rationale that had led him to his conclusion. Edward was noncommittal, puffing his cigars and nodding ambiguously.

Edward had turned fifty earlier in 1846. He had no family, but he still had hopes. He had a plantation in the fertile Missouri River Valley and he would be able to live comfortably with the money he had in American banks. Why should he upset his safe world?

Edward had listened as Matt made his case for becoming an American agent. Without knowing why, he felt the same insecurity that he had suffered when the Christian boys taunted him in Vienna forty years ago. Despite his discomfort, Edward had long since decided that it was better to be in position to have some control over events than to stand back and wait to be impacted by them.

He knew that his hesitancy had surprised Matt. In their dealings over the years, they had prided themselves on their abilities to study situations and make quick decisions. "To hell with it," he said out loud to himself while he was undressing in his cabin on the night before they were to dock at Independence. "I came to America to get away from fear. I owe America something. And I owe Matt." He put his pants and shirt back on and walked barefoot to Matt's cabin. "I'll help," he said. The partners shook hands without speaking, and Edward went back to his cabin and slept.

The *Missouri Queen* docked in the early afternoon and Matt and Edward rode to Independence in a hired carriage. They bought a Dearborn buggy, two spare wheels, and eight strong mules. Before sunup the next morning they were on the Santa Fe Trail. General Kearny's baggage wagons had cut deep ruts in the main trail, forcing the partners to find smoother ground to avoid breaking a wheel or axle. They pressed the mules hard, rotating fresh animals into the buggy's traces every two hours and traveling from before morning light until well after the sun set. They ate cold meals without stopping, bouncing along in the Dearborn. With plenty of grass from good spring rains, the well-fed-and-watered mules covered five hundred and fifty miles in two weeks.

Matt saw dust in the air in front of them. He stood on the Dearborn's seat, pointed his brass telescope west, and made out the blocklike solidity of Bent's Fort on the horizon. By late afternoon they were driving past army tents pitched on the rise above the Arkansas River. A guidon in front of an officer's tent identified the unit as the Mounted Volunteers, farmers and frontiersmen recruited from western Missouri. Farther on, they passed volunteer cavalrymen from St. Louis and the regular army's First Dragoons. When they approached a row of cannons, they stopped to chat with Meriwether Lewis Clark, the commander of the sixteen-gun artillery company.

In front of the Fort's *zaguán*, a Mexican servant trotted out and led their mules and buggy to the corral. After two weeks alone on the prairie ocean, the Fort's sounds were jarring—Son of a Bitch and God-damn pounding their hammers, peacocks screeching, and drunken men shouting.

Matt nodded toward the middle of the patio where a dragoon and a volunteer private were shoving one another. The dragoon turned to walk away and the volunteer smashed the back of his head with a blow that sent the dragoon reeling into the buffalo hide press. A regular army lieu-tenant ran out of the blacksmith shop and ordered men from his company to arrest the volunteer. They tied the offender's hands to the hide press and stripped off his shirt. At Lieutenant Dunning's order, a sergeant used a teamster's blacksnake whip to lay three lashes on the volunteer's back. "I didn't want to hurt him too much," Dunning told Matt later. "I just wanted to remind him he's here to fight greasers, not brother soldiers."

Matt and Edward found General Kearny's headquarters tent just out-side the fort's walls. "General, I'm Matthew Collins, and this is my part-ner, Edward Waterman."

"It's 'Colonel,' not 'General,'" Kearny said, leaning back in his can-vass camp chair and appraising his visitors.

"I've just come from Washington," Matt said, "and the president has authorized me to tell you that you've been promoted to brigadier gen-eral. You'll get the papers later."

"About time," Kearny said, grimacing. His face turned parchment white and he grabbed his stomach and rushed out of the tent.

"Is there a problem, General?" Edward asked when he returned.

"My apologies," Kearny said. "A touch of the shits. Feels like I've got a bellyful of copperhead snakes. It's this goddamned alkali water."

"No apology necessary, General," Matt said.

"What do you have for me?" Kearny asked, scowling from the pain rolling through his bowels.

"A letter from President Polk," Matt said.

Kearny read the letter slowly and looked over his glasses. "How do you figure your chances, Mr. Collins? Baca's supposed to be an unpredictable old rogue and they say Zambrano's as tough as a bois d'arc tree."

"Between Mr. Waterman and me, we know these men as well as anybody," Matt said. "I think we can get them to see reason."

"There are lots of rumors flying around," Kearny said. "I've heard that General Gomez is marching from Mexico City to Santa Fe with three thousand men. And that Baca has raised five thousand men."

"I don't believe the story about the Mexicans sending troops to Santa Fe," Matt said. "New Mexico is the last place the central government is worried about. They will concentrate their forces against General Taylor's army at Monterrey."

"We've seen the kind of soldiers Baca can raise," Edward added. "He'll round up Pueblo Indians and he'll force the *hacendados* to send him their peons. Even if he gets ten thousand men, General, you'll bowl them over."

"What has the president authorized you to offer, Mr. Collins?"

"Those orders are secret, General."

Kearny switched to his sternest voice of command. "I need to know so I can decide whether it's likely Baca and Zambrano will give up."

"I'm sorry, sir, but I can't."

"Goddamn you, Collins, I'm ordering you to tell me. My men's lives are at stake," Kearny flared.

"General, I know you have some fine gentlemen in your army—" Matt said.

"There are captains, lieutenants, and privates in this army," Kearny interrupted, "but there are no gentlemen. Damnit, what kind of offer can you make?"

"Sir, with respect, I can't comment," Matt said.

"If they decide to fight, it could be a mess," Kearny said. "Our supply line to Missouri is stretched thinner than a whore's nightgown. Now you, by God, tell me."

"I won't, General, but I can tell you this. I'm authorized to deliver cash payments that are many times more than the New Mexican government has ever had in its treasury. It's enough to accomplish our purpose."

"How certain are you?"

"Nothing is certain, General," Matt said.

Kearny, remembering that Matt was on a presidential mission, softened his tone. "I don't know a damned thing about what the Mexicans will or won't do, but I do know that you'd damned well better be right, Mr. Collins."

Matt watched as General Kearny, Lieutenant Dunning, and a corporal's guard pushed through a crowd of trappers, Cheyenne Indians, and soldiers that had formed a circle around William Bent and three Mexican peons in front of the *zaguán*. "What you got here, Mr. Bent?" Kearny asked.

"My hunters caught them just this side of Ratón Pass," Bent said. "At first, they said they were *ciboleros*. But they've admitted that Governor Baca sent them to do some spying."

"Do they speak English?" Kearny asked.

"No," Bent said.

"Lieutenant Dunning, these men came a long way to find out what we're all about. I want you to accommodate these greasers," Kearny said, pausing and looking closely at the prisoners to see if they reacted to his insult. When they didn't, he said, "Give them the royal tour."

The army camp was strung out for two miles along the Arkansas, making it appear that it was much larger than it actually was. Lieutenant Dunning and a guard detail took the captives to review the First Dragoons drilling in close order. And Major Clark's artillerymen demonstrated a twelve-pounder that shattered a cottonwood tree more than four hundred yards away.

After the Mexican captives toured the Army of the West, General Kearny received them in his white, conical tent. Sitting behind his campaign desk, with Matt beside him to translate, he motioned to the prisoners to sit on a bench. "Mr. Collins," the General said, "tell these Mexican gentlemen that I am going to release them unharmed. Tell them that I want them to go back to their country so that they can tell their governor what they've seen. Tell them . . ."

Matt broke in. "Just a minute, General. That's a lot to translate. Let me tell them what you've said so far."

After Matt translated, Kearny resumed. "Tell them that we have a well-trained professional army of three thousand men in camp and another five thousand troops who are three days' march up the Santa Fe

Trail," Kearny lied. "Tell them that I will crush any attempt to stop the Army of the West." After Matt translated, the guards led the three Mexicans to their horses and watched while they trotted toward the Arkansas River.

The general smiled almost benignly at Matt. "Mr. Collins, I have a rough draft of a proclamation to the people of New Mexico. I tried to address what I perceive to be the New Mexican's concerns, but I welcome your suggestions. Lieutenant, read the salient points." Dunning, his aide de camp, read in a monotone:

> "People of New Mexico. I have come amongst you to take possession of your country. We come amongst you as friends—not as enemies; as protectors—not as conquerors. I absolve you of all allegiance to the Mexican government. I now tell you that those who remain peaceably at home shall be protected by me in their persons and their property. My troops will not take a pepper, not an onion, without the consent of the owner and without paying for it. But those who are found to be in arms against me, I will hang."

Lieutenant Dunning looked up from the paper and indicated that he had finished the text.

"May I suggest," Matt said, "that you say something about religion and protecting them from Indians."

"Take this down, Lieutenant," Kearny said. " 'You have never received protection from the Mexican government. The Apaches and Navajos come down from the mountains and carry off your sheep, and even your women. My government will protect you against the Indians.' "

"That's good," Matt said.

"I don't know much about the papist religion, Mr. Collins. Can you suggest something?"

"What about this, General?" Matt began dictating: "I will protect you in your religion. I know that you are Catholics, and that some of your priests have told you that we will ill-treat your women. That is all false. My government respects your religion as much as the Protestant religion."

"That's good," Kearny said when Matt finished.

"We'll leave in the morning," Matt said.

"I've told my quartermaster to give you four good horses. How long will it take?"

"It's right at two hundred and fifty miles, General. We can make Santa Fe in five or six days."

"I'm going to rest the army here for another two days, and then we'll move out. I'll see you in Santa Fe, hopefully without a fight."

"We'll do our best, General," Matt promised.

CHAPTER TWENTY-ONE

1846

*"Polk says you are empowered . . . Don Mateo . . . to extend certain offers.
Putting aside for now the question of what a Mexican is doing negotiating on
behalf of a foreign country, what do you have to offer?"*

BEFORE NOON MATT AND EDWARD CRESTED A RISE THAT
looked down on Santa Fe. Matt stopped to watch a peon on the southern outskirts plowing his corn field with an ox and a wooden plow.

With his telescope, he made out his brown adobe home on the hill
north of town and tried to imagine what Celestina was doing. The two
men slapped their horses' rumps with their reins and rode off the Trail
to a piñon grove, where they hid their animals and stretched out to wait,
unsure of the reception they might receive.

After midnight, they rode to the Collins & Waterman store on the deserted plaza. Edward unloaded his belongings from his saddlebags and
went inside without lighting a candle. Matt walked the horses as quietly
as he could along the palace's east side, wishing that their scuffing hooves
made less noise. When he passed the palace, he mounted and then rode
to his house, where he tapped on the door with his riding crop until Timoteo came and unlocked it. He crossed the patio with a lantern and went
into their bedroom so quietly that Celestina did not wake until he sat
down and tickled a foot that was sticking out of the covers.

They took only enough time for her to tell him that the children
were healthy—and then they made love.

The next morning, they chatted by the fire in their bedroom until a
servant brought them a breakfast of scrambled eggs, sausage, and corn
tortillas. When they finished, he told her about his commitment to President Polk in as matter-of-fact a voice as he could muster. Celestina

asked no questions during the telling, but sat brittle and motionless with her hands in the lap of her silk dressing gown. While he was giving his rationale for his decision, she moved to her dresser mirror, swooped up her hair, and began placing pins to hold it in a French twist. Matt stared at her long, delicate neck, the feature that he remembered in the greatest detail whenever he was away from her.

"Why did you get involved?" she asked when he finished.

"I don't like being in the middle of this," he said.

"Can't you get out of it?" she asked. She took off her gown and went to their wardrobe to select a dress. "Why don't you let Edward handle it?"

"I gave President Polk my word."

"Help me with these buttons," she said, pulling up the dress and turning her back to him. Matt had thought through several versions of how Celestina might react, but her complete serenity was not one of them. *Surely,* he worried, *she's holding in something that might explode.*

Instead, Celestina listened placidly while Matt continued to make his case. He finished and went quiet, waiting for her response. For a long moment the only sounds were the miniexplosions of pine sap from the fireplace and the rustling of Celestina's dress while she adjusted it. In slow and deliberate Spanish, she said: "Your former countrymen have dressed up this manifest destiny in sacred robes. But the plain fact is that Mexico is weak, and America is going to take advantage of that to conquer New Mexico. I will say this only once, *mi amor,*" Celestina continued, looking straight at him with unblinking blue-black eyes. "I agree with some of your conclusions. Still, I am not comfortable with what is happening. But I am a Spanish wife. You are committed to this, and I will not object."

Matt was not sure whether to be relieved that she had gone along with him or fearful that she might harbor some lasting resentment. He stood and took her in his arms and kissed her, and she kissed him back. "That is enough of politics," she said. "This is behind us."

While he was dressing, Matt asked Celestina whether he might run into trouble if he appeared in public. "There haven't been any demonstrations for over a week. Besides, everybody knows you are a Mexican. Just don't wear that stovepipe hat," she said. They both laughed.

Later that morning, Matt went to the palace to arrange a meeting with Susano Baca but got no farther than the governor's secretary, who told him that Baca would not see him—then or at any other time. Matt left and immediately went to La Dama's establishment in Burro Alley. Through Payaso, the well-muscled man who kept the peace in the cantina, he arranged a meeting with her at her home that night.

After dark, Matt and Edward knocked on her door and a servant ushered them into the *sala*. Her parlor was sumptuous by Santa Fe standards. Red velvet was glued to the adobe walls and the two partners settled comfortably into oversized, stuffed chairs covered in purple damask. La Dama made her entrance, took her seat in a high-backed mahogany chair, and planted her feet on a puffy goose down pillow.

"Doña Julia," Matt said, "thank you for allowing us to visit. You look particularly beautiful tonight."

"For a woman of my age, all compliments are welcome," La Dama said, waggling a rhinestone-studded fan that caught the candle's flicker and sent light points flashing across the walls. "What can I do for you, Don Mateo?"

"Doña Julia, the American president has commissioned me to explore with Governor Baca and Colonel Zambrano the possibility of a peaceful settlement."

"I have heard that the Yankee army has left Bent's Fort," she said. "That is not all bad."

"I could not agree with you more," Edward said. "But I am surprised."

"What is there to be surprised about, Don Eduardo? I remember the days before the Americans came. There was no money. But your countrymen have made me quite comfortable. They gamble. They drink. They dally."

"The wags say you have more money than Governor Baca," Matt said, laughing.

"I do not know about that," she said, her smile revealing a set of ivory false teeth that she had had made in New York. They did not fit well and made her mouth sore, but she doggedly wore them. "Don Susano ought to welcome the Americans, too. With all the money they have paid him over the years, he is a rich man."

"Do you think his greed is satisfied?" Edward asked.

"If he had every penny in New Mexico, it would not be enough," La Dama said.

"Doña Julia," Matt said, "I asked for an appointment with His Excellency, but he would not receive me."

"Why would he be afraid? You are a Mexican."

"I know. But the governor's secretary says that an official meeting with me in these tense times would be indelicate. Could you arrange for Don Susano to meet us privately?"

"The anti-American sentiment is worse than I have ever seen it, and Don Susano is a prudent man. But I will try," she said.

Matt left La Dama's and hurried home for dinner with his in-laws and their nephew, Rubén Mondragón, who was visiting from Peñasco. Matt had spoken to Moisés Mendoza almost immediately after his return to Santa Fe. "There appears to be no end to the political swamp in which Mexico seems destined to loose itself," Moisés had said. "We have been trapped in an insular Spanish world that has seen barely a ripple of the Renaissance or the Enlightenment or the Industrial Age. But we are struggling to make the transition from a closed community to an open one; from being subjects to becoming citizens. We will get there a lot faster with the Americans."

A barefoot servant girl lit torches and they sat on the patio before dinner, admiring the spring blooms on the roses and day lilies that Celestina had brought from Missouri. Matt knew from Rubén's annual visits to Santa Fe that Celestina's cousin was instinctually conservative and intensely provincial. Matt kept the conversation away from the American invasion, reminiscing about his trip to Peñasco in 1827, when he had witnessed the *penitente*'s re-creation of Christ's crucifixion.

After they sat down at the dinner table, Matt spoke at length about a new breed of sheep he was thinking about bringing to New Mexico with the next year's caravan. When Sara asked about Matt's trip to Washington, Celestina cut her short with an avalanche of questions about Rubén's thirteen sons and daughters. Inevitably, however, the talk turned to the war, and for the first time that evening Rubén was animated. "What will happen to our family?" he asked Moisés. "We have been prominent in New Mexico for two hundred and fifty years. We have influence with the government, the Church, the community."

"My guess," Moisés answered, "is that the Americans will recognize that they will only be successful in New Mexico if they ally themselves with people like us."

"Have some more enchiladas, Mateo," Celestina said. "The cook made them especially for you." Her attempt to divert the conversation failed.

"The Yankees will send us a governor from one of their bizarre religious sects—Mormons or Baptists—and we will be nothing," Rubén said.

"That is not very likely," Celestina said. "Mateo says that President

Polk is more inclined to appoint someone who understands New Mexico. Someone like William Bent's brother, Charles, who is married to a Mexican and has lived in Taos for years."

"How do you stand on all this, Mateo?" Rubén asked while he freed a chicken leg from the carcass.

"Polk has asked me to try and facilitate a peaceful resolution to the problem. He sees the rascals in Mexico City as the enemy, not the people of New Mexico."

"You mean he wants you to spy for America!" Rubén shouted.

"Not to spy, Rubén," Matt said, raising his hands, palms out, as if to ward off Rubén's anger. "The president did not ask me to give information to the Americans. My only task is to negotiate with Baca and Zambrano to see if we can avoid violence in New Mexico."

"The damned Anglo-Saxons will tear the heart out of our culture," Rubén said, the rush of his breath fluttering the candles.

"Rubén!" Moisés barked. "Control yourself. We do not need such passion."

"Mateo, you are family, and I will not carry this any farther," Rubén said angrily. No one spoke, and nobody's eyes met. They sat in stiff silence while the maid served the next course. The only sounds were Celestina's silver Paul Revere knives and forks clacking on Pueblo Indian pottery plates.

The diners talked about the fine spring weather and the need to repair the gold leaf on the statue of the Virgin of Guadalupe in La Castrense—anything but the war, until the servant brought in the dessert—thin pancakes cooked to a toasty brown and smothered with maple syrup from America. They finished and Rubén stood and said his good-byes with strained courtesy.

The next morning, Payaso brought a message from La Dama to the Collins & Waterman store. Baca would meet them that evening in La Dama's private office behind her cantina. The governor, Payaso said, did not want to be seen going to her home, because many Santa Feans thought that she was too friendly to the Americans. But, if it looked like he was going to play a few hands of monte and then chat with Doña Julia in her office, that would not be unusual.

As La Castrense's bell rang eight o'clock, La Dama opened her office door for Matt and Edward, and left. Susano Baca was seated on a three-legged stool, and Matt and Edward took seats on a bench. "Governor, we appreciate your courtesy in receiving us," Matt said.

"I am always happy to see you, Don Mateo, and you, Don Eduardo." His wattles shook when he attempted a smile.

"You must be flattered, Your Excellency, that during these difficult times the central government has had the good sense to restore you to office," Matt said. "This is no time to have a Mexico City fop as governor."

"Thank you for you confidence. And how is Doña Celestina?" Baca asked.

"She is well, and my son and daughter are well," Matt said. "We have hired a tutor for them. Miguel is a particularly good student. But tell me, Don Susano, do you expect a good year with your sheep?"

"With this mild weather, the sun has not burned up the grass, so they should fatten nicely."

"I hope so. My herds have not had a good summer so far," Matt said. "The wolves have killed more than twenty lambs and ewes."

"Those damned peons always lie," Baca said, enjoying his own humor. "You will probably find those missing sheep in their cousin's corral."

"These men have been with me a long time," Matt said, "and they have never stolen anything."

The governor passed gas with the robustness of a bloated mule, but kept talking as if nothing had happened. "You claim to be a Mexican, Don Mateo, but you do not understand our people in the least."

"I hope your family is doing well," Matt said, choosing to ignore Baca's reminder that he was an outsider, a foreigner.

"Thanks be to God, they are all well."

"Are the farmers looking forward to a good harvest this year?" Edward asked.

"San Isidro has been kind to us," Baca said. "After two years of drought, he has given us rain at just the right time."

"We congratulate you, Don Susano, on getting your wagons to Santa Fe before General Kearny shut down the Trail," Matt said. "Eduardo and I were not so lucky."

"Tell me what kind of a man this General Kearny is."

"He is all military," Matt said. "Very abrupt. Very businesslike. Very American. He is a no-nonsense disciplinarian, and by the time the Army of the West gets to Santa Fe his troops will be well-trained."

"I have no doubt," Baca said. He crossed his arms and rested them on his stomach. The word *panzón*, potbelly, kept popping into Matt's head.

"Many of our citizens became hostile when they heard of the American invasion. There were inflammatory speeches and sermons."

"I can understand the people's concerns," Matt said.

"I do not have a happy populace. The humble people are terrified that the Americans will bring in Negroes to take over their work."

"President Polk has asked me to talk with you," Matt said. "And I have a letter from him that he instructed me to hand to you personally."

"May I see it?" Baca asked. His chins rolled over his collar as he leaned toward a candle to read the letter that Matt had translated into Spanish and Polk had signed. While he read, Matt quietly patted his knees in three-four waltz time and Edward gazed out the window without expression. "Polk says you are empowered to negotiate on behalf of the Americans, Don Mateo, and that you are authorized to extend certain offers. Putting aside—for now—the question of what a Mexican citizen is doing negotiating on behalf of a foreign country, what do you have to offer?"

"Your Excellency, I am proud of my Mexican citizenship, as I know you are. But there are certain practical facts which should be considered," Matt said.

"And those are?" Baca asked, assuming a calm, almost peaceful pose and snapping his dark eyelids shut.

"There are only a few regular army troops in Santa Fe," Matt said. "And, with all due respect, Your Excellency, they are not well-schooled in modern military tactics."

"Your point is well taken, Don Mateo," Baca admitted, warming to the game of giving tit for tat. "But our people will make up for that with their passion to defend our homeland. I expect thousands to answer the call to duty."

"Governor, I have no doubt that men will rally to you," Matt said, choosing his words carefully. "But neither you nor I can escape the fact that when these peons and Indians put their wooden lances and axes up against General Kearny's battery of cannons, they will not have a chance. A few rounds of grapeshot through their ranks will make these men turn tail and run. Many lives will be lost."

"Corporal," Baca shouted. The office door opened and a soldier in a faded blue jacket entered and saluted. "Go to the palace and tell Colonel Zambrano that I will be late for our meeting."

"I have only been home a short while," Matt said when the corporal left, "but I have heard soldiers in the cantinas grumbling that they have not been paid for weeks."

"What you say is true," Baca said. He explained that only a few wagons had made it down the Santa Fe Trail and that he had not collected enough taxes to pay the troops. Then the governor launched a bitter attack on the government in Mexico City. "I begged them for men and supplies, and all I got was a wagon load of rusted muskets and powder of such poor quality that the cannon balls barely dribble out the barrels."

"Everything goes back to that, Your Excellency," Edward said.

"To what?" Baca asked. Uncharacteristically nervous, he shifted his weight from one haunch to another.

"To the central government's failure to meet your needs," Edward said. "It seems to me that there are legal and moral grounds for breaking ties with a government that cannot protect its people."

"Your Excellency, you have been this region's most outstanding leader since independence," Matt added, "and I take the liberty of suggesting that you have a duty to the people who have supported and followed you."

"There is another consideration, Your Excellency," Matt continued. "You know that I have the greatest respect for Colonel Zambrano. But he has never confronted a well-officered army. Certainly, he has had successful skirmishes with Indians, but General Kearny has been a soldier for thirty-five years and many of his officers graduated from the American military academy at West Point."

"Colonel Zambrano may not have the latest books on military strategy, Don Mateo, but there is no one on earth who knows New Mexico's terrain like he does. And as long as I have Zambrano I have a man who will fight foreigners until he can fight no more. But, as you Americans are fond of saying, let us get to the point. What exactly is it that you want, Don Mateo?"

"Your Excellency, we are asking that you use your good offices to avoid a confrontation with General Kearny, and that this matter be settled by diplomatic means."

"You are asking me to surrender," Baca said. His flabby cheeks puffed out like a trumpet player's and his voice rose to a pitch well above its normal baritone. "You can tell Señor Kearny that we will fight for our homeland and our heritage. We will never give up! You can tell him that we have a plan for defense, and that we will send his so-called Army of the West back East with their asses dragging."

"Your Excellency," Edward said, "perhaps we should view this situation dispassionately. First, you should consider that General Kearny is a man of his convictions. If you fight and lose, Kearny says he will hang you. That is what General Santa Anna has done to his enemies, and I would expect the Americans to act no differently."

"This is a possibility, gentlemen, but, if we win, then none of this will come to pass—and we will be free of any threat."

"Governor, excuse me for asking this question. But how old are you now?"

"Fifty-six."

"Fifty-six. If you lose, the Yankees will take over your property and you will be too old to build up your fortune again," Matt said, pausing to let Baca think. "Rightly or wrongly, the people in Mexico City will blame you for a humiliating defeat."

"Have you spoken to Colonel Zambrano about this?" Baca asked. He stood and walked to the window to consider the grim picture that Matt had painted.

Matt and Edward sat silent until Baca took a deep breath and turned to face them. "We have not spoken to the colonel yet, Your Excellency, but we intend to," Matt said.

"I would appreciate your keeping me informed as to the colonel's response," Baca said in his most formal tone of voice.

"Certainly," Matt said, dipping his head in a deferential bow. Baca turned and went out the door, followed minutes later by Matt and Edward, who entered the cantina and found La Dama sitting at a corner table by herself. "How did it go?" she asked.

"The old scoundrel listened," Matt said, "but he made no commitments. He is going to wait to see what Zambrano does. Eduardo tried to contact the colonel, but he refused to see us. Can you arrange it, Doña Julia? We need to see him tonight."

"I will speak with Dixie Ledford," La Dama said. "But let me give you a word of caution. You will only convince the colonel if you offer him something that overcomes his sense of *pundonor.* Surrender would soil his honor, so you will need to give him something to cover the stain."

Just after eleven o'clock that night, Matt and Edward arrived at the house that Zambrano had rented for Dixie Ledford and followed her into her parlor. "Doña Julia tells me that you enjoy champagne," Matt said. He opened a wooden box and gave her the four bottles.

Dixie was dressed in a loose-fitting white satin dressing gown that clung to her body and, each time she moved, it revealed another aspect of her figure. She was tall and had an ample bosom, and, although her gestures had a certain grace, a slouching posture kept her from being elegant. She had loosened her abundant strawberry blond hair so that it fell to the middle of her back, and the candlelight brought out a luster that she achieved by frequent washings and brushings. She was heavily rouged and powdered, making it difficult to tell her age, but Matt guessed her to be in her late twenties or early thirties.

She told them that Zambrano was running late and clapped her hands to summon a servant. In halting Spanish, she instructed the girl to open a bottle of champagne. "Do not drink any of it," Dixie ordered. She switched to English: "These servants'll steal you blind."

"They're so poor that it's difficult to resist the temptation to take something," Matt said.

"I was poor and worked my way out of it without stealing," Dixie said, and deftly rolled and lighted a *punche* cigarette. "I think I hear the colonel's horse. Damned thing snorts and farts so's you hear him a mile away."

Zambrano was dressed in a new uniform and wore a gilt-handled sword. Matt and Edward stood to shake hands. "Are you going to speak in Spanish, gentlemen?" Dixie asked.

"Of course," Zambrano said, "this is not Washington."

"I'm going to the bedroom to fix myself," Dixie said, arching her back and running her hands through her hair. "When you people start rattling off in Spanish, I don't understand a damned thing."

"Colonel, I heard that the Navajos slaughtered a widow and her seven children up on the Chama River," Edward said.

"There is nothing I can do," Zambrano said. "We are spending all our time preparing to greet General Kearny."

Even though time was short, Edward and Matt launched into the obligatory litany of polite questions about farming, the weather, and families. Zambrano spent several minutes giving them the details of his wife's recent bout with smallpox and how the disease had left pock marks on her face and chest.

Matt judged that they had spent enough time on pleasantries, and shifted the conversation to their mission. "Eduardo and I want to thank you for seeing us. I know the climate is tense, and that you must handle things in a most tactful manner."

"You are right. Things are damned tense," Zambrano said, "with that *hijo de puta* Kearny on the march. Our spies went to General Kearny's camp and gave me a report on his army. But they are only peons. I would like your assessment."

"I would guess that he has close to seven thousand men," Edward said. "Regulars, dragoons, and Missouri volunteers. Those Missourians are as vicious as the scum who murdered Javier Otero."

"My informants tell me that Kearny's army is not that large," the colonel said, looking into Edward's eyes for signs of deceit. "What about their training?"

"The militia needed training," Edward said calmly. "That was the reason General Kearny spent so much time at Bent's Fort. When the Missourians were not too drunk, Kearny had them on the drill field."

"Weapons?"

"The latest government issue from Jefferson Barracks in St. Louis, and not a speck of rust on them."

"Cannons?"

"I counted thirty, mostly six- and twelve-pounders, and a good supply of grape shot," Edward answered, balancing his lie with enough truth to make it believable.

"My informants counted only sixteen cannons," Zambrano said, still assessing whether Edward was lying to him.

"When your men were there, all of Kearny's forces had not reached Bent's Fort," Edward said, "and they did not see everything."

"Could be," Zambrano said, taking a gulp of champagne. "This is quite good. Did you gentlemen bring it?"

"Yes," Edward said. "It is an eighteen thirty-eight vintage, the best we could find in St. Louis. Colonel, I apologize for being so abrupt, but it will only be a few days until the Army of the West gets here. With your permission, I would like to speak frankly?"

"What is your point, Eduardo?"

"President Polk has commissioned Mateo to make every effort to find a way to avoid fighting in New Mexico," Edward said. "We have spoken to Governor Baca and—"

"He is a thief and a coward," Zambrano broke in. "I told the people in Mexico City that New Mexico needed a military officer in charge when it was clear that we were headed for war. Since Baca got back into office, his stealing has been worse than ever. Only God knows how many bribes he has pocketed from men who want to avoid military service. If that charlatan had used the money to pay the army and buy horses and muskets, we would have a much better chance of destroying the *pinche* Americans."

"There are many of us who feel that you would make a better governor," Edward said. "But fighting the Americans will be a very risky business."

"Do you think I give a goddamn? God damn it, we are talking about our sovereign nation." Zambrano jumped out of his chair. "The Republic of Mexico! Land that we have owned and ruled for centuries."

"Colonel, we have been partners—" Edward said.

"Silent partners," Zambrano snapped.

"Silent partners," Edward confirmed. "You have had many years of good profits from our import business—"

"And Collins & Waterman has profited."

"Let me bring us back to the subject at hand," Matt said. "Don Diego, you may wish to consider whether fighting the Americans will benefit your people."

"I do not give a damn what the people think. What I do give a damn about is whether the Protestant, Anglo-Saxon, *pinche cabrón* Yankees are going to steal part of my country."

"Do you really think your troops can stand up to the Americans?" Edward asked.

"My men know they will be fighting to preserve not only their land but their way of life. And even though they might lack arms and training, I could stop Atilla the Hun's hordes at the narrows of Apache Canyon. If God ever made a natural fortress, it was there."

"I agree that the Canyon will be easy to defend," Edward said. "But the Americans might be able to blast their way through with their cannons."

"One hundred men are already at Apache Canyon digging trenches and cutting logs," Zambrano said. "Kearny's cannon balls will bounce off our breastworks. And, after those *pendejos* use up their powder, we will make General Kearny wish that he had never heard of New Mexico."

"We have heard a rumor," Edward said, "that the government sent you poor quality gunpowder."

"Those *hijos de la chingada* in Mexico City can go to hell," Zambrano said. "Whatever the quality of powder, we will defend ourselves."

Zambrano clapped loudly and a servant ran in from the kitchen. "Open another bottle of champagne, and tell Señorita Dixie to join us."

CHAPTER TWENTY-TWO

1846

"What you did down in Santa Fe is no less than a miracle. The president is delighted."

THE NEXT MORNING MATT GOT UP EARLY AND, WITHOUT HIS usual heavy breakfast, walked to town. When he entered the plaza, he heard a sergeant bellowing orders and stopped to watch him drill a company of Pueblo Indians. Matt was wearing a straw hat that hid his red hair, but his height made the sergeant stop and stare at him. He turned and went into the alley behind the Collins & Waterman store. His key tripped the lock, but Edward had barricaded the door. He shouted and banged on the door until he heard shuffling and the sound of boxes being scooted out of the way.

Inside, he and Edward went upstairs and opened tins of smoked oysters and crackers, and boiled water for tea over a candle. "Zambrano's harder to crack than a Brazil nut," Matt said when they finished eating. "But he's got to have a weak spot."

"He wants to protect every inch of Mexican soil," Edward said.

"We'd better get Baca in the tent first," Matt said. "Maybe it's time to throw a few gold pieces on the table."

"I agree," Edward said.

"But we've got to remember that Don Susano is still sensitive about his beating a retreat to Santa Fe when the Texians attacked in 'forty-three."

"Whatever we do, we've got to do it quick," Edward said. "General Kearny will be here in another ten days or so."

"You talk to Dixie about another session with Colonel Zambrano," Matt said. "I'll speak to La Dama and arrange a meeting with Baca."

Matt left by the front door and walked quickly across the plaza toward the corner of San Francisco Street, threading his way through the green peons and Indians that the regular army sergeants were trying to mold into soldiers. Adding to the confusion, a pack of stray dogs circled the plaza, barking and snapping at the sweating militiamen's legs. Those with sticks and farm tools for weapons swung at the attacking dogs, and one peon with an ax managed to behead a brindled mongrel.

Matt walked down San Francisco Street and turned into Burro Alley. Swarms of flies rose over the fresh burro droppings that a firewood pack train had deposited earlier that morning. He stepped gingerly around the piles and went in the main door of La Dama's cantina. At the center table, a Mexican was dealing monte for an American teamster and a French Canadian trapper. Matt found Payaso dozing at the bar and asked if La Dama was in. He came to, nodded, and led him to her private office.

"Could you arrange another meeting with the governor for tonight?" Matt asked.

"Susano will be here in a few minutes, if you do not mind waiting. He is out back in a crib with a new American girl."

"I need to speak to him alone."

"I understand. I hope you convince him that fighting is silly. An entire army of randy American troops! I might make enough to retire," she said, chuckling and stacking her arms on top of her bosom.

Susano Baca, clearly relaxed, came into the office, his shirt collar loose and his coat thrown over his arm. He nodded perfunctorily at Matt and took a seat on a three-legged stool. "Julia, the new girl is magnificent. She has had excellent training from somewhere."

"If your soldiers were as well trained as she is," La Dama teased, "you would rout the Yankees and send them running back to Missouri."

"What can I do for you, Don Mateo?" Baca asked when La Dama left.

"I have come to make a final proposal, Your Excellency. The American government has authorized me to offer you seventy-five thousand gold dollars if there is no armed opposition to General Kearny's army."

"You mean a *mordida?*" Baca asked, neither insulted nor surprised.

"Look at it more as payment for making a reasonable decision. I have seen the Army of the West, Governor, and even if your militiamen fight valiantly they do not have a chance against the Americans and their cannons. If General Kearny is not successful, the Americans will only send more men and more of our countrymen will be killed. Sooner or later, the Yankees will prevail."

"I know our weaknesses, and I do not need you to tell me what they are," Baca said. His coffee-brown eyelids slammed shut. "You know that *mordida* means, a 'bite.' But you did not offer a bite. What you offered was just a nibble."

"Governor, I understand that this is a difficult decision. I have authority for up to one hundred, but no more."

The thrill of bargaining took over. On countless occasions over the years, the two had haggled the amount of taxes and bribes, and they knew that, once the dickering began, they were on their way to reaching an agreement.

"Don Mateo, America is a rich nation," Baca said in his well-modulated baritone, his eyes still curtained by his eyelids. "I could not think of making this decision for less than two hundred thousand."

"One hundred and fifty is the maximum, Your Excellency. And, remember, this offer is for gold. Not silver. Not paper."

"Make it a hundred and seventy-five, and we will be agreed on the amount of money," Baca said.

"President Polk will not be happy with that number, Governor. He will think that I am a poor negotiator."

"Let him think what he likes. It is one hundred seventy-five or nothing."

"I will agree to your figure, Governor. And let me say that you have chosen a statesmanlike course."

"There is another requirement," Baca said, crossing one chubby thigh over the other. "You must swear on your honor as a gentleman that our business arrangement will never be made public."

"I give you my word, and the American government certainly has every incentive to see that our agreement remains strictly private. I will arrange for the gold to be deposited in your name at a bank of your choice."

"Put it in the Bank of Missouri," Baca said, his brown eyelids rising half way. "I already have an account there. I have another stipulation. Let's call it cosmetics."

"And?"

"You must convince Colonel Zambrano to lay down his arms. I do not want to be the only person in authority who decides not to fight. If the military commander joins me, it will be clear to everyone that I had no other choice. And my *pundonor*, my honor, will be preserved."

"I have already had discussions with the colonel," Matt said. "And when I leave I will talk with him again. I have no doubt that he will find the American government's offer to be sufficiently generous."

"As generous as mine?" Baca asked, his voice becoming a challenge.

"Yours is substantially more, Excellency," Matt answered.

"Unless—and until—Colonel Zambrano agrees not to give battle, I will continue with war preparations. Our army marches tomorrow at sunup."

"I understand, Governor."

Matt left La Dama's and walked to the plaza. He looked up at the Sangre de Cristo Mountains to the east and saw a spider web of lightning dancing across the peaks. He took a deep breath and sucked in the strong rain scent. An angry black cloud rolled over the plaza, but the sun's rays poked through it and created an eerie yellow-black light. Large raindrops, whipped by a sudden wind, pelted his straw hat, and within seconds a downpour swept over the capital. Matt ran under the *portal* in front of the Collins & Waterman store and watched the storm pass as quickly as it had come.

"How'd you do with Baca?" Edward asked when he went inside.

"We agreed on the money."

"Good."

"But there's a problem. Baca insists that Zambrano agree to surrender, too. If something goes wrong, His Excellency wants to be able to spread the blame."

"Matt, I'm not optimistic," Edward said, a gloomy look in his eye. "I don't know if we can deliver. I talked to Dixie and she says Zambrano won't meet us again."

Baca's secretary came into the store, handed Matt a folded paper, and waited to carry back a response. Matt read Baca's order that he and Edward accompany the army on its march to Apache Canyon. "It says he wants us to act as translators," Matt said.

"Why does he want me?" Edward said. "I'm not a Mexican."

"He says he would rather have you and Don Mateo where he can see you," the secretary said with no expression. Matt scribbled a reply that he and Edward would be ready at dawn.

The two partners went to Dixie Ledford's house, but Zambrano was not there. The corporal of the palace guard said he had not seen the colonel since before lunch. At Zambrano's house, a servant told them that his *patrón* had not been home all day. They walked toward the plaza and went into the *posada* bar. In a corner, Diego Zambrano sat at a table with Padre Domingo. They knew that approaching Zambrano while he was with Padre Domingo—who was solidly anti-American—was a risk, but urgency forced them to take it.

"Diego," Edward said, "would it be possible for you to talk with us for a few minutes in private?"

"No, it would not," Zambrano said, taking a sip of Kentucky whiskey.

"We have information of a private nature that we wish to pass on to you," Matt said.

"I do not want your fucking—excuse me Padre—information. I do not want to talk to you. I do not want to be seen with you. Get the hell away from me."

Matt and Edward stood at the bar. After another round of drinks, Zambrano waved at the barman, paid him, and he and Padre Domingo left together. Matt and Edward followed them out into the plaza, but the colonel and the priest walked arm in arm to the palace door, where Zambrano disappeared inside. Padre Domingo turned and gave them an angry look. *If he wasn't a priest*, Matt thought, *he would have accompanied that look with an obscene gesture.*

Matt and Edward spent the afternoon in their store trying to devise a plan that would persuade Diego Zambrano to lay down his arms, but they had come up with nothing. They toyed with taking the unused part of the bribe President Polk had authorized for Baca and adding it to the amount he approved for Zambrano. "Greed alone works with Baca," Edward said, "but that's not enough for Diego." The two partners stared at one another and said nothing for several minutes. Matt rose slowly, left without comment, and rode to Moisés Mendoza's house on the hope that his father-in-law could help him find something that would appeal to Zambrano.

Matt told Moisés about the colonel's refusal to speak to him. "I do not know how to break through," he said, rubbing his temples in frustration. There had been few times in his life when he wasn't able to find a solution to a problem or a way to skirt an issue to get what he wanted. He had prided himself on his ability to find just the right thing to say, just the right thing to dangle in front of someone.

"Have some of these *chicharrónes;* they're very good, not too oily," Moisés said, leaning back in his patio chair to let the setting sun hit him full in the face. "Perhaps you need to play to his sense of grandeur. Nobody thought a Corsican junior officer would rule France, but he did. Zambrano has always fancied himself a Napoleon. Maybe you could offer him a desert empire out West."

Matt reached for a handful of fried pork rinds from the bowl on the table and grinned broadly at what he took to be his father-in-law's joke. But, when he studied Moisés's face, there was no smile in return. "You're serious?"

"It may not be all that fantastical an idea," Moisés said. "There is logic behind it. When Santa Anna signed the treaty with the Texians, he gave Texas the eastern half of New Mexico, everything up to the east bank of the Rio Grande. But the fate of the western half was not clear."

Matt scooped another handful of *chicharrónes* and chewed them while he considered Moisés's plan. Then he said, "But President Polk did not give me the authority to cede territory."

"President Polk is two thousand miles away," Moisés said. "Living so far from Mexico City has taught me that one must improvise. One cannot always wait for instructions or grants of authority. *La audace! La audace! Toujours la audace!*"

"It may be a little crazy, but it might work. Maybe what we need is a little *audace.* At this point, anything is worth a try."

The next morning, Matt got out of bed before sunup and put on a Mexican homespun shirt, buttoned his suspenders on his pants, and pulled on the knee-high boots that a St. Louis cobbler had made for him. Celestina rolled over and watched him silently. Outside a coyote howled, until his mate answered with sharp, crisp yips. Matt kissed his wife and went to the back patio, where Timoteo stood holding the reins of his favorite horse, a palomino gelding.

Matt trotted down the hill to the Collins & Waterman store. Before he could dismount, Edward came out and got on his saddle mule. While the partners rode south to catch up with the New Mexican army, Matt thought through the offer he was going to make to Zambrano. "Zambrano's a stubborn son of a bitch," Edward said when they passed the last farmhouse. "There might not be anything that will sway him."

"He's ambitious and he craves a place in the sun," Matt said, having decided to keep the offer to himself. "We'll see what happens."

When the column stopped for lunch, the partners joined Susano Baca in front of a large tent. "We just completed our plans," Baca said. "Colonel Zambrano will lead our forces to Apache Canyon. I must return to Santa Fe to attend to some official duties, and I will come to the canyon later. Don Mateo, I want you and Señor Waterman to ride ahead with the colonel."

"But the colonel refuses to speak with us," Edward said.

"I have specifically ordered Colonel Zambrono to work with you. General Kearny has left Las Vegas and, if he wishes to treat with us, Don Diego will need your language skills."

"You two fall in behind me and my staff," Zambrano said as he mounted his horse. At Zambrano's signal, the trumpeter sounded advance and the march began. After covering eight of the twenty-nine miles to Apache Canyon, at sundown the colonel called for a halt to make camp. Matt, Edward, and Diego Zambrano shared a meal of jerked buffalo and French wine that Edward had brought in his saddlebags.

"Diego, I want to discuss the possibility of a peaceful settlement with you," Edward said. "Mateo has secured Don Susano's agreement to disband the army."

"I am not surprised," Zambrano said. The colonel looked as disgusted as if he had stepped barefoot into a fresh manure patty.

"Don Diego," Edward said, "excuse me for speaking bluntly, but we have little time. Our offer is fifty thousand gold pesos."

"Would I be getting the same amount you are paying the governor?"

Matt answered, "I gave Don Susano my word that I will keep my agreement with him secret, and I can assure you that we will hold any agreement we might reach with you in the strictest confidence."

"I cannot make a commitment of this sort," Zambrano said.

"But, Colonel," Matt said, "there is another—"

"There is nothing more to discuss."

At Apache Canyon, the peon and Indian militiamen marched into the Mexican camp, where officers directed them to work gangs that were digging trenches and grubbing out firing positions for sharpshooters up the canyon walls. A regular army corporal, whose ragged jacket had only one of its six buttons, summoned Matt and Edward to meet with Colonel Zambrano. The two men walked to a circle of officers surrounding their commander and listened as he gave orders for the defense. After the officers went to their units, Edward brought out a bottle of champagne and poured it into three clay mugs.

"I do not wish to intrude on your thoughts, Colonel," Matt said, "but I was hoping that we could discuss . . ." He stopped when Zambrano waved his hand and shouted, "*Basta,* enough!"

"I know that a possible settlement is the farthest thing from your mind, Diego," Edward said and gave Matt a glance that told him to keep quiet. "But General Kearny's advance guard will get here in a few days. If we are to reach an agreement, we must do it quickly."

"Eduardo, we have been friends for many years, but I do not want to talk about this until I have a chance to confer with Governor Baca when he arrives this evening." Zambrano raised his mug of champagne. "A toast to our victory over that arrogant *huevón,* Kearny. My spy says that the good general is bestowing American citizenship on all and sundry, like a bishop giving his benediction. Eduardo, give me some more champagne."

After sundown, Susano Baca and a guard of eight soldiers clattered into camp and found Zambrano's tent behind a thick grove of cedar trees. Matt and Edward greeted the governor and left the colonel's cook fire to stroll through the camp. The troops had marched hard for three days and then been put to work digging trenches. There were loud complaints that the supply wagons had not arrived and that all they had to eat was the food they had brought in their pockets.

A private sat cross-legged in front of a fire, drinking ersatz coffee and counting a stack of copper coins he had earned from sewing patches on worn-out moccasins. At another fire, men were drinking Taos lightning and Matt and Edward heard a corporal rolling out stanza after stanza of poetry, most of it obscene, and much of it devoted to how many *hijo de puta americanos* he was going to kill.

"Let's move on," Matt whispered. "If they get a look at our white faces we could be in real trouble." Walking back toward Baca's tent, they passed the latrine. Over thirty men with their pants down were squatting and groaning, suffering from water that had soured in their barrels.

"They're a pretty sad-looking bunch," Matt said.

"I don't think they would pass the Duke of Wellington's muster," Edward said. "A few blasts from General Kearny's cannons will have them on the run."

"I'd run too," Matt said.

"We have some brandy, Your Excellency," Matt offered when they took seats in front of Baca's tent. "Your aide will find it in my saddle-bags." After they finished their first cup of brandy, Matt asked, "Governor, have you and Colonel Zambrano come to a decision?"

"We are going to fight. The colonel has decided not to accept your offer. And, as I told you, I must refuse too."

"Your Excellency," Matt said, "we have seen your troops. Admittedly, there are lot of them, but they are in no condition to fight a well-organized army."

"Colonel Zambrano has convinced me that, even with the state of our men, General Kearny will never get through Apache Canyon. The Americans will have to bunch up to force their way through the bottleneck, and our sharpshooters will cut holes in their ranks as wide as a freight wagon."

"Your Excellency, let us have one more chance to talk with Colonel Zambrano before you make a final decision," Matt said.

"You have an hour."

Matt and Edward discussed what was clearly their last chance. Edward argued that, because of his special relationship with Zambrano, he should make the appeal. "There's no time to explain it," Matt said, "but I have something to offer him that will only sound convincing if it comes from me—as President Polk's personal envoy." They walked—almost jogged—to Zambrano's tent.

When they entered, the colonel dismissed his orderly. "Diego, I would appreciate your listening to the whole of Mateo's offer," Edward said. Then he lied: "Mateo has explained President Polk's proposal to me, and it is something that I, as your friend, think you should hear."

Zambrano nodded without speaking.

"Colonel, the time is short, so I will be brief," Matt said. "We have discussed the monetary component, but there is a more interesting part of President Polk's proposal. You know that the Americans only claim territory up to the east bank of the Rio Grande. And that leaves the west half of New Mexico in limbo."

Zambrano gave Matt an appraising look.

"You can create your own nation, Colonel. Few men in history have done that."

"That is silly. The Mexican government would send forces to take back their territory," Zambrano said, looking nervously behind him when his tent door flapped in a gust of wind.

"May I tell you something in confidence, Colonel?"

"Yes."

"General Taylor will continue his drive to Monterrey, and General Winfield Scott will open a second front. You know as well as I do, Colonel, that there is little or no money in the Mexican treasury. With the Mexican army defending itself on two fronts, Mexico will not be able to send troops across the Sonora Desert to attack your new nation."

"But, if the Mexican president did send an army, I would need soldiers to defend myself."

"The Army of the West will be here," Matt said. "And I can give you President Polk's assurance that if more troops are needed the United States will send them."

"How will I finance this new nation?"

"In addition to the fifty thousand for you, President Polk will advance another two hundred thousand to your new nation's treasury," Matt said.

"It sounds far-fetched," Zambrano said.

"Diego," Edward said, "when I first heard that the Americans were offering these terms, I also found it hard to believe. But, if you think about it, it makes sense for the United States to support you. Allowing you to set up your own nation will be much cheaper than fighting. And your nation will serve as a buffer between the United States and Mexico."

Matt scrutinized every twitch of cheeks and flick of eyes, and saw that, fantastic as the proposal was, the colonel was beginning to believe it. All he had to do, Matt told himself, was come up with one or two more credible points. "President Polk has agreed to enter into a treaty with you that allows the United States free passage across a carefully delineated road through your territory. Along that route, you will control the towns and cities that will be built to service the California trade."

"Control?" Zambrano said.

"However you see fit, Diego," Edward said, picking up the story. "And you will have the power to tax."

"How can I be sure that the American government will support me?" Zambrano asked.

Matt decided to back up his bluff. He pulled President Polk's letter giving him authority to represent American interests from his inside coat pocket. Nowhere in the letter was Matt authorized to make land grants. "I am going to allow you to read my instructions from President Polk."

"I cannot read English."

"I will translate for you." Matt did his best to give his made-up words the sound of a government document: " 'The bearer of this letter, Mr. Matthew Collins, is authorized and empowered to negotiate and conclude treaties on behalf of the United States of America which may relate to lands west of the Rio Grande and as far as the border with California. Said Matthew Collins may enter into agreements with such persons who said envoy may deem can be of assistance to the American republic.' I am not going to translate the entire document, Colonel, because there are confidential matters related to other persons."

"Eduardo, read that letter and tell me if what he says is true," Zambrano said.

Edward reviewed the letter and then glanced at Matt. "There is a mistake, Diego," Edward said. Matt swallowed and stared intently at a mildew stain on the tent wall.

"The letter," Edward continued, "does indeed bear the seal of the American president, and he has signed it. His signature is attested to by Senator Thomas Hart Benton. But, where Mr. Collins translated the words 'to conclude treaties,' I would translate them to read: 'to *finalize* treaties.' "

"Why would the Americans give this kind of power to a foreigner?" Zambrano asked. "The last time I looked, Don Mateo was a Mexican citizen."

Matt paused and coughed. "I have dual citizenship, Colonel. And I must tell you in all honesty that President Polk had doubts about granting me such broad powers. But I explained to him that you were an honorable man—a man to whom *pundonor* is crucial—and that money would be only secondary to you. I told him that, without the power to grant land, I would be unable to carry out my commission. He and Senator Benton debated this for some time while I was out of the room. In the end they concluded that I was right."

"Can you give me an assurance in writing?" Zambrano asked.

"That I can, Colonel. Do you prefer Spanish or English?"

"Do it in Spanish. Here are pen and paper."

Matt examined the quill carefully, sharpened it with his pen knife, dipped it in the ink bottle, and began writing. When he finished he made a second copy. He signed his name as agent of the United States of America and sprinkled sand to dry the ink. Then Zambrano signed and took one copy for himself. Matt wrote out a short statement saying that fighting the Americans would be futile and would only lead to needless bloodshed, and Zambrano signed it.

"Colonel, you have made a wise decision for your nation—and for yourself," Matt said, shaking Zambrano's hand. "I will notify Governor Baca immediately."

Matt showed the statement to the governor, who alternated puffing out and sucking in his heavy cheeks while he read. "I did not think that you would get the colonel's agreement," Baca sad. "Corporal, tell the militia officers and Colonel Zambrano to come to my tent immediately. Mateo, you and Eduardo stay here."

The militia officers assembled, and Baca, flanked by Zambrano, addressed them. "Gentlemen, Colonel Zambrano and I have discussed our military strategy and we have decided that the regular army can handle this situation. We are concerned that your men, who I know would fight bravely for our homeland, are not sufficiently trained to give battle to the Yankees. Our spies have informed us that the enemy has forty cannons to our four. And their men carry the most modern weapons."

"But, Your Excellency, with the fortifications we have built, those *pendejos* will never get through Apache Canyon," a militia officer from Chimayó said.

"You all know that I am as patriotic as any man here," Zambrano said, his face a mask of self-assured calmness. "But as your commander I have joined in this decision. Our quartermaster has given me a report on our supplies. We do not have enough food and water to sustain five thousand men during a long siege. In two or three days, our powder and shot will be gone."

"But we left our homes to come here and save our nation from the *pinche cabrón americanos*," the *alcalde* of Abiquiú said. "I say we stay and fight."

"Your love of Mexico is commendable," Baca said in a patronizing tone. "But which is better? To be killed by the Yankees or to return to your farms to take care of your families? The colonel and I have carefully considered every factor. We will remain here with the regular army and do the best we can."

"But the Army of the West is huge," the *alcalde* continued.

"We have a strong defensive position," Baca said, "and we can hold Apache Canyon for many days, perhaps weeks. When the foreigners see the futility of their effort, they will either turn back or negotiate a settlement that preserves our honor and our sovereignty."

"As your commander," Zambrano said, "I am ordering the militia to disband."

Word of their dismissal quickly spread through the camp and the men started walking back to Santa Fe during the night. By eight o'clock the next morning, only the regular army remained in the field. "Governor," Zambrano said, "I have called a meeting of the officers for two o'clock."

"Good," Baca said. "That will give us time for a nice lunch before we break the news. I will have a milk-fed kid roasted, and Don Mateo is providing excellent French wines."

After lunch, the officers gathered at Zambrano's tent. "Gentlemen, the governor and I have decided that it would be foolish to expose the lives of you and your men needlessly. We are not going to make a stand, either here or elsewhere."

"You mean you are going to surrender?" Lieutenant Vallejo asked.

"Not exactly surrender. We are simply not going to put up resistance," Baca said, glancing quickly at Matt and Edward, who were standing behind the officers.

"This morning," Baca continued, "I watched while my cook pulled a kid away from its nanny's teat. The little goat broke loose and started running in a circle, trying to escape his fate. The cook finally caught the kid and grabbed it by its ears. It was squealing and wiggling when the cook cut its throat. Gentlemen, trying to fight the American machine is as hopeless as that struggling kid's attempt to escape. I have no interest in making your wives widows. Carry what you can with you and go back to Santa Fe."

The next day, Matt and Edward rode beside Baca and Zambrano as they entered Santa Fe. They trotted into the plaza and stopped beside the Collins & Waterman store. Matt and Edward dismounted and shook hands with the governor and the colonel.

Baca rode to the palace, went inside, and made a bonfire of his papers on the patio. He found a corporal and two privates in the guard room and enlisted them to escort him to his hacienda near Albuquerque. Colonel Zambrano spent the day recruiting troops to ride with him to the west bank of the Rio Grande.

———

Two days later, in a drizzling rain, General Stephen Watts Kearny led an advance guard into Santa Fe. The acting governor, Juan Bautista Conde y Palacios, greeted the Americans in front of the palace, invited the officers in, and served Pass wine and brandy to the blue-clad soldiers. Kearny ordered a sergeant to strike the Mexican flag flying over the palace and to raise the American. Curious Mexicans gathered in the plaza to witness the end of the Spanish and Mexican rule that had begun in 1598.

Through an interpreter, Kearny made a speech in which he informed the crowd that New Mexico was now part of America. He told them that, if any American soldier took property or abused any person, he would mete out the harshest punishment. In addition, the Mexicans were free to worship as they wished and the American army would put a stop to Indian attacks. And, he announced, America was laying claim not only to the east bank of the Rio Grande, but to everything between Santa Fe and the Pacific Ocean.

"Matt," Edward said, a startled look on his face, "you never told me that Polk and Kearny planned to claim the land between here and California."

Matt said nothing, smiled, and turned to listen to the rest of Kearny's speech.

On an October morning Matt sat on the *Memphis Princess*'s stern, listening to the wheezing steam engine and admiring the way the sun illuminated the gold, orange, and red leaves on the oaks and maples along the banks. Just after noon, the Missouri River's current rushed the *Princess* into the Mississippi. The captain ordered full steam and its paddle wheel churned the water furiously until the ship slid ashore at St. Louis's mudflat docks.

As Matt walked toward the Perryman Hotel, he recalled the puzzled look on Edward's face when he had realized that Matt had not revealed the extent of President Polk's plan to claim everything from New Mexico to the Pacific. It was, Edward said later, the first time that Matt had held back something of such importance. After several days of awkward, curt conversations, Matt realized the extent of the damage he had done to their friendship.

During their trip up the Santa Fe Trail to Independence, Matt debated with himself whether to share the details of Polk's strategy for New Mexico and California. After an excellent, wine-enhanced meal in the *Memphis Princess*'s dining room, he decided that, with New Mexico in American hands and General Kearny on the march to California, there was no reason he couldn't tell Edward the specifics of New Mexico's and California's futures, even though the president had asked him to hold the plan in confidence. Edward listened quietly while Matt described his conversations with Polk and Benton. Without comment, Edward finished his cigar and port wine and went to bed. The next morning, when the ship stopped to let Edward off at his farm, he gave Matt a hearty *abrazo* before walking down the gangplank. Halfway up the path to his home, he turned, smiled, and shouted, "I'll see you in St. Louis in two weeks."

Ever since Matt had accepted Polk's mission, he had been conflicted. But, now that he had cleared away the last issue of his divided loyalty, Matt was comfortable with himself and his decision. He was an American citizen again, and Celestina, although still wary of where the Americanization of her Hispanic homeland would lead them, was supportive. And General Kearny had been so impressed with Moisés Mendoza's enthusiasm for the United States that he had appointed him territorial secretary in the new government.

Jim Perryman greeted his old friend on the hotel's front steps, took his arm, and led him to the tap room, where Matt saw Senator Thomas Hart Benton's pudgy figure profiled by the light streaming through a floor-to-ceiling window. When Benton noticed Matt, he broke off his conversation with a group of men and rushed over to shake his hand. "What you did down in Santa Fe is nothing less than a miracle," Benton said, his mastiff's jowls drawn back to frame a toothy smile. "The president is delighted. There are hundreds of American boys still alive today because of what you did. You saved the country millions and you've paved the way for our conquest of California. If you hadn't been acting covertly, you'd be a national hero."

"Thank you, Senator," Matt said, pulling his hand back from Benton's effusive pumping. For several minutes, the Missouri senator heaped praise on him. Matt tried, but failed, to force his lips into an appreciative smile. Suddenly, a wave of fatigue came over him. He excused himself and went to his room, where he slept through dinner until the next morning.

ACKNOWLEDGMENTS

I want to give special thanks to:

William E. Lokey, whose insightful advice on bicultural points of view was invaluable.

Rabbi Kenneth Roseman, whose profound knowledge of Jewish history made Edward Waterman's early years in Vienna come alive.

Professor Michael Olsen, who was generous with his time and counsel regarding the Santa Fe Trail.

David Jackson and Edward Koppman, who know enough about antique weapons to write a book of their own.

John and Mark Bauman and Emily Lyons, who provided background on Kaskaskia, Illinois.